KU-742-457

Unknown Male

British born of a Spanish father and a French mother, Nicolás Obregón grew up between London and Madrid. As a travel writer, Nicolás has had an extensive experience of Japan, but the beginning of his fascination with the country came from watching Japanese cartoons as a young boy. Nicolás Obregón is a graduate of the acclaimed Birkbeck Creative Writing Masters course and a former bookseller for Waterstones.

By the same author

Blue Light Yokohama
Sins as Scarlet

Unknown Male

NICOLÁS OBREGÓN

WATERFORD CITY AND COUNTY
WITHDRAWN
LIBRARIES

MICHAEL JOSEPH
an imprint of
PENGUIN BOOKS

MICHAEL JOSEPH

UK | USA | Canada | Ireland | Australia
India | New Zealand | South Africa

Michael Joseph is part of the Penguin Random House group of companies
whose addresses can be found at global.penguinrandomhouse.com

First published 2019

001

Copyright © Nicolás Obregón, 2019

The moral right of the author has been asserted

Set in 13.5/16 pt Garamond MT Std
Typeset by Jouve (UK), Milton Keynes
Printed and bound in Great Britain by Clays Ltd, Elcograf S.p.A.

A CIP catalogue record for this book is available from the British Library

HARDBACK ISBN: 978–0–718–18995–2
OM PAPERBACK ISBN: 978–0–718–18996–9

www.greenpenguin.co.uk

Penguin Random House is committed to a
sustainable future for our business, our readers
and our planet. This book is made from Forest
Stewardship Council® certified paper.

For my father

'Will you walk into my parlour?'
    said the Spider to the Fly,
''Tis the prettiest little parlour that
    ever you did spy;
The way into my parlour is up a winding stair,
And I've a many curious things to
    show when you are there.'

– Mary Howitt

0. Still There

The boy loved everything about these rare car journeys – the smell of the leather, the gleaming dashboard, the seatbelt's embrace against his chest. But most of all he loved to watch the city flashing past him. Sometimes weeks would pass without him leaving the house. To the boy, Tokyo was more magnificent each time he saw her. Tokyo was freedom.

That day, it was cold and bright, skyscrapers glinting in the late-afternoon sun. The chauffeur was grumbling about the traffic more than usual. Even though they hardly ever spoke, the boy liked him. He liked his calm, steady motions, and he liked his pristine white gloves, barely moving on the wheel. But his favourite was when the chauffeur fiddled with the radio dial. The boy had never been to the ocean, but even so, the fuzzy static made him think of waves.

The car turned on to the big street where people sold wind-up toys. Plastic robots shuffled along the pavement, as though mimicking pedestrians around them. A few metres away, men in suits sat on wooden crates along the kerb, their faces hidden behind newspapers. Crouching figures frantically buffed their shoes.

Seeing them, the boy felt the sickness. Looking away, he tried not to think about his father. His father's shoes were shiny too. Shiny and heavy and always growing closer.

He kept his eyes on the chauffeur's gloves until the sickness passed and it felt safe to look out of the window again.

Tokyo was bigger by now: taller, louder, more awake somehow. Through the zoetrope of the car window, the boy saw the city growing, soaring, unfurling. If he looked away for a moment, he'd find that Tokyo had changed behind his back – as though she were always trying to trick him.

The car slowed now. 'Not again,' the chauffeur hissed.

Through side streets, the boy could see a crowd of people marching together, punching the air in time, bright orange flags fluttering above them. Someone was leading them on with a megaphone. Every few seconds they all shouted as one.

'Who are they?' the boy asked.

'Anti-nuclear marchers.'

'What do they want?'

'To save the world.' Sighing, he turned on the radio and the DJ introduced the next song, 'Crazy' by Patsy Cline.

'Isn't that good?'

'Nobody can save the world. All these people do is slow the traffic.'

The car passed under the train tracks and stopped at a red light alongside a concrete mixing truck. The boy wondered what the concrete would be used for, what they would build. He pictured police stations, theme parks, zoos – places he had never known. His trips outside were so rare and the world was so full of things he didn't understand. Sometimes he would make himself dizzy with the wondering.

The lights turned. Pressing his small face to the glass, the boy looked for his favourite billboard now – the big yellow Nikon one. The sunset was such a dazzling gold he had to squint. The song on the radio was interrupted by an urgent newsflash: a plane had crashed into Tokyo Bay. Muttering to himself, the chauffeur veered off the normal route. The boy wanted to complain, he would miss his billboard, but the idea of a new route excited him too much to say anything.

They were soon on a narrow street, barely wide enough for the car, passing through stacks of traditional houses. Dusky thrushes hopped along the branches of low-hanging snowbell trees. Up ahead a moss-swallowed temple composed long shadows. This Tokyo seemed much older and smaller; nobody was selling anything here, nobody was building, nobody was marching.

Another turning and the chauffeur groaned – another, smaller crowd was blocking the way. Then the boy saw it. Heart thudding, he watched as the children swarmed through the big green school doors, a battlefield charge of happiness. He saw identical uniforms. Classrooms emptying out. Books on shelves. Gymnastic bars. Wooden horses. Teachers glancing at their watches as they hurried children outside. Everyone belonged in that place.

The boy received his education at home, at a single desk in the gloomy study at the back of the house. Though it looked out on to the garden, his father always kept the screens shut, denying him a daydream landscape. A series of private tutors would come, occasionally Americans. None would ever stay for long. On the days where nobody came the boy would scavenge through the house for books, rejoicing when he found a new one, a secret trapdoor to the world.

If he couldn't find any, he'd just sit and stare at the screen. Sometimes bird shadows would dance across the rice paper and the boy would follow them in his mind. On clear mornings, sunlight might stream through the wax myrtles in the garden and paint the room jade for a brief moment. For the boy, those were the good days.

Now a great sadness filled him: a lonely anger in his stomach, stinging his eyes. He watched the last of the children pass through the gates, reunited with smiling parents. The boy knew he would never be one of them, he knew he would never belong in that place.

The chauffeur returned to the main road and there, after all, was the Nikon billboard. Turning away from it, the boy pictured the children in their classrooms. He cursed them all.

'Every which way is blocked,' the chauffeur announced. 'The appointment will have to be rearranged. I'll take you back home.'

Feeling like he couldn't breathe, the boy pulled the seat-belt away from his chest. It wasn't an embrace any more.

Home.

Home was a place where the lights were left off. Home was the terrified squeak of a windpipe as it was gripped. Home was the purr of a leather belt leaving trouser loops. Home was the boy's whole world.

The gold in the sky had faded now, replaced by the sad blue bleeding into the Tokyo dusk. A quiet rain began to fall. Journeys back were always so fast, as though the car were attached to an elastic band snapping back into place. Another Tokyo trick.

The boy closed his eyes and imagined running into the marching crowd, chanting with them as one. He imagined falling into that poured concrete. He imagined crashing into Tokyo Bay. He tried to imagine anywhere, anywhere but *home*.

The rain grew heavier, thrumming on the car. All too soon, the city became silent suburbs, a trillion sandcastles washed away. The streets were empty here, houses hiding behind high walls. The chauffeur hummed along with the radio, nodding at colleagues as he passed them. His speed-ometer glowed like embers. The boy wanted to scream. Wanted to plead with him. Beg him to take him away. But he knew it was no use: the chauffeur worked for his father. Everything in the boy's world belonged to his father.

Home came into view now. The boy began to shake. He closed his eyes and heard the crackle of gravel beneath the wheels. The car stopped. The chauffeur got out to open the passenger door. The boy counted six crunches of gravel; he knew them by heart, the saddest sound in the world. The car door clunked open and cold air took his breath away, the rain much louder now. The glass lanterns tinkled madly like pachinko.

'Come on, you'll get wet.'

The boy started walking, feeling the gravel chomp at his soles. Home's windows were all dark. It was such a big house, from the outside it might have looked like it was full of things. No one would be able to tell how empty it was inside.

Scrunch scrunch scrunch . . . the gravel had all run out now. Reaching the door, the boy listened but heard nothing. All he wanted was to sit with his mother and tell her about the things he had seen today, to ask what nuclear was, to ask why concrete had to churn in big mixers. Or, if she wasn't feeling well, he would just be in his room under the covers with his Captain Tsubasa manga.

Swallowing, he pushed open the door as gently as he could. Inside, there was only darkness. For a second, the boy's heart leapt with hope. But then he saw the telephone – plugged in. If his father left the house, it would be unplugged. In the *genkan*, big black shoes gleamed like river stones. Above them, a suit jacket was on a hanger, dark as closed eyes. The blackness of the fabric was so rich, so shiny, it mesmerized the boy.

He took one last look back. The chauffeur was bowing, his eyes on the ground, the rain in his headlights like sparks. Waving, the boy shut the door softly, the world outside muted.

And then the footsteps came. *Thump thump thump*, down the stairs, heavier and heavier. The boy froze, the air in his throat cornered. He kept his eyes on the suit jacket.

The footsteps stopped. His father stood there, filling the hallway. In the gloom, his face was a blurry blue. He was breathing steadily today, his fists in his pockets bulging like rocks.

'You're back early.'

The boy nodded.

'The plane crash.' It wasn't a question. His father never asked questions. The boy thought about the voice on the megaphone earlier, all those people following it. His father's voice was like that too; you did what it said.

'Where is Mother?' The boy clenched and unclenched his fists in his pockets.

'Not feeling well today. Take your shoes off.'

The boy undid his laces, praying he wouldn't wet himself. The suit above him swayed slightly in the draught, almost trying to waltz, its silken lining blood in moonlight.

'Did you hear me, Kosuke?'

'Yes, Father.'

The boy obeyed and walked slowly towards his father.

'Didn't Noboru urge you to hurry inside?'

'Yes, Father.'

'But I saw you through the window. You didn't hurry. And now you've made puddles in my corridor.'

The boy heard the tinkling of the belt being unbuckled. He kept his eyes on the jacket instead. Black buttons looked back at him; they seemed to watch him somehow.

Kosuke Iwata woke up punching at the air, panting like an animal, a noose of soaked sheets around him. Down the years, the nightmares had sometimes been vague and distant, but lately Iwata woke up with the belt buckle tinkling in his ear. He would have to lie there until the anger dissolved before he could start his day. Sometimes it took hours.

A knock at the door. Iwata realized now it was what had woken him.

Santi came in, rubbing his eyes, the home phone held out. 'Thought it was a wrong number, but he keeps saying your name.'

'Thanks.' Iwata took the phone. 'You good?'

'I'm good.' Throughout much of his childhood, Santi had suffered from nightmares. Iwata stayed by his bedside each night, as though nursing some physical affliction in the boy. Then one day the nightmares just stopped. Either that, or Santi started lying.

He allowed Iwata to ruffle his wild hair now, then shuffled away. 'Tell whoever it is it's 5 a.m.'

He bumped the door shut and Iwata held the phone to his ear. 'Yes?'

'It's me.' The voice on the line was slow and wheezing. 'Kid, you don't wanna know what I did to get this number.'

It took Iwata a moment to find the words; he hadn't used his Japanese in several years. 'Who is this?'

The laughter was like a steam train coming to a halt. 'Figures you wouldn't recognize my voice. Been long enough.'

'. . . Shindo?'

'I know what you're thinking – *he's still alive?*'

Iwata had not spoken to his old boss in a decade, the man long since consigned to unpleasant memory. Yet here he was, rasping in his ear. 'You know what time it is here?'

'Something has come up, kid.'

'If you're calling me, someone is dead.'

'Still sharp, I see. All right, here it is: I have a murder on my hands and I need you. But before you tell me to go screw myself, there's something else. You remember Hideo Akashi?'

Iwata felt a distant nausea at the name. 'I try not to.'

'Well, he remembers you. It's his time, see. Three days from now. And he's asked for you.'

'Nobody in this world owes Akashi a damn thing. Least of all me. Why would I do this?'

'Because it's my time, too, Kosuke.' Shindo's voice lowered, an old man ashamed to be asking for help. 'I haven't got long left and I need you to come home.'

Iwata thought of his mother. She had died five years ago. Sometimes, he still found himself forgetting the fact, then reliving the pain in lonely moments – in bed, at red lights, in the swimming pool. Every day since her death he had regretted not knowing more, not giving more, not loving her more. He sorely wished – sorely – that he had asked her everything, every detail, every choice she had made, that he had charted the shape of her life, blood archaeology.

But there was a reason for all this.

Iwata closed his eyes and saw his father's gleaming shoes. For years he had avoided Tokyo, the past. He had put 6,000 miles between him and the city; he had lived a whole life-time away from it. And yet the nightmares were always there, always driving him back to his father's house. To the man that had sown his life with pain. The man who had raped his mother then blackmailed her into marriage. The man who had kept him in a prison of fear.

Iwata opened his eyes. Perhaps it was time to finally accept where the nightmares were taking him.

'Kid, you still there?'

PART ONE

1. Tokyo, Somewhere

Mr Sato glanced around the carriage as he nibbled off the nail from his little finger. Confident that nobody had seen him, he plucked it out from between his lips and dropped it into his breast pocket to be with the rest. Keeping them was his little habit, his little secret.

The train was heading south, past the airport, out towards the fringes of the city. Not that Mr Sato knew where Tokyo started and ended any more. The carriage jolted in the warm evening, a mobile sauna, so tightly packed the passengers swayed as one. Unlike the others, however, Mr Sato did not crane his neck for a view out of the window or a glimpse of newspaper. He simply looked at his shoes and accepted the journey, occasionally closing his eyes.

Mr Sato was of medium build, of middle age. His hair was neatly cropped and his shirt impeccably pressed. Tie: seasonal. Watch: functional. Suit: bland yet elegant. Everything about him said mid-range. He had no birthmarks, no scars, no distinguishing attributes. His face was ordinary. His only unharmonious feature was his eyebrows, at once sparse and long, like the hair on a spider's legs. He had a habit of blinking too much, his irises two flies trapped in a web.

Mr Sato worked in the corporate headquarters of a confectionery conglomerate that specialized in chocolate bars, dairy products and dietary supplements. He had joined the company straight out of university and had never worked a single day anywhere else. For the first ten years, each spring, an innocuous little slip of paper would arrive on his desk announcing a raise in salary without any kind of explanation. When Mr Sato's wife became pregnant, he swore he would redouble his efforts and aim for top management.

But in the following years the pay rises diminished and while his 'classmates' were promoted Mr Sato was quietly farmed out to his current dead-end division. Soon he found himself lost in a quagmire of sleepless nights and stress.

His wife told him not to worry, things would work out, they would be okay. Hard times were just part of life. After all, *stress* was the most common English loanword in Japan.

Mr Sato tried everything. He went to mind gyms to relax with special light goggles and soothing music. He visited stress-relief salons for aromatherapy sessions in vibrating cubicles. Bars where he paid a small fee to smash plates. Even IV drips at a fashionable new clinic. When the new-fangled failed, he fell back on the more traditional methods: massages, hostesses, drinking with old friends. Nothing helped.

The economy contracted yet again. There were rumours the company had hired downsizing consultants. At his lowest, Mr Sato considered ending it all.

But then one day, his father spoke to him. From beyond the grave, on the car radio. He didn't say anything special – it was the usual – stop whining, stop daydreaming, knuckle down. *And while I'm at it, when are you going to put things right in the village? Your own father, shamed. You're just going to leave things the way they are? You were born in Ōkuromori.*

Mr Sato worried at first; he had to be losing his mind. But when it happened again a few days later he admitted to himself how comforting it was to hear the old man's voice

4

now and then. His father began to speak to him more and more frequently. Mr Sato simply accepted it. After that, as if by magic, the stress vanished.

By then, he had been working at his company for over twenty years. If Management had forgotten about him, then he would respond in kind. They paid his salary. He fed his family. Put gas in his car. He refused to worry about needing anything more. For the first time in his life, Mr Sato swore to be his own man. Swore to put things right in the village.

The train gave off a low moan as it trundled over narrow tracks, a tiny ventricle in the never-ending Tokyo heart. It ran past the backs of apartment buildings, dirty billboards, and offices now operating on unpaid overtime. There was a brief stop at an elevated station and a few commuters got off, free of the heat. Along the sagging telephone wire above an unkindness of ravens huddled, throwing up their throaty *kraa kraa* calls at the deepening dusk.

A woman in a sleek grey pant suit boarded and apologized quietly as she brushed past Mr Sato. Admiring her silk scarf, he thought of the boutique nearby that his wife loved. It would probably still be open. He gauged the amount of bodies in his way while juggling thoughts of what kind of present he would even begin to look for. But as he wondered whether a voucher would make for an anticlimactic gift, the doors hissed shut. *Tomorrow, maybe.*

The little train rose high over the streets, then down through level crossings, where flocks of home-bound bicycles gathered. Not a single person in the carriage knew another; not a word was spoken. The sky was a soupy orange, the last of the sun flaring through the apertures in the cityscape.

The thoughts in Mr Sato's head were unremarkable – his work, the village festival he was organizing, his son. He was a good boy. A little quiet, a little wide-eyed, but a good boy. Thinking about him made Mr Sato's chest feel like a cuckoo clock, as though at any moment his secret pride could burst out. He inhaled deeply, tasted the sweat hanging between the bodies, the stench trying to hide in perfume and colognes. But Mr Sato didn't mind smells.

Mr Sato arrived home a little after 8 p.m. He ate a pleasant dinner with his wife and son then helped out with the home-work. Afterwards, he sat with his wife to watch the news while she read her book. Another government reshuffle was expected. There was a time when current events would have provoked some feeling in him. That time was long gone.

At 11.30 p.m, Mr Sato tried to kiss his wife, but she turned him down.

'I'm sorry, I just don't want to shower again.'

'It's okay.'

'If you want I can use my hand?' She marked the page in her book.

'It's okay,' he smiled. 'Another time.'

Mr Sato got up and went into the kitchen. He climbed on a stool and took out a maroon-coloured Thermos from the highest cupboard.

'I forgot to ask,' his wife called out. 'How are the arrangements for the *matsuri* coming along?'

'Fine,' he called back. 'I found a good recipe for venison stew.'

'Controversial choice!'

'Yes,' he laughed. 'The village will be talking about it for years.' Looking over his shoulder, he opened the Thermos.

6

A viscous pork smell escaped. He slipped his hand inside his breast pocket, dropped in his nail clippings then quickly fastened the lid again. Wafting the smell away, Mr Sato washed his hands and returned to the living room.

'I'm going back into the office,' he said apologetically.

His wife looked up from her book with a sympathetic pout. 'You have to?'

'Afraid so. Deadline approaching.'

'Please rest a little during the day.'

'I'll try.'

'Will you make the last train?'

'I still have time.'

'Good.' She nodded at the Thermos under his arm. 'What's that?'

'Just some tea.'

'You get through so much these days!'

'We all have our vices.' Mr Sato said goodnight and left.

Outside, instead of turning right for the train station, he headed for the small parking lot. Getting into the family car, he flipped through digital albums on the dashboard before settling on Céline Dion's *The Power of Love*.

It took Mr Sato ninety minutes to reach the winding Ibaraki mountain roads, his car like a stray firefly in the darkness.

By the time he was cruising along the narrow country lanes north of Lake Ōkuromori, it was a strain to contain his excitement. But he soon spotted the familiar sequence of chinquapin trees followed by the unmarked turning. Mr Sato loved the slow, crackling, popping sound of his tyres over the twigs and dead leaves. It made him imagine himself as a giant worm, slithering through the warm earth.

He parked in the usual dense grove and got out. Mr Sato

swapped his shoes for rubber boots, then he took the tarp sheet he'd hidden in the nearby tree and covered the car. Now he was ready. With his keyring torch, he found the old path.

The low buzz of crickets was constant, a triggered burglar alarm. There was a chilly current through the trees, branches screeching gently. Beneath it, the sound of little animals bolting away in the blackness. The woody tang of the forest smelled like life. Mr Sato filled his lungs with gusto.

After a while the path gave on to a secluded lake. He squelched his way along the muddy shore to the jetty. There he texted his wife to tell her he hoped he hadn't woken her but that he was making good progress at work. Then he crept along the rickety jetty and lowered himself into the old boat that had belonged to his father.

Mr Sato began to row, his intrusion rippling out across the water. Sleeping birds flapped out of low branches, grazing the surface of the lake. He heard his father in the creaking of the oars. *It's good to see you're finally taking things seriously, son. Even if it did take you all these years.*

The islet was about 400 metres away. There was nothing special about it to the eye, simply a patch of inaccessible trees in the middle of the lake. But Mr Sato knew what lay beyond those trees. His heart hammered for the knowing.

He was sweating by the time the boat scraped on to the shore of the islet, steam rising off his icy shoulders. Carefully climbing out, he steadied his breathing and luxuriated over the exquisite commingling of nerves and anticipation. Then he raised his torch and made his way through the thick knot of cedars.

On the other side of them Mr Sato saw what he had

come for at last: a simple A-frame cabin, little more than two telephone boxes in size. The country air was strikingly fresh on his lips. He licked them.

Feeling the key in his pocket, he recalled what his father would say whenever he asked for chocolate as a child: *Look at you, your hand is reaching out of your throat for it.*

He worked the locks briskly and the chain fell to the grass. The soundproofed door opened. From the darkness, a woman screamed.

2. Enjoy Your Stay

Rainy season. Hot air from the south had embroiled itself with Siberian cold, burying Tokyo in a shallow grave of humid cloud. In the depths of the city snakes were slithering out of gutters. Herons nested along the concrete banks of nameless canals. And ten million plastic umbrellas were opening and closing, a never-ending bloom of jellyfish in propulsion.

In the north-east of Tokyo, purple neon letters spelled out the name of a love hotel – *Starlet*. The businesses hiding in this narrow alleyway were easy to misconceive, tinted glass doorways designed to be overlooked by those not in the know. Ordinarily, nobody but the desperate would linger. But tonight the alleyway was packed. Tonight there was a special guest.

Blue tarp cloaked the entrance to Starlet. Policemen shuffled in and out of the alley, hungry pensioners at a cold buffet. At the end of it, a squad car blocked the way, lights flashing but no siren wailing. Instead an automated female voice entreated locals to carry on about their business:

PLEASE DO NOT DWELL HERE, POLICE
OFFICERS ARE WORKING. KINDLY
REMEMBER TO OBSERVE TRAFFIC
REGULATIONS AND COOPERATE IN
THE PREVENTION OF ACCIDENTS.

In another part of the city the crowd might be bigger, but few asked questions here. In San'ya, trouble was nobody's business. The rest was business as usual. Despite the police presence, the shabby sex grottos still opened their doors as the sun went down. Chinese prostitutes in sci-fi coloured wigs merely moved a few metres up the road, the strands of denim on their skirts stirring in the warm air. They seemed more worried by the threat of rain than by the law, dispassionately chirping their mantra at every passing male: *Massaji? Massaji? Massaji?*

Inspector Shingo Hatanaka had no trouble pushing his way through the half-hearted congregation. His burgundy armband identified him as Division One: Homicide. He was a large, balding man with small eyes, thick lips and a mole over his left eyebrow. His shirt collar was tight around the thickness of his neck, giving him the impression of a tortoise emerging from its shell. Though he was mid-thirties, his body was a decade ahead of him. His weight didn't exactly help.

Hatanaka swallowed another antihistamine and scowled up at the clouds. This weather always made him paranoid. He could almost hear the rustle of the dust mites, smell the mould colonies spreading through the dank interstices of this crumbling district.

Hatanaka turned his attention to the love hotel. It didn't look that old. He guessed the owners had banked on gentrification after the Olympics had been announced. But seven years had passed and the Games were now just two weeks away. San'ya was still San'ya.

It was a place that could not be found on maps. Even asking for directions would not help. Most locals would say, 'You're not too far.' It had been the Shogun's execution grounds centuries ago, home to meat packers, tanners and undertakers, those who worked with blood, those tainted by death. Later, it became known for trouble – agitators, drinkers, prostitutes, political extremists. In the sixties it had been erased from the map by a squeamish city authority. Dissected and renamed, today – officially speaking – San'ya no longer existed.

'What a place to die.'

Lips tingling, Hatanaka dipped his head under the blue tarp and entered the love hotel. It smelled of mildew and detergent. The cramped hallway was dim. There was nobody at reception, not that he would have been able to see anyone, given the screen. A master keycard in the shape of a star had been left out for him. Hatanaka took the elevator to the eighth floor. As he ascended, it occurred to him that a love hotel wasn't a bad place to kill a person. *No faces. No windows. No questions asked.*

The elevator pinged open to a silent, featureless corridor. Assistant Inspector Itō, a younger detective with a quiet voice and a sober haircut, was waiting for his superior. He led the way.

'Sir. First-responding officers have made their reports, forensics team en route, the prosecutor has been notified. Victim is female. Young. A foreigner. Pretty clear blunt-force trauma. Killed several days ago. Likely somewhere between the 7th and the 8th of July.'

'Who found her?'

'Anonymous tip. Responding officers discovered the body tonight at 9.30 p.m.'

'Good. Means my crime scene won't be too wrecked.'

The doors were all closed except for one room, 806. The plastic sign outside read: *Andromeda.* Snapping on nitrile gloves, Hatanaka entered. The walls were painted a cartoonish purple galaxy, little electric stars projected on the ceiling via a cheap lighting system. On the radio, Tokyo 1 Gold was playing an old *kayōkyoku* song – 'Goodnight Baby' by the King Tones.

The girl was lying face down on the floor, bare and pale, her head caved in. Her blonde hair was wine red on one side, in coils and ringlets, as though she had just emerged from the shower.

Hatanaka crouched over her and smelled a wink of perfume. 'Who is she, Itō?'

'Here's her alien residence card. Name . . . Mackintosh, Skye. Twenty-two. From the United Kingdom. Exchange student.'

In the photo, Hatanaka saw a pretty young woman with large, brown, almond-shaped eyes and a wide, conquering smile. The ID card told him she was from London and that she went to Rikkyo University, on the other side of Tokyo. It would have been her birthday the week after next.

Hatanaka took out his torch and ran his beam over the woman's body. The backs of her knees had pale little grooves, like pink soldering on a doll belying its manufacture. Her heels were calloused. There was a small mole on her lower back, one on her right breast. The stretch marks about her hips shone like seashells.

'I don't see any of the usual bruising.'

'Agreed, sir. Sexual assault not obvious at this stage.'

'I wasn't asking for your opinion, Itō.'

Skye's eyes were open, the pupils a rye-whiskey colour. Despite the fact that she had been dead for several days, her forearms and calves still had a reddish tan. She had no tattoos on her body, no birthmarks.

Hatanaka returned to the main wound: a dark, deep breach on the right side of her head. He guessed perhaps just one or two blows with the weapon, but enough to cause catastrophic damage. Her small nose was smashed flat, twice its size compared to the photograph. Her forehead and cheeks were puffed up, as though inflated.

'He beat her severely, but this looks like the blow that finished her. Hammer, or something similar.' Hatanaka indicated the site of the *coup de grâce* with his little finger.

Itō nodded but kept his opinion to himself this time.

'Find anything else?'

'Not much, sir. Just her clothes in the bathroom. She'd drawn a bath.'

Grunting, Hatanaka stood back up. 'How do you see it, Itō? Was she meeting a boyfriend or selling spring?'

'I'm not sure, sir.'

'How did nobody find her sooner?'

'The room was rented for a week. Receptionist said she remembers it because that length of time stood out to her. It was paid for by –' He referred to his notepad now. *'A scruffy-looking man. 174 to 178 centimetres. Had buck teeth. Looked homeless.'*

'We need to find that man. Did the girl come in with him?'

'No, she came in alone. Looks like she ordered some takeaway pizza, but the delivery guy was up and down in two minutes. We're looking for him right now, too.'

'This scruffy man, he could have been waiting in the room for her.'

'Apparently not. Reception confirms he paid then never returned. The only other people who have been up to this floor in the last five days were a couple who stayed for an hour. And a young woman by herself. But she didn't stay for long at all.'

'Itō, this girl didn't smash her own head in.'

'No, I realize –'

'While I'm at it, do you see a murder weapon?'

'No, sir, whoever killed her must have taken it with him, but –'

'And where's the pizza box? Does the killer hate litter, too?'

'Perhaps he took it with him. Didn't want his employer to be identified.'

Hatanaka sighed and stepped over the dead girl. In the bathroom, a bra hung from the only chair, the clothes bundled. The cold bathwater was pink, its scent artificial cherry.

Through a tiny window slat Hatanaka peered out over the electric black skyline and saw the blimp that had appeared in recent days. An enormous electronic display on its side replayed the same message over and over:

TOKYO WELCOMES YOU –
PLEASE ENJOY YOUR STAY!

The screen ran through a loop of inane facts: 339 gold medals with more than 11,000 athletes participating from 206 nations! 6,000 hours of television coverage to be beamed across the world! Millions of visitors! Over ¥800 billion spent!

San'ya was only eleven kilometres from the National Stadium but there was little for the tourists here – homeless camps, gambling dens, long-closed labour exchanges, shutters slashed by graffiti. Men huddled in gaps to drink beer from flasks, faces wizened beyond age, eyes dulled by all. Alleyways smelled of piss and cigarette smoke. In the mornings, workers gathered at the crossroads hoping for off-the-books employment, once abundant, now scarce. Along with the gambling and prostitution, what was left of the illicit day-labour trade belonged to the gangsters, themselves squeezed by an ever more obdurate government.

Along the banks of the Sumida River, plywood boxes contained the homeless in all their variety, from the elderly living out their last days to the secretly redundant salarymen, briefcases still in hand, aimlessly walking the streets of Tokyo in the day then returning to their hutches beneath the freeway at night. The hopeless wagered their last few yen on unlit street corners. Strange shouts could be heard not too far away. Shadowy figures approached abandoned buildings and tested locks. Prostitutes led clients into empty lots.

It was a far cry from Kabukichō, Tokyo's most ostentatious red-light district, where sex could look and feel and taste any way one wanted. But Kabukichō was another Tokyo altogether. And that puzzled Hatanaka. A foreigner found murdered in a love hotel was one thing – rare as that was. But a foreigner found murdered in a love hotel in San'ya? That was odd.

Not that Hatanaka cared. He was here, and he was here *first*. Somewhere, on the other side of the world, a mother's phone would ring and announce a cataclysm. But not for Hatanaka. For Hatanaka, this was something else altogether.

'An opportunity,' he whispered.

It had taken him years to finally move up from Assistant Inspector. While countless younger detectives had been fast-tracked through the ranks, Hatanaka had drifted from station to station, fielding more rubbish bags mistaken for corpses than actual dead bodies. By the time he was promoted to Inspector it had become something of an embarrassment. No matter, he had joined Kappa Unit in Shibuya HQ, one of the most respected homicide teams in the country.

Hatanaka quickly found himself out of his depth, working under a fanatically strait-laced senior detective. But the bastard had retired at last, the decision to replace him still up in the air, and the English girl was dead on the ground.

In the alley below he saw a frail figure being helped toward the love hotel, cane out in front like a small antenna. *Commissioner Shindo? But he never comes to crime scenes.*

Swearing excitedly, Hatanaka hurried out of the room. As he took the elevator down, he ran through different responses in his head. Should he respond normally? Or with extra formality? *Relax, just let it happen,* he scolded himself. *The old man isn't going to promote you on how low you bow. Just keep your head in the game. Maybe it's not a promotion, maybe he's putting you in charge of Kappa temporarily. Either way, this is finally your chance to win the old man's trust.*

The doors slid open now and Hatanaka bowed deeply. 'Commissioner, thank you for coming.'

'Does me good to see the sky sometimes.' Isao Shindo, once burly, was now gaunt. After his stroke, one eye had drooped, his lips bunched to one side. The good hand gripped a walking stick, the back of it spotted purple.

'Commissioner, the murder of this young woman is a tragedy. But rest assured, already I have identified some promising –'

Shindo held up a finger. 'We need to talk.'

'Of course,' Hatanaka bowed again and hoped sweat hadn't dripped off his forehead.

The officer who had accompanied the commissioner took his cue and left Shindo leaning against the counter. 'That thing upstairs? That is not a tragedy, Hatanaka. It's a *problem*. A very big problem.'

'Yes, sir. I completely understand. That's why –'

'In a few hours there'll be a circus camped outside this shithole. We're going to be so busy we'd borrow a cat's paw to help.'

'Yes, I agr—'

Another raised finger. 'The Olympics are around the corner and the eyes of the world are going to be on us. The one thing we cannot be is an embarrassment. We *cannot*.'

'No, sir. Absolutely.'

'We need a result here. It has to be done right.'

'Sir, I appreciate that. Which is why –'

'I'm transferring you.'

'. . . What?'

'You're out of Kappa Unit.'

The immediate, irrevocable truth of the statement was a boot in Hatanaka's guts. He knew Shindo was not someone to plead with. Certainly not one for changing his mind. This was happening. Hatanaka was going backwards yet again.

'. . . Out?' He could only murmur it.

'I need you to work the missing prostitutes.'

'Who will lead Kappa Unit?'

'I'm bringing someone else in.'

Jealousy spread through Hatanaka's chest. '. . . An outsider?'

'Yes and no. As it happens, you know him.' Shindo

coughed wet and deep, his half-frozen mouth unable to keep in the spittle. When he could breathe again he unapologetically wiped away the pink flecks from his shirt and gestured for his human walking stick to return.

Shaking, Hatanaka realized this was what passed for an explanation in the old man's mind. 'Commissioner, have I let you down in some way?'

Shindo did not face him. His sigh was long, his response considered. 'You have not.'

'So then may I ask why it's necessary —'

'It's Kosuke Iwata.' He nodded, as if that name were a statement of fact — everything that Hatanaka was not. 'This is just how it has to be.' The officer helped Shindo outside.

Trembling with anger, Hatanaka glared at his hunched back as it darkened with rain.

3. Just Visiting

Iwata's old gunshot wound ached. The rains never failed to revive it, like some tiny creature that had lain dormant within him. As the train crossed over the Arakawa River, he tried to focus on the view out of the window.

Seguro-sekirei birds shuffled along the grassy banks, little plump chests cream white. Though he could not hear them, he knew they would be making *tzi-tzi* calls. After so long away, he was glad they were still here.

It had been almost ten years since Iwata had been back to Japan, a long time anywhere but a Tokyo lifetime. Travelling in from the airport, almost everything felt different to how he remembered – louder, sharper, faster.

And yet, even as an outsider, it was strange to him how comfortably he blended in. For all the time passed, for all the Los Angeles streets he knew by heart, for all the life he had lived since being here last, in just a few hours he had become a Tokyoite again. Though the city conveyed absolute disinterest in who he was these days, who he had become, it still whispered to him: *If you're here, you're mine.* And though it would never be home, Iwata still felt like he belonged somehow. It was a contradictory feeling, but then maybe that was true of all hometowns.

The train driver announced the next station in the gently monotonous tone most Tokyo train drivers employed. Iwata stood. The screens showed it was 11.20 a.m., twenty-seven degrees, and humidity was tickling 90 per cent.

Forty minutes left.

Despite the heat, Iwata wore a black suit, a black tie. Half the people on board were dressed similarly, except for the tie. A black tie meant something in this city. Death.

Glancing around the carriage, he read the headlines – the first few athletes and officials arriving at the Olympic Village amid spiralling costs, and an English girl found murdered. *No doubt she belongs to Shindo now.*

Iwata puffed out his cheeks, his empty stomach knotted. The jet lag pressed down on him, sweat trickling down his thighs and back. He clenched and unclenched his fists in his pockets, trying to keep a steady, calming rhythm.

At Kosuge station the train rolled to a halt and the unique jingle played. Every station in Tokyo had its own. Iwata got off and saw his destination in the distance. The hulking structure dwarfed the little neighbourhoods around it, a strange white building that looked more like the headquarters of a pharmaceutical giant. On the map it resembled an hourglass.

Iwata took the escalator down and exited the station. It was a narrow street, all available space used, every angle appropriated. Little houses stood beneath the arches, as though built for the sole reason of fitting. Featureless apartment blocks hunched over them. Iwata headed for the small pre-war house at the end of the street, its ceramic roof tiles shiny in the rain.

The warm air was thick with cigarette smoke here, with hot laundry and the wet wood of old houses. All around Iwata the rain hissed, a sticky patter through concrete runnels, droplets loudly hitting leaves and bicycle frames.

Turning right, he followed a small grey canal heading east. There was no risk of getting lost, even if he wanted to, the building in the distance too large for that. Just the sight of it exhausted Iwata.

Ordinarily, at this time on a weekday morning, he'd be in his Los Angeles office, his desk cluttered with papers. Or, if he wasn't at his desk, he would be in the borderlands, combing the desert emptiness for lost souls, for bodies, for answers – men and women disappeared while attempting to cross the American border for a better tomorrow.

He wished now that he had not taken Shindo's call. Iwata was a man who always treated telephones respectfully, lifting and dropping them delicately, as though misfortune might be provoked through their mistreatment. In his world, a ringing phone usually preceded tragedy. His work took him to the most desolate corners of the southern borderlands in search of a missing father, mother, daughter, son, cousin, friend.

At night, in motels throughout the deserts of California, Arizona, New Mexico and Texas, he would go over his case files. Jawlines, earrings, student ID cards, a necklace, a tattoo – in the pre-dawn hours, lying in beds that always smelled of loneliness, he would try to connect human memorabilia to the emptiness of the desert. If he was lucky, he would have a whole body. Usually there was nothing.

It was strange work. If he found a sun-bleached fibula next to a torn Reebok running shoe, it was the shoe that reminded him that this person had been human. Had made choices. What to walk in. Where to go. How to stay safe.

Iwata was a chronicler of bones and his career was a sad déjà vu that differed only administratively – names, ages, genders, physical descriptions of the missing. It was his job to find them. It had been for the past five years. But all that had changed with the call. Shindo had spoken the name of a ghost from the past. Now Iwata was here.

For a long time Japan had been an abstraction to him; it had existed only in the past tense. But the bawdy buzz of the cicadas in his ears was too real. The eggy grease drifting in from the Arakawa River too strong. Arakawa meant 'raging river' and thoughts of water always led Iwata to the rocks beneath the lighthouse in his mind, his wife and child smashed on them like foam.

His memories always felt like free fall – places where he had kissed, laughed, failed – all of them crevasses. Cleo and Nina were an abyss.

Fighting nausea, Iwata clutched the canal railings and fought to control his heaving. Closing his eyes, he concentrated on sounds – a bicycle bell, the distant bickering of Tokyo's endless trains. He concentrated on all that was not him. Normally, he thought of Santi to get him through these moments; he thought of those who needed his help. Today it was Hideo Akashi.

You are doing this. Start walking.

Breathing deeply, Iwata opened his eyes. Koi fish lulled in the water below, their little mouths gaping wide 'O's, hopeful for crumbs. Tokyo brought back bad memories. He was glad not to be stopping for long.

By 11.40 a.m. Iwata was inside the Tokyo Detention House and had passed through the rigorous security checks. He was joined by a group of men, their suits and ties also black. They were Metropolitan Police, as he had once been, but they were the new breed – sleeker and shrewder, politicians with badges. Iwata recognized no one and no one looked at him twice.

A guard led them deep into the building, a never-ending labyrinth of windowless corridors and steel doors. The cold air was tinged with bleach and cheap incense. There were no voices, only quietly moaning vents and soles squeaking on the polished floor. The deeper in they went, the more unfathomable the building's function became.

Finally, after three sets of security gates and two elevators down, the group stopped at an unmarked door.

'It will begin in ten minutes,' the guard announced.

Iwata entered to find himself standing on a glass balcony facing a cedar chamber. The chamber was divided in two by blue curtains, the thick carpet a pleasant cream colour. It looked like an ordinary hotel function room, but a Buddhist sutra could be heard distantly, like spiritual muzak. Beneath the cedar chamber was an empty concrete space, featureless except for a small drain in the centre of the floor. A stairway to the left of the balcony led down to it. The smell of persimmon air freshener turned Iwata's stomach.

The suits leaned against the glass balustrade. Everyone was making small talk – how the Olympic Games would lead to headaches, how the English girl would affect things, how taking a morning off would eat into case progress. One detective told an anecdote about a suspect having an epileptic fit mid-interrogation and everyone laughed.

Iwata ignored them, instead concentrating on keeping his breathing even, the clenching and unclenching of his fists rhythmic. The detective standing next to him gave him a nudge. 'Which division you with?'

The clock read 11.59 a.m.

'None,' Iwata replied, his eyes fixed on the chamber. 'Just visiting.'

The man frowned. 'You're family, then. But how? Family are never told in advance.'

Iwata shook his head. 'This man has no family.'

'So then why are —' The curtains ripped open and the suits fell silent.

A tall, blindfolded man stood in the centre of the cedar room. Hideo Akashi was old now, his wild hair pelican white, yet he was still muscular, his grey prison sweats tight against his broad frame. Seeing his old enemy for the first time in a decade triggered a deep, arcane fear in Iwata. Akashi was in a sealed room, his hands and feet bound. Yet Iwata knew what the man was capable of, as though some homicidal Houdini, too large for his small cage.

A rope was cinched around Akashi's neck and ran up to a pulley on the ceiling. Though he stood perfectly still on the red square painted on the floor, he was breathing hard, his chest rising and falling rapidly.

Iwata knew the last face Akashi would have seen was that of Kannon, the goddess of mercy, her statue in the antechamber smiling serenely — she, too, had been sentenced to death. He hoped the sight of her had given Akashi some comfort in these final seconds. Perhaps the priest had been able to get through to him. Or maybe it was possible that Akashi's mind was no longer the warped morass it had been ten years ago. That he no longer lived in his own imaginary world, a fanatical realm of blood sacrifice and purification. But then he opened his mouth.

'Iwata!' he bellowed.

Akashi's voice tore through Iwata, the horror of its familiarity as sudden as a flick knife.

'Are you there!?'

Iwata opened his mouth. The word *yes* fell out.

Akashi smiled, exactly the way Iwata remembered it. It was still a winsome smile. His voice softened a little. 'Thank you for coming.'

The clock struck twelve. Somewhere a telephone call was placed and one word was spoken. Three unseen guards pressed three identical green buttons. There was a loud clank and the trapdoor gave way. Akashi dropped four metres and a quiet but distinct crack filled the air.

After a few seconds of awkward silence the suits began to shuffle out. The man standing next to Iwata gave him a poisonous glance. 'Betrayed his own kind. Better than the mad bastard deserved,' he muttered. Then he was gone, too.

In the corridor their small talk started up again, as though they had just attended some underwhelming briefing on statistics.

When Iwata was alone, he slowly descended the stairway. Akashi's body was swaying gently, the drain beneath gurgling on the piss that dripped down his still-trembling leg.

Iwata delicately removed the blindfold, and tensed. For so long, this face had been in Iwata's nightmares, at first ever present, later surfacing at longer intervals, but never gone. Now he saw it was just the face of an old, crazy man.

Akashi's jaw was still pronounced, but the skin was sagging. Up close, there were little white thorns of stubble that had been missed by the final shave. His head was at an unnatural angle, slumped forward as if disappointed – a kid grounded unfairly.

Iwata slipped his fingers inside his own clammy shirt

and traced the scars Akashi had given him. The knife had delved deep, the blade never really retracted. It had been almost ten years since Iwata had solved the murder of an entire family and identified Akashi as the Black Sun Killer. Ten years since he had confronted him on Tokyo's Rainbow Bridge. On that day, Akashi had almost fallen to his death, but Shingo Hatanaka had caught him. Ever since, Akashi had been suspended in that moment, locked in his own madness, a prison within a prison – waiting out the inevitable.

Now, at last, he had hit the nethermost.

Iwata reached out and touched Akashi's foot lightly. 'Rest,' he whispered.

Outside, it was raining hard, but Iwata was grateful for it. He hailed a taxi and looked back at the Detention House through the mist. How many people had Hideo Akashi sent there himself? How many had he killed? Now he was gone, too.

Iwata was glad it was over. Now the work would begin.

4. Shiny Happy People

Mr Sato woke early. Before he had even stretched out a yawn, he was in a sensationally good mood. He had the day off. *Doesn't mean I don't have work to do, of course.* Allowing himself a few moments more, he breathed in the smell of the house – a soft lemongrass. Then he heard the moan of the vacuum cleaner downstairs.

Sighing, Mr Sato got up and did his stretches. He was no Adonis but he went jogging at least three times a week and lifted weights at the gym most days. He inspected himself now. He was pale. Almost hairless except for his shins, his pubic region and the sparse rings around his nipples. It was a taut and sinewy body, an intertwining of pronounced veins. He liked that his muscles couldn't easily be discerned beneath a shirt and tie.

Sitting on the edge of the bed, Mr Sato checked his testicles for lumps. As he did this, he thought about the girl in the cabin. He knew she would be hungry; the little glucose drip he had set up would run out fast. Another little thing he would have to fix – there were always little jobs to carry out in the cabin. *A handyman's work never ends.* He wondered if the girl was asleep right now. Perhaps she would be crying. Screaming.

Looking down, he saw he was getting hard. He scolded himself and tried to think about something else. Every other minute of the day he thought about his cabin and its contents. He was always dreaming up excuses to get away – he lived in pretext.

Yet he was disciplined. He knew the risks of drawing attention. That was how others got caught. But he wasn't like them. He was smart. He was cautious.

Mr Sato showered, shaved then brushed his teeth. Downstairs, he kissed his wife and drank a cup of black coffee. He dressed in workout clothes, slid 'Slow Hand' by the Pointer Sisters into his ancient Walkman and went outside with a bucket. He always cleaned the car thoroughly, really taking his time over it. The car transported him to the cabin, to his secret, joyful place. The least he could do was keep it clean.

As Mr Sato ran the sponge affectionately along the chassis, his head full of wonderful thoughts, the front door opened and his wife called out to him. He took off his headphones. 'What did you say?'

She looked up and down the street. 'You'd better come in for a moment.'

Inside, Mr Sato sleeved away the sweat from his forehead. 'What is it?'

'Are you going up to the village today?'

'I was planning on it. Time's running out before the festival and there's so much left to do. I was also hoping to take a few hours for myself, maybe shoot a doe or two.'

She smiled. 'Maybe I might come with you for once? Bring the boy, too.'

Though the words enraged him, he grinned. 'Of course, that would be nice. But weren't you going to go running with your friends today? The marathon dry run is coming up.'

Her smile faded. 'I have some bad news.'

For some reason, Mr Sato immediately feared for his cabin, even though he knew it couldn't be that. 'What is it?' he asked, trying not to sound too alarmed.

'I just got a call from the school. He's being sent home for the rest of the day.'

Mr Sato was shocked. '. . . What? Why?'

'Something about an altercation with a classmate. I wasn't given many details.'

'He's never done anything like this before. It must have been the other boy's fault.'

'It was a girl.'

Mr Sato paced the hallway, trying to contain his anger. 'This is unacceptable.'

'I know.' His wife chewed her lips. 'But he's still young and —'

'*Unacceptable!*' He smashed the Walkman against the wall.

After a few moments of silence Mrs Sato reached out and touched his shoulder. '. . . Itsuki?'

'I've had that Walkman twenty years.' He shook his head ruefully, the black fragments shiny at his feet.

'Are you all right?'

He nodded. 'I'm sorry.'

'It's okay. You won't shout when he gets home, will you?'

'Of course not.' He kissed her on the top of the head. 'Why don't you pack a bag? It will be nice.'

She smiled. 'What a man I married.'

Mr Sato watched her hurry up the stairs and tried not to imagine kicking her to death.

Ōkuromori was a reasonable drive north-east of Tokyo, a mountain village of two hundred or so. It had been born

30

out of potato farming, a remote place known for its pines and winding roads. The biggest problems facing Ōkuromori were deer eating the mushrooms before they could be picked and, like many small villages, its old ways dying out.

Mr Sato was known in the village as a quietly successful man with a love of cooking. People were polite to him, despite who his father had been. Some grumbling aside, no one objected when he offered to take over the running of the *matsuri* following the death of the mayor a few months ago. It wasn't much of a festival – some fireworks, home-made beer and a communal stew – but Mr Sato wasn't about to slack off.

Unlike the other villagers, Mr Sato's father had built his house up in the forest overlooking Ōkuromori. In life, he had not been the sort of man to pay any mind to notions of forest spirits or witches. But in death, it was as if Mr Sato's father still inhabited that house somehow, looking down on the village below – distant and watchful. In his honour, Mr Sato made a point of keeping the place clean and ready for the changing seasons. Besides, his son liked playing in the forest.

The Sato family unpacked the car together then started preparing lunch. When the boy left the kitchen, Mrs Sato nodded in the direction of the fishing rods. Mr Sato grinned.

A little after midday, at the bottom of a shadowy forest ridge, Mr Sato and his son were wading through knee-high water. When they found a good patch, they stopped. The water babbled over the metallic melancholy of the cicadas. Father and son stood without moving a muscle, their traps set, spiders in their web. Mr Sato again thought about the cabin. He looked up at the sun in the sky, urging it away, hungry for the moon.

31

By 1 p.m. he had admitted defeat and sat down on the leafy bank. The boy sat next to him, fiddling with a torn piece of rubber on his boot. Mr Sato took out a little foil rectangle from his pocket and snapped it in half. His son took his half and they munched on the chocolate, the sunlight dappling through the branches above them. There was a mountain finch up there somewhere, its sporadic song shrill and toneless.

'So, are you ever going to tell me what happened to your face?'

The boy looked away.

'Come on, you took my bribe.'

'Father.'

'Look, I know about what happened. I just want to hear your side.'

'Someone scratched me. That's all.'

'A girl?'

'Yes.'

Mr Sato balled up the foil and crushed it in the palm of his hand. 'Why did you let her get the better of you? She's just a girl.'

The boy looked up at his father curiously. 'I was taunting her, I didn't expect her to –'

'Oh, yes?' Mr Sato smiled now, for some reason. 'Why were you taunting her?'

'I don't know why. She's nice . . . but I only say mean things to her.'

'What's she like?'

The boy's cheeks reddened.

'Come on, you can tell me.'

'I don't know. She's nice.'

'You like her?'

'When I'm near her I feel afraid . . . but in a warm way.'

'What do you mean?'

The boy looked at the shadow embossed on the grass beneath his feet. He ran his fingers through the blades. 'It's like this shade. Different from the grass, but the same.'

Mr Sato laughed. 'My son, the poet.'

The boy looked away, his blush darkening.

'This girl, is she shy?'

'I don't know.'

'Well, is she similar in behaviour to your mother? Or is she loud and obnoxious?'

'I don't know.'

'If she hit you, she can't be a nice girl. You shouldn't bother with her.'

The boy looked at his father now. 'But why?'

'One day you'll see that although some girls may *look* nice, inside, there's only poison.'

'. . . Poison?'

'Listen to me, boy. The older they get, the worse the poison becomes. It's like –'

They both turned to see Mrs Sato standing behind them, a strange look on her face. She cleared her throat. 'Lunch is almost ready.'

That night in bed Mr Sato stared at the wall, his back to his wife. He was waiting impatiently for her to fall asleep. Instead, she rolled over.

'Itsuki?'

'Yes?' His voice came out warm and gentle despite the squall that churned within him.

'Why did you say that today?'

'What?'

'What you said at the stream to the boy. I overheard you.'

He turned to look at her. 'We were just joking.'

She searched his eyes for a long time. They were smudges in the half-dark, small and cold as riverbed pebbles.

Mr Sato kissed her forehead. 'Sleep now.'

It was gone 3 a.m. by the time Mr Sato could finally seize his chance. It had taken his wife a long time to fall asleep, a silent battle of wills between them. Several times, he'd caught himself nodding off, too. Now he drove towards Lake Ōkuromori at high speed, the dashboard clock cruelly reminding him how many hours he had lost already. Seeing the chinquapin trees, he screeched into the unmarked turning. He left the car in the same place as before and again covered it in the tarp. Mr Sato hurried through the forest, snagging his arms on thorns in the darkness. He was making more noise than he would have liked, but he knew there was no danger of seeing anyone. Nobody came up to this part of the lake. After a catastrophic algae outbreak, it had been cut off years ago. When Mr Sato made the offer to buy the land, the local authority jumped at the chance to sell off the dead space. To them it was worthless, but to Mr Sato it was a wooded lagoon oasis.

He reached the water now but didn't bother with the rubber boots. Even though it was summer, the muddy shoreline was freezing – the shock of the cold delighted him as he squelched his way to the jetty. The boat was heavier than ever, the oars loud through the water. Finally reaching the islet, he leapt out of the boat, ran through the knot of trees and out towards his beloved cabin. *At last at last at last.*

Mr Sato's breath was short and squeaky, his penis hard. He fumbled with the chains and then *thank god* the metallic release. The sound made him bite his tongue in pleasure. *Inside inside inside at last I'm inside again I'm home.*

The door opened. Moonlight painted his kingdom silver. He stood in the doorway and looked at the naked girl the way he always did, his eyes taking in every cut, every bruise, every welt.

'Good evening, Number Seven.' Mr Sato's voice was deeper in the cabin. Jollier.

The young woman in the dentist's examination chair was facing away from him. He knew all she wanted in this moment was to pretend it was all a nightmare. But he could read her, just as he had read the others: she would know this wasn't a nightmare. She was in some kind of cabin somewhere, somewhere with trees and grass outside. These things were all real.

Mr Sato always left the portable surgeon's tray close by but just out of reach. The keys to the handcuffs were there too – some positions required him to free a limb. But he also liked the idea of the girls being just a few centimetres away from their freedom. He knew they would torture themselves with the thought: *If I can just get that tray a little closer, I can get out of here.* He loved the idea that they would hope – there had to be something he had missed, something he'd left out, something that could help them. Instant surrender was a turn-off.

Mr Sato closed the door behind him. The radio was on. He always left it tuned to an eighties channel. In the reddish darkness, he could see the girl's legs open wide, her feet tied to the stirrups. On the portable tray, he saw his utensils. They were sharp. Ready.

As he stared at them, they seemed to take on their own life, the weight of them in the air, their pink, stainless gleam, their proximity to Number Seven – as if they had their own hungers and personalities. They were all wonderful toys, but the hook blade was his favourite.

'Did you miss me?'

The girl was still facing away. She didn't respond. Until now, she had always screamed. This disappointed him, but he retained his cheerful tone. 'You're learning to accept your new world. That's good.'

He turned on the light and began to take off his clothes. Now he paused. The girl was in the chair and naked. All was as it should be. But he realized that her head was slumped at an unnatural angle. He checked her pulse. 'Seven? Speak to me.'

She did not move. He put his fingers beneath her nostrils – nothing. Mr Sato slapped her hard across the face. Her head snapped to the side, but she was still limp. Panicking, he laid his ear to her mouth. The woman went for his jugular vein. He yelped as she bit down on his earlobe. Instantly, he lurched out of reach.

'I'll kill you! *Kill* you!' She bucked against her restraints, blood all over her lips and teeth.

Mr Sato was holding his ear, laughing madly, as if she had just told him a marvellous joke. When he finally collected himself, he applied a small bandage to his wound. 'You're a bad girl.' Another soft chuckle. 'Still, you almost had me there, Seven.'

He sniffed the air now. Checking under the dentist's chair, he tutted. 'You've missed the bucket again. Next time I'll have to bring nappies for my silly baby.'

He took out wet wipes and mopped up between her

legs, the base of the chair, the floor. The girl screamed out the last of her rage.

'Who do you think will hear you? Nobody comes out here. And even if they did, you're just a rutting fox.'

Exhausted, she began to cry.

Mr Sato slotted REM's 'Shiny Happy People' into the cassette player and pressed play. He bounced around with glee as the opening jangled around the cabin, clapped in time.

'I love this song!' He sang along in broken English. 'Don't you love it?'

The girl kept her eyes closed.

When it was over Mr Sato pressed stop. He stood there and licked his lips. 'Seven? I understand you want to kill me. But did you really think it through? Even if you had, then what? Nobody knows you're here. You'd be in trouble, wouldn't you?'

The young woman had no words. The cabin was a whirlpool of surreality and brutal, unrelenting fact.

'I know you're not happy here, Seven. But I'll be honest,' he smiled, almost embarrassed. 'There is nothing more delicious than us in my life. *Together.* When I close my eyes and think of us, that's the song I hear in my head.' Mr Sato took out the Thermos from his bag and poured the black liquid into a pink bowl.

'Oh, god.' The girl whispered. 'Please, not that.'

He placed it in the microwave and keyed in a few seconds. 'I love this cabin, this secret world of ours. You see, when I'm here, that's who I really am. So in a way, that means that I love you, Seven. And together we're going to do something very important.'

The microwave dinged. He took out the bowl and

brought it over, waving a baby spoon. The girl gagged on the stench – a pork-bone broth mixed with semen, saliva, pubic hair, nail clippings and scalp flakes.

'Please.'

'I know, I know,' he soothed. 'But it's the only way, Seven. We need to fuse together. That's how we'll show them.'

'I can't do it any more.'

'Yes you can. If you don't . . .' Mr Sato pointed to his scalpels on the tray.

The young woman opened her trembling mouth.

5. Life is an Adventure

Iwata reached Nagasaki at dusk. He left the central station and headed north. High up in the green hills above the city, the ashes of his old partner – Noriko Sakai – were buried. Iwata calculated she would have been almost forty years old now. From up on those hills, she would have fireworks, city lights, seasons. It suited her somehow.

A hazy red sun was melting into the glassy bay. Like so many others, she had fallen victim to Hideo Akashi. Iwata closed his eyes for a moment. *It's over, Noriko. He's gone.*

The route heading north through Nagasaki was long and hilly. The city behind Iwata was phosphorescent in the darkness, harbour lights reflecting on the water. His footsteps carried on wet cobblestones as he passed lonely shrines, little clouds of steam escaping from ancient bathhouses. Old trams still ran through these streets, one of the few streetcar networks in Japan never to have lost any of its lines.

When he reached the neighbourhood he was looking for, Iwata checked a public information board against the address he'd written down back in Los Angeles. He wasn't far.

The house turned out to be a rain-blackened concrete box hiding behind a disused warehouse. Iwata could tell the man lived alone. That would make things easier.

He knocked, waited a while, but received no answer. It didn't matter; Iwata would wait as long as he had to.

A woman in the house across the street opened her window and started hanging clothes on the line.

Iwata called up to her. 'Excuse me, do you know the man who lives here?'

'The whole street does,' she answered, without looking down.

'Any idea where I find him?'

'Probably the bar on the river. I forget the name, but it has a neon tomato outside.'

'Thank you. Sorry for the disturbance.'

'You're not the first debt collector who's come looking for him.'

Iwata was about to correct her but realized there was nothing to correct.

The Drunken Tomato was the sort of place a man came to drink alone. Except for one red neon strip behind the bottles, the bar was practically pitch black. It smelled of cigarettes and urinal cookies. There was a jukebox in the corner. Iwata saw his mark at the end of the bar, nursing his drink slow. *Savouring it.*

Dropping some coins into the jukebox, Iwata chose Patsy Cline's 'Crazy' then ordered whiskey. The barman laid the glass down, but Iwata pointed instead at the old man. The barman frowned; this wasn't the sort of bar where anybody picked up anybody else's tab. When the whiskey was set down, the old man snapped out of his daydream.

Iwata sat with a thin smile. 'Hello, Noboru.'

The old man looked at him with slow, pink eyes. 'Do I know you?'

'Oh, we go back a long way. Drink up.'

'What's it going to cost me?'

'From the looks of it, you've already paid.'

'Real funny guy.' Noboru necked the dirty gold and winced with relief. 'I've never met you before. You've got the wrong guy, pal.' The old man tried to shuffle off his bar stool, but Iwata held him in place with a hand on the shoulder then motioned for a top-up.

'It's not you I'm looking for, Noboru.'

'So what's it got to do with me?'

'You used to be a driver. Real good one, as I recall.'

The man sipped again, this time the whiskey less sweet. 'That was a long time ago.'

'Not to me. Let's reminisce awhile.'

'You think I'm going to spill my guts just because you bought me a drink?'

'That was just a kind gesture. No, you're going to spill your guts because I'm a cop.'

'Bullshit.'

'I didn't come all this way to bullshit an old drunk.'

Noboru downed the rest. 'What do you want?'

'You were a chauffeur once. Ryoma Hisakawa was your boss.'

'At one time, but . . .' The old man peered at Iwata now, the shock cranking open his lips. 'It's you, isn't it? The little boy.'

'Where can I find him? Give me an address.'

Noboru scoffed. 'How should I know? That bastard canned me the second you and your mother disappeared.'

'Did you get the feeling he wasn't a very nice man?'

'Look, it wasn't my business, all right? I just drove the car, I didn't –'

'Save it. *Hisakawa* – talk.'

41

Noboru ordered another drink and scowled at the red neon. Iwata figured that's where the man did most of his thinking these days.

'Come on, I'm not leaving till you give me something, Noboru.'

'Shit. This doesn't come back to me?'

Iwata held up his hand: *Scout's honour.*

'All right, look. The only thing I know is that Hisakawa was getting involved in politics back then. Man like that would find himself at home in that world, I'd say.'

'People. Places.'

'I used to drop him off at a lounge bar near the National Diet Building. I don't remember the name. Real close to Nagatacho station. Swanky place. Sometimes he'd be in there for hours. Every so often he'd bring councillors into the car and they'd talk.'

'About what?'

'No idea. That was always my cue to take a smoke break. I figured he was sowing his political seeds. But like you said, this was all thirty years ago. I doubt the place is even still there.'

Iwata tossed money on the bar and stood. 'Take care of yourself, Noboru.'

'What is this about, anyway – you going to save the world, Mr Hero Cop?'

Iwata paused at the door. 'Nobody can save the world. Only slow down traffic.'

Puzzled, the old man watched him go.

Iwata checked into a budget business hotel. In a tiny room that looked on to a fire escape, he ate a tuna sandwich and tried to read *The Buenos Aires Quintet* by Manuel Vázquez

42

Montalbán. On the rare occasions that he read for pleasure, Iwata always chose books in Spanish – he was determined to help Santi keep his mother tongue. But tonight he was unable to concentrate on the words. He turned on the TV instead and watched a documentary about green heron.

When it finished, Iwata showered, got into bed and waited till eleven o'clock before phoning home. Six thousand miles across the Pacific, his landline in Los Angeles rang.

'Hey, it's me,' he said when Callie answered.

'Hey.' His ex-girlfriend's voice made him feel at once warm and lonely. 'You okay?'

'Just glad it's over.'

'I can only imagine how horrible it was. Still. You did what you came to do.'

'How's Santi?'

'He's good. Still sleeping. We made *chilaquiles* last night.'

'Thank you for this, Cal.'

'I love spending time with him, you know that. Not like I ever turn you down.'

'I know.' There was a melancholy pause, the space between reality and their happy days as tremendous as the distance between the two telephones.

Callie spoke softly. 'You miss him, huh.'

Iwata wondered if *him* meant *us*. He was almost sure it did not. 'Even when he's in the next room.'

'Since when did you become so sappy?'

'Always was.'

She had no reply to that. 'I'll tell him you said hello.'

'Thanks, Cal. See you soon.'

'You get some sleep.'

Iwata hung up and thought of Santi. After the death of his wife and child, Iwata would walk along the craggy strand where they had fallen. Sometimes he would sit among the rocks and let the tide come in, till it reached to his chest. Life after Cleo and Nina was an empty, grey shore. Even long after leaving Japan he was still present on that beach. But then five years ago, the desert had given him the boy to care for, a pearl spat out by a careless sea.

Santi was the closest thing Iwata got to peace, his only remaining thread to human feeling. He lived for the boy.

They searched for Clash LPs at flea markets on weekends, learned how to cook new dishes by watching YouTube videos in the evenings, practised Spanish nonstop. By now the boy's mother tongue had been overtaken by his English, a perfect little American accent. Yet Iwata always took him to buy groceries at Mexican supermarkets, took the car to Mexican auto repair shops. He wanted the boy to hear his own people, see them, be around them.

Theirs was a strange relationship. They never called each other father and son. They never spoke of the past. They just existed together each day, as though both were aware that this was the only kind of reality this world tolerated.

Iwata had not been a good father to his own child, Nina. He doubted he was to Santi. But he was there. Every single day, he was there – silently fighting despair inside himself to be a stanchion for the boy against the world outside. Iwata preferred not to put things into words, but if that was atonement, so be it. Maybe that's what love was.

On the TV, a cartoon about a talking police car was

44

playing. Though he had muted it, the lyrics to the theme song bounced along the bottom of the screen:

Come play in flower town! You'll see all your friends there, new ones, too, everyone playing in the sun. Even if we lose our way, we won't cry – after all, life is an adventure!

Iwata turned it off. Opening his wallet, he took out a folded photo. Iwata and Santi at Chuck E. Cheese's, bear-hugging one another by the air-hockey machine. Half of Callie was in the background, smiling.

Iwata was a mess of this but also that. Though he never set foot in churches and shook his head at TV preachers, he had memorized whole swathes of biblical verse and found himself silently reciting prayers on morning runs. Even so, Iwata believed wholly in one truth alone: loving those who were close to you until you died.

He was a born drinker with a poetic love of antidepressants, yet he looked away from liquor stores and pharmacies. There was a temper in Iwata, shark-fin quick, a secret and luxuriant rage looking for a way out.

Sometimes he blamed his father, another unwanted inheritance. Other times he claimed his past transgressions as his own. But when he woke up in the morning, trembling with anger, he calmed himself by remembering that he lived for others. That was all.

And in this, a final oxymoron; Iwata had gone to the ends of the Earth for the dead, risked everything. Yet in life he had hurt those who loved him, his own blood. He had hurt them to carry on running from who he was, where he had come from.

You're so good, aren't you? So good at finding other people.

45

But Inspector, tell me something. Have you ever searched for yourself?

A lost woman had once asked him that. At the time, he had not answered. Now, five years later, in a lonely Nagasaki hotel room, Iwata realized it was finally time.

Iwata woke before dawn, trampled by jet lag. His plan was to catch the 5.58 a.m. limited express to Hakata. From there, he would change on to the Tokyo-bound bullet train, *Nozomi*, meaning 'hope'. Iwata didn't dwell on the fact that this had been his mother's name. He had dreamt about her again. Fragments of her – upstairs somewhere, muted sobbing through walls.

Iwata had buried these fragments deep within him for years. But ever since Shindo's call, it was as if his flesh had pushed them out. Things could never go back to how they were. Iwata looked out of the window. It was still dark outside. The rain shrouded the hills above the city. 'Ryoma Hisakawa,' he whispered. 'I'm coming.'

6. Above and Beyond

Anthea Lynch hadn't expected the Metropolitan Police Service to pay for business class, but it pissed her off that the best they could manage was a middle seat in the back row of a twelve-hour flight. Her immediate irritation was the tubby American business type next to her. Between the fat arms and the sideways glances, she pegged him as trouble not long after take-off. In the end it had taken him seven hours and three delicately sipped vodka and tonics to pluck up the courage.

'You from London?' he offered with a nervous grin.

'Yeah.'

'First time to Japan?'

'Second, as it goes.' She looked away.

'Am I picking up one of those cockney accents? I didn't know that was still a thing.'

Lynch looked up at the grey panel above her and prayed the oxygen masks would drop down like angels.

The American persisted. 'So, uh. How come you're going to Tok—'

'Work.'

'And what do you do? Other than talk in short sentences I mean, haha –'

Lynch got up and headed for the toilet, trying to massage her migraine away. She thought about ordering a bottle of wine – plane-sized, harmless. Surely Powell would understand, in these circumstances.

Lynch entered the galley but instead of cabin crew, she found Dylan White – a tallish young man with messy brown hair and unfashionable spectacles over bloodshot eyes. He had an affable face, but his exhaustion was so clear he looked like a walking Lemsip advert.

'All right, Dylan?'

He stared at her as if they had never met before.

She understood – grief was a fog. 'We met yesterday, I'm –'

'DC Lynch, I remember.' He gave a shy, crooked smile now. 'Can't sleep either?'

'Never can on planes. How are you holding up?'

'. . . I'm doing my best to keep it together. You know, for them.' He nodded towards the curtain behind him, where the family of Skye Mackintosh were seated. 'This is all just so mad.' After that, he ran out of words.

'You're doing well, Dylan.' Lynch held his shoulder. 'Honest.'

He smiled sadly then faded back into the moaning gloom of the cabin.

In the toilet Lynch puffed out her cheeks and caught sight of herself in the mirror. She had always cut a striking figure, whether she liked it not – height, hips and wiry limbs. She had her Nigerian mother's big eyes and mulberry lips, her Irish father's freckled cheeks and reddish hair, which she kept buzz-cut short.

But the last few months had taken their toll. She looked older. Tired. The evaluations had flagged hypertension, post-traumatic stress. That sounded a bit much to Lynch, but it was true that she had lost pleasure in things. She would feel faint for no reason. When the insomnia wasn't there, the hazy nightmares were. The truth was, Lynch

48

had reached breaking point. That she lost control when she did didn't surprise her. Only that it took so long.

She'd been put on gardening leave for a month then quietly ushered back in. For the past few weeks she'd been working on the fringes of a routine murder case. Then, yesterday, the call came.

She'd only seen Chief Superintendent Powell once before, on graduation day – some puffed-up speech about the future and how the new recruits would shape it. He'd barely seemed real at the time, epaulettes and silver pips gleaming in the sun, more of a football-club mascot than a copper. Yet in his top-floor office, with his seafaring eyes, Powell looked like a man who lived in a world of unsavoury choices.

'DC Lynch.' He said it like it was a pleasant surprise, despite her file lying open on his desk. 'Sit.'

'Thank you, sir.'

'Get here all right?'

'All the elves know the way to Santa's grotto.'

He smiled politely and returned to the file, his eyes flicking from side to side. Lynch looked out of the window. She had travelled in her time, seen her fair share of bleak cities. But London had its own particular grey emptiness, its old stone crannies holding loneliness like nowhere else.

'Can't be good news, can it, sir? Personnel folder on your desk and that.'

'Tell me something, Anthea.' He closed the file, took off his spectacles and leaned back in his chair. 'How are you getting on?'

'In the Grant case? Well enough, I'd say. There's a lot of back and forth with CPS about whether or not we're looking at –'

49

'Not what I asked.'

She shrugged one shoulder, hoping her smile looked natural. 'Calvin, yeah. You know, busy. I mean, how is anyone?' In her mind's eye she replayed the door being kicked down. The screams. The smell. 'Anyway, sir. Main thing is, I've been cleared to return to duty.'

'Provisionally.'

'And I'm happy to be back.' She wondered how something could be true and a lie at the same time.

'I ask because there's been some –' Powell tinkled his fingernails on a Charlton Athletic mug as he tried to find the right words. 'Concern. Expressed. Regarding your . . .'

Lynch dug her fingernails into the palm of her hand. 'Return?'

'Well-being.'

Lynch blinked, anger unfurling in her chest. 'And where has this *concern* been expressed? From a magic cloud?'

'Now, Anthea, hang on a minute –'

'Sorry, but I do my *job*. I do it to the best of my ability.' Interrupting the Detective Chief Inspector with direct oversight of north-west London's Homicide Command didn't feel like a clever move, but Lynch wasn't that kind of clever. 'I'm out there every day, same as everyone else. I know what I did shook a lot of trees. I do, sir. But either I'm cleared or I'm not.'

'Anything else?'

'I think I deserve to know who is flinging mud in my direction.'

'It was DS Barrett.'

Shopped by her own boss. Lynch had hoped she'd been summoned for a warning. Now she saw her mistake. She wondered if Powell was expecting her to grovel for another chance. Truth was, she didn't have that in her. Lynch looked out over the London skyline. Solving this city's murders was what she had become. Who else could she be now?

'Anthea, look. Barrett says you turn up stinking of alcohol some days. That you're easily provoked by colleagues. Aggressive, even. He's worried about you.'

Lynch stood. 'Suppose I was right, then. Bad news after all.'

'We're not finished.'

'You've been clear enough, sir.'

'Sit *down*, Lynch.'

She held his gaze a few moments too long then took her seat again.

'Concerns were raised, yes' – Powell slurped his tea as if tasting his proposition before making it – 'but it was also made clear that you're one of the finest talents in Barrett's unit. You're an asset to this police force, Anthea. And I want it to stay that way.'

'I don't understand, sir.'

'I'm talking about a *second chance*, girl. They don't always come around.' Powell put his spectacles back on and opened the file again. 'You went to SOAS university, yeah? Studied languages.'

'Linguistics.'

'But you speak Japanese.'

'*Intermediate* Japanese – I'm not following.'

'There's been a homicide, DC Lynch. English girl out in Tokyo. Someone smashed her head in and you can bet it's going to be a right sodding Elliot.'

'I don't see what that's got to do with . . .' She saw.

'The Tokyo nick have formally invited one of my inspectors to shadow their investigation. In the spirit of "openness", you see. I'm sure the Olympics being days away has zero to do with it. 'Course, the Foreign Minister is all over it like a pisshead on a chicken shish.'

'Chief, if you're suggesting that I –'

'I'm not *suggesting* anything. You'll liaise with the family of the victim initially, gather any pertinent information concerning the victim, then accompany them out there.'

'But I'm not . . .'

'What?'

'They should have a proper FLO.'

'They'll have support from the Foreign Office instead. Besides, Tokyo Police said *one inspector*. The gods have chosen you, Anthea.'

'Chief –'

'You'll also keep an eye on the investigation itself. Now look, I'm not expecting you to solve anything, you're just a sock puppet out there. But you will report back to me regularly. Goes without saying that you'll praise their lot every time a mic gets put under your nose. You fly out tomorrow.'

'I didn't sign up for babysitting.'

'Then fuck off out of my police station.'

Lynch stood reflexively, but caught her tongue at the last moment. She sat back down.

Powell glared at her over his mug for a few seconds, then softened. 'Look, I know you've been through the mill recently. After what you've had on your plate, that's normal. But whatever you signed up for is sod all to the people who decide your fate. And it's sod all to me. If you're going to *stay* in this job, you need to do this, Anthea. And without being indelicate, I'm saying stay off the sauce while you're at it. This is going to be very public and you'll be the face of the Met out there. The face of *London*.'

Lynch dug her nails harder into her palms. 'I could say no.'

'And if you did, DS Barrett – the very respected DS Barrett – would almost certainly find himself before the Directorate of Professional Standards with his concerns about you.' He lifted the teabag out of his mug and dropped it in the bin. 'That said, if you could muck in on this one, that'd be a great help for me in trying to allay those concerns, don't you think, Detective Constable? *Japan* is a long way away, after all. You'd be going above and beyond, I'd say.' Not waiting for a reply, Powell took out the Mackintosh case file from his bureau and tossed it over.

Without another word, Lynch collected it and headed for the door.

'Oh, and Anthea? Just to be clear, I'm not saying you have to crack this. But you fuck it up? Well, let's just hope they have an opening for you in Tokyo.'

She bit the insides of her mouth hard before answering. 'Sir.'

'Dismissed.' He slurped his tea. 'Or should I say *sayōnara*?'

In the plane toilet, Lynch splashed her face again and returned to her row. The American was asleep. Easing herself back into her seat, she closed her eyes. '*Above and beyond*,' she whispered to herself. 'Wanker.'

7. Family is Important

Iwata arrived back in Tokyo at 1 p.m. Half an hour later, he was standing outside Maximilian's Lounge. The door plaque told him it had been established in 1971. *Old enough. Close to the National Diet Building. Spitting distance from Nagatacho station. Has to be the place.*

The bar was as swanky as Noboru had described it. Pink ivory wood panels, a concrete feature wall, crimson alligator leather chairs. The half-dark was perfectly calibrated. A piano version of 'What the World Needs Now' tinkled away inoffensively in the background. Cigar smoke gauzed the ceiling, toads in tailored suits guffawed in corners. They stared now as one at the newcomer.

At the bar, Iwata ordered ginger ale with bitters. The barman's tuxedo jacket was a brilliant white, his carnation a deep blood red. He set about preparing the drink as though it were a complex alchemy – aromatic bitters in a tiny glass dropper bottle, fresh pulp from a gleaming lime, imported ginger ale. He served it with a deep bow.

Iwata took a sip. 'Not bad.'

'Thank you, sir.'

'You been working here long?'

'Eight years.'

'You must have overheard some talk in your time.'

The barman smiled emptily. 'I lost my curiosity a long time ago.'

'Diplomatic.' Iwata nodded. 'You could probably show these guys a thing or two.'

The barman laughed uncomfortably. 'Are you in politics, sir?'

'Me? No. I'm in town on business. Tell the truth, I'm taking care of a few things for my recently deceased father. Thing is, he often spoke about this place. I wanted to see it for myself, raise a glass in his honour.'

'Very good, sir.'

'He used to meet a close friend here. Mr Hisakawa? Ryoma Hisakawa? I was hoping to catch him before I leave. You wouldn't know him, would you?'

'I'm afraid not, sir. I don't look at the names on the gold cards, I just charge them.'

Iwata scanned the room and decided the local pond life wouldn't have much to say to him. Thanking the barman, he settled and headed for the door. Passing the last table, a thick hand shot out and grabbed his wrist.

'Haven't seen you before.' The man was the largest of the toads. His bulbous nose shone with grease, the leathery pouches under his eyes folding with a wide, cruel smile. A lifetime of Montecristos and Glenfiddich had scratched his voice raw. King Toad sucked his cigar and puffed out inquisition. 'What was your father's name?'

Iwata glanced down at the thick fist, a gold signet ring glittering. 'Let go.'

'I come here a lot, that's all. Might have known him.' With a shrug, he released Iwata's wrist then adjusted his own gold cufflink. 'But *Hisakawa*? Now him, I do know.'

Iwata's breath caught. 'Where can I find him?'

King Toad smiled the way men with power did when they identified weakness. 'Friend of the family, is he?'

'Something like that.'

'Haven't seen him recently, but you might want to have a look at this.' The huge man double-tapped ash on an open newspaper, his eyes lolling down to the page. 'Family is important, wouldn't you say?'

Reading the cue, Iwata swiped the ash off, picked up the paper and left.

PRIME MINISTER HEDGES BETS IN CABINET RESHUFFLE – APPOINTS OLD HANDS AND RESPECTED LAWMAKERS

DEFENSE MINISTER: RYOMA HISAKAWA

Known for his expertise in national security and defense strategies, Hisakawa assumes the ministry for the first time. He formerly oversaw the Lower House Committee on Security as chairman and has long been a vocal proponent of expanding military operations overseas. In relation to North Korea, he has been a documented advocate of the development of pre-emptive strike mechanisms and is known to be strongly in favour of extending the current arms trade pact with the United States. Currently in Virginia on business, Hisakawa will join his colleagues, many of whom have argued that a superior agreement may be sought elsewhere, in the Cabinet this week.

Other known issues close to his heart include corporate tax reform, boosting rural economies and tough crackdowns on crime. In joining the Cabinet, Hisakawa relinquishes his role at ATLA (Acquisition, Technology and Logistics Agency) as commissioner for weapons development, procurement and export. He is the father of two.

Crashing into the gap between two garbage dumpsters, Iwata vomited violently. Somewhere nearby, a grey tatter of pigeons flapped away. Breathing hard, he fought blackout.

When it had half passed, he staggered out of the alley-way behind the bar, still clutching the newspaper. His head was swimming. The biography in the article meant nothing; they were words about a stranger. But next to the text box there was a photograph.

Iwata had not seen his father's face in over thirty years, but there he was, suddenly flesh, suddenly human. In his sharp ink-blue suit, he looked an amiable man – mostly bald, pink cheeks, a smile beneath the small, neat moustache.

It seemed impossible to Iwata – to know he existed because of this blithesome man. Every moment he'd ever lived, every breath he'd drawn, every case he'd solved or failed in, all of it had been caused by Ryoma Hisakawa. After so many years of pushing him back down into nightmares, the *sight* of him now was like being hit by an eighteen-wheeler.

Panting, eyes streaming, he slumped against the wall. For most of his life, he had suppressed the memories of his father. Now it was as though the truth, which had receded before a tsunami, were roaring back.

Brushing away tears of guilt, Iwata looked down. He was still gripping the newspaper in his hand. He let it drop to the floor.

His father grinned up at him.

Iwata was due at the police station at 3 p.m.; Shindo would be expecting him. The subway was crowded and he ended up next to a stressed young man in a suit holding a musk melon in a gift box. The price tag had not yet been removed – ¥146,000 – easily half a month's salary. Iwata figured it was a gift for a new boss, or perhaps in-laws.

On a whim, he got off one stop early to walk his old route. He passed the nameless canal which still hid behind cramped, overpriced apartment blocks. The graffiti was gone and the restaurants that had once lived on the lonely hours of salarymen had long since failed. Billboards no longer advertised vague concepts such as DVD, SET-MENU, REMEDY. But Tokyo rain still brought out the smell of sewage, commingling with soy sauce and exhaust. Ten years, twenty years – Iwata supposed it always would.

Turning on Meiji-Dori, he saw it: Tokyo Metropolitan Police Shibuya HQ. The last time Iwata had stood across from it, he had been a different person – a lost, uncertain man living an empty life. He had not, of course, found some magical clarity, some kind of pop-psych book resolve. But he had learned to accept life, invested in it, taken the risk of loving again. He had become someone.

Yet now, looking at headquarters, an old fear gripped him. Iwata knew it was only a building – he could walk in and walk right out; it wouldn't change who he was. But there were too many memories there, too much pain, too much yesterday. Not to mention potential enemies.

Ten years ago Iwata's investigation hadn't just ended with the capture of Hideo Akashi – the Black Sun Killer. Dozens of inspectors, officers and officials had been indicted on corruption charges. The sclerosis that for so long had spread through the inner workings of the MPD had been cut away.

Iwata was not expecting to be greeted by well-wishers.

The lights changed and pedestrians flowed around Iwata, checking watches, eyes on phone screens, plastic umbrella skins rasping against one another. It would be so simple just to turn around and head for the airport. Go back to Santi as if nothing had ever happened.

Family is important, wouldn't you say?

King Toad's words sparked in Iwata thoughts of his mother. He had never asked Nozomi why she'd left him as a child while she was alive. But the truth was it had always eaten away at him, gnawed at him. Only after her death had he learned the truth about his father and the rape. If Hisakawa had moved into government, it would be harder to get at him. But by accepting Shindo's offer, he could at least get closer. Iwata would need to step back into his old shoes, revert to what he was at his core – a chaser of bad men – he would need to find Skye Mackintosh's killer, hidden somewhere in the Tokyo depths.

The lights changed. Iwata took a breath and crossed.

8. City of Smiles

After receiving his temporary pass from the front desk, Iwata took the elevator up to the twelfth floor. The elevator was wall to wall with mugshots and missing-persons posters, just as it had been a decade ago. The largest poster was the same one that was plastered all over the main foyer. On it, Pipo-kun, the MPD mascot, a little orange fairy with an antenna on his head, was outlining his vision for Tokyo in 2020 – *The World's Safest City*.

No. 1 Preparation for emergencies! Threats will be handled by our crisis management team.

No. 2 Fighting invisible enemies! We'll protect cyberspace with our sophisticated methods.

No. 3 Fighting organized crime groups! Tokyo will be safe and secure, without violence.

No. 4 Reinvigorate our ties with all communities! Tokyo is an international and diverse city.

No. 5 Hard work will lead to achievements and Tokyo will be the city of smiles!

Directly beneath this was a garish red-and-yellow poster related to a murder with a metal bat in a Roppongi nightclub a few years ago. The suspect was stocky, with scars on his face. A ¥6 million reward for information leading to his arrest was being offered, the words in Japanese except for one phrase in English:

Oh?? Do you know this man? Any little piece of information you have may be helpful. Please give us your tips!

The doors slid open to a large open-plan office, more cramped than Iwata remembered, with a few token pot plants dotted around now. The huge digitized map of Tokyo, black except for wherever incidents flashed red, now seemed dated, but the computers were new. Everyone in the room was working frenetically.

'Iwata!' a familiar voice rang out. 'Don't you recognize your old protégé, bastard?'

'Hatanaka?'

'That's *Inspector* Hatanaka to you.'

Laughing, the two men took each other in. 'It's good to see you.'

'Shame it's in these circumstances.' Hatanaka mimed a noose cracking his neck.

'I was expecting you to witness the execution, too. Being the hero of the day, and all.'

'If I recall correctly, that's not how the press saw it. Not a single mention of my name in any of the articles.' Hatanaka's tone was too sour for the joke. He scratched the irritated skin on his jowls. 'You're here for the English girl, I take it.'

'That's right.' Iwata saw that one of the meeting rooms was packed with schoolkids watching an educational video, Pipo-kun flying around the screen, explaining the importance of remembering the emergency number, 110.

'Well, I was the first inspector on the scene, as it happens. If you want to compare notes, I know a great teahouse not too far away. The house special is really something. They grow it in the shade and brew it at a milder temperature. Fine grade. Full-bodied yet mellow –'

'I'm happy with plain green tea. Listen, I told Shindo 3 p.m.'

'Of course, of course. I'll take you.' While evidently irritated by the rejection, Hatanaka spoke brightly, though with more volume than actual enthusiasm. 'How's life in America?'

They began to make their way through Division One. 'Can't complain.'

Hatanaka shook his head. 'Ten years and a new life on the other side of the world and you reduce it to two words. You haven't changed, then.' They passed a frosted-glass meeting room and he considered their reflections.

Iwata was still slender, unremarkable, though pleasant-looking. His face was fatigued but his eyes, which blinked rarely, belied the focus of a man who established the exact contents of a room as soon as he walked into it. Except for the suntan and grey hair, time had seemingly passed him by. Hatanaka knew the same did not hold true for him and that Iwata would undoubtedly have noticed the weight gain, the loss of hair, the handkerchief kept in his sleeve for mopping sweat.

'So,' Hatanaka said. 'You're American police these days? Joe Friday?'

'No, I set up a small foundation a few years ago.'

Hatanaka hoisted an eyebrow. 'Foundation for what?'

'Finding missing people.'

'Then you should open a branch in Japan. You wouldn't be short of customers. We get more than a hundred thousand a year.'

'I wouldn't use the word *customers*.'

They had reached Hatanaka's cubicle. 'This is me, Kappa Unit. Finest homicide team in the country. Let me introduce you to Tanigawa and Ideguchi. You'll be working with them.'

Two unimpressed detectives looked up. Ideguchi, a bearish man with a buzz cut, said nothing. Nor did Tanigawa, a clean-cut man in his early fifties. He wore braces, his hair slicked back. Iwata could see their rota on the whiteboard; it was plain that neither of the two had had more than a few hours off in the last week, yet Tanigawa looked like he'd just picked up his suit from the dry-cleaner's off the back of a good night's sleep. Iwata figured him for the brains, Ideguchi for the muscle. Immediately, he re-christened them in his head: George Milton and Lennie Small.

The former spoke first. 'So, you're the American Shindo has put in charge.'

Iwata bowed. 'I look forward to working with you.'

George smiled as though the gesture were quaint. 'Welcome back. I think I speak for everyone when I say that I'm keen to learn from your special methods.'

Lennie grinned like a pumpkin.

Hatanaka led Iwata away. 'They take a while to warm up.'

'I take it I'm stepping on some toes being here.'

'Not theirs.' Hatanaka smile was lopsided. 'I'm the one off the Mackintosh case.'

'I didn't realize. I'm sorry.'

'You weren't to know. The old man has me investigating some missing hookers. Might as well be looking for farts in the wind.'

They had arrived at Shindo's office. 'I have to say, it's strange seeing you, Iwata. You look just the same.'

'Except for the grey.'

Hatanaka nodded. They had run out of things to say.

'Well, let me know if you want to compare notes. Like I say, I was first on the –'

'It was good to see you.'

'Okay. Oh, one last thing. I don't know if you know but Shindo is . . . unwell.' Hatanaka shuffled back to his cubicle, where George and Lennie ignored him.

Iwata turned and read the plaque on the door:

COMMISSIONER ISAO SHINDO

Bastard makes Commissioner but keeps his old office. Knocking once, Iwata entered and saw an old, yellowed man standing by the window, taking little drags on his cigarette. When he turned, his face distorted, his teeth greyed, Iwata was shocked to see that it was Shindo.

'Kosuke. Been a while. Come on, sit.'

The two men regarded each other in silence. Whenever Iwata had imagined this reunion with his old boss, there were always fond words and glasses raised to ghosts. But sitting once again with him after so long, the matter-of-fact silence was the only way it could have been.

'So. You watched that fucker hang?'

Iwata nodded.

'I hope you pissed on his swinging body.'

Iwata understood his hatred. Shindo was the only other person left in this world to miss Noriko Sakai as much as he did. 'Anyway. How you doing, kid?'

'Jet lagged. You?'

'Dying.'

'You haven't lost your optimistic outlook.'

'Yeah, yeah. We're all in the gutter, but some of us have pancreatic cancer.'

64

'Maybe you should be at home.'

'I am home.'

Iwata looked around Shindo's little cell of an office. It was absolutely unchanged – endless stacks of paper, a bin overflowing with crushed cans, little dust drifts in unused nooks. He knew Shindo had no wife, no real family to speak of. He wondered who the man might have been, had he not pledged his life to the MPD. Iwata pictured a house with bookshelves and open windows for spring breezes to slip through – downstairs a wife on the phone, their son, now grown, and doing so well at university.

Instead, Shindo had grown old before his time and reached his end in a labyrinth of crimes, a burial hall of paper plinths, his valediction an endless stream of names, dates and distinguishing marks. 'You should think about retirement, boss.'

'Fuck that, I'm in the prime of my life.'

'At least give up the smokes.'

'A hit is a hit.' Shindo crushed his cigarette against the windowpane, dropped it into a can of coffee then grimaced into his seat. 'And a fox is a fox, when all is said and done.' With great effort he stifled a cough, only one half of his face moving. 'I need eyes that see here, Kosuke. Someone with their wits about them.'

'I should tell you to go fuck yourself, Shindo. You know that.'

The old man grinned. 'Not many men talk to me like that in my own office.'

'And not many men on death row are given more than an hour's notice before hanging. Someone gave Akashi a few days. Would you happen to know anything about that?'

Shindo revealed a few grey teeth. It might have been a smile. Or it might have been a wave of pain.

'It was you, wasn't it? You knew you needed me for the English girl's murder, and you tossed my name Akashi's way, knowing he'd request my presence. That shifted the burden of turning down a condemned man on to me.'

'The English girl is a calamity. If I had just asked, you would've said no.'

'For many reasons. You have other people.'

'The capable ones are gone, Iwata. This new lot may have PhDs, but most have never seen a drop of blood. Frogs in a well won't ever know the ocean. You can close this.'

'I went over the file this morning. This case is a blue ruin, Shindo. Based on how little you have, you must know that.'

'We've worked with less. What are you so afraid of?'

'Whoever murdered Skye Mackintosh is smart. Knew the scene before he worked it. Exited on his terms. Didn't leave much of anything behind and he has a big head start. You're trusting me, but it's because you're the one who's afraid. Truth is, I'm not so sure I can get him. Maybe not me, or your Kappa Unit out there, either.'

'I don't believe that. My gut is rotten but it's made more calls than yours. And it's telling me you'll find him.'

Iwata stood and looked through the glass at Division One. It used to be a plaster wall. The new decade was one of transparency. 'I spent a long time trying to put this job behind me. This place. I swore I'd never come back.'

'Yeah, well. We both know you've broken promises before.' With a trembling hand, Shindo dumped out some smokes on his bureau. 'When I was made Commissioner in 2014 we had 127 homicides or attempted homicides.

We cleared 124. I could put my name to that.' With a struggle, he lit up and fell back into his seat. The nicotine hit gave him a millisecond of pleasure in the half of his body he could feel. 'But, Iwata, if this case isn't solved, the English girl will make those stats insignificant. I wasn't joking before. I am dying and, for better or worse, Division One is all I've got left in this world. It's all I am. You look down the barrel of a gun, kid, and I promise you, you start thinking about how what you are sounds like when it's in the past tense. I want to go out with my head held up high. Kosuke, I won't be remembered as the commissioner that shamed Tokyo.'

Iwata exhaled. 'You know, for an old rock, you tell a good sob story.'

Shindo laughed an ugly laugh. 'Consider it my last request. You've already honoured one.'

'If I do this, I have one condition: I investigate as I see fit.'

'That's the only way you know, anyhow.'

'No interference.'

'None from me. What about your work in America? Your son?'

'It's taken care of.'

'So be it. Officially, you'll be a consultant. In practice, you're the lead inspector. Of course, you'll have full support – I have the ear of the Justice Minister – he built half his career on my results. And I'll see to it that your pay will match that of the senior detectives in this division.'

Iwata nodded.

'Oh, I almost forgot.' Shindo opened a drawer and tossed over a leather pocketbook. 'Made a good paperweight all these years.'

Iwata opened his old *techou* and saw the *asahikage*

emblem, a jagged, gold morning sun, the symbol of Japanese law enforcement. Next to it, a photograph of his much younger self, his eyes somehow bigger. Iwata wondered what he had been thinking about in that moment, if his proud smile was real or not.

Now from the drawer Shindo produced handcuffs and a small black snub-nosed revolver. He looked at the clock with his good eye. 'Almost time. The victim's family arrived today. They're going to formally identify the body. Given the attention this is already getting, I want you to meet with them and extend our condolences. We've been accused of being uncaring in similar cases in the past, and I won't have that here.'

Iwata pocketed the gun and the cuffs. 'Understood.'

'There'll also be a press conference tomorrow – the usual suspects, but international outlets as well. I want you to lead the English segment. You'll be on for just a few minutes and you don't need to say much beyond, *We're investigating multiple leads at this time, I can't talk specifics regarding an ongoing case.* The identification will take place this afternoon. You'd better head out there now. You'll be meeting' – Shindo peered at the page in front of him – '*Detective Constable Lynch* from the London Metropolitan Police. She'll be shadowing the investigation. The minister thought it would send a positive message.'

Iwata stood, gazing down at the gold morning sun emblem that he had kept close to his heart all those years ago.

Shindo nodded. 'You'll catch the bastard. I have faith.'

'I don't –' Iwata picked up his *techou*. 'But if this man has made any mistakes? Well, then, there's nowhere in this city that he can hide from me.'

9. A Terrible Thing

Raindrops pattered through the leaves of plane trees; the mating song of the cicadas tinnily buzzed away at the sweltering afternoon. Bunkyō ward was quiet, as though cowed by the belch of distant thunderheads.

Iwata had arrived at the medical examiner's office – a white block building opposite Ohtsuka Hospital. As he crossed the road, he noticed the grey Suzuki Escudo. There were two men inside, both of them staring straight ahead.

Ignoring them, Iwata entered the building and approached the front desk. While waiting for clearance, he looked at the wall. Statistics used to be displayed there: how many dead received last year, how many autopsies carried out. Now the wall was bare. He wondered if displaying last year's statistics meant being held accountable for the following year's.

Iwata was buzzed through secure doors into a quiet corridor. At the end of it, a tall, arresting woman was standing against the wall, arms folded. She wore a black jacket and trousers. On her left arm, like him, she now wore the burgundy armband of the homicide unit. She was holding a large manila envelope in her hand.

Lynch addressed him in Japanese. 'I look forward to working together, Inspector.' Her tone was respectful though contained.

'Likewise, Detective Constable. Should we proceed in English?'

'Yeah. Cheers.' Her own gratitude seemed to annoy her.

'I take it you've already met the family?'

'Yes. They were all interviewed in London before flying out. The boyfriend, too. I was told you'd be provided with the transcripts.'

'I've read them. Is there anything you'd like to go over before we begin?'

'No, let's get this done.'

Iwata took a deep breath and they entered. The small waiting room smelled of orange rind. It was quiet except for an inappropriate vending machine humming nervously at the back. The Mackintosh family had come straight from the airport; their luggage was bundled in the corner of the room. There were four of them, including the boyfriend, Dylan White. He stood at the back of the room, looking out of the window, hands in his pockets, his shoulders slouched forwards.

The mother, Karen, was a short woman with grey, mushroom-cap hair. She was shaking her head and staring off into space, as though searching for answers before an infinite paradox. The sister, Geraldine, was slumped against her father as she wept softly. Her resemblance to the victim was clear. The father, Philip Mackintosh, was a stringy man with a pink face and reddish hair. He kept on taking little sips of water and complaining about the 'terrible noise'. It took a moment for Iwata to realize he was referring to the distant cicadas.

Iwata had seen all these responses before. In the face of the most extreme abnormality, all was normal.

Lynch quietly cleared her throat. 'Hello again, everyone.'

The family looked at her, dumbstruck.

'This is Inspector Iwata of the Tokyo Metropolitan

Police Homicide Division. He will be leading your daughter's case.'

Pink eyes drifted over to Iwata.

'I'm so sorry for your loss.' He bowed. 'I'll be happy to answer any questions you may have at this –'

The father cut in. 'Inspector, we've come a long way. We'd just appreciate it if you could tell us whether it's Skye or not.'

'I understand. However, formal identification requires the involvement of at least one family member.'

'But you must *know* it's her.'

Lynch stepped forward and placed the manila envelope on the table. 'Mr Mackintosh, in this envelope there are photographs, okay? Both police forces believe they are of your daughter. I'm afraid I'm going to have to ask you to look at them.'

The man drained the last of his water and began to shake his head. 'Maybe now isn't the right . . . the right time.'

'Dad!' Geraldine wailed.

'I'm sorry, but no –' He was shouting now. 'We haven't been here more than five minutes and we're being forced –'

'For god's sake, Phil.' His wife was holding her chest. 'Don't make this about you controlling everything –'

'This is nothing to do with me! It's them! What if *they've* made a mistake?'

'Dad, we wouldn't be here unless –'

'No! They make mistakes. We've seen that before. The girl – what was her name? You know the one. How long did her killer give them the slip? Years!'

'Mr Mackintosh?' Lynch sat down on the free sofa and slit the envelope open. 'This is a terrible thing. I can only imagine what you're going through.' Her tone was at once gentle and uncompromising. 'But I'm afraid there is no alternative. I'm sorry.'

Drained of his anger, the father nodded. He accepted the hug from his daughter and tried to take another sip from his empty bottle.

'All right, so ah, how do we . . . I mean, how . . . ?'

'One of you, or all of you, whichever is most comfortable, will sit down next to me. Then I will show you the images one by one. I won't lie to you, they will be hard to look at. But I'll describe what you'll be seeing in each one beforehand. You'll tell me anything you recognize from the images: scars, birthmarks, and so on. The process won't take more than a few minutes. Do you understand?'

Philip Mackintosh nodded. Lynch looked to the mother, the sister, the boyfriend in turn – they all nodded, too. 'If any of you need someone to talk to afterwards, that will of course be arranged.'

Iwata considered Lynch with a distant curiosity. He had initially figured her for the junior stuck with the chump job. How many London Met Police detectives spoke Japanese? But Lynch had taken control. Not through wanting to make an impression but out of habit – she was used to dealing with death. Iwata would have to be careful with her, he concluded.

Feeling his eyes, Lynch looked up at him. He glanced away.

Karen Mackintosh sat down on the sofa.

'Whenever you're ready,' Lynch said softly.

The mother took a long, shaky breath and nodded her consent. Knowing the worst was better than fearing it.

The first photograph was taken out of the envelope. Iwata knew it would be as delicate as possible, the injuries barely visible, no gore. Even so, he knew it would destroy the family.

Before it was turned over Iwata quietly left the room. His work in Los Angeles and the border deserts was one long, sorry procession of grieving relatives, his job to manifest the worst for the most vulnerable. He knew the fewer present in that moment, the better.

Outside the waiting room Iwata clenched and unclenched his fists in his pockets, again searching for that steady, calming rhythm. As he did this, he reached for positive thoughts. They always centred on Santi. But even this made him anxious now.

Often he would lie awake at night, fearful of what would happen one day when questions were asked. When Santi's falsified records landed on the wrong desk. The story was that Iwata had adopted him. He'd been very young when they'd both crossed the desert together, from Mexico into the US – Iwata on a case, Santi with his mother, fleeing violence in search of a better life. She hadn't made it out alive.

Santi hardly ever asked about her. Perhaps he didn't want to know the truth. Either way, Iwata knew, one day, he would have to speak to him of that desert. Take him there, even. Allow the boy to face the landscape of his childhood nightmares. Explain what had happened to his mother. Admit how close the desert had come to claiming them, too. The thought of it made Iwata nauseous. What was happening next door made him nauseous.

This whole place did.

Ten minutes later the Mackintosh family emerged in a stricken silence. The horrible mistake scenario they had clung to on the flight from London was now fully dispelled. There was no denying the beauty spot, the little scar on the shin, the depth of Skye's whiskey-gold eyes.

They drifted past Iwata, the walls of the corridor lined with notices, the kanji like a secret code they would never comprehend.

Lynch came out a second later. 'The boyfriend is still in there.'

'I'll get him.'

Dylan White was in the corner by the window. Up close, Iwata saw that the younger man was taller than he'd thought; his slenderness gave him the bearing of a shorter man. Dylan was chewing his lips as he gazed up at the branches of the plane tree outside. The rain had stopped and a bird was shivering itself free of droplets. 'Is that a jay?'

'I think so.'

'Skye loved jays.'

A short silence followed, tiny dust motes sparking in the brief grey sun.

'You've seen the photographs?' Dylan asked.

Iwata nodded.

'I looked at them, too . . . It was her. It was Skye. But she was so . . . gone. Just gone.'

'I'm sorry.'

'Inspector –' He turned to face him with wet eyes. 'The person who did this . . . you'll find them?'

Iwata placed a hand on his shoulder. 'We're going to try our best.'

Dylan White took one last sad look at the bird. Iwata started rolling the suitcases out, but the younger man brushed him off. 'I'll get mine.'

'I've got it.'

'No, no. Couldn't have that,' Dylan muttered.

Once they were clear of the building, Lynch explained to the Mackintosh family that a Foreign Office representative would be waiting for them at their hotel to go over the next steps, including the press conference tomorrow morning. She asked if there were any questions. There were none. For now the only relevant question had already been answered.

A car arrived and the family got in without another word. Then they were gone.

Iwata and Lynch returned to the medical examiner's office and took the elevator to the basement. The doors opened to a darkened corridor with low ceilings. They heard whistling – 'Row, Row, Row Your Boat' – and a short woman in her fifties emerged out of the gloom. She wore a lab coat with ink stains about the pockets, her grey hair in a ponytail, her fingers yellow from tobacco.

'Doctor Eguchi,' Iwata said. 'Long time.'

'I'll be damned.' She smiled a smoker's smile. 'Inspector Iwata.'

'This is Detective Constable Lynch from London. She'll be with me.'

'I see.' Eguchi eyed her for a moment. 'Well, Forensic Pathology will be in touch in the next day or two' – she pointed to a dim side room – 'and you can suit up in there.'

Iwata and Lynch turned away from each other to put on scrubs, face masks and eye goggles.

Then they entered the gleaming main chamber.

The body of Skye Mackintosh was on the furthest autopsy table, illuminated by powerful lamps, like a lost pharaoh. The ventilation system clunked, the strip lighting was stark; a good venue for appraising demise. There was formalin in the air, irritating Iwata's eyes despite the goggles. Eguchi stood behind the bare body, hands behind her back, a waiter at a posh restaurant.

Iwata took a secret breath and glanced down. The girl had been pretty, early twenties, dark blonde hair which death was quickly turning straw yellow. She was fairly tall, longish limbs, the body of a swimmer. But gravity had already taken effect on the stagnant blood inside Skye, the lividity evident – some areas were white, others a blotchy purple.

'Time of death likely sits between 8 p.m. and midnight on 7 July,' Eguchi began. 'She wasn't in bad condition when she was found, considering the heat. Air con obviously helped somewhat. Death is by blunt-force trauma. One major cranial penetration to the left side of the head concentrated on the temporal lobe. Linear fracture on that side of the skull. Some abrasions to the face and forearms. The body doesn't look to have been moved after death. And no sexual interference. Blood and stomach contents all typical.'

Iwata had no response. This was the very same table where Sakai had lain in death. He had identified her – she had no one else. The memory of his murdered partner was too real, an echo heard too close. He closed his eyes and shook his head. He knew it now: he should not have come back – his body was shaking, it was telling him *no*.

'Inspector?' Eguchi said.

'The weapon,' Lynch cut across. 'Any idea?'

Eguchi looked up at her, taken aback by her Japanese.

'Uh, actually, that's the only interesting part.' Eguchi addressed Iwata once more. 'Initially, I assumed it to be a hammer, but the signature is somewhat odd. Definitely something heavy – a tool of some kind, I'd say. Though that doesn't tell you much.' The phone began to ring. 'Excuse me, Inspector. I need to take that. But in any case, there's not much more to add. I will of course let you know if there's anything else.'

When she had gone, Lynch turned to Iwata. 'Everything Calvin?'

'What?'

'Calvin Klein. Fine.'

'That's cute.' He jutted his chin down at the body. 'What do you see, Detective Constable?'

She held Iwata's gaze for a moment before looking back down at the girl. 'Common defensive wounds. Looks like the victim fought for her life. She doesn't dye her hair. Her nails look like they've been done recently, salon job. But they've been cut hastily. Could be that she managed to scratch the killer, but Clever Clogs didn't want his DNA under her nails. Either way, he's right-handed, I reckon.'

'Anything else?'

'Her pubic area has been recently waxed. Now maybe she just prefers it that way, 'course. But this, and taking into account where she was found? You ask me, she had another boyfriend, someone else she was seeing. And if I'm on the money here, then whoever that man is would be my first port of call.'

Iwata nodded. 'Mine, too.'

10. Spider in the Corner

Iwata and Lynch got into the unmarked Nissan Altima and soon reached Metropolitan Expressway 6. For the second time in two days Iwata crossed the Arakawa River. In the distance, the white frame of the Detention House rose up. He looked away.

The colossal grey expressway flyover curved along the river. In the shadows beneath its concrete supports tiny, ragged figures were hunched, piles of cans between their legs. They crushed them underfoot, or with bricks and rocks, some using old steel tampers. The homeless of San'ya had been crushing cans as long as cans had been around. As Iwata's eyes lingered on them, he felt he'd been wrong. Maybe Tokyo hadn't changed all that much. Nor had his place in it: to seek out those who took away life. *We all have our cans to crush.*

Iwata turned into an alleyway near the Namidabashi crossing – 'The Bridge of Tears. Centuries ago, the condemned had bid their final goodbyes here before being taken on to the execution grounds. Long since built over with railway tracks, there was little left now beyond the Kubikiri Jizō, the Decapitation statue, its arcane smile slowly fading through rain and time.

Iwata killed the engine and Lynch woke with a start.

'Sorry,' she said, her voice rough.

'Don't apologize,' Iwata replied. 'The jet lag is no joke.'

They got out of the car, holding the case files, and heard the *snick-snack* of the trains overhead, their warm eddies mixing in with the smell of wet concrete. Both of them glanced up at the statue looming over the small cemetery. Big black butterflies bobbed through the gravestones, glad of the break in the rain.

A few hundred metres down the road, passing the Tamahimeinari shrine, Iwata and Lynch reached the crime scene. It was hard to miss: the paparazzo huddle crowded the police tape. Seeing the two detectives now, they turned as one, Kodak-crazed tourists catching their first glimpse of the *Mona Lisa*.

Do you deny the rumours, Inspector?! Are we dealing with a murdered Western prostitute?!

Is there a murderer on the loose on the streets of Tokyo?

Inspector Iwata, this way!! Face the camera!!

Barging their way through, Iwata and Lynch cleared the police perimeter. They made their way down the alleyway, both of them automatically scanning for details.

'How did they know your name?'

'Same way they knew to be here in the first place,' Iwata answered, without looking up from the case file. 'Bribes.'

The photographs from the case file hadn't done the love hotel's smallness justice – it was definitely a *starlet*, not a star.

He pointed to the fire exit at the side of the building. 'Probably how the killer escaped. Staff don't have the alarm activated to allow for cigarette breaks.'

'Why not just smoke out front?'

'Prying eyes scare customers away.'

They considered the fire exit. Beyond that, there was only the main entrance and a finite list of people who had used it in the last few days. Iwata and Lynch already knew the details of the case; the musical notes had already been put down on paper for them. Now it was time to see if the piece played in tune.

A detective in his late twenties was waiting by the entrance. He was wearing a cheap rain jacket, drinking 7-Eleven coffee. Seeing Iwata, he leapt up to bow but scalded himself.

'I'm Assistant Inspector Itō, sir.'

'Iwata.'

'It's an honour. You're the replacement, then?'

'Yes, I'll be substituting for Hatanaka.'

'Oh. You know him?'

Iwata nodded, reading a hidden loathing in the word *him*. 'You were to him what he once was to me. This is Detective Constable Lynch from the London Metropolitan Police.'

Itō bowed, less deeply, but added in English. 'A pleasure to meet you, Detective.'

Lynch returned the gesture but said nothing.

Iwata pointed to the bin by the entrance of the love hotel. 'Assistant Inspector, has that trash can been searched?'

'Yes, sir. Only cigarette butts.'

'What about the other trash cans?'

'We searched all the ones in the love hotel, yes.'

'I mean on this whole block.'

'Oh. I don't –'

'Have every single one searched. Look for gloves, a cellphone, anything the killer might have left behind. I know it's unlikely we'll find anything after almost a week, but it won't hurt to look.'

'Absolutely, sir.'

'Also we need the victim's cellphone records.'

'They've been requested, but they'll take some time.'

'Ask Shindo to light a fire – he's good at that.'

Itō led them inside. At the elevator, he handed over the master keycard. Iwata pressed the button and, almost as an afterthought, added: 'You can wait down here.'

'Sorry?' Itō was too slow to hide his incredulity.

'I said you can wait down here.'

'But . . . I'm assigned to the Mackintosh investigation. It's my job to assist you.'

'I understand. You will assist me by waiting here.'

Itō glanced over at Lynch. 'And her?'

'She's with me.'

'Forgive me, Inspector. But I thought her role was simply to *observe* this investigation.'

Iwata's tone frosted over. 'And it's mine to lead it. If you have an issue, you can take it up with Commissioner Shindo.'

Itō bowed. 'I'm ready to help in any way I can, sir.'

'Good. I believe I already gave you a task.'

The elevator arrived and Iwata and Lynch entered. After a few seconds of strained silence, they stepped out on the eighth floor, put on nitrile gloves and silently entered *Andromeda*. It was a small room, the purple satin bedsheets hardly disturbed. The purple walls and painted star systems looked silly in the grey daylight. Everything in the bedroom and bathroom had already been bagged and tagged, corresponding perfectly to the information contained in their case files.

Iwata stalked through both rooms methodically, occasionally looking down at the notes in his hand. It felt like Mass at a church he had not attended in a long time. Lynch did the same, though she wasn't able to understand everything in the case file.

They started at the fringes of the rooms and worked their way in, combing for any missed detail, any hidden component. When they met in the middle, she replayed the smashing motion of the killer, while Iwata imitated the body's fall. They both inspected the body outline on the floor and pored over the images of Skye's final position. The two officers found little to disagree on.

Lynch chewed gum to help her think. Iwata stretched his legs. In the bathroom, he surveyed the city through the window. In the grey amplitudes, vast yet remote, he saw the two rivers – the Sumida and the Arakawa, curving away from, then towards, each other, two lusting snakes.

During the last five years that Iwata had been working missing-persons cases in those infinite deserts, answers had been almost always a rarity. Still, there were often commonalities – points of entry into the US, certain supplies they carried, cellphone numbers. And the goal was always the same. Iwata could understand what that person had been doing in the desert in the first place. And he understood the myriad dangers that awaited them.

Yet *Andromeda* was a small vacuum. *What was Skye doing in this love hotel? And who wanted to kill her?*

In Iwata's experience, homicide was rarely more than an instance, a single breath, almost never orchestrated. But here was a murder that, despite its conventional appearance, did not sit right with him. A murder without fingerprints, seemingly without DNA. Just a body left behind, the only necessary component; nothing more, nothing less. And a murder which, in just a few hours, was going to belong to everyone.

Iwata sleeved away the sweat from his forehead and returned to the bedroom. 'Thoughts?'

'No good ones.' Lynch pursed her lips. 'At this point all I know is he's right-handed. If I'm guessing, I'd say this girl meant something to him. Reckon he probably arranged for her to meet him here, so let's bet he knows this area. Maybe he lives locally. Works nearby. At the very least, he feels comfortable around this way. Other than that, pretty much sweet FA.'

'Let's go over what we do know. When was Skye last seen alive?'

'We know she came here alone on the night of 7 July. A takeaway pizza arrives sometime around 10 p.m., and, as it stands, that's the last person that would have seen her alive. Her clothes were left here, her purse and money, but no travel card, no phone. As for *how* she arrived here, we still don't know.'

'CCTV would tell us more.'

'Thinking caps on. Why did Skye come here?'

'This is a love hotel. We have to guess she was either meeting a partner or a friend. We can't yet discount the possibility of the murderer being a client. Any of these seem a more likely murderer than a pizza deliveryman in a bad mood.'

'Even so, we need to find him.'

'We do.'

'So what next?'

'I'm due to brief the team back at HQ. I want to look into something first, though.'

They made to leave the room, but Iwata paused at the door. He took a step back and gazed down at the corner farthest from where the body would have been. In a little patch of gloom, a tiny object lay supine. It was a spider lying in the shape of an 'X' – bright yellow and black in colour, almost like a cartoon. Crouching down, Iwata gently slipped his hand underneath it, its weight negligible. He held it up to the light, its tiny hairs silver, like dandelion wisps.

Lynch grimaced. 'That's a big bloody spider. You normally get them that size in Tokyo?'

'Not like this, I don't think. Could be it was left here by the killer. Trying to send a message to us?'

'Then he's taking the piss as well as being an escape artist. Marvellous.'

Iwata dropped the spider delicately into a plastic evidence bag and slipped it inside his pocket.

Lynch wrinkled her nose. 'So what's this thing you want to look into?'

'What's British for "hunch"?'

11. Priority Number One

Wedged in beneath the expressway and the river, plywood shacks dragged on as far as the eye could see. Beneath concrete arches and under stairways, in nooks and crannies, the homeless crushed their cans, the clanking sound marking the beat of the last of the evening commute above.

In a concrete niche, a cluster of homeless people had come to sell their aluminium. The middle man was writing down weights and converting them into prices. He was chubby, his notebook twitching as each haul was placed on the scales. Little fingers crept over the calculator and he announced his price.

As Middle Man paused to drink tea from a flask, an elderly man in a Hiroshima Carp hat stood on the scale. Middle Man again ran his fingers over the calculator and the old man laughed.

'The bastard is working out my price!'

Parking under the flyover, the detectives approached. Iwata flashed Middle Man his *techou*.

'Mind if I ask you a few questions?'

Middle Man glanced at Lynch for a moment before pocketing his notebook and leading them away from the group. Iwata took out his own notebook and recorded the man's details. 'You know why we're here, sir?'

'The murdered foreign girl, I'd guess. Everyone in San'ya has heard about that.'

'And what has everyone heard?'

'Just the sirens, the buzz. But I wouldn't say anybody knows anything here. I sure don't.'

'You run the can collection. In the last week, have you noticed anything out of the ordinary?'

'Not especially.'

'You mind flipping through your notebook, just to satisfy my curiosity?'

Middle Man didn't argue, his pudgy finger scanning down columns, names and prices until he stopped and tapped the page. 'This is probably nothing, but I guess it could be classed as "out of the ordinary". It's Ueda, one of my best collectors. He missed the last sale. I've never seen that before. Hasn't shown up today either. Nobody's seen him.'

'What do you know about him?'

'Not much. Lives in one of those shacks. About my height. Late thirties. Slim. Buck teeth. Then again, he's probably just drunk somewhere.'

Iwata wrote this down and underlined the name UEDA twice. 'Tell me about the sale here.'

'Collection every Monday and Wednesday at dawn. The truck comes by and everyone gets their cut.'

'Is there anyone here who might have been keeping an eye out in the last few nights? Particularly over at the riverbank.'

'People here don't really keep an eye out.'

'Some things get seen without meaning to.'

'I wouldn't know.'

'What about whoever lives there?' Iwata pointed to the shack farthest away from the rest, nearest the water's edge. 'He's in a good spot.'

'CEO? You're wasting your time, Inspector.' Middle Man chuckled. 'But what do I know? I don't get paid to be curious.'

'Appreciate your time.'

The two inspectors made their way over to the isolated shack, smelling the grease creeping up from the river. This shack was smaller than the others, holes visible through the rotten wood. Even so, a sign had been placed outside the entrance which read: PRIVATE PROPERTY. Before Iwata could say anything, a small old man emerged and glared at him, his eyes spilled ink on yellowed paper.

'I'm busy. What d'ya want?'

'You live here, sir?'

'I stay here when I'm on business, yes.'

'Since when?'

'Can't recall. Hold on,' CEO went back into his shack. After a minute or two he emerged again, wearing a moth-devoured pinstriped jacket and a bluetooth headset. 'Did those maggots send you over here to bother me?'

'No, sir. It's just that I noticed you have a good view of the bend in the river.'

'Not a bad view. I rest here sometimes, that's all. My work takes me all over Japan.'

'What do you do?'

The old man smiled, half his teeth missing. 'Can't tell you that.'

Iwata took out his *techou*.

'Lawman, eh? Okay, I guess I will admit I used to be . . . *involved*. You know what I mean.'

Iwata raised an eyebrow. 'Yakuza?'

'Look at this.' CEO glanced around and lowered his voice. From his inside jacket pocket he took out an old cellphone with a thick plastic antenna, at least twenty-five years old. 'You think the clan would have entrusted just anyone with this? This *means* something.'

'So maybe a man as well connected as you would be able to help me.'

'I can make things happen. What are you after?'

'Did you see someone come through here six or seven nights ago? They might have thrown something in the river. This would have been late at night, after ten. And something heavy.'

CEO nodded. 'You're talking about George Harrison. I saw him, sure.'

'*The* George Harrison? Or someone who looked like him?'

'I actually met him once. Summer 1966. Beatles tour. They laugh at me, but it's the truth. I was running security backstage. I did a good job and George gave me chewing gum. Ever since then, I've liked gum.'

'Lynch.' She handed over her packet of gum, which Iwata passed to CEO. 'This man you saw. He *looked* like George Harrison?'

CEO emptied out the pieces of gum into his blackened palm and counted them.

'Sir?'

'Hm?'

'The man you saw. Was it someone who looked like George Harrison?'

'What are you talking about?'

Lynch sighed. 'This is a waste of time.'

'You saw a man throwing something in the river,' Iwata persisted.

'Oh yes, I saw him. He was tall, but hard to tell what he looked like, exactly. Still, he threw a green sports bag in the river, of that I'm certain.'

*

Midnight. The briefing room at MPD Shibuya HQ was packed. Iwata recognized several faces from Akashi's execution. Lynch was off to one side, drawing a few furtive looks.

It was to be a joint task force comprising Shindo's most trusted homicide men, Kappa Unit, and, as the body had been found on their turf, detectives from Minami-Senju. Though nobody spoke, doubt hung in the air, thick as the sweat, as though the task force had been asked to go through some ridiculous trust exercise.

Shindo had arrived first, not wanting everyone to see him walking with a cane. The second he cleared his throat, two things happened. The door was shut and the room fell pin-drop silent.

'Sit,' he said.

The room complied.

'This is Kosuke Iwata, formerly of Division One. As I'm sure many of you already know, he worked here some years ago and was responsible for bringing the culprit to justice in the Black Sun Murders. Before that, he solved various cases throughout Ibaraki and Chiba. He currently works as a private investigator in the United States.' He glared around the room, daring anyone to take issue. 'So that's story time over. Now, officially, he is acting as a consultant, but all you need to know is that he is lead investigator in this case. His word is my word. Is that clear?'

The room clamoured in agreement. *No* was not an option.

Iwata took the stage, feeling like a triangle player in a room full of composers. But feelings didn't matter. Not his, nor theirs. 'You all know what we're here to do so I won't waste your time.' He flicked off the lights and the projector flooded the entire back wall with a photograph of Skye Mackintosh. It was the image taken from her resident ID, that same wide, conquering smile.

The task force, cast in blue, all gazed up at her. Then Iwata hit a button on the remote control and the image was replaced with a close-up of her smashed head. There was no audible response to the gore, but several of the younger detectives blanched.

'From here on in, those of you from Minami-Senju will form Team A. Kappa Unit, and anyone else from Shibuya HQ, you will be forming Team B. You will be examining the victim herself: Skye Mackintosh.' Iwata held up his hand to her face like a pastor beneath his god. 'Take her life apart. Who were her friends? Who were her enemies? Who was she sleeping with? Who did she drink with? Who were her classmates? Her lecturers? Did anyone bear a grudge? Did anyone hold a candle? I want her bank accounts dissected, her emails read, her Facebook scoured. I want the whole picture – priority number one.'

Shindo pointed at a young woman sitting near the front. 'Iwata, for computer stuff, I'd talk to Negishi here.'

The young woman bristled with pride at the name-check and Iwata nodded at her before turning back to Team B. 'Relevant intelligence regarding the victim has already been gathered by Detective Constable Lynch over there and her colleagues in London. Each of you has a copy of those findings, along with interview transcripts. I want you to get up to speed as soon as possible.'

The task force leafed through their copies now, while stealing glances at Lynch.

'Lastly, the victim's phone and Suica card are both missing. I want them found. Any questions?' There were none, only questioning looks.

Iwata transferred his attention to the other side of the room. 'Team A, as this murder took place on your patch, your focus will be the love hotel and the surrounding area. That's where your expertise lies and I plan to lean on it.' There were a few earnest nods. These guys didn't know HQ politics and their faces told Iwata they were unlikely to care. This was an opportunity for them to bat in the big leagues.

Iwata continued. 'Now, it's improbable the victim was hanging out at the love hotel for fun. This means the killer likely arranged to meet her there. You will discount no possibility, but it's a good bet that he picked that love hotel for a reason. I want to know what that reason is. Is it significant to him in some way? Is he local? Is the choice of room significant? I also want every employee checked out. Stands to reason they'll say they've never seen Skye before, they don't make it their business to pay attention to faces. So push them. Are we clear so far?'

A murmur.

'Additionally, I want the homeless camps along the river near the love hotel canvassed. Put the word out that we're searching for a man named Ueda – homeless, possibly mid-thirties, he's a can collector in the area. He turned up religiously to sell his aluminium but hasn't been seen since Skye's murder. Ueda is somewhere between 174 to 178 centimetres tall. He also has buck teeth and, as you all know, the man who rented the room in Starlet also had buck teeth. So, while he's not officially a suspect, he's the main suspect. Along with everyone else in Tokyo. Understood?'

Assistant Inspector Itō doodled a man with buck teeth holding a hammer.

'One other possible line of inquiry – an elderly homeless man who lives by the Sumida River saw a tall male dispose of a green bag in the water. Now, I've already requested divers to search for it. It's not much to go on, but he described this man as looking like George Harrison – as in The Beatles.'

There was an amused ripple until Iwata clicked the remote again. This time the image was of Skye's upper body, dark bruising concentrated across her left side. One of the Minami-Senju detectives made a quip about her breasts. There was a burst of laughter but Iwata glared at the culprit until there was silence again.

'Lastly, a word on the murder itself. As you can see, the victim tried to defend herself; there are multiple injuries before the fatal blow – here. Given the meeting place, the lack of forced entry and the aforementioned violence, at this early stage I'd have to assume we're dealing with a killer known to the victim. As for the murder weapon, it seems that we're looking for a tool of some kind. Something heavy with a pointed edge, that's the best we've got. In any case, hotel management have confirmed that there was nothing of that nature lying about in any of its rooms, meaning that the killer brought the murder weapon in with him.' Iwata flicked on the lights and the room squinted up at him. 'That's all I've got. Questions?'

A young Minami-Senju detective with a port-wine stain on his cheek put his hand in the air and leapt to his feet when Iwata nodded at him.

'Inspector, uh, *Consultant* Iwata, the area around the love hotel attracts a lot of drifters. Would you consider it prudent to make inquiries at the building sites and labour exchanges?'

'Certainly can't hurt.'

The next detective, in his late fifties with cauliflower ears, put his hand up. When Iwata nodded at him, he didn't bother standing.

'Your, uh, theory about the killer knowing the victim makes sense to me. But let's be logical about this. What about her family or a boyfriend? Has that been looked at? Were they in the country? In my experience –'

'The victim's family and boyfriend flew in from the UK this morning. Like I said, their statements are enclosed in the file provided to us by the London Metropolitan Police. Anything else?'

At the back of the room, Lennie announced his question by blowing his nose. 'Yeah, I'm just wondering. Are we looking for a guy with buck teeth between 174 and 178 centimetres tall? Or a *tall man who looks like George Harrison*?' One side of his mouth curled up. 'I'm not trying to rain on your parade here, uh, Consultant. I'm just saying, they can't have both killed the girl.'

'Thank you, Inspector Ideguchi. As you say, these two descriptions diverge. For now, the aim is to rule out both men from the inquiry.' Iwata looked around for stragglers. There were none. 'All right. Report back to me via Assistant Inspector Itō. Dismissed.'

Shindo slapped the desk and the task force was mobilized, its detectives shuffling out to complete their duties.

Iwata closed the door after them. Only Shindo, Lynch and Itō remained. It was the latter who spoke now. 'Sir, the CCTV from the local area around the hotel will be ready for viewing soon. Also, we're trying to track down where the pizza was delivered from, but there are a few hundred places within a reasonable radius so it'll take a while.'

'Oh, and the trash from the alleyway behind the love hotel and the surrounding area is in the room next door, ready for you. Unfortunately, no cellphone or gloves.' With a crisp bow, Itō left.

Iwata and Lynch entered the adjoining room, where the contents of nine trash cans had been laid out across two tables. Used condoms, empty cans, stinking noodle cups, banana peels, a broken umbrella – nothing of interest. Putting on nitrile gloves, Iwata cautiously fished through the pile, trying to breathe through his mouth.

'The glamour never stops,' Lynch said. 'Anything?'

'Nope.' Hatanaka knocked on the glass door panel and mimed sipping tea but Iwata ignored him. 'There's a newspaper that's a week old here, so at least it seems the garbage truck has missed some of the cans.'

Lynch picked out a dog-eared ticket for the Golden Koi hydrofoil from Busan to Hakata. 'A ferry ticket?'

'It's dated 6 July. Day before Skye's murder. Could be anyone's, though.' On a whim, Iwata placed the grubby ticket in an evidence bag and pocketed it.

Defeated, the two detectives returned to the briefing room. It was a gloomy blue again, the projector back on.

'That was a nice touch, kid. Assigning the letter "A" to the smaller police department. A little gesture for the Boy Scouts.' Shindo smiled through cigarette smoke then raked at his silvery stubble. 'You went to the crime scene?'

Iwata nodded. 'He left nothing behind. Not a thing. Except this.' He took out the dead spider from his pocket and held it up to the light from Skye's face. 'Could be that the killer left it for us.'

'How do you know it didn't just die there by itself?'

'I don't.'

'Okay, let's say he did. What are you thinking, kid?'

Iwata gazed up at Skye again. 'That I like this less and less.'

12. The Loneliness of Melon Rinds

The high street thronged with midnight life, a bustling vein of neon and noise, international calling card offers, electronic jangling from arcades. It was one of the city's most diverse areas – Vietnamese, Malays, Indians, Filipinos, Arabs, Turks – but Shin-Ōkubo was known as Korea Town. Korean restaurants, Korean stores, Korean markets, Korean boyfriend bars, Korean girlfriend bars, K-pop street performers hoping to be scouted. Up until a week ago, it had also been home to Skye Mackintosh.

'That's where we turn.' Iwata pointed at the huge pachinko parlour. It was painted bright yellow to convey fun and enjoyment. The addicted queued around the block. Cigarette smoke from the building could be smelled two metres away.

As the detectives made the turning, Iwata paused. Across the street, he noticed the same grey Suzuki Escudo from earlier. Peering through the neon glare of the glass, he thought he saw two men in black suits. *The same two from outside the medical examiner's?*

'You recognize them?' Lynch asked.

'It's nothing. Let's go.'

Taking the turning was like a trapdoor to suburbia. The narrow street smelled of wood shavings and cooking oil. Dead wasps in puddles made little crunches underfoot. A child's rubber boot had been forgotten in an empty playground.

Skye Mackintosh's apartment block was at the end of

the street. Like many other new-builds in the area, it had been given a pretentious French name – *Sérénité*. Iwata was glad there were no press camped outside. He figured that would just be a matter of time, though.

On the telephone wires above three fat ravens dozed, black and shiny – rich salarymen in suits.

Iwata pressed the button and the main door buzzed open. A man in his twenties emerged, a roll-up hanging from his lips.

'You're Miyake, the landlord?' Iwata said.

'Yeah, that's me.'

'We appreciate you meeting us, despite the late hour.'

'I'm a night owl.' He answered without looking at them, busy lighting his smoke instead. Despite the heat, Miyake wore a red bobble hat and a diamond-patterned Pringle jumper. He was unshaven and had dirty nails, but Iwata figured it for hipster grunge.

'We're from the MPD, sir. I believe you know what this is about.'

He nodded dispassionately and led them into an L-shaped courtyard of bamboo, flower beds and neat recycling bins.

'She's in number four.' Miyake pointed to the last corridor. 'Or was, I guess.'

'Can I ask how she came to lease your property?'

Miyake blew out smoke that said this was a waste of time, even though he had it to kill. 'Through her university. Some of my properties are listed in their housing catalogues.'

'Mixed gender?'

'No, female only.'

'And did you know Skye Mackintosh?' Lynch asked.

He looked at her sidelong. 'Not really, no.'

Iwata followed up. 'I'd ask you to be specific, sir.'

'Just the occasional greeting. Nothing more. Still, it's a real shame. Word gets out she lived here and it'll be curtains for my property values.'

Iwata ignored the comment. 'Where were you on the night of 7 July?'

Miyake paused for a cautious puff. 'What's that got to do with it?'

'Just routine, sir.'

'I was at home until about half eight, then I headed to a club.'

'Which club?'

'Black Widow. It's not far.'

'What time did you arrive?'

'Around nine, I'd guess.'

'And you live here, correct?'

Miyake pointed up to the top floor.

'Good view of the comings and goings.'

'I don't take an interest.'

'Isn't that part of being a landlord? Taking an interest?'

'What would be the point? People eat, people shower, people go to work. Nothing irregular to see here.'

'Sir, if that were true, you and I wouldn't be having this conversation.'

Miyake shrugged, handed over the duplicate key then leaned against the wall to make another roll-up.

'We'll need you to come in and give a statement, Mr Miyake.'

'Fine.'

They left him and approached Skye's door. A Burberry umbrella hung from the handle. Like everyone else in this block, she had been unconcerned about petty theft.

Iwata slid the key home and they entered. The mess

seemed organic; nothing out of place on first glance. Skye had a collection of paper cranes on the bedside table, a stack of Japanese language books, her laptop charging under her pillow. The *genkan* was overflowing with shoes, battered Adidas Superstars, Converse, a pair of Christian Louboutin heels.

The apartment smelled of floral body mist and stale laundry. There was a portable turntable in the corner next to a potted sugar vine. Beneath it, in a basket with spare candles, Skye's collection of LPs – Stevie Nicks, Grace Jones, O. V. Wright, Lee Fields & The Expressions, The Yeah Yeah Yeahs.

Lynch took the bathroom. She saw hair straighteners, Muji face creams, hair pins. In a glass on the sink there was a single toothbrush and a half-strangled tube of paste. In the bin, used cotton pads, stray hairs and a balled-up receipt for a box of strawberries and hairbands. For Skye's loyalty, she had made a ¥200 saving on her purchases. Lynch sighed.

Iwata's eyes roved around the main room. The bedding was tasteful; she hadn't scrimped. There was a beanbag with a flowery pattern in the corner. It still held a human-sized crater. The wardrobe hung open, though it was only half full – beneath it, an archipelago of clothes strewn across the floor. Fairy lights lined the walls. The windows were locked shut, the air-conditioning had been left on. Above the bed, Skye had tacked up a scratch-off map. *Well travelled*, Iwata thought.

His habit was always to start with the right wall and go from there. He wasn't sure where the quirk came from. Perhaps it was because it worked in mazes.

Lynch joined him in the main room. Between them,

they went through the objects that made up Skye Mackintosh's life. They had already searched the room in which she had died. Now, it was the turn of the place in which she had lived.

Iwata considered the items that had belonged to the girl – a spangly nail varnish that hadn't been touched. A vibrator under the mattress. A universal plug converter. They seemed smaller than normal, emptier for their lack of owner.

In a shoebox, he found a letter from SMBC Bank offering gold credit. The bank's mascot, Midosuke, a sort of green-and-white beaver, was grinning up at the client. *Did you know that I'm one of the most popular emojis used on the LINE app? Why not become my friend and you can send me in your messages to your friends!*

'She's not visible to any neighbours,' Iwata said as he checked the window.

'Or her smarmy landlord.'

'Smarmy?'

'He was very quick to let us know he's not interested in his tenants' lives.'

'I noticed that.'

Lynch moved into the kitchenette, little more than a fridge, a stove and a sink. There was hardly any food here beyond a few cup noodles and two sour-plum rice balls. In the fridge, there were only a few cans of *umeshu*. Lynch caught herself automatically reaching for one. *Stay off the sauce.* That's what Powell had said. But she was exhausted and he was thousands of miles away. He hadn't seen what she had seen. Lynch bet he slept just fine at night.

Hand encircling a can, she looked up and noticed a photograph of Skye. She was next to her sister, screaming on a rollercoaster mid-plunge. Swearing, she closed the fridge.

In the bin she found a used teabag, string beans and melon rinds. Picking up one of the rinds, there were teeth-marks in the dried flesh. To Lynch it felt like the loneliest thing in the world.

After they had searched every inch of Skye Mackintosh's apartment, Iwata and Lynch had local MPD officers take statements again from the neighbours – despite it being 3 a.m. The tenants that answered could only repeat what they had said a few days ago: they hardly saw the young English woman, she kept to herself and made little noise. Nobody had ever seen any strange men in the area, no peeping toms, no flashers, no trouble to report. Certainly nobody had seen her leave the apartments on the evening of the 7th.

It was dawn by the time the detectives left, taking with them Skye's laptop. Back in the car, Iwata headed south.

'Where are you staying?' he asked.

'A budget place near headquarters.'

The news was playing on the radio, the top story focusing on the Olympic Games and problems relating to ticket resales for the impending opening ceremony.

'Anthea, you said you interviewed the Mackintosh family.'

'Front ways and back ways.'

'Are they wealthy?'

'The mother is a council worker. The father's in electronics. I wouldn't say they're "wealthy", but they're comfortable enough.'

'Were they paying Skye's rent?'

'No. They wired her money from time to time, but she had savings, apparently. We looked at her bank accounts on our end and she didn't have two bob to rub together. When do we get access to her Japanese account?'

'Should be this afternoon. But doesn't this seem strange to you? An apartment that nice should be out of reach for her. Fairly large by Tokyo standards, too.'

'And designer clothes all over the gaff.'

'She's a student. She's been in Japan a little less than a year. Yet she has her own apartment in a new complex and she's getting high-end credit-card offers?'

'Seems like there was more to Skye than meets the eye.'

Twenty minutes later, they pulled up outside Lynch's budget hotel. This time, the car stopping didn't wake her up. Iwata touched her arm. She woke with a shout and slapped it away. Her eyes were wide, her fist drawn back.

Iwata's palms were out now. 'Anthea, you're okay. We're here.'

Lynch rubbed her eyes hard then gripped her skull. 'Fuck's sake.'

'Are you all right?'

'Just tired.' She got out of the car, unsteady on her feet.

'I'll pick you up in a few hours.'

Lynch nodded and headed for the lobby, her eyes already falling shut. Iwata watched her enter then started the engine. He recognized nightmares when he saw them.

Within a few minutes he was back at Shibuya HQ. Parking the car, he took the elevator to the second floor, the Cyber Crime Taskforce.

There were still several people working, all of them wearing the dark blue MPD overalls and armbands. Each desk had at least three monitors, piles of wires everywhere, stacks of tablets, laptops, cellphones, hard drives, digital cameras. None of the investigators spoke, not that there would have been any point, given the loud humming from the servers.

Seeing the young woman from the briefing, Iwata approached. 'Negishi, wasn't it? The computer whizz.'

She smiled. 'What can I help you with?'

'I need you to break into this.' He passed her Skye's laptop. 'It belonged to the victim.'

'That won't be a problem. I'm assuming you want the passwords for her email, social media, messengers, bookmarked pages, and so on?'

'Anything at all that tells me who she is.'

'Give me a few hours.'

Iwata thanked her, wrote down his number, then turned to leave.

'Inspector?'

'Hm.'

'I just wanted to say, what you did earlier on? When that guy made the joke about the victim? It was the right thing to do. I know they need their gallows humour, but it's not right.'

He nodded. 'See you later, Negishi.'

As the sun rose, Iwata walked through Shibuya, along catwalks, through underpasses, into backstreets. Everywhere he looked, cranes criss-crossed the kindling sky, men in hard hats hurried to and fro, sparks from behind construction barriers flared up. Shibuya had not changed in that it was always changing, never sticking, forever modifying. On a metal scaffold, someone had graffitied: *TOKYO IS YOURS*.

A few blocks away, Iwata approached a cheap capsule hotel. He looked over his shoulder and stopped still. Had he caught another glimpse of the grey Suzuki Escudo turning off down a nearby side street?

At the hotel reception, Iwata paid for seven days and took the elevator to his floor. Unlocking his capsule, he gave it the once-over. It was the size of a wealthy man's coffin, beige plastic walls, a built-in TV, a panel to control temperature.

Iwata dumped his bag in a locker and changed into his robe and slippers. On the top floor, he entered the male changing room. He put his capsule key and robe in a spare locker. In the first shower cubicle, he sat on a small plastic stool and began to clean himself thoroughly in near-scalding water. He scrubbed his skin hard, the profound ache of his muscles almost taking his breath away. When his entire body was pleasantly raw, he showered himself off.

Next door, the bathing room was like a large green-house looking out over Tokyo. The sun had gone in. Iwata padded over the wet tiles and lowered himself into the hot water. He gasped as his tired bones were enveloped and covered his face with the hand towel. Exhaustion was all there was. His eyes closed, he could hear only the gentle hiss of the sauna, the pattering of rainy season on glass, a distant helicopter snickering somewhere far away.

When Iwata came to, he heard feet splatting loudly on tiles. Peeking out from beneath the towel on his face, he saw a man lower himself into the bath. He was around Iwata's age, his body lean and pale. His facial features were even, his black hair swept neatly to one side. Nothing about the man's physique stood out to Iwata, it was the one thing he was wearing that caught his eye – a gold signet ring.

'You look like you're working too hard.' The man's voice was sedate, a demure smile about his lips.

'Do I know you?'

'No, but I believe you met my boss earlier at Maximilian. My name is Ozawa.'

King Toad. Iwata felt a warm disquietude. 'He sent you?'

'It's not too bad up here. All we need now is whiskey, eh?'

'I don't drink.'

'I can't say that surprises me. You strike me as a sober man,' Ozawa mopped the sweat from his forehead. He switched to English without warning, heavily accented but almost perfect. 'As my superior understands it, you're here investigating the English girl? Terrible business.' He tutted at the ceiling.

Iwata eyed him. 'Your superior – given the bar's location, I'm guessing he's in government. Which department?'

'*The arc of the moral universe is long, but it bends towards justice.* Theodore Parker said that, I believe.'

'So Justice Department.'

'Soon to be.'

'What's his interest in Skye Mackintosh?'

'In her? Zero. And you, Inspector?' Ozawa covered his face with his hand towel. 'You've come a long way for this case. Or was it, perhaps, a pretext to cover another motive?'

'I don't have time to waste on errand boys.' Iwata stood.

Ozawa smiled under his towel, the indent from his mouth moving as if he were some cursed mummy. 'I do what my superior asks of me. And right now he wants to know why you're looking for Ryoma Hisakawa.'

Iwata got out, wrapped himself in the towel and made for the locker.

'Inspector,' Ozawa called. He removed the towel from

his face and smiled with small but prevalent teeth. 'It could be that you and my superior could provide value to each other. Depending on your intentions, of course. He wants to get to know you a little first.'

'Is that why I keep on seeing the same grey car everywhere I go?'

'Oh, them? Who knows who they are.' Ozawa laughed. 'But I wouldn't think you'll be seeing it again after today.'

'Why not?'

'They'll switch cars.' He stood up and towelled water from his body. Lifting his leg on to the rim of the bath, he scratched his balls absently, as though Iwata had been a pleasant but romanceless fuck. 'Think on what we discussed, Inspector.'

13. A Tokyo Skye

Mr Sato was sitting at his desk, clock-watching. The open-plan office was almost empty, its drab silence deafening. He rolled a hard-boiled sweet around his mouth, enjoying the sound of it hitting his enamel. He had always had a sweet tooth.

He had had Number Seven for three weeks now. She had lost a lot of weight; her shine was gone. And now she was sickly. The last thing he wanted was to get sick himself. The smart thing to do, he knew, would be to get rid of Number Seven. After that, he could go to Kabukichō to look for another one. In a rose garden, nobody missed a few blighted petals.

But the thought of the cabin being empty made Mr Sato sad. Number Seven had been his favourite so far. Still, for Number Eight he wanted to go younger. *What if I snatch a new girl tonight and bring her to the cabin? I could get rid of Seven and have a replacement ready to go. Could even make her watch the disposal – that would be some welcome!*

Though even as Mr Sato thought it, a small sadness tugged at him. He had formed a vague affection for Number Seven. She was the first to fight. She had even drawn blood. It stood to reason after what he had done to her. Picturing it, Mr Sato was trance-like now, his body tensed, his mouth open, a string of saliva dripping down his chin.

'Damn it, Sato! Are you deaf?' His colleague was standing over him. 'Your phone is ringing.'

'Oh!' He chuckled. 'Sorry, I was half asleep.'

The man noticed the saliva dripping from Mr Sato's chin, the erection. Saying nothing, he walked off.

Sleeving away the saliva, Mr Sato answered the phone. 'Yes?'

'Itsuki, it's me. I'm thinking of getting home delivery tonight.'

Mr Sato stopped himself from punching the desk. 'Good idea.' He cleared his throat. 'That would be nice.'

'Are you leaving soon?'

'Yes, I can't wait to see you both.'

Mr Sato hung up and looked at the phone murderously. All he wanted was to drive around Kabukichō searching for Number Eight, but he knew it was impossible now. He refused to arouse suspicion in anyone. Especially not his wife. Normality was his cloak and he wore it assiduously. There was only one place in the world he would remove it – his cabin.

No suspicions. And dispose of one before I bring another one in. The formula works. Follow the rules. The TV screen up on the wall was playing the evening news on mute. Though the anchor was a young, beautiful woman, he heard his father's voice coming from her lips. *Don't you let me down, boy.*

Iwata woke with a shout. It was the falling dream again – his wife jumping from the cliff with their baby in her arms. In the warm dark of the capsule, he felt the familiar evisceration of their loss, the end of every dream another small bereavement. He would give anything for another moment with them, even if it was to see them falling again.

The alarm buzzed and the lights flicked on inside the capsule. Iwata stared up at the dim beige ceiling for awhile, just a few inches from his nose. Crawling out, he looked up and down the hallway; with its countless small doors, it resembled a carpeted morgue. He took his clothes to the laundry room downstairs. While he waited for them to dry, he phoned home, but realized Santi would be out somewhere with Callie. He sent the boy a short text saying that he hoped he was having fun and that he would call again tomorrow.

He signed off: *Back soon. Love you.*

Iwata dressed and walked the short distance to Shibuya HQ. Negishi wasn't there, but Skye's laptop was. Next to it, there was a smaller black laptop resting on a small pile of printed pages. There was a Post-it note on it with the words: *As promised.*

At 9.15 a.m. Iwata knocked on Lynch's hotel room door. She answered with a toothbrush in her mouth. He held up the pages Negishi had printed for them and the doppel-gänger laptop.

'We're in.'

Lynch drew the curtains and groaned at the grey morning light. At the table Iwata opened the laptop.

'Skye's social media footprint was pretty minimal, but you had already gleaned as much from her parents. There was nothing particularly interesting in her internet searches, purchases, photos. Most of her online activity seemed to be on her phone, anyway, and her finance records should come through later today. But there is this – Skye's blog.'

'*A Tokyo Skye.*' Lynch browsed through. The background was of a Tokyo cityscape, the sky above it vivid pink. She had two pages on her website: MUSINGS and PHOTOS. The latter was empty. The former contained a few disjointed diary entries.

'Doesn't look like there's too much here, Iwata.'

'About twenty entries. She meanders a lot, almost stream of consciousness at times.'

'Christ, it's too early for that.'

'Not a lot in the way of dates, places or concrete names. But she does mention *someone*.'

My name is Skye Mackintosh, but nobody ever really knew me. How's that for an opening? I'm not using the past tense to be morbid, even if all the girls think there's a crazy man out there snatching young women. I reckon it's bollocks, though. Tokyo is as safe as it gets. If something happens to you here, maybe it's just your time. No, I was using the past tense because I plan to be honest for once. Leave the OLD Skye behind. Hey, maybe that's a kind of death in itself.

Anyway, it's been a while since my last entry. Not that anybody knows this blog exists. Still, reading old posts feels like a different me. Can a diary ever be truthful? Aren't they always written with the secret, pathetic desire to be read? Still, I'm going to try. If only because it gives me something to do before my shift begins. So yeah, this is the new me. And the new me will try and be open. Open as the sky.

Something I've recently made my peace with: I don't have what you would call a dream or a goal. Don't know where I'll be in a year. I let life carry me along. I don't see what's wrong with just existing. I act and talk as if I'm driven by purpose, like everyone else, but I really don't know what I'm doing. I was always like that.

When I was younger I'd make plans with people with no intention of keeping them. Then I'd curl up in bed feeling terrified for some reason and ignore my phone as it buzzed. I don't know why, but I would think of a nest of furious bees and me, the honey lost. There would be days when a new man would absolutely motivate me; I'd hang on his words. I would <u>hunger</u> for his bones. Then the next day I wouldn't be able to bring myself to look at him, everything he said a childish irritation. I've never really known whether I'm coming or going.

I have always liked spur of the moment things. Travel. One thing I've always been sure of is that I wanted to come to Japan. It's always been there in my subconscious, whispering to me. And now I'm here. Funny how life works :)

I don't know why it had to be Japan. My father brought me here once when I was a child; we went to Disneyland. He used to work here for a time – thought that touchscreen digital watches were going to change the world. Or change Hertfordshire, anyway.

I don't really remember the visit all that well, I was only small. I just remember feeling special because my sister was too young to come and it was just me and Dad. I suppose it was magical. After that, there was a Sailor Moon phase. A tea ceremony obsession. Kurosawa box sets and Murakami books for Christmas. I never really grew out of Japan.

Dad's business partner from Osaka came to visit us once. For the life of me, I can't remember his name now. Dad was nervous. His employees, too. It was meant to be a barbecue, but of course it pissed it down. I remember looking out of our window and feeling embarrassed that he'd come all that way to end up with cold sausages in Hatfield. But when he turned up, he was dead polite. Quite handsome in an old, quiet way. He spoke to Dad and his colleagues about new designs. I just remember Dad going red with the effort of trying to impress him, constantly telling Mum to bring out another bottle.

III

At one point, I saw the man sneak out of the garden and into the field behind us. I don't know why but I followed him out. When he saw me he told me in broken English that he was just calling his wife. When I pointed out that he'd left his phone in the kitchen he laughed and asked if I wanted to sit under the chestnut tree with him. He didn't say much of anything, we just watched the clouds getting darker and darker in that chilly field. Then, when it started to *really* rain, he didn't move. I remember his white shirt going see-through. I told him that he'd come a long way just for Hertfordshire. He smiled, put his hand in his pocket and took out a digital watch that glowed blue. When I put it on my wrist it was so big it fell off.

'It doesn't fit me,' I whined.

'We can hide it,' he said, like nothing I did could ever be wrong. 'You can get it when you are bigger.'

He buried it under that chestnut tree. I never saw him again. But that man always stayed with me. I would think about him from time to time. Imagined coming to Japan one day wearing the watch. Wondered what he'd say. Not that I ever found the thing. For all I know, it's still there under the tree.

Years after the visit, G got a digital watch for Christmas. We would play a game with it in the car – the countdown game on the stopwatch – trying to get the milliseconds to stop as close to zero as possible. Every car journey we would do that. One time, I got 00:01. G said it wasn't possible, it hadn't happened. Back then, I was so sure it was real. I don't know any more. Maybe my sister was right and it was all a dream. While I'm at it, maybe my dad's Japanese business partner never buried that watch for me either.

I just know that I like thinking about it. Imagining it buried safely in the warm dirt, nobody in the world knowing it's there except for me. It used to be that thinking about it made me feel better when I was anxious or lonely – imagining time slowly dripping away. It used to make me feel better to think that anything – anything – will pass. It used to make me feel that nothing really mattered all that much in the end. Like, if enough time passed, anything would be OK.

But things have changed now. Everything has changed. Now I feel like I'm running out of time. Everything is happening too fast and I want to be able to savour it all, not miss a single beat. I'm HERE. In Japan. And finally I'm me.

I know I'm putting off writing about it. It's hard to put into words. But I don't want to forget a single detail so I just should fucking start.

It happened in the canteen at Rikkyo. It's all marble floors, Gothic windows and high, vaulted ceilings with wooden beams. Very Harry Potter. All they're missing are the floating candles. That's what I was thinking to myself when K sat down next to me. Can you imagine? What an inane little observation. I was totally oblivious to the fact that my life was about to change.

K was talking to me about something or other, I don't remember what. But I do remember the taste of the sour-plum rice ball we shared. It was such a simple thing, to taste something together. K smiled at me as we chewed and, all of a sudden, I felt something inside me. Simple as that.

God knows I wasn't expecting to meet anyone here. Over here I stand out as it is. I feel the tension of older Japanese men, my height, my hair colour, the loudness of my laughter. It's like my entire existence serves to emasculate them. But K's different. Different to anything that went before.

If I'm honest, I never believed people could be happy. I mean, truly happy. Or at least not the sort of people I am. But now – ridiculously – I'm in love. I realize that doubting real love was like doubting malaria because you've never had it. I thought love was a silly lie, essentially bollocks but lovely fanfare – a Christmas of the heart. But when I look at K I realize now that it is real. Love is everything subtracted except for the terrifying certainty of itself. And now I'm nothing but a container in which to keep these feelings for K. That's all I am now.

Poor D. I understand his behaviour, looking back. I did love him. But I just know I can't ever go back. I'm addicted to my own feelings and I have no space in me at all for anyone else but K. Maybe in the end love is just a balancing act with two distinct weights. If I'm a seesaw, D is the grasshopper, K is the boulder. For the first time in my life, I realize that I'm being who I really am. That's why I had to change. To make the clean start. For me and for K. Just realizing there's no difference between those two things makes me grin like a nutter.

Course, we argued a bit. Work is hard to walk away from when the money is so easy to get used to. But I've already told MM I'm quitting. She didn't seem so bothered. I think she understood, really. Still, I don't feel bad about it. I don't feel much of much about it.

Maybe drained. Tired of men. Fucking <u>men</u>. I gave them my time the same way one stranger lights a match for another. So boring. So empty. So scared. Endless men. Suit after suit after suit. As if it's some kind of costume that says success, belonging, providing. But to me all it says is want, want, want. Well, I don't want anything in my life any more. I have everything I need. I have K. And I think we'll be OK.

Lynch closed the laptop. 'Skye mentions *the girls*. *Shifts*. *Quitting*.'

Iwata nodded. 'Clearly she was working over here in some capacity.'

'And if it's related to the sex industry, that could explain her money.'

He looked out of the window. 'She also mentioned a man *snatching up girls*.'

'Sounded like a rumour.'

'It did, but Hatanaka – an old colleague of mine in Division One – he's working on a case involving missing sex workers.'

'There could be a connection,' Lynch conceded. 'Still, one thing seems pretty bloody clear.'

Iwata stood. 'We need to find K.'

14. Tokyo Removals

Standing in the love hotel room, Kaori Harada had told herself it wasn't real. It couldn't be real. The medication played tricks on her sometimes, that was all it was. Now and then it took a second for reality to snap back into place.

Kaori had shut the door, bile rising in her throat. Closing her eyes, she begged the world not to have changed. But when she looked again, Skye Mackintosh was still lying there, eyes open, blood silently blooming out from her head across the carpet. Her legs were wide apart, feet pointing towards the door, her palms facing up, as if she were resigned to being exposed. Everything else about her naked body seemed as usual, alive and familiar, the downy hairs illuminated by a fallen lamp, like cactus needles in the dawn. But it was her eyes that gave it away, the gold-brown warmth completely gone, now porcelain-doll still in death.

'Skye . . .' Kaori Harada whispered. 'Please get up.'

There was no reply, only the soft hum of Tokyo. And in that tranquil murmur, the loss of love had engulfed her. It had been real. Skye was gone. Everything had changed.

Sinking to her knees, a strange howl left Kaori's body. Unable to look at Skye, she reached out for her foot. It was shockingly cold. Holding the soft, icy object, she wailed and heaved at once.

Somewhere at the fringes of her consciousness, Kaori knew she should call the police. But the thought terrified her. With her past, they would draw the wrong conclusions. They wouldn't understand.

Sobbing in that hotel room, Kaori told herself she could not have done it. She loved Skye Mackintosh. Loved her in a way she had never imagined to be possible. Every moment with her was elation and fragility, felt as one single emotion. Skye was a wondrous assemblage of gestures and mannerisms, a golden bunch of keys, each one opening some new, small part of Kaori.

I could never hurt Skye. That isn't possible.

But Kaori doubted herself.

Before Skye, she had always pictured love to be a tender undertaking. Now she knew it was a lustful anarchy. And in that chaos, there was always fear, always envy. It was true that Skye had given herself to Kaori. But she always wondered if she had given herself *completely*. Kaori understood Skye's job. She had known it from the beginning. Money didn't grow on trees. Her rational side accepted it. Yet her heart did not.

Every moment spent without Skye was a churning, envious misery. Kaori would torture herself with sickening questions: what if there was some small fragment of Skye, not of her mind, or of her heart, but of her *body*, that could not give up those men? What if, deep inside her, there was an animal demand that she could never escape, no matter how much she loved Kaori? Was that why she insisted on keeping their relationship a secret? Why did she linger in quitting Black Widow? And what if there was some tiny parcel of Skye Mackintosh that could never be fully possessed? In the rabid extremity of her love, Kaori Harada wondered: What if she *had* lost control? Truth was, she had been violent before.

'Never,' she had whispered to herself. 'I wouldn't hurt her.'

Desperate to kiss her one last time, Kaori crawled towards Skye's body. She stopped when she felt the stickiness. Like a whirlpool, the blood puddle was darker in the middle. There were flecks on the walls, on the ceiling. It wasn't all blood; there were little chips of bone too. She couldn't kiss Skye now, she wasn't there any more.

Reality seesawed above Kaori, beneath her. *Why would Skye bring me here?* It made no sense. Nothing in this shameful little room made sense, its walls painted like galaxies that smelled of sweat and secrets.

Kaori had struggled to her feet. Then, in slow, serene horror, a spider had emerged from a shadowy corner of the room. It was large, a vibrant black and yellow.

'Manami . . . Is it you?' Although it was the right subspecies, Kaori realized at once it wasn't *her* spider. This one was too small, stumbling, her abdomen shrivelled, close to death.

But if it's not Manami, then why is this spider here? Retching, she came to the realization. *Someone knows about us . . . Someone knows about me.*

Kaori staggered out of the room, into the corridor, down the fire exit stairs. Stumbling into the alleyway, she gasped at the feel of the lashing rain on her skin. Hyperventilating, she ran down the stinking alleyway and clattered into a phone box. *Skye is dead. Skye is dead. Skye is dead.* Hands trembling violently, she dropped the receiver twice. The glass was already steaming up in the hot night. Kaori's finger hovered over the emergency numbers, but she couldn't bring herself to dial.

Dread consumed her. *Why had Skye wanted to meet here?*

Who would do this? Why the spider? Someone knows. Someone knows. Someone knows.

As Kaori tried to calculate outcomes, she peered through the mist. There was a man on the other side of the street. The large silhouette lingered a moment. *Is he looking at me?*

But he was already walking off. With no other options, Kaori opened her wallet and took out the scrap of paper, its numbers faded. It had always been there, like a lifejacket beneath the seat of her existence. With a shuddering breath, she lifted the receiver and dropped in a coin. The glint of silver into the mouth felt like there was no way back.

'Tokyo Removals.' An unremarkable male voice.

'I need your help,' Kaori had whispered.

'Full service?'

'Yes.'

'Tomorrow. 3 a.m.' The man hung up.

When the time came, Kaori Harada was ready. The street-lamp buzzed, the slim moon blotted out. Black puddles glimmered electric orange. Trains groused past overhead. In the distance, skyscrapers pulsed gold in the hot night rain. But that was another Tokyo. These were shabby out-skirts sleeping fitfully under train tracks – streets without names, populated only through lack of choice.

Kaori glanced over her shoulder, her face hidden by a scarf. The area was deserted. That was good. Beyond the level crossing, she found the alleyway. Passing empty lots belonging to feral cats, she stopped at the end of the alley-way. Before her, a decaying warehouse. The sign read:

TOKYO REMOVALS COLLECTIVE

Men in overalls were unloading boxes from unmarked vans. One of them pointed to the back door. 'Upstairs. Wait in the office.'

Kaori entered what had once been a fish-gutting factory and passed through tall stacks of cardboard boxes overflowing with all manner of articles, a vast lost-property room. At the end of it, she climbed a flight of stairs to an office. Inside, it was well ordered, though much of its contents seemed redundant – obsolete computers, dusty radio equipment, tubes of rolled-up tidal maps.

Kaori took off her scarf, brushed the sweat from her brow and sat down across from an old bureau. A sickness had ferreted into the back of her throat, between her shoulder blades. In this empty office, she could only keep on replaying images of Skye's dead body.

The door opened and a woman in her late fifties entered without greeting. Sitting with a groan, she considered Kaori before opening the file in front of her. She plucked out a photocopy of a birth certificate. 'This you?' Her voice was hard, its warmth from whiskey rather than good will.

Kaori nodded.

'Not any more.' The woman scrunched up the page and threw it in the bin. 'You are no longer you. You're nobody. Forget Kaori Harada. It's a bad joke you heard a long time ago. You have a new name. New blood type. New birthday. If you want the world to quit you, you have to do the same. You understand?'

Again, Kaori nodded.

'Good. Now. That scar on your chin, it's not so big but it's the sort of thing people will remember. You make sure to cover it – make-up should work.'

'I understand.'

'So, what are you running from?'

'It doesn't matter.'

'No, it doesn't.' The disinterest in her face was as clear as groundsel in cracked concrete. 'Did you withdraw the money the way you were told to?'

Kaori passed over a small gym bag. The woman opened it and ran her finger along the spines of money bundles. Zipping it up, she nodded. 'You didn't bring anything much with you.'

'I was told not to. Is that what all those boxes downstairs are for?'

'You weren't born yesterday, huh? Most people realize on the big day that they can't live without their trinkets. People pay me for their knickknacks to collect dust. They never come back for 'em, of course.' The old woman peered at Kaori's bag now. 'What did you bring?'

'My clothes. My laptop. My spider.'

'Spider?'

'I like spiders. I raise them.'

'Whatever works for you. But that laptop? You can't ever go online with it. Ever.'

'I understand.'

'All right, then.' The old woman glanced at the clock. 'Well, I hope you're ready, because you'll have to make your own way from now on. We can hide your tracks to a degree, but you'll have to live off grid for the rest of your days. Is that clear?'

'It's not the first time I've had to start again.'

'What about family? Loved ones? They'll look for you. Bring the police into it.'

'Not for me.'

'Very well.' She wiped her fingers in the dust and blew.

A little silent explosion whirled in front of her face. 'Then you are now one of the *johatsu* – you just disappeared.'

As if on cue, a truck could be heard outside now, its engine rattling the windowpane. Business concluded, the woman stood. 'By sunrise, it'll be as if you never lived in this world.'

Kaori wrapped herself in the scarf again and left the warehouse. The removals men kept watch as she got into the back of the truck. Creditors and private detectives could show up at the last moment. Not for nothing did the men keep blades under their overalls.

Inside the truck it smelled of feet and tobacco. Six or seven figures clustered around her, no faces visible in the darkness. The door slammed shut on them, like soldiers bound for an unwinnable war somewhere far away.

A cellphone rang. Someone barked an order. The truck jerked away. In the darkness there were relieved sighs. *Goodbye, Skye*, Kaori thought. *Goodbye, Tokyo.*

The truck went back the way Kaori had come. She saw the lone streetlamp she had passed. The puddle beneath it quivered in a sudden, sour wind. Kaori thought about Skye. She felt a deep, all-encompassing regret that she had wasted so much time with her – arguments and recriminations. *I should have treasured and worshipped her every single moment I had.* Kaori held her head in her hands now. *But there were others that interfered. Others wanted her. Paid for her. Lusted after her. Got in the way of us being together.*

Kaori was trembling with a sudden rage now. She could scarcely believe she had blamed herself at first. *It was him. Of course it was him. How could it have been anyone else?*

She slammed on the back of the cab. 'Stop the truck.'

Kaori was not ready to disappear. Not yet.

15. Who Hurt Me?

The British Embassy was built on some of the most expensive land on Earth, a stone's throw from the Imperial Palace. The Union Jack snapped from side to side, a summer storm brewing above it.

In a basement toilet cubicle, Iwata was vomiting. He knew it was ridiculous; it would only be a few minutes answering rudimentary questions. Nobody was there for him – he was little more than a voice box. But Iwata also knew that it would mean standing in front of the world and revealing himself once more. He retched again.

Ozawa entered wearing an expensive suit and a government party lapel pin. He went to the urinal, unzipped, then looked over his shoulder. 'My superior asked me to come and wish you good luck today.'

'How gracious.' Iwata flushed then went to the sink to wash his face.

Shaking himself off, Ozawa stood alongside Iwata and turned both taps all the way. He leaned forward and spoke softly, in English now, his words barely audible over the gushing water. 'My superior is a man on the rise, Inspector. Understand: a change is coming.'

'You're not going to quote Theodore Parker again, are you?'

'Amusing. Did you consider what we discussed?'

'There's nothing to consider. He wants to see my cards while he's not even at the table.'

'He simply seeks to understand your interest in Hisakawa. As I said before, you may find you have common ground.'

'You'll forgive my reservation.'

'The Ministry of Justice will soon be under his leadership.'

'Which is just another way of saying, *My boss is your boss.*'

'At least a useful man to be friends with.'

'Friends don't send Ozawas.'

'Well, Inspector, you should know that he's not a stupid man – he's well aware of what Commissioner Shindo has done in appointing you.'

'He's earned the right to make his own calls.'

'You're quite the call.'

'He trusts me, that's all.'

'Inspector, you are the desperate move of a man two turns away from checkmate. Shindo doesn't have to live with the fallout of a stupid decision. The Ministry he serves, however, does.' Ozawa slicked back his hair and considered himself in the mirror. 'If I were you, I'd finish this, and finish this fast. There are a lot of people watching.'

Iwata turned off the taps and stepped into the man's space. 'Believe this: you hold nothing over me. Not you, not your boss, nor whatever office he's about to hold. Now you tell him to stop sending his dogs my way. It only wastes time.' Iwata brushed past him for the door.

'The old man,' Ozawa called. 'Don't forget about him.'

Iwata stopped. 'Is that a threat?'

'The new Minister recognizes the great contribution Commissioner Shindo has made over the years. It would be regrettable if his legacy were . . . *sullied.*'

'Shindo has given his entire life to –'

'Everyone has secrets, Inspector. Whether they're real

or not. *You're* responsible now. So even if you don't care about yourself, think about the old cripple at least.'

Iwata swallowed his anger. 'What does your boss want with Ryoma Hisakawa?'

'That doesn't concern you. In the meantime, I leave you with some advice: when the tsunami looms, Inspector, it's prudent to stand on higher ground.'

The door opened and a janitor entered. It was Ozawa who brushed past Iwata now. 'Oh, and Inspector? Do yourself a favour. Get yourself a new suit.'

The press room was mobbed, a morbid buzz in the air. Every seat was taken, sweating reporters jostling for a good view, the TV lights giving the room a harsh pallor. At the front, there was a long table heaving with microphones. The curtains behind it were an ugly red. A few hushed jokes were shared around. Others remarked on the late start.

At nine minutes past eleven the door opened. Iwata entered first, followed by Lynch, the embassy press secretary and the Mackintosh family. The family members all wore the same white T-shirt with a photograph of Skye's face, as though they were fans of some new pop idol. Above and beneath Skye's photo, in both English and Japanese, a message was printed alongside a phone number:

WHO HURT ME?

In gentle tones the press secretary announced the tragic death of Skye Margaret Mackintosh, twenty-two years of age, from Archway, North London. She went on to introduce the members of the Mackintosh family.

Then it was Philip's turn. As he cleared his throat into the microphone, Iwata noticed the journalist in the front row. He was bald, wearing a pince-nez and staring openly at him – eyes intent, unblinking, a slight smile on his lips.

'I am Skye's father . . .' Mackintosh stated, as though the room might implode at this statement. It was met only with expectant looks. 'Less than twenty-four hours ago we were asked to identify the body of our little girl.' His tone was bitter, his expression one of disgust. 'Skye was the sort of person who could light up a room. Indeed, she was the light of my life. That of my wife, Karen, my daughter, Geraldine, and her loving boyfriend, Dylan. Skye never harmed anyone. She had only kindness and compassion for all that crossed her path.'

Karen Mackintosh began to cry now, the breath caught in her throat coming out in high-pitched yips, but Philip did not waver. 'Skye came to this country to study in your fine institutions. To experience your great culture. To learn your language. She loved Japan. And now someone has taken her away from us.' He glared around the room, as though the killer might work for the *Yomiuri Shimbun* or Reuters. 'So now my family is appealing to you, the people of Japan, for any information to help find the individual responsible for Skye's death.' He took out a photograph from his breast pocket of Skye smiling to camera. At this, the cameras starting snapping, bright flashes and the sound of Hungry Hippos – this was the shot. 'If anyone knows anything – anything at all – please contact the police. Please come forward.'

He sat back down. He thanked no one. There was no bow. Ostensibly, the right words had been used, Mackintosh had spoken earnestly and confidently. But Iwata knew he had been too confrontational in his tone, too composed, given his position. There wouldn't be enough sorrow for the liking of the reporters, certainly not enough tears. They liked their articles to follow a neat narrative, something with a clear beginning, middle and end. *Girl is killed. Father distraught.*

As the Mackintosh family was led out of the room there was a respectful silence. The door closed and now the press secretary was introducing Iwata. Before he had a chance to gather himself he was standing at the lectern and squinting into the glare. At the back of the room he saw Ozawa, who gave him a thumbs-up. The room was silent but thrummed with expectation and agendas.

'Good morning. My name is Kosuke Iwata, lead inspector assigned to this case. As you know, I can't answer explicitly on matters relating to ongoing investigations, but I will take questions in a moment and share what I can. At this time a Homicide Division task force is investigating multiple leads, though again, I won't be able to give specifics. One final note.' He motioned to Lynch and she nodded. 'This is Detective Constable Anthea Lynch of the London Metropolitan Police. In the spirit of openness, she will be shadowing the investigation. We are confident her insight will be an asset to the task force – Skye was a Londoner, after all.'

Hands shot up into the air.

'I'll start with you.'

'*Asahi Shimbun.* Can you confirm how the victim died?'

'Blunt-force trauma. At this time, I can't give any further details.' Iwata pointed to the next reporter.

'*Yomiuri Shimbun.* We've had some indication that the victim was found in a love hotel in the old San'ya area. Is that something you can confirm? And if so, what was she doing there?'

'At this stage, I can only confirm that she was found in lodgings in that area. As to what she was doing there, I wouldn't think it wise to speculate. Next.'

'*Mainichi Shimbun.*'

'Yes, I remember you – Tetsuya Suda.'

Suda, a plain man in a simple blazer and jeans, bowed. Iwata had always respected his work and had given him the scoop on the corruption scandal in the MPD all those years ago after the arrest of Hideo Akashi. 'Any word on a suspect, Inspector Iwata? Any description?'

'No. As Mr Mackintosh said, we are appealing to the public for information. If anyone saw a person or persons acting suspiciously between 7 and 8 July in the second *chome* of Kiyokawa, particularly near the Tamahimeinari Shrine, please come forward. It's absolutely vital.' Iwata pointed to a woman in the back row.

'*Tokyo 24.* Inspector, should the people of Tokyo be worried? Is this a one-off? We note the MPD is currently investigating the disappearance of several sex workers in the Kabukichō area.'

'Citizens should, as ever, remain vigilant. However, we currently have no kind of indication that the suspect will act again. For now, the disappearances you mentioned remain unconnected to this case. Individuals working in the Kabukichō area are not typically easy to pin down but, as I understand it, there's no suggestion of foul play. With that said, I would like to remind the public that Tokyo remains one of the safest cities in the world.' Iwata glanced up at the clock. 'We have time for just a few more. You, sir, third row.'

'*Keizai Shimbun.*' The reporter stood, his hair slicked back, a gaudy polka-dot tie. 'Inspector Iwata, this is obviously a most significant case and comes just over a week before the commencement of the Olympics. The world's media is here in our capital. And yet, as we understand it, you are not one of the senior detectives in Division One. Are we to conclude that you have been placed in this role only because of your relationship with Commissioner Shindo?'

A salacious murmuring broke out.

'I'm here to answer questions relating to the case itself, sir. Not debate the commissioner's staffing choices.' Iwata's response was decisive but the question had shifted the tone in the room.

The next reporter stood without invitation. 'Inspector Iwata, we at the *Tokyo Tribune* respectfully recognize your experience in the MPD. But even so, aren't you concerned that your reassignment to Division One may cause a distraction among your colleagues, given your *controversial* past?'

'I don't know what you mean by controversial.'

The reporter smiled awkwardly. The question had been pre-approved by his editor; consensus had been reached. Clarification was now required. 'Well, uh, given the corruption scandal of 2011 and your, ah, role in that. Many police officers and law enforcement officials went to jail. Some say unjustly.'

Iwata had to raise his voice to be heard over the noise. 'It is my job to catch criminals, sir. It's that simple. There was no controversy then. And I see none now.'

Coarse laughter pierced through the racket and the bald man with the pince-nez in the front row stood up. 'Except there *is* controversy, isn't there?' The room fell quiet. 'I'm with the *Kantō Times* and I think you and I both know, *Inspector Iwata*, that you're not even officially a homicide investigator any more. You see, myself and many of my colleagues here have been doing this a long time. We have relationships in the police. Nobody in the MPD knows what you're doing here either. So my question to you is: since your resignation was accepted almost a decade ago, what *exactly* is your official capacity in this investigation? And why did this case have to wait a full week before it had someone to lead it?' Pince-nez sat back down in satisfaction.

Iwata looked around the room. There was no way around it, they were already on the scent; there was no point in lying. 'Officially, I am acting as a consultant on this case –' There was uproar now, furious questions overlapping. 'But frankly, this press conference has not been called to examine my credentials. There are over fifty investigators focusing on Skye Mackintosh's murder around the clock and who have been since the first moment –'

The chaos was total. The press secretary stood and apologized. Reporters barked over her. The battle had been lost. She bundled Iwata out of the room.

In the service elevator, Lynch yawned. 'Well, that went well.'

The Kanda River was swollen by the rain. In the distance, skyscrapers were hidden by mist. Traffic was gridlocked. From up on Expressway No. 5, Lynch looked down at the pedestrians crossing shiny black roads. They inched forwards, the window-wipers bleating against the glass. 'Iwata, you realize that was an ambush back there?'

'I noticed.'

'I've been here for all of five minutes, but it's obvious someone leaked. Those wankers practically said as much.'

'Mm.'

'Aren't you going to do something? Maybe Shindo –'

'Shindo will say the same thing I'll say to you. You know what *shou ga nai* means?'

'It can't be helped.'

'Get used to hearing that.'

The dashboard lit up with an incoming call from Itō. Iwata answered. 'Assistant Inspector, you're on speakerphone.'

'I'm with Team B at Rikkyo University, but I just wanted to let you know the bank records have come through, Inspector.'

'Go ahead.'

'The victim had two Japanese accounts, one with Japan Post Bank – nothing out of the ordinary there. The interesting one is with SMBC.'

'Go on.'

'As you suspected, she had a job. At least temporarily. She drew a salary from a club in Kabukichō for four months, starting last autumn. A fairly low hourly rate with a few bonuses here and there. She worked no more than two or three nights a week.'

'Not enough to bankroll the designer clothes and the nice apartment.'

'No, but get this. On *nine* separate occasions since last December her account received significant cash injections – ranging from ¥100,000 to almost a million. She made the deposits herself. Cash.'

'Who from?'

'It's a business account, but from a different bank – they're refusing to trace it without a court directive. That will take a while.'

'All right, what's this club called?'

'Black Widow.'

'Good work, Itō.' Iwata ended the call.

'Well, well, well,' Lynch said. 'We've heard that name before.'

'The landlord, Miyake – he said he went there the night she was murdered.'

'But according to her bank records, she left the club months before her murder. I suppose it's possible this Miyake bloke didn't know she'd worked there. Either way, whether at Black Widow or out of it, sounds like someone was giving Skye a lot of money. I'd like to know who.'

'Black Widow sounds like a hostess bar. Skye would have been popular, as a Western girl. Maybe she met someone. A *wealthy* someone. She's encouraged to go on a *dohan*.'

'Eh?'

'Basically compensated dating – a nice meal with Mr Big or whatever. The club gets its cut. But maybe after a while Mr Big tells her not to bother with the club any more. Now she has his money, she quits. That explains those deposits.'

'And you think Mr Big is the one who killed Skye?'

Iwata shrugged. 'I don't think anything yet.'

'But for you the slipper fits.'

'You don't think this is the most pressing lead?'

'You ask me, I reckon we need to find the "K" in her blog – love can go wrong, Iwata. Or look, maybe it wasn't K at all. Maybe it was just a guy in class who was jealous of them. The admirer. The spurned friend.'

'But you've already interviewed Skye's family and Dylan. All of them said she had no enemies. Nobody with a grudge.'

'True. Then again, none of them knew she was seeing someone behind Dylan's back, did they? Let alone that she worked at this hostess bar. Clearly, Skye had secrets. If she had an angry boyfriend on the side, she was keeping him quiet. Either way, I'd look at her university. And the men who put their eyes on her every day.'

'But what about the money in her account? That's unlikely to be coming from someone she met in the canteen.'

'Fair dos. I can't explain the money yet. But I've just seen it too many times, Iwata. The nice guy in class. In your office, whatever. You give him an inch of friendship and, before you know it, he's a black hole of greed and possessiveness. So whether it was someone she loved, or someone who wanted her from afar, you ask me? That man will probably be part of Skye's everyday. I'm not saying the hostessing isn't a logical angle, it makes a load of sense. Only that we don't really know if Mr Big even exists yet, just that she made the money. But what we do absolutely know for certain is that she fell in love.'

'She said so herself,' Iwata admitted.

'And that doesn't happen at the Black Widow. That happens in Skye's real life.'

He nodded. 'Okay. Black Widow later. Right now, we find this K.'

16. No Such Thing as a Stranger

Rikkyo University was one of the city's 'Big Six', a liberal arts institution with a focus on international programmes. The main campus building caught the eye, an ivy-laden affair with tall trees and red bricks – a mini Hampton Court Palace in the middle of Tokyo. Students spoke in hushed tones on corners, lips were chewed, pencils tapped. Exam-week tension hung in the air as clear as the cicada song.

The rain had let up but the heat was still stifling as Iwata and Lynch crossed the gardens. Little brown birds hopped along the rich lawns in search of worms. There were no bills posted on walls, no political slogans, no puddles of dried vomit. Only pleasant gardens and the pungency of wet leaves.

Iwata and Lynch entered Skye's old classroom. Lynch regarded the wooden tables and chairs, the dark floor brought to a high varnish. 'Reminds me of my school,' she said.

'Really?'

'Well, that bit does anyway.' She nodded at the crucifix on the wall.

He was about to reply when the door opened and a dozen tired-looking detectives muddled in, led by Tanigawa and Ideguchi – George and Lennie. Iwata thanked them for coming but their silence stated the obvious – gratitude was immaterial, this meeting was not optional.

'Victim's tutor is called Morley Holford,' George began.

'He's Australian. Specializes in "business strategy within the East Asian context", apparently. Speaks excellent Japanese, something he didn't want to escape my attention. That said, he really didn't give me much. Quote: *Skye was a good student, a bright young woman. She delivered good work. Certainly, she never came to me with any issues or problems. But to be frank, I never really got to know Skye.* Now when I asked if he had any concerns about her, he did make it clear that they were in frequent contact throughout the first term but that he had hardly heard from her this term. Holford recently tried to arrange a tutorial, but she ignored two of his emails. He didn't know of anyone she was particularly close to. When I asked him about *their* relationship specifically, he said it never went beyond the confines of Rikkyo. I found him credible.'

'Thank you, Inspector.' Iwata turned to Lennie, who breathed out loudly through his nose before speaking.

'Uh, yeah. I canvassed the vic's classes, study groups, local cafés – pretty much anyone she might have been in contact with. Couldn't find any lovers, any problems, any gossip. Seems like she was on good terms with pretty much everyone. Even those who didn't really know her described her as nice or outgoing.'

'Friends?'

'That's the odd thing. It doesn't look like she had any real friends here. Not a single student or member of staff could give us the name of someone she was close to. The best we got was a dark-haired young woman who was apparently friendly with her. But nobody could put a name to her, nobody knew which class she might have been in. Maybe an *outsider*.' Lennie met Iwata's eyes as he spoke that word.

George took over now. 'We've spoken to the security department about CCTV, but there's a lot of it. Now beyond that, we looked for people with names beginning with "K", like you asked. A few students mentioned a guy that had been paired with the vic in a few projects in her business class. Then there was also another guy in the same academic year as her. Zero connection to her, but by all accounts, not the type to play nice. I questioned them; both have solid alibis. That's all we have.'

Iwata's phone rang. 'Itō . . . You're certain?' There was a long pause. He looked up at Lynch. 'Make sure it's photographed immediately and that nobody touches it. And I mean *nobody*. We're on our way.' Iwata hung up. 'Seems like they've found the murder weapon.'

Far below the elevated freeway by the river, homeless men were playing dice. A woman in her nineties was doing callisthenics with a cigarette in her mouth. Middle Man and his cronies were nowhere to be seen. Can-crushers were sitting outside their plywood shelters. Others sat in corners, in dank gaps between piping, the residual concrete crevices. Wind chimes had been fashioned out of plastic, vegetables planted in cut-up Coke bottles. On a piece of wood, a poem had been painted in awkward characters:

> In the cherry blossom's shade
> there's no such thing
> as a stranger

Commuters on their way home drove over this domain, cycled past it, averted their eyes as their river boats sailed by. Life under the buttresses was ordinarily of no interest to the outside world. But tonight was different. Tonight, for once, the homeless camp near Shirahige Bridge contained something the outside world wanted.

Local police officers, under direction from the detectives in Team A, were tossing tents and pulling apart shacks. Those who dwelled in them had been corralled into the nearby park and were being grilled on the whereabouts of the missing can-crusher: *Where's Ueda! We know you know him! Tell us, or there'll be consequences!*

A few metres away, police divers were sitting on the concrete banks of the river. They were smoking and drinking tea, their work done, their wetsuits glistening black.

Iwata and Lynch got out of the car. Assistant Inspector Itō hurried over. '*Blood*, sir.' He spoke the word with almost starstruck glee. 'A lot of it.'

'Itō, this area was meant to be searched, not demolished.'

'I know. But it seems our Team A colleagues have their own way of doing things here.'

'Look, there's an old man who lives in that shack right over there. He'll be wearing a pinstriped suit. Tell those idiots I want to talk to him.'

'Yes, sir. But I do have an update.' Itō took out his notebook. 'The landlord, Miyake? He came in to give his statement. Nothing interesting there. Then I looked into him: it turns out he was accused of rape several years ago. Kicked out of university along with two of his friends.'

Iwata and Lynch looked at each other.

'He got out of it, though. No prosecution. But there were consequences for him. Seems like Miyake was expected to take over the reins at his old man's corporation. Evidently, that didn't happen, as he's now managing property instead.'

'What about his alibi on the night of Skye's murder? Does it check out?' Lynch asked.

'That's the thing. Several witnesses place him at Black Widow; he didn't leave till 4 a.m. But I can't get corroboration for his time of arrival. He says "around nine-thirty or ten" but we only have his word on that.'

'Okay, Itō. I want you to look into this Miyake on the side. Use your imagination. He has money, we know he goes to hostess clubs – including the one where Skye worked. Dig into his finances. Given his past, we shouldn't have a problem getting hold of these records.'

'Yes, sir. I'll see about that right away.'

Lynch climbed over the river barrier now. Iwata held his breath against the grease and followed her. The divers helped them down into the dinghy and they gathered around the object, a bizarre nativity scene. At their feet, swaddled in plastic sheets, was a green rubber sports bag.

The dinghy bobbed softly. In the distance, the Tokyo Skytree rose up like a dystopian Eiffel Tower. A tepid wind blew and the nearby zelkova trees burbled. Rush hour was droning above in absolute mundanity – surprised commuters glancing down at the blip in their everyday.

'Bag wasn't weighed down,' the diver said.

Iwata zipped it open. Foul river smells seeped out. Sure enough, inside was an old steel tamper. It was the length of a household broom but, instead of bristles, the head was a thick steel square – the size of a beer mat. It was covered in blood and clumps of hair, tiny gobs of brain visible in its grooves.

'It's a tool?' Lynch asked.

Iwata regarded the rubber grip and resisted the urge to touch it. 'Used for paving, dirt packing, gravel levelling – that kind of thing.'

'Who would use this? A construction worker? A gardener?'

'Maybe. Then again . . .' Iwata nodded at the can-crushers beyond the police cordon. There were at least forty of them.

In the sky above them a press helicopter circled. Iwata turned to the police diver. 'Okay, let's get this zipped up and out of view, please.'

Itō's face appeared over the river barrier. 'I found him, Inspector.'

'You!' CEO screeched. 'I might have known this was *your* doing.'

'Hello!' Iwata called up.

'*Hello!?* You assholes are killing me here! Some of us have work to do!'

'I'm sorry, this wasn't my call.'

'Birds of a feather.'

'I'll have them out of here as soon as I can, you have my word on that.'

The old man scowled.

'One question: you answer, we all vanish. Fair?'

CEO waved his hand. 'Fine.'

'When we spoke the other night, you remember you mentioned George Harrison throwing a red bag into the river?'

'Yeah, I remember. But it wasn't red, I said it was green.'

Iwata parted his feet to reveal the green rubber bag. 'Was it this one?'

'Could be.'

'It's very important, sir.'

CEO looked at Lynch. 'She got any more of that gum?'

*

139

After statements had formally been taken and the tamper had been sent off for testing, Iwata and Lynch got back in the car. Itō gave the signal and the recently arrived mass of journalists were parted to let them through. But as Iwata started the engine the young detective from Team A with the port-wine stain rushed over.

'Consultant Iwata, the missing can-crusher, Ueda? We found his shack. It's empty except for trash. But there was this –' He handed over a paper menu. On the front of it there was a fat Italian chef who bore a striking resemblance to Super Mario. A speech bubble was coming out of his mouth: PIACENZA PIZZA!

'Inspector, you think that Ueda could also be the man who delivered to –'

Iwata snatched away the menu and floored the accelerator.

Yanaka was one of the few city quarters where the old Tokyo was still clinging to life. Fishmongers next door to cake shops, watchmakers next door to butchers. Chocolate-box houses and little shrines clustered together as if trying to ward off the future and her big ideas.

Along the main shopping street, fortune cats waved robotically. Tourists eyed ceramic knick-knacks and fried mince croquettes. Couples took selfies at the top of the Sunset Stairs.

Piacenza Pizza was a shabby little store surrounded by money plants and mopeds. A bell trilled as Iwata and Lynch entered.

'*Buonasera*.' A portly man in a dough-caked apron emerged.

'Police,' Iwata replied. 'We spoke earlier.'

'Will this take long?' He addressed Iwata but kept his eyes on Lynch.

'Just a few minutes.'

The owner called for his colleague to mind the counter and led the two detectives into the alleyway. He sat on a tower of empty beer crates and lit a cigarette. 'So. You're here for Ueda, huh?'

'We'd like to speak with him. Routine, you understand.'

'What did he do this time, knock someone over?'

'We can't divulge that.'

'Well, it doesn't surprise me you're after him.' He blew out smoke as thunder rumbled. 'The guy had a short fuse.'

'Violent?'

'I didn't say that. Just a short fuse.'

'But you hired him anyway,' Lynch cut in.

Momentarily taken aback, the man shrugged. 'It's pizza delivery, not charm school.'

'So, a short fuse but not violent.'

'Nothing major. Just a few outbursts.'

'How long has Ueda been working for you?' Iwata asked.

'One year and eleven days. All part-time.'

'Good memory.'

'I looked at his file this morning.'

'You were thinking about firing Ueda.'

'Nothing gets past him, huh?' Pizza Man winked at Lynch. 'Yes, I was thinking about firing him.'

'Because he hasn't shown up since 7 July?'

'It's not the first time he's disappeared. My drivers are all local and I can always get cover. That's not the issue.'

'So?'

'I've had one or two complaints from customers. *Don't send that guy next time, he smells bad. He gave my girlfriend a funny look and now he has our address.* That kind of thing. Anyway, I hired Ueda in the first place because I felt sorry for him.

141

He was a smart guy and a hard worker. But like I say, he was prone to outbursts. Acted like everything in life was unfair. Throw in the negative comments from customers and yeah, I was thinking about firing him. Now that you guys are sniffing around, I'm done.'

'One of your pizzas was delivered to the Starlet Hotel at 9.52 p.m. on 7 of July. You can confirm it was Ueda who did that run?'

'Yes.'

'How do you know?'

'He was the only driver on shift when that order came through. I hit my bell, the box was picked up, then off it went.' Pizza Man stubbed out his smoke. 'Speaking of which, I should get back.'

Iwata handed over a card. 'If he shows up, you call this number.'

'*Buonasera*.' At the end of the alleyway, the man looked back. 'Oh, and detectives, if you do find Ueda? Tell him from me he's fired.'

Iwata turned to Lynch. 'This fucking guy. Metropolitan Police Homicide Department and Human Resources for Piacenza Pizza, at your service.'

'Something tells me that when we find this Ueda he's going to have bigger problems than a job hunt.'

17. I ♥ Kabukichō

Kabukichō. Sleepless Town. A neon pleasure circus that indulged the full rainbow of human perversion. Soap-lands, grope trains, gay bars, fake classrooms, pink salons, cabarets, bath houses, massage parlours, S&M dungeons, trans clubs, happening bars, maid cafés, hostess bars, host bars – it didn't matter what it was called, what was spilled, who was used, who was gratified, who was scammed – pleasure was money and pockets weren't judgemental. Kabukichō was a gold mine and it was just metres away from Shinjuku station, which spat out 3.6 million potential punters every single day.

Beneath the electric-candy cavalcade, in thimble-sized bars sloppy shots were poured high. Men in suits whispered in narrow alleyways. And everywhere the human symphony resounded – footfall, laughter, shoulders brushing. Above it all, a neon sign flickered in the warm rain:

I ♥ KABUKICHO

As Iwata and Lynch crossed the road, a group of drunk salarymen weaved in front of them and made a comment about Lynch being an escapee from the zoo. Before the next sentence was half finished, Iwata had a fistful of shirt and was snarling into the ear of the comedian. One of his friends tried to intervene, but Iwata silenced him with his *techou*. Within moments, Mr Comedian was bowing profusely, almost holding back tears.

Iwata pushed him away and caught up with Lynch.

She glanced at him. 'You all right?'

'Fine.'

'So. What was that?'

'He said something I didn't appreciate. Better that you don't understand.'

'Oh, I understood him. But Iwata, do me a favour? Next time you want to swing dicks, save yourself the hassle. I don't need my honour defended, thanks.'

Iwata looked up at the neon signs. Bars, barbecues, brothels. Cartoon hookers, cartoon sushi, cartoon arcade-game characters, vertical commerce: 1F, 2F, 3F, 4F. On and on it went, five hundred thousand lifetimes of unknowables.

'You know, Lynch. That's a bad habit of yours.'

'What's that?'

'Being right all the time.'

'*Shou ga nai*, Iwata. *Shou ga nai.*'

They had arrived at Black Widow. The bouncer solemnly shook his head. 'We're full.'

'Regrettably' – Iwata tapped his *techou* on the man's chest – 'you're going to get the hell out of my way or I'm going to regrettably arrest you.'

The bouncer stepped aside. Lynch noted the aggression in Iwata's voice tonight. It had been there ever since the British Embassy. She stole a sideways glance at him. He was a strange man – warm but without any trace of friendliness. His tone shifted sharply, muted resignation to outrage in a single breath. She had seen him lift his shirt in the morgue, seen the scars beneath – meandering cicatrices from a knife, an old gunshot wound on his arm. She had also seen him lick his lips at the sight of sake, look longingly at the *umeshu* in Skye's fridge. Iwata seemed a simple man, but she sensed there was a past in him, a shipwreck beneath those still waters.

Then again, Lynch had her own past. That wasn't any of Iwata's business. And his was none of hers. They were working together in the spirit of *openness*. It didn't have to mean anything, just look like it did.

'So what's the deal here?' Lynch asked.

'This is a hostess club. Mostly it's business types entertaining clients who want to be surrounded by pretty girls to fill their glasses, light their smokes and keep the bullshit flowing.'

'No sex, then?'

'Not here. Sometimes the hostess might make arrangements with clients outside of the club but that's not meant to be part of the deal.'

Inside Black Widow a sleek hallway led off to several side chambers. The walls sparkled with diamante spider webs. Grace Jones's 'I've Seen that Face Before' was playing somewhere. Beneath chamber doors, cigarette smoke beckoned them in.

The reception podium had a gold spider motif. Standing behind it was a woman wearing a midnight-blue suit and an earpiece well hidden by expensive earrings. Iwata figured her for an ex-hostess that had bought her way into the industry, now the madam of the club.

'Evening.' She smiled. It looked genuine from a distance. But Iwata saw the fatigue beneath it – a lifetime of men. Still, she didn't bat an eye at Iwata and Lynch as they approached; Black Widow had catered to every kind of party.

'For two?'

'What do you think?' Iwata took out his *techou*.

'I'm Madam Madoka.' Her smile was demurely controlled now, a woman accustomed to men of authority, whether real or perceived. 'What can I help you with, Inspector?'

'We need to talk about Skye Mackintosh.'

'I don't think I'm familiar with that name.'

'Don't follow the news much, huh?'

'Perhaps if you could come back tomorrow? We're very busy tonight –'

'*I'm* busy tonight. You run a kindergarten for losers. Now I know Skye Mackintosh used to work here, so either you answer my questions – right now – or I develop a curiosity as to whether everything here follows the letter of the law.'

Madam Madoka gave an empty smile then led them into a small side office. It was barely big enough for a desk. On the back wall was an enormous whiteboard depicting an elaborate ranking system: a column of female names, their corresponding salaries and how many customers they were pulling in, how many dates they were securing. Behind her desk, there was a large glass tank containing twigs and dead leaves. It took Iwata a moment to notice the black widow in a shadowy corner – absolutely still.

The woman sat behind her desk. Lynch leaned against the wall. Iwata took the seat opposite and noticed the employee manual on the desk. Without asking, he flipped through:

- Often the guest will be dressed in a suit. Never miss an opportunity to compliment him on this.

146

For instance: *I just love how guys look in a suit.* If he is wearing a colourful tie: *I love your tie, you have really unique taste.* Alternatively, if he is dressed casually, go the other way: *It's so nice to see a guy just being himself. I like a man comfortable in his own skin.*

- Direct compliments and flirting work well with many guests. But consider playful, subtle and indirect comments that intrigue the guest and leave him wanting more. Instead of overtly praising his looks, why not mix in some uncertainty with your flirting? *You look just like a guy I used to have a crush on.* Instead of telling him he is special directly, <u>imply</u> that he is better than other men. *You're fun, you make this feel like it's not work.*

- Always turn a guest's physical traits into a positive. If he is overweight, why not say: *I bet you make your girlfriends feel taken care of with that manly physique!* If he is skinny, compliment him on his body tone. If he is old, his maturity should be praised. Whatever type of guest sits down before you, it's your job to repackage him as a desirable man.

Iwata tossed the manual back on the desk and nodded to the glass tank. 'Nice spider.'

Madam Madoka nodded. 'Loved them ever since I was a little girl. I would watch them mating in my garden, the female eating the male. I found it fascinating.'

'So fascinate me: when did Skye Mackintosh work here?'

'She started last October, I think. Left after a few months, which is normal enough. The exact date would be in our files.'

'Why'd she quit?'

'I didn't ask. Girls come and go.'

'We're going to need her file.'

The woman flipped through some documents for a moment, then handed over Skye's file. It contained only her basic employment information.

'Your girls.' Iwata nodded at the board behind her. 'When they go on dates with the guests, you keep records of these men?'

'Of course. But those are totally confidential.'

'I could come back with a subpoena.'

'And when you do, I'll comply with the law.'

Iwata relented. 'So Skye met a lot of men here.'

'It was her job to be friendly.'

'Did she ever go on a *dohan*?'

'Naturally. She was a beautiful girl – good earner, too. But she wasn't particularly enthusiastic about it. None of the girls are, you understand. I just mean she could have gone on more dates, they could have been lucrative.'

'Did she ever meet a man called Miyake?'

'I can't answer that, I'm sorry.'

'And you can't employ a foreign national on a student visa either. But that didn't deter you, did it? I'm not asking to look through all your dirty laundry. I'm just interested in Skye.'

Madam Madoka clucked her tongue. 'I can't give you the details of every man Skye met; I'd lose fifty clients in one day. But this Miyake – I know who you mean, he's a regular. What do you want?'

'Two things: you tell me if he met her outside of this club. And you tell me if he came in here on 7 July.'

The woman nodded. 'Give me a day or two to get that information.'

Lynch spoke now. 'Did Skye ever have any problems here? With Miyake or anyone else?'

The woman shook her head. 'We have signals. Security. Microphones.'

'What about friends?'

'Not really. She was the only girl who was –' the woman hovered over the word – 'foreign. But she was professional, like I say. Good Japanese, too.'

Iwata smiled thinly. 'Having some exotic eye candy in the window didn't hurt, that it?'

'Everything here is eye candy, Inspector.'

'So Skye Mackintosh just floated through this place? No one knew her, no one was close to her. Then one day she just up and left.'

'How else would you like me to describe it?'

'I want to talk to your employees.'

'I'm afraid everyone is busy.'

Iwata walked out of the office. He opened the first door he came to and entered a small room with sofas, booths, mirrored walls and plastic chandeliers. Built into the walls were large glass habitats filled with spiders, illuminated by blue neon. Faux-pearl cobwebs laced the alcoves. The dresses of the hostesses were cut low, the music turned up high – Dusty Springfield's 'Spooky'. The tables were squat, hostesses having to reach down to pour drinks, cleavages revealed. Men were talking, hostesses laughing, lighting cigarettes, pouring drinks.

Iwata sat at a free table. Lynch sat awkwardly next to him. Madam Madoka appeared in the doorway and glared at Iwata for a moment. Then, glancing at her other guests, she closed the door with a scowl.

'I don't think you made a good impression,' Lynch said.

'That's the idea. If the hostesses pick up on that, they might respond more positively to us.'

'And if they don't?'

'I'll use my charm.'

On cue, a woman in a skimpy cocktail dress dropped into the empty chair like a lozenge on a tongue. She looked around twenty – by design – her make-up heavy, her contact lenses gold, the glitter on her cheeks princess pink.

'What's your name?' Iwata asked.

'Where are my manners?' She gave an over-modest grin. Passing across her hostess card, she added, 'I just love your suit! You don't dress the same as everyone else in here. It's refreshing.'

On the card there was a cartoon version of the hostess, her puppyish eyes much larger, her skin lightened, her face almost infantile, her breasts greatly expanded. It said her name was Coco and that she was eighteen.

'Is this your friend?' Coco asked.

'My partner.'

'Kinky! Foreign girlfriends must be more open-minded.'

'Not that kind of partner.' Iwata flashed his *techou*. 'Real name, please.'

Although irritated, Coco loosened up. Nothing was in play now, one less person to impress. 'Miki Sugita,' she said, inspecting her nails.

The bartender arrived and Iwata ordered three Cokes. Sugita continued to audit her nails, pink acrylic daggers depicting tiny rainbows. But the porcelain-doll aesthetic was itself the product, just another fake Gucci bag. There was a hardness beneath the naivety. In that muted misery of a thousand nights with a thousand men, an emotional brawn had been forged in Miki Sugita. Iwata saw it in all the hostesses here. It was in their faces, in their voices. And if one listened closely, beneath the Dusty Springfield and the giggles one could hear the sound of the mournful nightly blues of this place: a hymn to brushing off the gropers, laughing away leers, parrying the passes of dark figures in dark suits. This wasn't a flirting parlour, it was a gladiatorial chamber.

'So am I supposed to be in trouble?' Sugita's voice was flat now, unaligned with the pop-girl image. 'If you're going to tell me I should be back in school, I'm twenty-four.'

'We're here about Skye Mackintosh,' Lynch replied.

She looked up from her nails, a flicker of real emotion. 'I was sorry to hear about that.'

The drinks arrived, along with little trays of wasabi peas and rice crackers, the bill demanding an amount worth a full dinner at a decent Ginza restaurant. Sugita sipped her drink, careful not to spoil her lip gloss. 'It's not like I really knew Skye, but she seemed . . . nice.'

The last word stalled, as if it might be caught trespassing.

Iwata understood. 'Nice' had no place here. Every soul in this room was a prisoner to desires, physical or financial; everyone here wanted something and nobody wanted to give. Beneath the neon, the mirrors, the glitter, all was darkness – only the spiders belonged here. Iwata's head was spinning.

'Was there anyone Skye was close to?' Lynch asked. 'Anyone she trusted?'

Sugita shook her head. 'I won't talk about the other girls. But I'll say this: this isn't really a place to make friends. All of us are here for the money. Though I don't know why – we get paid sparrow tears most of the time.'

'What about men? Anyone that was taken with her or gave her trouble?'

'Maybe, I don't know. Skye was the same as the rest of us. We're toys. Pull the cord, we giggle. Light your smoke. Fill your glass. Skye was no different. But she was beautiful. Foreign. She probably had to deal with more of these . . .' She bit her lip and, remembering she was on show, smiled glassily: 'Guests.'

'Miki.' Iwata spoke. 'Someone beat her to death. I think you know something and we really need your help.'

'*You?*' Her smile concealed her anger poorly. 'No, *we* need your help.'

'What do you mean?'

'Oh, come on. Don't tell me you don't know what I'm talking about. Every single girl in here knows about *him*. Black Widow and every other hostess club in Kabukichō. There's a man out there and he's been making us disappear for a long time. None of you lift a finger.'

'Who?'

'I don't know *who* exactly. No one does. But he'll dress like they all do. He'll sit at a desk somewhere. He'll kiss his wife. Take his kids to the park. Then one night when he has the chance, he'll come to Kabukichō and one of us will vanish. And where will you be then? Where will I be? Same place as Skye?'

Iwata considered this before answering. 'Miki, I can't

promise you things will ever be fair. But if this man is out there and there's a chance that he's the one who murdered Skye, you have to tell me what you know.'

Sugita looked up and saw one of the CCTV cameras panning towards them. 'I'm sorry, I can't talk to you any more.'

'We'll leave you alone after this, you have my word.'

The young woman steadied herself then remembered her role. She laughed convincingly at the nonexistent joke then threw a wasabi pea at Iwata. She glanced up at the camera then whispered. 'Swear?'

Iwata nodded.

Sugita took out a pink pen from her Gucci handbag and scrawled something on a napkin. She kissed it for the cameras and slid it into Iwata's pocket. 'Thanks for the drink.' She said it loudly in her girlish voice. Then she slinked away to another table, where two sheepish salarymen had just sat.

Iwata stood.

'Wait,' said Lynch. 'Look.'

Through the neon smoke they saw him. Miyake was surrounded by hostesses and knee deep in the telling of his anecdote. The hipster look was gone; instead, he wore an expensive grey suit. He was batting his eyelids at the hostesses as if he were the one in make-up. His story reached its climax, the laughter of the hostesses piercing.

Taking one last look at Miyake, the detectives stepped out into the corridor. Beneath a cobweb chandelier Iwata took out the folded napkin Miki Sugita had slipped into his pocket:

SKYE MET SOMEONE. I DON'T KNOW WHO BUT SHE SEEMED DIFFERENT

BEFORE SHE LEFT. LOOK FOR A <u>KAORI</u>. IF
ANYONE KNOWS, IT'D BE HER.

PLEASE DON'T COME BACK HERE, I NEED
THIS JOB.

18. Sea of Glass

Skye Mackintosh's memorial service was held in the Anglican chapel at Rikkyo University. Her parents had worried about whether or not this was inappropriate before her funeral took place in London, but in the end Karen was adamant: Skye needed the blessing of a priest.

Lynch enlisted Itō to help find an English-speaking priest at the last minute, a for-hire Belgian in his twenties with a solemn beard and a strange accent. Of course, he wasn't a real priest, he worked at a 'wedding centre' in Takadanobaba – although only a fraction of Japan was Christian, 'Western-style' weddings were wildly popular, catching on after the televising of the marriage of Charles and Diana. A Western 'priest' could be hired to officiate for authenticity – often English teachers moonlighting for extra cash.

Lynch decided it would have to do.

During the service Iwata observed the family. He had gone over Lynch's transcripts. They had all shared a great deal with her, painfully personal details, most of it largely irrelevant to the case. He filled in the blanks with his own suspicions.

Karen Mackintosh and her family sat in the front row. Her husband was next to her, sitting absolutely upright, breathing stiffly through his nose. Geraldine Mackintosh and Dylan White were holding hands, both of them staring blankly at the priest. It was peaceful in the chapel, almost empty. The echoes carried. It seemed impossible that outside there was a mob of reporters lying in wait for the grieving money shot.

The priest was pink-cheeked, chubby, prematurely balding. Grey morning light glinted off his spectacles. His cassock was loose and tight all at once.

'And I saw as it were a sea of glass mingled with fire.' He looked around. *'And them that had gotten the victory over the beast, and over his image, and over his mark, and over the number of his name, stand on the sea of glass, having the harps of God.'*

Iwata watched as Karen let the strangely spoken words wash over her. He could see they made little sense to her. There was no making sense of this. For her, every waking moment was a paper airplane expected to reach the moon.

He saw the bewilderment strongest in her. She had lived for Skye. This abyss in her heart would never be sealed. Skye was dead.

Karen begged Iwata for details he did not have whenever she saw him. Had Skye been wearing one of the bras she had bought for her on her last birthday? Had she cried for her mother at the end? What kind of man could murder someone like Skye? Was he short or tall? Japanese or foreign? Would he have wondered what sort of family she had?

With Lynch, Karen confided her regrets. Phrases she regretted using with Skye. *Cheer up, lass. You're a long time deid.* Parts of Scotland she had never taken her daughter to. Sentiments she was waiting to share later on in Skye's life. Maybe when she became a mother.

Karen began to cry.

Philip pulled his wife to him, hard, as if he could crush the grief from her. Little more than three days had passed since they had arrived in Japan, yet he had not experienced them in real time – it had been a slow-motion blur of disorientation and pain.

Philip's way of dealing with it had been through irritated silence, an impatient vigil before the ineptitude of the Japanese. If he focused on what they were doing wrong – what the police were mishandling, what the media were mis-cueing – then he could preoccupy himself with reining in his anger, and that was better than yielding to grief.

To Philip, accepting Skye's murder did not feel like accepting the truth, it would be endorsing a monstrosity. And though Karen and Geraldine did not need his strength – they never really had – he felt like he had no option but to maintain his silent-hardman routine.

Skye had always had a way of reducing his posturing to a silliness, affectionately undermining his authority with just a few words.

All right, Moai Man?

She had likened him to the Easter Island statues as a little girl, the name quickly adopted by the rest of the family. And while he had rolled his eyes each time, he secretly loved her teasing. Later, Skye would stagger home at 5 a.m., drop on to the armrest of his chair and slink an arm around his long neck. *Moai Man angry with daughter? Yes, Moai Man furious. Skye stay out late. Very dark outside. Daughter must make cup of tea for peace.*

Philip would have been mentally perfecting the bollocking all night, yet he couldn't help laughing. She had always had a knack of avoiding trouble through jokes. In fact, he'd always thought of his daughter as somehow magically fortuitous, trouble always present in her life but

157

never quite grazing her. Whatever Skye did, wherever she went, she came up roses.

But there was no avoiding trouble this time.

Philip gave out a shuddering sigh. Skye had died thousands of miles away from home, alone, close to no one who loved her. He clenched his fist under the pew, the hatred thrumming inside him as constant as the rainsong outside. *We'll find him. We'll find the fucker. And when we do, maybe I'll get to him first.*

Geraldine was almost glad this was happening here, so far away from home. She imagined the funeral back in London and how different things would be there. She pictured her sister's wake at home, the women in one room, the men in another. They would have the door closed and there would be angry talk about who had done this. That was the unbearable thing about her father. He could never accept that there were some things in life he couldn't do anything about. Her mother went the other way. Everything was fate.

Geraldine was glad Dylan was here. She was holding his hand like a scared little boy. While his face was expressionless, she could feel him trembling next to her. She felt so sorry for him she wanted to embrace him. *Poor Dylan.*

Geraldine hadn't ever said it out loud, but she knew her sister would leave him. Dylan had always so clearly been in Skye's thrall. It would never occur to him that he was more than good enough for her. That had always been Skye's trick. This effortless aura that had somehow always been there, that of Skye's superiority to everyone else – especially those who loved her. All throughout her childhood, Geraldine had glowered with indignant envy. All she had ever wanted was for her big sister to be conscious of her good luck. But

Skye only ever drifted through the world, as though life itself were her own personal lilo.

Geraldine wondered if Dylan had intuited Skye's abandonment. *Not Dylan. Look at him.* For all his brain-power, the man was surprised when a Tuesday followed a Monday. Geraldine had always liked Dylan. Perhaps it was just one underdog recognizing another. Or maybe it was something else. Something she couldn't allow herself to put into words. When he gave up his PhD programme, Skye had torn into him. But Geraldine understood. She helped him with his CV, even secured him an interview at a travel agency where a friend worked. To her delight, he took to the job like a fish to water, his airy demeanour and silver tongue selling dream holidays with ease. To her annoyance, he was saving up his commission for a flight out to see Skye.

Geraldine took out a tissue as a pretext for letting go of Dylan's hand. It was appalling, indulging in her fantasy at her own sister's funeral. She told herself she was only filling her head with ridiculous thoughts to avoid confronting the real ones.

She turned around and glanced at the English detective, who nodded back at her solemnly. Geraldine liked Lynch. No-nonsense but still empathetic. Not like the Japanese detective off to the side, who kept glancing at them. He said the right things but his words were completely empty somehow.

Geraldine remembered what Lynch had said walking out of that morgue place. *You're going to feel a lot of things in the next few days, Geraldine. None of them are abnormal and none of them are wrong. Just concentrate on keeping it together as best you can.*

'You okay?' Dylan whispered.

'Yeah.' She reached out and squeezed his hand. She couldn't help herself.

Dylan returned his gaze to the priest. He had been feeling only a numb dread these past few days. And so he ordered himself to experience everything, see everything, listen to everything – he didn't want to miss a single moment, didn't want to forget a shred of this. Dylan had loved Skye in life, memorizing every achievement, every place they went to, every second shared. He wasn't going to stop now in her death. On the altar, a framed black-and-white photograph of Skye smiling. *God, I miss you.*

As the ceremony reached its conclusion Iwata and Lynch slipped out. The ashen morning was hazy in the warm downpour. Cops in black suits were trying to blend in with their surroundings, their heads swivelling this way and that, looking for anything they deemed 'out of place'.

The two detectives approached Itō, who stood off to one side.

'I'm guessing *he* didn't show up,' Iwata said.

'No sign of anyone suspicious, sir. If the killer has come to gawp, then he's doing it with a telescope.'

'All right. Where are you with Miyake's financial records?'

'I'll have the subpoena tomorrow morning. Then I'll head straight to the bank.'

'What about my surveillance in the red-light district?'

'Kabukichō has now been flooded by Team B, as you requested. Shindo pulled in cops from Vice, too. Team A has turned over the building sites and labour exchanges in San'ya, but found nothing except down-and-outs.'

'And the CCTV around Shirahige bridge?'

'It should be ready for you by the end of the day. Tomorrow morning at the latest.'

'All right, good work. One last thing: I need you to look into a woman by the name of Kaori – that's the only name I have. We think it's a colleague of Skye's at the hostess club. Potentially the "dark-haired friend" at Rikkyo. I know that's not a lot, but do your best.'

'Understood, sir.' Itō bowed.

'Well,' Lynch said. 'We haven't found Mr Big, the rapist landlord has his alibi and Ueda has fallen off the map. Not to mention this K is still out there.'

Iwata nodded. 'He's still out there. Somewhere.'

The apartment block was on the fringes of Tokyo. It had been abandoned long ago, the entire neighbourhood emptied and sealed off after a toxic gas leak. The must of human absence lay thick in the air.

Although the room was full of webs, there was only one spider. Kaori was lying on her makeshift cardboard bed, listening to the crickets. The room was filled with them, their chirping noise throbbing in the darkness, desperately scraping their bodies on their wings in the hope of attracting a mate. But there was no mate here. Here there was nothing. Only the large yellow-and-black *Argiope* spider.

Kaori had named her Manami – *beautiful*. The entire room was hazy with her web, as though a field of dandelions had been frozen in the moment of their breezy destruction.

She spun her webs low to the ground to trap the crickets. But the webs were distinctive in their patterns, little silken doodles in a childish hand.

Like a tiny bodybuilder, Manami was on a strict diet. Steadily she grew larger, she grew stronger. Kaori had been raising the crickets on a protein gel and spraying the webs with vaporized energy drinks.

Kaori marvelled as she watched her slowly abseil through dark space like an assassin. Finding the perfect hiding place, Manami could spend entire days in silent ambush. Her webs carried her secret signature, the *stabilimentum*, a thick band of silk ribbon that reflected ultraviolet light to lure prey. And the quality of Manami's silk was exquisite. The crickets would never bounce off the web but neither could they break free – once the crickets entered, they could never leave.

At her own leisurely but undeviating pace, Manami would descend on her prey and work it into a silken strait-jacket. When she was finally ready, she would stab her venom into her victim's body. Kaori loved the moment the cricket gave up its struggle, resigned to her perfect dominance. As it sagged under the paralysing effects of her venom, chemicals from Manami's stomach juices would begin to liquefy her prey, allowing her to suck up the rich nourishment.

Kaori would gently encourage her as she fed: *There you are, my love. Take him. Take him. Take everything you need.* It seemed like a perfectly adequate exchange. Some pathetic, mindless drone to sustain a goddess.

Sometimes, Manami would crawl over Kaori's body. Up close, she could see her eyes gleaming in the dark. Despite having so many, Manami didn't rely on them. Instead, she used the hairs on her body to decipher the world around her – she lived through feeling, through minute sensation, with no concept of boredom or emptiness, living every second as it flowed through her perfect little body. Manami was ready to fight. She was strong. She was merciless. She didn't understand what it was to hesitate. And soon she would be ready.

Kaori opened her eyes to look for her but couldn't see

162

her in the gloom. Manami would only be seen if she wanted to be. In the abandoned apartment there was only the mad dream of her webs, a bridal veil ripped to shreds.

Skye had recoiled at Kaori's secret love of spiders. *They freak me out.*

But you don't understand, they're amazing. One teaspoon of their silk can weave ten thousand webs. In ten minutes, they can produce half a mile of thread. They're just misunderstood.

Like you?

Maybe. Why don't you touch her?

No way!

If you love me, you'll touch Manami.

One corner of Skye's mouth had curled up. There was nothing she wouldn't try, even if she was afraid of it. That was the fearlessness in Skye Mackintosh which Kaori would never understand but always be in awe of.

She rolled over on the mattress now. It was dusty and dank, but comfort didn't matter any more. Her eyes fell to the newspaper. The pet-shop owner hadn't intended anything by it, of course, but the latest box of crickets had been wrapped in this evening's edition. There, on the front cover, was a grainy picture of the detectives on Skye's case. Next to it was a photograph of her family emerging from a chapel. She recognized that chapel but she didn't want to think about Rikkyo. That place didn't matter anymore either.

Kaori tossed the paper away into the darkness, immediately hoping she hadn't harmed any of Manami's webs. She told herself that she had to move as delicately through the room as Manami. *In this room and everywhere else.*

Chest heaving, overwhelmed with solitude and grief, Kaori rushed over to her rucksack and pulled out her old laptop. She looked at her favourites bar and saw the tab for *A Tokyo Skye*. More than anything she wanted to click on it, but she knew it was impossible. It wasn't just that there was no internet here, nor was it that the Removals Collective had forbidden her any kind of online activity. Besides, she knew the blog posts by heart. Kaori's English wasn't perfect, but it was good enough for the words to hurt – as though Skye had cut them, not typed them. She just wanted to see that stupid font and that photo of the sunset. A reminder that Skye had been real.

Before they had met Kaori would spend entire days in bed, skipping class, not eating. It was hard to generate the energy just to leave her room. If it weren't for her spiders needing food, she might not have bothered at all. The business classes at Rikkyo had been a throwaway choice, wishful thinking for the Kaori she knew she would never be. *You don't honestly think you'll ever amount to anything, do you?* her father had always jeered when she was a young girl. Beat her. Worse.

Afterwards, he would lock her down in the basement. It was always dark and wet down there. *With the spiders, where you belong!* But they never hurt her. Bothered her. They were always gentle with her. Hour after hour, night after night, she would watch them. Learn from them. In time, Kaori came to love them. To mirror them. She became like them. Still, silent, merciless.

One day when her father was sleeping she went at him. When the police came, they found her in the basement, covered in dried blood and cobwebs.

The years that passed after that were hazy – institutions, medication, evaluations. And then, without warning, she was released, expected to make her own way. Kaori floated from city to city, surviving on her knowledge of spiders. She always found the underground betting dens.

Eventually she ended up in Tokyo. That's when she saw Skye. Followed her. Even paid to see her at the hostess club. That the place had a spider motif seemed like an omen. Kaori gained the trust of the madam, helped her with her spiders. Another excuse to watch Skye.

When she finally made her move in the canteen and Skye smiled at her, everything had changed. Wondrously, somehow, they had gone drinking. An eighties-themed bar that took song requests and sold cheap drinks. Skye got up and sang along with 'Damn I Wish I was Your Lover' by Sophie B. Hawkins and Kaori felt her stomach implode with lust and admiration. Outside, in the alleyway, their breath mingling in the cold, they had kissed.

After that, every day that Kaori woke to a world with Skye in it there was only glory. At night, she could barely bring herself to close her eyes. Not with Skye's body next to her, her breathing like secrets she had no right to hear.

But then the jealousy began. The squabbles. The men that intruded on their love.

And now Skye was gone and Kaori was on the run. Japan was an empty room full of webs and she was the cricket, chirping for nothing. Everything had been taken from her. Everything but vengeance.

Wind blew rain through the broken window. Kaori realized how late it was already and how few crickets were left. Sighing, she forced herself to get up and covered the scar on her chin with make-up before putting up her hood. She left the empty apartment block through the back, then zigzagged through a small cedar forest to the street. The forest ended at the exclusion fence. Kaori climbed over it and was now on suburban back streets. The sun had almost set. This far out, nobody would recognize her, though she knew she needed to move on soon. *I need to find* him *first. Then I can leave Tokyo for good.*

19. Michael Bolton

The conference was out in Nagano and would last for two whole days. To Mr Sato, it felt like a glorious forevermore. It was 6 a.m. and he was already on the road. On clear days, particularly in winter, there was a sharp, precise beauty to the Ibaraki countryside that he had always loved. But today's sombre dawn promised only rain and thunder. The silver family car wound through a monotony of sad forests braided in mist, cold brooks lost amid mossy trees.

Mr Sato, of course, was not heading west, to Nagano, but east, to his cabin. The only place in this world where he could truly exist. But first, he had to take care of some things. He would overshoot Ōkuromori by more than an hour, heading north to Takahagi. It didn't have to be there; it could be anywhere, so long as it was somewhere he had never been before. But Mr Sato liked the idea of being by the ocean today.

He reached the outskirts of Takahagi in good time and stopped for breakfast at Denny's. The waitress, a pretty but dozy country girl, took Mr Sato's order, the Morning Sunny Side Up Set: two fried eggs, one rasher of bacon, one small sausage and a creamy salad. For his side, he went for the pancakes with cream-butter and syrup, and for his drinks a drip coffee and a melon soda. Normally he would never eat something so unhealthy, but he had a long day ahead of him. Breakfast arrived promptly and Mr Sato tore through it. As he carefully slit open his eggs and dripped yolk concentrically on his pancakes, he watched the waitress and wondered what the total length of her small intestine would be if it were stretched out.

When Mr Sato was finished he asked for the bill. The waitress had drawn a little cat in blue pen thanking him for his custom. Taken aback by the little detail, he blinked rapidly for a few seconds. Smiling, he folded it up into his wallet on a whim. He paid at the counter but, to his disappointment, a different waitress served him. When he was done he went to the bathroom, cut his toenails and took out the Thermos from his bag. Working up some phlegm, he spat into it and added the nail clippings. He left the Denny's with a cheerful goodbye and the doodle waitress smiled.

Back in the car, Mr Sato decided that he liked her. She was probably just being friendly – after all, women were always masking their true feelings. But what if she wasn't? *Maybe she likes me back?*

Mr Sato looked down at the receipt, but the cat doodle had lost its smile. Its little mouth opened. *You dumb bastard. Go back in there and ask her out? Have you forgotten our rules?*

He looked down at his lap. 'No, Father.'

Recite.

'Never speak to anyone unless absolutely necessary. Always avoid eye contact. Never wear bright colours or brands and keep clear of symbols or patterns. Always seem serenely purposeful.'

Good.

Like a spy in deep cover, Mr Sato honed his skills not to stand out. Wherever he found himself, he would always seek out the social baseline and immediately submit himself to it. If he were passing through a town of farmers, he would remove his tie and jacket and roll up his sleeves. He always carried spectacles and sunglasses, a copy of that day's newspaper to hide behind. Frequently, he practised accents and studied regional quirks so that wherever he travelled to in the country he'd be able to get by. Mr Sato worked tirelessly to become the Grey Man, a man who nobody would notice, a man who would drift through any memory undetected, a man who slipped silently into the extraneous background information the brain would filter out.

Folding the Denny's receipt into his wallet, Mr Sato drove around Takahagi until he was satisfied he had seen all his options before finally choosing a hardware store in the centre of the city. He put on some spectacles he did not need, then went inside and bought industrial-grade plastic sacks. Completing his purchase uneventfully, he loaded them into the back of his car, safe in the knowledge that there was zero chance that the sacks could carry any fibres from his home or workplace. In a nearby music shop, he bought a new violin case for his son and loaded that into his car, too. Then he parked on the eastern edge of the town and walked along the concrete esplanade for a while.

Filling his lungs with briny morning air, he looked at the grey waves and recalled a trip with his father to the beach. Mr Sato had gone in search of gleaming shells for his mother. Then, later, smashed rocks into stranded jelly-fish. He dug his little toes into the dark, slimy sand and wished as hard as anyone could wish that his father would notice him. Mr Sato laughed now at his infantile silliness. It was a quiet laugh, lost in the ocean breeze.

On the way out of Takahagi he stopped at an outdoor-supplies shop and purchased a large rucksack, again paying in cash. He drove the three-quarters of an hour to Naka, where he stopped again. This time it was the pet shop.

'Something for the little one, is it?' The owner asked.

'A cat.' Mr Sato simulated a stutter. 'I just can't help but make him happy.'

So far, he had bought four dogs. They were an essential element of his disposal procedure, but they weren't cheap. Mr Sato couldn't risk his wife's curiosity. He bought a tabby cat at a good price and set off for Ōkuromori. The cat meowed the whole way.

Mr Sato arrived just before 1 p.m., feeling delighted with his progress. If he factored in ten hours' sleep over the next two days, the amount of time he would get with Number Seven was tremendously exciting. He'd already dug the hole up on the mountain, so disposal wouldn't take long, either.

Seeing the chinquapin trees, he slowed to make the turning on to the hidden forest lane, brimming with optimism and alacrity. But as he looked both ways his heart sank. There was the walking tub of lard, his neighbour. He was waving now, a timid grin widening grotesque cheeks.

Having no other choice, Mr Sato smiled and rolled down his window.

'Itsuki!' he called as he hurried over. 'Been a while.'

Mr Sato nodded. 'Sure has.'

'You're out here early.'

'Couple of days off. Thought I'd carry on with the preparations for the *matsuri*. What are you doing all the way out here?'

The neighbour patted his belly. 'Making some repairs of my own, and I've started jogging. Taking a leaf out of your book!'

'Great.' Mr Sato tried not laugh in the man's face. 'That's great.'

'Hey, if you're free tonight, we could get a beer in the village?'

'Sure, that would be good. Let me see how I get on and I'll call you.'

The neighbour beamed as he turned and plodded on down the lane. Mr Sato glared at the small, rotund figure dwindling in the mirror. His hand hovered over the gearshift. There was a moment. But Mr Sato ordered himself not to put the car into reverse and crush him right now.

Chest heaving, mood completely ruined, he made the turning.

The cabin door opened and, for the first time in days, Mr Sato allowed Number Seven to see daylight. Stepping inside, his breath caught. The stink made him think of his old biology classes, the smell released when slicing through pig hearts. It was as if the air in the cabin had been pumped through those slimy porcine valves, the stench astonishing now.

The girl was shrivelled and raw-boned, her body's stores of sugar and fat long gone. The drip had done what it could but, without vitamins and minerals, her immune system had shut down. For Mr Sato, the silver lining was that it meant minimal cleaning up of faecal and menstrual waste. It was clear now that Number Seven had run her course.

He flipped through his tapes, settled on Tasmin Archer's 'Sleeping Satellite' and hummed along as he set about removing her drip and washing her body.

He didn't bother closing the door; even if there had been anyone to hear her, her vocal cords were completely shot. He cleaned her face with wet wipes and it reminded him of caring for his son as a baby.

Next, he cut her fingernails and trimmed her pubic hair, putting the takings into his Thermos. She faced away from him as he worked. Every so often, he would pretend to dig the scissors under her fingernails like he had in the beginning, applying just enough pressure to make the nail go white, but she no longer flinched. He realized the sensation was likely gone. Or perhaps she was simply resigned to the pain. Either one was a disappointment.

Mr Sato decided to leave her feet alone. The smell of infection from where he had removed the small toe on the left foot was unpleasant, even for him. He had never been the sort to be put off by a few specks of mould on his bread or a sourness to his milk, but he had to admit, by now the girl was a mess. Besides, his Thermos was full.

Carefully, he poured the Mixture into a bowl, put it in the microwave and looked at Number Seven as it warmed. 'How are you doing?' He asked this in the same tone he had used with his neighbour.

She said nothing, her eyes agleam in the dimness of the cabin.

'Tell me something, Seven. What do you think about when I'm gone?'

Silence.

'Please answer my question.' His voice was even, a man commenting on the weather. 'I don't want to have to take another toe. I'd use my teeth this time.'

'Nothing.' A tear rolled down her newly fresh face. 'I think about nothing.'

'Oh, that can't be true. Nobody thinks about *nothing*.'

She shrugged one shoulder, the one with the most bite marks.

'Come on. You can tell me the truth.'

'I think about dying.' She gazed at the cassette tape. It had finished long ago.

'Ah, yes. Don't worry, that's probably normal.' Mr Sato stepped out of his shoes. 'Now tell me something else. Do you tell yourself that this is all a nightmare?'

'No. I know this is real.'

'Or maybe it *is* a nightmare. But a beautiful one.'

She had no reply.

'What about your family, Seven? Do you miss them?'

'We lost contact a long time ago. I already told you.'

'You did. But I like to check your consistency.' He smiled sheepishly. 'I'm a nit-picker.'

Both of them looked out of the cabin door. The sky was a blue-grey enamel. Distantly, they could hear coots on the lake.

'Mr Sato? . . . I'm very hungry. Do you think I might have –'

'Seven, do you ever wonder why I've done this to you?'

She closed her eyes. 'No.'

'Really? You don't? That's interesting. But I *want* you to know why. I think that's important for someone in your position. You see, there's a village not too far from here, it's called Ōkuromori. Pretty little mountain town. Thing is, it's full of bastards. You could run into town covered in blood right now and they would lock their doors on you. You think I'm exaggerating, but I know these people. Years ago, my father was the mayor, you see. Everyone respected him. He was an important man. Then there were some financial misunderstandings, but the way they treated him . . . In the end, people always forget themselves.'

Mr Sato waded into a bitter recollection which lasted

173

until the microwave pinged. At that, he remembered his smile and took out the Mixture.

'But they'll see, Seven. We'll make them see.'

'Please don't make me eat any more . . .'

Carefully, Mr Sato poured the now-steaming dark liquid back into his Thermos. Screwing the cap back on, he returned it to his bag. 'Oh, don't worry, we're past that phase now. We've already fused completely. Do you know what that means, Seven?'

He began to unbutton his shirt and she closed her eyes.

'Oh, come on, don't give me that. You didn't think this would last for ever, did you? Or were you secretly hoping we'd get married?' With a chuckle, he pulled down his trousers and smoothed down his pubic hair. 'Seven, I'm going to be very clear with you – you deserve that much. The truth is that I'm going to kill you. Within the next few minutes. Then I'm going to bury your remains in a place where they'll never be found. It's a shame, I know. But that's just how it has to be.' He hung up his clothes neatly and turned to face her, now as naked as she was. 'But before we get to that, there is something else we need to discuss.'

From his bag, he took out his broken Walkman and held it in front of her face.

'Do you see this?'

She was shaking violently, but he chose to assume it was a nod.

'I owned this for a very long time. I bought it before you were even born, Seven. It's given me a lot of happiness down the years, but now it's destroyed. What do you think about that?'

'I–I don't know.'

'Do you feel badly?'

174

She nodded.

'Do you really?'

'Yes.'

He booted her chair hard. 'Fucking *mean* it!'

'I mean it!' she yelped. 'I'm sorry!'

'You did this.'

'W–what?'

'You broke it.'

'Nuh – No, I didn't! I swear –'

'Apologize to me.'

'I'm sorry, I'm sorry.'

'Now fix it.'

'What?'

'You caused it to break. You fix it. I'll let you out of the chair if you can fix it.'

'I–I don't know how.'

'*I don't know how,*' he parroted in a whiny voice. 'Of *course* you don't know how. You know why? Because you're just a female. Just a stupid fucking female. Which is to say, you're nothing. You receive and contain. You're an absence. I've got no further use for you.'

'I'm sorry.' She was weakly hysterical, her voice barely able to rise above a whisper. 'Please don't kill me.'

Mr Sato put the broken Walkman back in his bag and flipped through a small box of tapes under his workbench. He stopped at Michael Bolton's 'How am I Supposed to Live without You?' and stroked the case lovingly. Putting it into the cassette player, he jumped up and kissed Seven on her riven shoulder.

'Apology accepted.'

As the music began Mr Sato slipped one of the new plastic sacks over her head and pulled it taut. Her face became a glazed grey mask, as if a mannequin had taken on life. He slow-danced with Seven from behind as he smothered her with the sack, his penis waggling, the metal stirrups of the examination chair clanking quietly while she struggled.

Mr Sato sang along with the chorus in broken English, his happy crooning dueting with the final dry sucking sounds.

When the carving was done and the hosing down was finally over, Mr Sato was left with mostly bloodless chunks and cleaved limbs. He stuffed them into the large rucksack he had purchased that morning and put it in the boat along with the cat carrier and set off. The tabby meowed angrily the whole way.

On the other side of the lake, he moored the boat and looked up at the setting sun. Then he hefted on the rucksack and started his hike up the mountain, the uphill slog familiar by now.

Darkness fell and it began to rain. Mr Sato didn't complain. Rain was good. The cat in the mesh carrier, however, was mewling loudly. He stopped, took off the rucksack and dragged out the cat by the scruff of the neck. It seemed confused, its wet fur spiky. Mr Sato walked over to a cedar tree and slammed it against the trunk until there was no more noise. Then he stuffed the broken thing back in the carrier.

At last, he reached the abandoned pig pen. This high up on the mountain, it was cold. Far across the misty range, thunder could be heard. Mr Sato ducked inside an old wooden shack that was barely standing and stood over the deep grave, droplets of his sweat falling in. Unable to resist, he opened the rucksack and took one last peek.

Seven's head was looking up at him, the elastic drawstring tight against her brow, one eye open like a doll's.

'Don't worry,' he whispered. 'I'll be with you soon.'

Quit dawdling, boy, do you want to get caught?

'Sorry, Father.'

Mr Sato booted the rucksack into the grave and began filling the hole. As he worked, he thought about how far he had come with his project.

At first, the killing had been incidental. He needed the girls for the Mixture – their death was simply a necessary part of that. But as he progressed in his work Mr Sato realized the pleasure it brought. He'd never known a thrill comparable to controlling another human being's existence, forcing them to consider their own final moments slipping away, the absolute joy of possession.

Possession.

First, of their lives; then, of their corpses. Mr Sato had lived all those years without understanding that the true meaning of life was to *possess*. By now, he was finding it harder and harder to look at women – even men – and not see them for what they really were: human remains in waiting. To Mr Sato, the feeling of killing was natural and unstoppable, like kissing in the haze of love.

Of course, he had started off blunderingly. Granted, his plans were all meticulous, the method watertight, but in the moment itself his voice had faltered, his hands had trembled, his lunch had crept its way up his throat. When he stopped the car and called out to Number One he had been terrified, as though offering a contract to the devil himself. But the devil had signed on gleefully. The girl had got into the car.

By now, Mr Sato's amateur phase was far behind him.

He had learned, he had honed, he had shrugged off all apprehension. As far as he was concerned, he had reached his apex.

When the grave was mostly filled Mr Sato mopped the sweat from his face with his collar. He threw the dead cat in, along with some wildflowers, and buried them shallow. It would trick cadaver dogs, the hole's true contents hidden far below the decoy.

Starting back down the mountain, Mr Sato felt glum. He would miss Seven.

The disused Ōkuromori community centre was a small, cheerless single-storey building in the shadow of a bamboo grove, its peeling walls dishwater grey. It was out of the way and had been replaced with a newer building in the centre of the village long ago. Mr Sato overshot and parked a full kilometre away from it, then walked back. At the door, he surveyed the rice paddy across the road, the grass silently shivering in the moonlight. He saw no one.

Mr Sato unlocked the door and slipped inside. He didn't turn on any lights but made his way to the small kitchen at the back. He took out another key for the padlock, which he had installed himself, due to 'vandalism'.

In the kitchen, he took out the last key, this padlock securing the old refrigerator at the far end. It hadn't come cheap, but he had specifically installed an American model for its capacity. Opening it, he moved the dummy products out of the way and found his metallic vat at the back. As he lifted the lid, he turned his head and the stench wafted out, a cold, meaty foulness. He opened his bag and emptied the contents of his Thermos into the vat, then sealed it once again. Finally, Mr Sato locked the fridge and looked up at the calendar. It wasn't long until the *matsuri*, but he was making good progress.

Good, my son. One more should do it.

Arriving back at his house overlooking Ōkuromori, Mr Sato took off his clothes and methodically incinerated them, flushing the charred scraps down the toilet. He showered, made himself a simple dinner of mushroom soup with green onions then phoned his neighbour. He apologized, explaining he had lost track of time with the *matsuri* preparations, and wondered if he still felt like a nightcap. To Mr Sato's delight, the man said he was tired but that they would definitely go for a beer next time.

Locking up the house, Mr Sato then cleaned the car thoroughly, going over every surface with a UV light torch. Satisfied nothing was out of place, he got into the driver's seat. The dashboard read 12.40 a.m. There was still time to make it to Kabukichō.

Mr Sato's body was weary, but his mind was whirling with excitement. He started the engine and chose 'It Ain't Over 'Til It's Over' by Lenny Kravitz.

Soon, he was back on the highway, sticking exactly two kilometres below the speed limit, the perfect verisimilitude of a normal motorist.

PART TWO

20. Mood Music

Anthea Lynch was lying on the hotel bed. Another day had passed, the Skye Mackintosh task force still lost in innocuous facts that led to nothing. She was standing amid a pack of dogs, chasing their own tails as one.

Lynch did not want to be here, in the comfortable purgatory of her featureless hotel room. She did not want her face on the ten o'clock news she had muted. She did not want her name on the front page of every newspaper printed that day in Tokyo. But Lynch knew that wherever she was she'd still be locked in her own mind, back in that bathroom, the sound of the aluminium baton over ribs ringing out.

Her phone started buzzing. Groaning, she swiped into the call. Chief Superintendent Powell's big face filled the screen. 'Anthea, how is everything in the Land of the Rising Sun?'

'Terrific. Wish you were here.'

'That's the spirit. How's that Inspector Itawa working out?'

'*Iwata*. Fine.'

'You don't sound convinced.'

'There's something off about him.'

'What do you mean?'

'I don't know what I mean, but my gut does.'

'Well, Detective Constable, you make sure he doesn't –'

'I know, sir. Don't worry, I'm all sweetness and light.

Anyway, to what do I owe the pleasure? Spelling mistakes in my homework?'

'No, your reports have been exemplary. Everywhere I look, I see you in the background.'

'All in the spirit of openness, sir.'

He nodded then took a serious slurp of tea. 'Look, I'm calling because there's a problem with your *situation*. You being out there. The face of London . . . Well, let's say that not everyone agrees with me that this was a good idea.'

'What are you saying?'

'Your disciplinary hearing couldn't be avoided in the end. I tried my best, Anthea.'

'Sir. You told me that if I came here –'

'I know what I said, but they've got their fucking magnifying glasses out now, haven't they? And that ties my hands. It's not like you got caught speeding.'

Lynch looked through the lambent haze of the window. There was life present out there, but it was unintelligible to her. 'When?'

'I'll email you the details now. Look, Anthea, I'll try to make sure you're given every opportunity. This isn't a foregone conclusion, all right? Maybe when you get back –'

Lynch ended the call and lay back down on the bed. A few seconds later Powell's email came through:

Notice for hearing to be held in public, 14–19 August 2020

Detective Constable Anthea Lynch, based at North-West London's Homicide Command Unit, will answer allegations that her conduct amounts to a breach of Standards of Professional Behaviour. It is alleged that on 19 May 2020, whilst on duty DC Anthea Lynch entered into an altercation involving a member of the public during an intelligence-led police raid. In the course of said raid, DC Lynch was assaulted. It is further alleged that she used excessive force and verbally abusive language during the arrest of the suspect. It is alleged that in doing so DC Lynch breached the Standards of Professional Behaviour in respect of: <u>Use of Force, Honesty & Integrity, Authority, Respect and Courtesy, and Discreditable Conduct</u>. The hearing will start on Friday, 14 August 2020 and is listed for four days. The hearing will start at 0930 hours and will be held at Empress State Building, Lillie Road, SW6 1TR. The identity of victims/witnesses will be protected during the hearing as appropriate.

Lynch closed the email. She felt only an intense detachment, hardened by jet lag and hatred. If her career was over, then maybe it was for the best.

Whereas, before, she had been able to remain professional while interviewing suspects, now she felt violent urges. Big men at home with their women turned to paper tigers as soon as she pressed RECORD. The ham-fisted fictions revolted her, their raw knuckles hidden under the table.

And it wasn't just in the interview room. She would read personal attacks into everything, somehow unable to tolerate a harmless smirk between two colleagues in the changing room. At her desk, Lynch was barely able to sit still. She'd never been particularly affected by the brutality of her day-to-day before, the brass tacks in the blood. But it had got so that she avoided looking at the whiteboard in briefings. Her eyes glossed over photographs, just pink blurs at the fringes of her disgust.

Lynch was at her limit – she simply couldn't face inspecting images of another child's crushed oesophagus or listening to another evidence tape of a doomed 999 call.

Even before joining the Met, she'd heard the screams. Thumps behind thin walls. She'd grown up on the Wendling Estate, a labyrinth of brown brick hutches and white uPVC windows, all concrete recesses, unused walkways and emergency doors that led nowhere.

Lynch had learned early on what it meant when the man next door turned the TV volume all the way up. And why, despite grey skies, his wife would be wearing sunglasses the next day. Once a week, a Wendling door would get kicked in, police jackboots would rumble up stairs and someone would be dragged out, shouting. Lynch's mother offered the coppers cups of tea with ginger biscuits and they'd chat about this and that.

She never expected her daughter to become a pair of those jackboots.

Lynch closed her eyes and searched for a black-box solution in the wreckage of her life. But she could only replay the nightmare in her mind – the moment that, on 14 August, would end her career.

A quiet rapping resounded. She opened the door. Iwata stood there, holding two coffees. In the ugly light of the hallway he looked older, as though he, too, had been trapped in a hotel-room purgatory for a long time.

She watched him as he entered and realized she could

not understand his place in all this. It was obvious to her why the task force would see *her* as an outsider. But Lynch couldn't fathom why Iwata was seen that way.

From what she could tell from the whispered conversations and hushed gossip, most referred to him as American. He certainly had the accent when speaking in English. But his Japanese sounded no different to theirs. She had once walked in on him speaking Spanish on the phone. When she asked him who it was, he had merely responded *home*, seemingly irritated that she had seen that side of him. The darkness around his eyes told her he hardly slept. She was yet to see him eat.

On the one hand, Lynch sensed a searing determination in Iwata. He had devoted himself to the case and applied good, clear logic. On the other hand, she couldn't help but doubt his motives. He disappeared now and then. He spoke to men in corners. When Itō had jostled for her position, Iwata had shut him down immediately. At the time, she had appreciated it, but now she realized she had never done so little to earn trust. Had he done this simply so she would not question him?

Yet she had from the beginning.

Ultimately, it was clear that the murder of Skye Mackintosh concerned Iwata. But Lynch did not believe that he *cared* about it. She had no basis for feeling this. She just knew she was right.

'What is it?' he asked, as if hearing her thoughts.

'Nothing. What's up?'

'I just spoke to Itō. He managed to find a Kaori who was part-time at Rikkyo. She didn't show up in the initial searches as she was just doing summer classes, she wasn't an actual student.'

'You made contact?'

'She's not answering her phone, but I have an address.'

As the clockwise Yamanote Line hummed through the rainy night, Lynch looked out of the steamy windows and thought about the anime films she had sneaked out of her brother's room as a little girl. She remembered the vivid feeling of wonder sewn into those infinite neon and concrete panoramas, flesh and machinery fused together, an outlandish jumble of supernatural and tech-noir cyberpunk. The never-ending anonymity of those animated worlds felt more real to her than dragging shopping bags along Holloway Road with her mother. But now Lynch was here, Tokyo felt flatter, drabber, less vivid than her little girl's imaginary version.

Lynch drifted through old memories: the glorious painful tugs when her mother did her hair, how rare and warm her hands were. That wonderful French book she had been given by an old classmate: *I am an aspirin that dissolves in Tokyo*. The whiskey-sour words an old lover had wooed her with: *Language is the only homeland*. Only later had she realized he had stolen it from Czesław Miłosz. Memory somehow seemed more real in this place. And though Lynch felt a disconnection from this strange city, it also seemed impossible that she would ever return to London, to the Met, to face consequences.

At Shinjuku they changed on to the Chūō-Sōbu Line. The carriage was packed, despite the late hour. People in suits rested their heads on each other's shoulders, exhaustion trumping social reservation, the unspoken kinship of the grind allowing this isolated intimacy. Salarymen, pink in the face from post-work drinks, hung their heads between their legs as if they regretted existence itself. One or two glanced at Lynch, but sharply looked away when she met their eyes.

The detectives reached Asagaya at 10 p.m., a residential area of zelkova trees and jazz bars which had once been home to the city's literary bourgeoisie. Indigo House was on a quiet backstreet not too far from the station.

'This is it,' Iwata said. 'Kaori Harada's place.'

'Let's hope she's a night owl.'

The housing officer, a portly young man with a ponytail and a turtleneck, answered the door. Although he grumbled about the lateness, he seemed thrilled by their arrival. Upstairs, he solemnly opened the bedroom door, as if it were a responsibility that could be executed only by him.

Iwata and Lynch looked around Kaori Harada's small room, its mauve curtains closed, the bed unmade. Lynch opened drawers and cupboards. They were all full – clothes, trinkets, toiletries. Nothing obvious missing. Iwata went through the small desk and found Kaori's passport and student identification card.

'Kaori keeps to herself,' the man said as he primped his ponytail. 'I'm the only one who ever sees her, really.'

'Ever have any problems with her?'

'No. Well, not really.'

'Go on.'

'Oh, just a few tenants have mentioned it to me: sometimes you can hear a strange sound coming from her room.'

Iwata looked up at him. 'Strange how?'

'Kind of like a low buzz. I assume it's mood music or something.'

'When will Kaori be home?'

'Late, usually. But I haven't seen her for a few days.'

Iwata and Lynch glanced at each other. 'When did you last see her?'

'It would have been on the seventh or the eighth – in the morning. Funny, though, isn't it? Judging by all these cobwebs, you'd think her room has been empty for weeks. I guess it is spider season after all.'

Iwata ran his fingers through the empty webs, delicately destroying the silk traps. 'Where was Kaori Harada going when you last saw her?'

'She had her book bag. So university, I guess.'

'We checked. She hasn't been to Rikkyo in several weeks.'

'Oh. Well, Kaori did what she felt like doing, that was the vibe I got. Try talking to her family?'

'She hasn't got any.' Iwata crouched down over a cobweb in the corner of the room. It was full of cocooned crickets. 'What about visits from friends?'

'Never. She often came home late, but always alone.'

'I'll let you know if we need anything else.'

The housing officer turned away, disappointed, as if excluded from school gossip. Lynch closed the door after him and looked at Iwata. 'What are you thinking?'

'I'm thinking Kaori was friends with Skye and now it looks as if she's missing, too. You?'

'Same. But is she missing because of *him*?'

Iwata had no answer. Only more of that bad feeling.

Shindo rolled his cigarette slowly between his thumb and forefinger and considered its shrinking tip with what little sympathy the good half of his face could manage. Between twitchy drags, he spat into his bin, his natural acerbity returned in the gesture.

Iwata was standing by the window, peering out of it as though it were not opaque. Assistant Inspector Itō was hovering by the door, anxious his presence might offend his superiors at any second. He had lit Shindo's smoke and was nervously flicking the Zippo shield open and shut, the metallic chinking the only sound in the room.

The phone rang and Iwata hit the speakerphone button. 'We're listening.'

'This is the Third Biology Section of the National Research Institute of Forensics. My name is –'

Shindo rolled his one eye. 'We're *listening*.'

'. . . Yes, of course. Well, um, sum and substance: you won't be shocked. The tissue on the recovered weapon matches the victim. Blood. Skin. Hair. As for the room at the love hotel, it's swimming in DNA. Excluding the profiles of staff and cleaners, who've all been checked out, we're left with any number of guests.'

'What about the criminal database?' Iwata said. 'Any hits?'

'Two, but nothing compelling. One is a woman who's been tagged for prostitution. The second is a male who served a few years in the nineties for fraud. In any case, he's already been located and was out of the city at the time of the murder.'

'Great,' Shindo muttered. 'Case closed, then.'

'Understood,' Iwata said. 'Please thank Third Section for their work.' The call ended.

'Well, then.' Shindo took out another smoke. 'The mystery continues.'

Itō snapped the Zippo shut.

Shindo fixed him with his eye. 'Aren't you meant to be with Team B?'

'Yes, sir.'

'Well, get to it. And give me back that lighter – it sounds like a goddamn metronome in here.'

Itō put the Zippo down, bowed and swiftly exited.

When he was gone Shindo sighed. 'See what I mean? These fucking kids today. Never had to lift anything heavier than chopsticks their entire lives and they're fast-tracked into major cases.'

'Itō's no different than the rest of them. He just wants to impress you.'

'The boy is dense.'

'He's done a decent enough job for me.'

Shindo coughed hard, the effort of it draining him. 'Pass me the lighter, would you?'

Iwata handed it over and went back to the window. 'Didn't I say you needed to quit?'

'We both know I'm beyond quitting.' Shindo clumsily lit up, took a little puff and sat back low in his seat, a vanquished dragon in its cave. 'But what I want to know is where *you* are, Inspector Iwata.'

'Right here, looking through a window out of which I see nothing. And it's *Consultant*.'

Shindo snorted. 'You think I care what the press say? The fact that you're leading this case was going to come out sooner or later. But, Iwata, listen to me. Soon as you put this one to bed? The press, Division One, the Justice Minister – we'll all be having sweet dreams.'

'Speaking of the Minister, I thought you said you had his ear.'

'I do.'

'Well, before the press briefing at the embassy I was threatened by a Justice Ministry goon. Said he worked for the man who will be taking over.'

Shindo frowned with one side of his face. His was an industry of transfers, rotations, upheavals. He had survived this long, clawed his way to the top, forged the necessary connections without trading in his integrity. But he was old and no one could stay on top for ever. Shindo didn't need Iwata to tell him he was blind to what was happening behind the scenes.

'It doesn't matter. But Shindo, there is something else you need to know. Skye was friends with a young woman called Kaori Harada. We went to her house tonight. It looks like she could be missing, too.'

Shindo scowled at the glowering tip of his smoke. 'So, if I'm understanding this correctly, we've already got worldwide attention on the Mackintosh murder, and now you're telling me the killer may be branching out?'

'And Hatanaka is looking for a man kidnapping young women. The cases could be connected, but Tokyo is home to 38 million people. It's entirely possible there are two bad men out there somewhere.'

'Well, that's just fucking great.'

Through the beclouded window Iwata could see only red aircraft warning lights blinking.

'Iwata, tell me: you really think there's a chance this English girl is connected to Hatanaka's missing sex workers?'

'There's a chance, of course. But that's not what my gut tells me. His case centres on prostitutes out walking the streets. Skye Mackintosh and Kaori Harada weren't out on the kerb. At least, we have no evidence of that. Then again, there's a lot about Skye that we don't know. And we know next to nothing about Kaori. However, the chances of a killer picking them both up by coincidence is likely inferior to him knowing them both.'

'Yes, you said these two girls were friends.'

'And that's what I can't work out – if the killer knew both women, then he's part of their circle. But that's not somewhere he could hide, not with the scrutiny we've applied.'

'This Harada woman.' Shindo took a drag. 'No body yet, right?'

'No. As far as I know, she's alive and well.' Iwata stood now, as if this thought had compelled him.

'Then carry on doing what you're doing. But before you leave, remember your briefing with Team B. I'm sure they've made popcorn.'

'We'll talk tomorrow.'

'Iwata?'

He paused at the door.

'. . . You will find this son of a bitch.' Shindo flicked on his Zippo and stared at its flame. 'You'll find him, just like you found the rest.' There was a stony certitude in his voice, but in his withered face Iwata saw a decrepit naivety, an old widower convincing himself his marriage had been a happy one. The blindness of the faith bothered him, as though his former boss had become someone else. The real Shindo only ever believed in things begrudgingly. Yet this misshapen elderly man was desperate to believe in anything.

Iwata closed the door. He supposed, for some, when facing the end, anything was better than nothing.

21. Unknown Male Three

On the ninth floor of Shibuya HQ, the last remaining inspectors of Team B were packed into the briefing room, yawning behind their coffee cups. Their glassy eyes took in the footage once again. Thirty windows were projected on to the screen, different angles of San'ya.

Negishi, the insomniac computer cracker, was manning two laptops. George Milton was standing at the front. Lennie Small was sitting in the first row, teacher's pet. Iwata was in the corner. The familiar smell of armpits and shitty aftershave turned his stomach.

'First things first.' George cleared his throat. 'We've now established the victim's route to the crime scene.'

The screen showed Skye Mackintosh crossing the road and hurrying towards a train station. The time stamp showed 8.26 p.m. 'This is Shin-Ōkubo Station. She uses her Suica card, checks her phone – both of which are still missing. She takes the Yamanote Line clockwise to Ueno station. There she switches on to the Hibiya Line and arrives at Minami-Senju station at 9.16 p.m. From there, she dips in and out of coverage, as you can see, but she's alone the whole way and certainly doesn't look distressed. It's about a ten-minute walk from the station to the love hotel. Now, on to the suspects.' George stood beneath the screen, his face illuminated a dim blue. 'There is one scooter that approaches the Starlet Hotel at 9.50 p.m. on the night of the 7th. We can't get an angle of it approaching the building itself, but it's the only one that enters the alleyway. Looks blue, perhaps a later model. Crucially, there seems to be a pizza box attached to the rear storage box. Now it's difficult to tell, but he appears to fit the description given by the love-hotel staff of the male who rented the room – *between 174 and 178 centimetres*. As for looking homeless and having buck teeth, it's impossible to tell, given the helmet and the quality of the footage. Here you can see that he enters and leaves the alleyway in little over a minute, the only difference is: no pizza box on the way out. He certainly doesn't appear to be rushing.

Now, assuming for a moment the deliveryman is not the culprit, we have identified twenty-five males in the vicinity around the time of the murder that match some or all of the physical descriptions given by the hotel staff. But only three of them cross Shirahige bridge before the murder, then cross back some time later.' With a laser pointer, he indicated three grainy figures on the screen. 'Of this handful, Unknown Male Three is the only subject with a bag large enough to contain the recovered weapon. Unfortunately, he sticks pretty close to his umbrella the whole time. Negishi, please isolate him and play.'

She nodded and the footage whizzed back to the start on a single window. It then played on fast-forward but at a pace the human eye could track.

'As you can see, the subject doesn't have the bag with him heading in the direction of the love hotel.' George criss-crossed the blurry figure with his laser now. 'But about an hour later he walks back over the bridge . . . here . . . And *this* time he has a bag. So if this is the killer –' he flipped on the main lights, took off his glasses and inspected them for smudges – 'then perhaps he finds the weapon near the love hotel, or he has it stashed in the vicinity. In any case, even with Negishi's best work, we still can't be sure it's the same green bag as the one recovered from the river. Moreover, he looks significantly taller than 178 centimetres. Though we can't be certain, of course.'

Iwata balked. 'You're saying you don't think it's him?'

'I'm saying this footage isn't all that much to go on.'

'Inspector Tanigawa, this is the only male in the area at the right time holding a bag that resembles the one found containing the murder weapon. Then there's the description given by the old man at the river. Look at this guy.'

'Ah, yes. You're referring to the testimony of the mentally unstable man. Well, the build he described is undeniably similar to Unknown Male Three, it's true. And evidently, this individual is tall. But this description was issued by an eyewitness who isn't exactly what you'd call . . .' George searched for the right word.

'Sane?' Lennie offered.

'Demonstrably credible.'

Iwata pinched the bridge of his nose, his head spinning with fatigue. 'Maybe he's not all there, but he saw what he saw: a tall man who threw a green bag into the river. I made a point of testing his memory on the colour. He corrected me.'

'Consultant Iwata, with respect' – Lennie took the laser pointer and circled Unknown Male Three's face like an angered hornet – 'the witness, if he can be called that, described a tall man who looked like George Harrison. And yes, the subject is tall. But he's also got an umbrella and is wearing a face mask. Same kind as you could buy in any 7-Eleven in Tokyo or a million other places. He may well resemble George Harrison. Or he may resemble Michael Jackson.'

'Thank you for that, Inspector Ideguchi. But this Unknown Male Three is the only individual that could have murdered Skye Mackintosh. He had the weapon with him and he disposed of it. The man by the river described what we are looking at, even if we can't see his face. I understand you may have doubts, but I would ask you to please refrain from unnecessary observation from here on in.'

'*Unnecessary?*' Lennie laughed, his thick neck rippling with hate. George tried to talk him down, but it was too late. 'Consultant Iwata, we've all sat here and listened to your briefings, followed your orders, which you give without explanation. And I think I speak for everyone when I say –'

'But you don't.'

'What?'

'You don't speak for everyone. I do. If you don't like it, you can walk.'

Lennie looked around the room, his face red. He hadn't expected to lose this exchange, but Iwata had bared his teeth; there was no backing down now. He gave him one last rancorous look then walked out. The door slammed shut.

'If anybody else here has an issue with my direction, now's the time to be clear about it.' Iwata scanned the briefing room. 'No? Then let's finish. Inspector Tanigawa, where does Unknown Male Three go next?'

George sighed. 'We lose him not long after he crosses the bridge. He walks along the river under the freeway, but there's no coverage there. We think he cuts through the park then out into the backstreets somewhere around

Kanegafuchi station. It could be that he disposes of the bag in the river. Or it could be his gym bag and he's going to do his laundry.'

'No, it's the murder weapon and he's going to dispose of it.'

'How do you know the green bag wasn't hidden in the bathroom? How do you know the deliveryman didn't have it stashed in his scooter's storage box?'

Iwata turned to Negishi. 'What's the best angle you can get on his face?'

She keyed in a few commands and the entire screen was consumed with a blocky mess of pixels. Beneath the umbrella, they saw Unknown Male Three's face. It was covered by a medical mask, ubiquitous for the Tokyoite, his eyes nothing more than black and grey holes.

'Sorry,' Negishi said. 'That's the best I can do.'

Iwata walked over to the screen, his shadow embossed on the face. 'Team B, this is who we're looking for. Circulate the photo among your men in Kabukichō – both the uniforms and the undercover guys. They're looking for anybody who could be this man. Someone tall. Possibly Western.'

George, the most experienced hand in the room, shook his head. 'Consultant Iwata, the Olympics are here. You know what'll happen if we start hassling foreigners now? With all the shit the press is already throwing at us? As for this *image*, it isn't worth looking at. If you circulate that and ask –'

'Inspector Tanigawa, let me simplify this: I don't care. This investigation is under my command. As such, if officers see a man who looks suspicious, I want him stopped, I want him questioned. If he acts suspiciously, I want him stopped, I want him questioned. If he tries to pick up girls out in the open, particularly Western girls, I want him stopped, I want him questioned. Is that understood?'

There was no reply, but Iwata wasn't waiting for one. He opened the door. The meeting was over. Team B grumbled out of the room, glancing up at the clock with quiet curses. Lennie, standing just outside, was consoled by almost everyone as they passed.

Iwata left the police station and gingerly crossed over the walkway above the intersection. Now he had disagreed openly with the respected Tanigawa and publicly humiliated Ideguchi, what had been a mutual distaste between him and the Team B detectives would be venomous.

Iwata wondered if he should have trodden more carefully, but he knew he simply didn't have the time to indulge these men. His loyalty was to Shindo. And even then, he had been distracted for too long from his real motivation in returning to Tokyo – Ryoma Hisakawa.

As if reading his mind, Iwata's phone buzzed.

GOVERNMENT OBSERVATORY BUILDING IN 1 HOUR.
NIGHTCAP.

The number was unknown, but the message was in English. The identity of the sender was obvious.

Closing his eyes, Iwata heard the whoosh of the surface traffic below and the drone of the traffic on Metropolitan Expressway No. 3 above him. He pictured himself floating through Tokyo, a foreign virus interpolated within the city's blood vessels. He rubbed his eyes and saw phosphenes, his body a leaning tower of pressure and exhaustion.

All he wanted was to return to his capsule, where he could find the relief of non-being.

But then he recalled Ozawa's words: *You may find you have common ground.*

The last train had long departed and he couldn't risk falling asleep in a taxi. Instead, Iwata started walking north, a storm rumoured in the low, marbled sky. Except for the brief green interlude of Miyashita Park, Tokyo barely changed on this wide boulevard – all flagship stores for global brands, interminable gingko trees and an unending consecution of beige office blocks. Beneath the skein of cables above the street cyclists veered around salary-men who looked dead on their feet, their suitcases like anvils at their sides.

Iwata tried to recall the last time he had come this way but drew a blank. Was it possible he never had? So much of the city looked like versions of itself.

As he walked, he inhaled a cologne of rubbish, exhaust, wet concrete. No city had more nameless streets or alleys. Tokyo was too vast for numerics or nomenclature. To walk through her ways was to be inveigled in her web.

The city spoke to him in the rumble of bus engines, in the mechanical clank of rubbish trucks, in the din of late-night restaurants. She murmured from steam vents and snickered from overflowing gutters. She could be heard in the subterranean whispering of freight trains. *So. You told people you were through with me, didn't you? But here you are.* Tokyo laughed in trilling bicycle bells, in a blaring car horn. *Honey, don't you realize you're not the one who decides who's through with who?*

1.40 a.m. Iwata was walking through the empty streets of the city's financial district. A few miles to the east, Kabukichō would be packed, its neon ruelles buzzing with human traffic. It was the spiritual home of *mizu-shōbai* – 'the water trade' – the traditional euphemism for nocturnal entertainment, an industry that lived and died on fickle factors: bad weather, bad marriages, bad economy. And, tonight, on every corner of Kabukichō, policemen and women dressed in the plainest of plain clothes would be trying to act casual in the scrutiny of the irregular, their eyes scanning the streets for a murderer – Unknown Male Three.

But here in Marunouchi – an area of wide, sweeping boulevards and sleek skyscrapers – there was no one. Only the sound of hot, bitter eddies through the corporate emptiness.

Iwata crossed the deserted road, the traffic lights changing for no one. The streetlamps here only tinted the darkness with a hazy tangerine. Up ahead, the Tokyo Metropolitan Government Building was an 800-foot-tall Gothic cathedral made of motherboards and sockets, a sharp upward stab.

Iwata was peering up at it when he became aware of footsteps. A pair of them, increasing their pace. By sound alone, he knew they carried weight and intention. He picked up his own pace and forced himself not to look back.

Instead, he glanced to his left as he passed a parked car. In its reflection, he saw them. Two men. Anonymous black suits. Heavy-duty yet assimilable in a crowd. *The two from the grey Suzuki Escudo?* They were looking over their shoulders, scanning the area, checking to see if they were being observed.

Being observed before what?

Iwata snapped off to the left and knocked on the window

of a parked taxi. The driver jolted awake. He swore, but seeing Iwata's *techou*, wound his window down sheepishly.

'Help you, Inspector?'

'You can't park here, sir.'

'Oh! I'll be gone before you know it.'

'Not just yet. Licence, please.'

The driver fumbled it out and Iwata made a show of
inspecting it. The two black suits passed by behind, their
riptide almost perceptible in the thick air. Iwata watched
them go before handing the licence back to the driver.
The taxi slinked away.

Fifty feet away, one of the suits turned to look over his
shoulder. It could have been a squint. It could have been a
wordless threat. Iwata couldn't be sure in that half-dark.

22. I Found You

Inside the observatory the lights were kept low to maximize the view. Soft jazz played. Couples shared slices of gateau and gazed out over the city while holding hands under the table, drunk on the panorama, abetted by the overpriced cocktails.

Tokyo did not illuminate, it ignited. Aircraft warning lights blinked red everywhere, a swarm of fireflies reborn each night. Even the pockets of darkness shone somehow, as though made of beetle shell.

Ozawa was sitting at the end of the bar, drinking whiskey. He was reading the evening edition, nibbling his thin lips as his eyes scanned the pages.

'Next time' – Iwata sat next to him – 'a little notice would be appreciated.'

Ozawa didn't look up from the paper. 'I don't think either of us inhabit a world of suitable notice, Inspector.'

'I need to sleep.' Iwata ordered coffee.

'Ah, but that midnight oil flows through your veins.' He raised his glass. 'Besides, you're *hunting*. Speaking of which, how goes the hunt?'

'That depends.' Iwata sipped his coffee. 'On which end of the gun you're talking about.'

Ozawa laughed. 'Well, according to the fine people at this paper, it's not going so well. There's a lot of gnashing of teeth over a lack of arrests, while they've come up with several theories of their own. A few scapegoats mooted.'

'Scapegoats are easy to find.'

Ozawa's smile was a vacuum, a human 404 Not Found. The jazz ended and a muzak version of Debussy's *'Clair de Lune'* followed.

Iwata looked around then spoke in English. 'Ryoma Hisakawa is my father. You can tell your boss that my interest in him is personal.'

'Oh, we already know that. You're not the only dirty secret Hisakawa has buried in his backyard. What my superior wants to know is what *kind* of personal.'

'I'm sure he didn't get to where he is by having everything spelled out for him.'

Ozawa mulled this over then nodded once, almost to himself. 'Very well, Inspector. I think we can afford to be candid at this stage. Ryoma Hisakawa is not a man of integrity. He represents the past, in many ways. In fact, my superior considers him a danger.'

'To him?'

'To the people of Japan.'

Iwata looked at the man's whiskey a moment too long. 'I don't need to know details. My business with him is my own, like I say.'

Ozawa took a delicate, considered sip. 'Inspector, am I to understand that you bear ill will towards Hisakawa?'

'You could say that.'

'An eye for an eye?'

'At least.'

'Well, in that case I'm sure my superior would understand. And when that time comes, you'll be protected.' Ozawa necked his whiskey. 'Good evening, Inspector.'

'Wait, you said *common ground.*'

'Open your eyes. You're already standing on it.'

Iwata watched him go, too exhausted to respond. Last orders were called. He was about to push himself off the bar when he noticed the newspaper Ozawa had left behind.

The article he had been reading was on the Cabinet reshuffle, speculation that the Prime Minister would make further changes in the coming days.

Again, the article meant nothing to Iwata; it was the grainy black-and-white image of Ryoma Hisakawa that made his throat tighten. But, this time, beneath the old man's grinning face something had been scrawled in small English letters.

An address.

Iwata returned to Police HQ for the Altima then stopped by his hotel to drop off the scrap of newspaper Ozawa had left on the bar. He didn't want it on him if by any chance he was stopped.

The drive took twenty minutes. Den-en-chōfu was a leafy district to the south of the city, home to artists, singers, business leaders. And now, the new Minister of Defense – Ryoma Hisakawa.

Iwata left the car near the train station and went into the 24-hour coffee shop to try and muster up the courage. Dawn wasn't far off. There was only one other customer, a young woman surrounded by English textbooks.

'*Tom knows that Meg* loves *him*,' she announced. '*Tom knows that Meg* loved *him*.'

Cursing the past tense, she took out a hand mirror from her handbag and muttered to herself as she searched for imperfections. '*Tom knew that Meg loved him? Tom knows that Meg loved him.*'

Iwata left the coffee shop and walked through rain and

shadows. The handsome tree-lined avenues of Edwardian villas and Swiss-style chalets seemed a strange backdrop for a reckoning.

A few minutes later Iwata was looking at Ryoma Hisakawa's house, stomach churning. He stood under a tree, staring, disbelieving, his clothes darkening in the downpour. The anger inside him kicked like a baby.

Whereas before he clenched and unclenched his fists in his pockets to calm himself, now he stroked the grip of his revolver.

The windows of the house were dark, the street was empty, the rain unrelenting. Iwata's body was weak, but his thoughts were clear. He was an inspector. He would always be an inspector. And now, he realized, after so many years, the real culprit had finally revealed himself. His father had always been here, in this garden suburb, waiting for him.

In the darkness, Iwata spent a long time watching the house.

'I found you,' he whispered. 'I found you.'

Shin-Ōkubo station. The Mackintosh family were in the thick of the rush-hour scrum, handing out flyers. They were wearing the same T-shirts as they had at the embassy press briefing – Skye on their chests, smiling to camera, three words running beneath her:

WHO HURT ME?

They searched the faces in the crowd, as though waiting for someone in particular, their expressions stuck somewhere between embarrassment and determination. They carried placards in Japanese, laminated for the rain, and a small group of bilingual volunteers were on hand to help. Commuters flowed around them, trying to avoid eye contact. Those who stopped would take a flyer, talk politely with the volunteers, occasionally steal a rueful glance at the parents.

Philip and Karen stood apart from each other, the former looking thunderous, the latter sadly overwhelmed. Geraldine was assiduous in her work, frequently going back to the box for more flyers. Dylan, as the only one of the group who could speak some Japanese, seemed animated and willing enough to talk to the public.

By 7.50 a.m., the rush hour was at its vertex. Lynch stood off to one side. She had seen the cram for the Northern Line six bodies deep, but this was like one of those world record attempts at fitting people in a Mini. And with every passing train, the crowd's panic grew, clean-cut disarray in black and grey. She understood why Shin-Ōkubo station had been chosen for the photo op; Skye had used it every day to get to class. But with only one entrance and just a single elevated platform, it was a mess.

The press, of course, were present. The whole event was in their honour, after all. Every time a Mackintosh handed a flyer to a member of the public, their cameras would desperately snuffle down the moment.

Two uniformed police officers, the male handsome and muscular, the female tall and attractive, were there to keep watch. But Lynch noticed they stayed in shot whenever the press cameras flashed.

Iwata was sitting in the café up the road. It was packed with students on laptops scouring for jobs, suits in need of a caffeine lifeline and old men crammed in the smoking section.

There were few things that galled Iwata as much as wasting time. Certainly, he wasn't about to strike any poses for the press. For the last few days they had painted him as an interloper out of his depth, even a 'foreigner'. Like a bullied kid, everything he did would only spark further scorn. No doubt being photographed next to the family would be seen as an empty gesture. Then again, avoiding it would be seen as disrespectful to the Mackintosh family. And Shindo had been clear. Or, perhaps more accurately, the Justice Minister had been clear: the photo op was not optional.

None of this mattered to Iwata. It was background noise. After all, he now had what he had come to Japan for: the whereabouts of his father. He just didn't know what he was going to do with that yet. The memory of standing in front of the house in the early hours of the morning barely seemed real now.

Behind him, a voice broke his train of thought.

'Inspector, I didn't know you were here.'

Iwata turned to see Dylan White standing behind him. 'Can't start the day without coffee.'

The younger man nodded. 'I'm the same. Mind if I join you?'

'Not at all. Hey, I noticed your Japanese is good.'

'I'm out of practice.' Dylan laughed sheepishly as he sat. 'The press relations lady told me to have my coffee here, out of sight.'

'If she had any sense, she'd have you in front of a camera speaking in Japanese.'

'I thought you lot were meant to tell the truth.'

'I'm not kidding.'

'Says *you*.'

'Well, I grew up between two countries. You just some kind of linguist?'

'No, nothing like that. I used to teach here in Tokyo. That's actually how I met Skye.'

'I thought you met in London.'

'Well, yes. I was in the Japanese Society at university and Skye just walked in one day. She came right up to me and announced she was thinking of coming out here when her degree was over to do a Masters. She had all these questions.' He laughed then cast his eyes down at the Skye on his T-shirt. 'I guess that was it for me.' Self-conscious, he changed the subject. 'Last time I was in Japan I remember reading about the government trying to get rid of these smoking sections. Suppose they didn't have much luck.'

'Old habits die hard here.'

'It's the same in England.' He took a sip of his sesame marshmallow latte and looked out of the window, his top lip foamy. There was something childlike about his manner, Iwata thought, a vulnerability.

'How are you holding up, Dylan?'

He shrugged. 'I don't really know.'

'You're doing great.'

'I don't feel like I am.'

'Take it from me. For example, those T-shirts? That was a good idea.'

Dylan nodded. 'They were from the print shop near Skye's parents' house. When the owner found out why I wanted them, he didn't charge me.'

'I've seen a lot of people in your position fall apart completely, but the interviews, the flyers, the T-shirts – you put that all together. You should be proud. I know it means a lot to Skye's family, you being strong like this.'

'Thank you.' Blushing, Dylan looked around then lowered his voice. 'Though if I'm honest, I can't help wondering . . . How is the case going? I know you can't tell me much. I just can't stop thinking about *him*. You know. What he did to Skye.'

'I can only say that we're trying our best, I'm sorry, Dylan.'

'I understand, you're just doing your job. And I want you to know that I appreciate it, Inspector. No matter what these newspapers are saying about you.'

They sat in silence for a while.

'So you taught English out here?'

'*Teach* is a strong word.' The younger man laughed at himself. 'I just worked at a language school after university. I was terrible, though. No, it was actually the volunteering I did that really helped me learn the language.'

'I didn't know about that. Good for you. Whereabouts?'

'It was a homeless shelter in Adachi. Closed now, I think. God, I met some characters there.' Dylan's eyes glazed over at the memory, a small smile playing on his lips.

Iwata nodded. Shit things happened to good people.

Assistant Inspector Itō held up the subpoena and the bank manager's eyes widened as though it were a shotgun. Within ten minutes he had been given a small side office and Miyake's financial records were bring rushed out like late entrées.

Closing the blinds, Itō took out his phone, put his earphones in and selected 'Diminished Responsibility' by the UK Subs. As the music crashed around his eardrums, he placed Skye Mackintosh's financial records alongside those belonging to the man who had been her landlord. With a pen, he checked the first significant deposit in her account – ¥300,000 – against Miyake's. There was nothing of note leaving the man's current account on or around that date, but then Itō looked at the business account: a ¥300,000 withdrawal.

Breath quickening, he skipped ahead a few weeks to the second deposit in Skye's account – ¥400,000 – there it was, the exact same amount leaving Miyake's business account the day before. It was the same for Skye's third deposit. And the fourth. And the fifth. By the ninth, Itō's hands were shaking as he dialled Iwata.

'Sir, I've got Miyake's records in front of me. Those big sums of money Skye was getting? They're from him. Every single one.'

Iwata shunted the table out of the way and hurried for the café door. 'Then gather those records, Itō. It's time to bring him in.'

'Inspector!' Dylan White called after him. 'Is everything all right?'

Iwata looked back and, against his better judgement, nodded. 'It seems there's been a development.'

The younger man's face broke into a shocked smile, foam still coating his upper lip. Dylan glanced down at Skye on his T-shirt. He seemed to whisper something to her.

23. Always Two Sides

As Iwata and Lynch were preparing to enter the interrogation room, Iwata's phone rang. Staring through the two-way mirror at Miyake, he answered.

'Inspector? This is Madoka, the manager at Black Widow.'

'How could I forget?'

'About that information you wanted: I can confirm that Mr Miyake did indeed visit us on 7 July. He arrived at 11.02 p.m. I've made copies of the CCTV tape and his credit card payments that night. The girls don't want to talk to you, but they did tell me he was in that night; they remember him talking about the eclipse. Now, Inspector, I trust the matter is concluded?'

'You're absolutely sure of all this?'

'Absolutely.'

'Then I wish you and your spiders all the best.' Iwata hung up and turned to Lynch. 'That was the manager at Skye's club. The landlord lied to us again. He didn't show up on the night of the 7th until after 11 p.m.'

'Well, well, well. Looks like it's time we had a word with the good Mr Miyake.'

There was a knock at the door and Negishi came rushing in, holding a stack of papers. 'Iwata, NTT Docomo came through –'

'These are the victim's phone records?'

'Yes, but –'

'Okay, good. I want you to go through these line by line, Negishi. Find me a pattern, anything out of place – was she confiding in anyone? Was she afraid for her life? And when do the actual call logs come through?' Iwata flipped through the rows of numbers, times, dates.

'They've said that should be within the next two or three days. But I did find something odd up front; Skye didn't order pizza on the night of her death.'

Iwata looked up at her. 'That is odd.'

'Someone else must have, but there's another thing –'

Iwata stopped at the final page. He held it to his face now. 'Negishi, this last text message that Skye received. Who does the number belong to?'

'That's what I've been trying to *say*, sir. It was from her landlord –' Negishi noticed the man in the interrogation room now. 'Oh. Him.'

Lynch smiled. 'When it rains, it pours.'

'Son of a bitch.' Iwata shook his head as he passed the page to her.

'*You . . . won't . . . ignore me ever again.*' Lynch read out loud. 'Did I get that right?'

Despite the smallness of the chair in the interrogation room, Miyake was lounging in it, watching his smoke drift upwards. He wore a baggy black T-shirt and a large beanie pulled down low over his brow. When the detectives entered, he didn't bother looking at them.

Lynch leaned back against the door and folded her arms. Iwata sat opposite him. 'Mr Miyake' – he placed a file on the table – 'We meet again.'

No reply, only a serene drag.

'I take it you know why you're here.'

Smoke. 'Do I?'

'Come on, Mr Miyake. We both know you're in trouble.'

Miyake chuckled on another drag. 'News to me.'

'News, huh? Let me tell you what was news: when we found significant sums of money leaving your business account and going into Skye's checking account. *Headline* news when we unearthed your history of violence towards women. The accusations made against you.'

'That was dismissed a long time ago. I never hurt –'

'You lied to the police, sir. You lied to *me*. Told me to my face that you didn't know Skye. Repeated that in the statement you gave.'

'I didn't lie. I said I didn't *really* know her.'

'I'm sure the judges would see it that way. Miyake, look: we know you were paying her for sex. And we know you used love hotels. What was it you didn't want the other tenants to know about your little arrangement?'

Miyake kept his eyes on his smoke, but his jaw had tightened. 'I've got nothing to say.'

From the file, Iwata took out a sheet of paper and placed it in front of him. 'Mr Miyake, please read this. It's a simple outline of the crime of which you stand accused.'

Miyake's eyes took in the first box at the top of the page: Article 199 of the Penal Code. '*Homicide?* This is bullshit.' His voice quivered, which he tried to hide by taking another drag. 'I didn't kill her. My father –'

Iwata slapped the roll-up from his hand. 'He can't help you here, Miyake. Because *your* money is in her bank account. *You* had the keys to her apartment. *Your* fingerprints are all over her bedroom. *Your* DNA is everywhere. And now she's dead.' Iwata crushed the roll-up underfoot. 'So, tell me again this is bullshit.'

Miyake shook his head, his face pale. 'You can't talk to me like this.'

Iwata moved forward, his face only a few inches away from his cheek. 'You're not the landlord here.'

The younger man leaned away, his face white with disgust.

Iwata shrugged as though they had simply agreed to disagree. 'Do you remember my colleague, Miyake? Detective Constable Lynch from the London Metropolitan Police. She's come 8,000 kilometres to be here in this room with you. And why? Because they know you killed the girl, too.'

Miyake clutched his temples. 'I didn't kill anyone.'

'Save your breath. It's not a question of your *guilt* – we're not here to determine that. Hell, we could bring you down with half of what we've already got. No, see, we're here for the *why*.'

'I'm not going to confess to something I didn't do.'

'You paid her for sex, didn't you? On at least nine separate occasions. That's how she could afford that apartment, isn't it? Because you were charging her next to no rent whatsoever. Is that your tactic? Lure them in from campus with an offer of cheap lodgings?'

Miyake hunched forwards.

'That's how it started. We know that. But then what? Tell me. Did things get out of hand? She got sick of your needs, told you the arrangement was off. And you lost your temper?'

'That has nothing to do with . . . !' Miyake stared up at the ceiling. 'I didn't kill her. I've never killed anyone. This is *madness*.'

'Okay, Miyake.' Iwata softened. 'We're not unreasonable.

You must understand we see this kind of thing fairly often. And we know that there are always two sides. Now, as it happens, we also know the sort of person Skye was . . . Deceptive. Two-faced. Am I wrong? Come on, it wasn't all one-way traffic, right? So help us understand.'

'Understand *what*?'

'She tried to blackmail you, didn't she? That would explain the shitty love hotel.'

'I've never been there.'

'Did she start the fight? Your agreement got out of hand, didn't it?'

'No –'

'You only wanted a little fun and she tried to twist it into something else, something dark – maybe that was it. She found out about the accusation against you in your past? She'd been threatening to expose you. You'd been under pressure for a long time. It was just a *moment*, wasn't it? Just an understandable moment of madness? We all react now and then.'

'No!' Miyake was snarling, yet Iwata leaned in as though for a kiss.

'I *understand*. I know why you lashed out. I would have done the same thing. I just want to help you.'

'You're lying –'

'Shh, Miyake, listen to me.' He smiled like a father. 'Confess. Just let the burden go. Write it down on that paper and I will do everything in my power to make them see that you cooperated with us, took responsibility. That will count for something.'

Trembling, Miyake shook his head. 'I never hurt Skye. I was never at that love hotel.'

'Fine.' Iwata sighed, and his tone reverted to its previous

acerbity. 'Miyake, your alibi is that you were at Black Widow all night, correct?'

'It's the truth.'

'Unfortunately, the problem is that hostesses see a lot of men in a night. Not many of them seem to have good memories.'

'They'll remember me.' Miyake spoke defiantly, despite quivering lips.

'Okay, I like that. Let's talk about Black Widow. You never mentioned that Skye worked there.'

'She'd already left that place by the time you came to search the apartment.'

'You didn't think it was relevant?'

'I don't know. I guess not.'

'Tell me something, why are you so sure the girls at Black Widow would remember you?'

'I go a lot. I spend a lot. I'm not old or fat, I don't disrespect them. I know they like me.'

'Well, as it happens, they do remember you. We spoke to some of them already. They all said the same. That you liked Skye. She was your favourite. The manager confirmed as much. Said she knew that you were going on dates outside of the club.'

'Look, we met sometimes, sure. I'm her landlord, we had things to discuss. But that's all.'

Iwata referred to his file. 'You told me on the day we searched Skye's apartment that you arrived at Black Widow *around nine*. Yes?'

'I couldn't exactly be –'

'Yet you gave a statement to us the following day rather generously estimating your arrival at between nine-thirty and ten. Where'd that extra hour come from, Miyake?'

'I'm trying to tell you, I wasn't paying attention to the time.'

'Evidently. Because you arrived at Black Widow at two minutes past eleven that night. They have you on camera. And the walk from your apartment to the subway station passes at least three prominent clocks I can think of just off the top of my head. You saw the time, Mr Miyake. No, the reason you're so fuzzy about the time of your arrival is because reaching the club at eleven means you could have been in San'ya beforehand. Yet you say you were at home alone before that, nobody to vouch for you.'

'Okay, I made a mistake with the time. But I wasn't lying. I'm –'

'I told you. There's no need to try and talk your way out of this. We already know what happened. We just need to ascertain why. So tell us, Miyake. You were only trying to defend yourself, was that it? Maybe you just wanted to scare her a little and it went too far?'

'No.' Miyake's eyes were pink. 'I could never kill her. I could never do that. I grew up without my mother, I know what it is to lose a –'

Iwata nodded enthusiastically now. 'See, that's good. You're telling me that you're a good guy, you would never *plan* to hurt Skye. It was *beyond your control*. I understand that. We all understand that, right?'

Lynch nodded sympathetically.

'No, you're not listening to m—'

Iwata took the final page from Skye's phone records from the file. The last text message was circled. 'You recognize that number, sir?'

Miyake peered at the page through tears.

'Oh, God.'

'Who is that from?'

'Okay, okay. Listen, I know that sounds bad. But I wasn't threatening her. I was just sick of being ignored, that's all. I had feelings for her, all right? I tried to tell her but —'

Iwata slammed his fist down on the desk. '*Enough.* Your shithole of a mouth might be saying *no*, but we have your DNA in the girl's apartment, on the girl's clothes. Do you understand what that means? Your DNA is confessing. Your bank account is confessing. Your phone records are confessing. All of them are telling us that you're a liar. So why don't you just stop being a coward for once in your little life and take responsibility for your actions?'

Miyake wiped away his tears and nodded. Something in his demeanour had changed. 'All right. I did pay Skye for sex. I can't remember how many times. But I *never* hurt her. Never. And I know you can't have any evidence of that, because it didn't happen. Not once. Now, it's true I've been accused of things in the past, but I learned my lessons. And if you want to charge me with this, then so be it. Still, I'm not signing anything. I have nothing else to say.'

'In that case' – Iwata gathered the papers together and stood – 'I'll see you in the next life.'

Outside the interrogation room the detectives stood by the coffee machine. It hummed as though in thought. 'You think he did it?' Lynch asked.

Iwata shrugged. 'There are things against him. A lot of it looks bad.'

'But not enough for you.'

'I'm not discounting any possibilities here.'

'Do you ever say what you mean?'

He looked at her. 'Do you?'

They fell into silence again, watching Miyake through the window as he tried to stop crying.

'Get me one of those weird spiced coffees, would you?'

'One thing Miyake is right about.' Iwata dumped a few coins in the machine. 'We can't connect him to the love hotel. His DNA profile isn't present and, although he's taller than 178 centimetres, he doesn't "look" like Unknown Male Three to me. I don't think we can make him for homicide.'

'So what next?'

'I have to announce the arrest.'

'And Miyake?'

'We can hold him for twenty-three days without charge.' He handed over her coffee.

'Twenty-three *days?* Fucking hell, we get twenty-four *hours.*'

Struck by an idea, Iwata peered at Miyake through the two-way mirror. 'Still, if we were to turn him loose today and he *is* the murderer, I'd be willing to bet he'd be in the mood for a spring clean.'

Lynch smiled. 'We catch him in the act of tying up loose ends and Bob's your uncle.'

'I don't even need to know what that means. I'm going to talk to Shindo now. I'll ask him to pull a few surveillance guys out of Kabukichō and beg him to approve bail for Miyake.'

24. Running

By nightfall, it was all in place. The police media room was wall to wall, not just every type of local and national news organization but global ones, too. Standing space was at a premium. A cluster of hastily seconded sports journalists were packing the doorway.

A different police station had been chosen for the occasion to throw the media off the scent. The press director announced the arrest of a suspect – his gender and age – but refused to release any further details, to the audible displeasure of the room. The decision to quietly release Miyake on bail – a rarity at the best of times – was not mentioned.

The briefing was over in a matter of minutes and the journalists shuffled out incredulously. Outside, Tetsuya Suda was fumbling inside his blazer for a lighter when he heard his phone ringing.

'Iwata? Nice of you to call. Didn't see you at this pointless briefing.'

'My apologies. Been a little busy.'

'Tell me you're going to throw something my way.'

'You still fighting the good fight, Tetsuya?'

He raised an eyebrow. 'We're not talking about the English girl any more, I take it.'

'Bigger. And closer to home.'

'Don't tease me, Inspector.'

'We'll talk soon.'

*

The next day, across Tokyo, Miyake was released from Shibuya police station. He rubbed his face – a man waking from a nightmare. The sun through the thick cloud was a coppery glare, the early-morning traffic already heaving. Cursing the new world, Miyake hailed a taxi and got in.

As it pulled away from the kerb, a white sedan followed. A few seconds later a grey van with a sign for a non-existent delivery company pulled away, too.

– Buzzard 4 to Buzzard 9, confirm visual. –

– This is Buzzard 9, visual confirmed. Subject is travelling northbound in a dark green Toyota Comfort, taxi registration 66-5B. –

– Buzzard 9, be advised. Aerial drone is reading heavy traffic up ahead. Some kind of demonstration? –

– Copy that. HQ is telling us it's the practice run for the marathon, switched over to our district at the last minute. 'Security measures.' –

– Nice to have the notice, as usual. –

Itō listened to the garbled patter from the back of the surveillance van. He knew the only reason Iwata had asked him to come along was because he couldn't go himself. Still, he couldn't help but feel pride that he had been chosen for this.

In the past week he had requested subpoenas, CCTV, criminal histories. He had gone through student records, phone numbers, bank details – even garbage. *At last*, he thought. *Some real action.*

Itō had joined the police for want of any better ideas. He had assumed it would be better than a dead-end desk job. But years of a featureless beat, domestics and stolen bicycles put paid to that. By the time he was promoted to Assistant Inspector he realized that, more or less, he had ended up in a desk job anyway.

Yet here he was, in the back of a surveillance vehicle – *under cover* – shadowing what in all likelihood was a murderer. Itō knew assumptions were enemies, but he had watched the Miyake interrogation himself. He knew the facts. The man had lied about a girl who mattered to him and now she was dead. His alibi was weak.

Itō had to admit Iwata had made a clever move – letting the lawyer in early to talk to his client. He knew Miyake would want to be bailed, a rare and highly expensive move. Yet the Miyake family were good for the money. Within just a few hours, the papers had been signed and the suspect was now back on the streets. *With any luck, he'll show his hand.*

– Buzzard 9, be advised. Subject just got out of the taxi. Traffic is at a stand-still up ahead, we got swamped in it. Recommend immediate foot pursuit. You're on your own now, gentlemen. –

The van slammed to a halt and the door slid open. The two other surveillance cops casually hopped out. It took Itō a second to remember his instructions. He slipped his earpiece in, took a deep breath and got out. The street was bustling but, immediately, he saw Miyake up ahead.

Itō took a flyer from a traffic cop outlining the last-minute street closure for the practice marathon and pretended to read it. He was the farthest back out of the three, about thirty metres away. One of the surveillance guys was on the other side of the street, the other was tailing Miyake fairly closely.

– Buzzard 6, copy? –

'Oh, uh, yeah. That's me. I mean, *copy.*'

– It looks like the subject is heading for the subway station. We'll follow him down; you stay up here just in case. –

'Understood.' Itō swore under his breath.

The morning was already stifling. He looked at the current of faces drifting by, thousands of people scurrying around each other. Tokyo was a shingle beach of crossed purpose.

– HQ, be advised. Subject is in the station. He's just passed through the barriers, heading for the Hibiya Line. –

Sighing, Itō headed for the newspaper vendor and searched his pockets for change.

– Fuck. Buzzard 6, subject just doubled back. He's headed your way. –

'Are you sure?'

– Yes, I'm sure! He got a call on his cell, turned around, hopped the barriers. If we'd turned, too, he would have made us for sure. Get on him, right now. –

Itō scanned both exits to the subway station, one on either side of the street. He spotted Miyake now, hurrying north, into the crowd.

He bolted after him. 'He's taking a left at the lights.'

– Wonderful, then he's headed straight for the marathon. This is a shit show. –

Itō bundled through bodies, hopped the traffic barrier and zigzagged through idling cars. He took the same left as Miyake and scanned the crowd. The marathon dry run was under way, steel barriers blocking off the street. There were huge speakers, the announcer blaring joyfully. A large CITIZEN digital clock was running above. Sponsors on feather banners fluttered in the warm breeze – a sports brand, an investment bank, a nutritional supplements company. A helicopter could be heard overhead. As another volley of runners passed by applause rippled through the crowd.

'I don't see him.'

– Buzzard 6, this is Buzzard 4. We've ditched the car, we're a way behind you but we're heading in your direction. –

Itō had him again now. Miyake was climbing the stairs to the pedestrian bridge crossing over the road. Itō gave him a few seconds then hurried to the stairs. As he reached them Miyake was merging into the crowd on the other side of the street.

At the top of the bridge Itō stopped, took out his phone and pretended to be looking for directions. He saw Miyake nudging through the crowd.

'Subject still heading north.' Itō stepped into the bodies. 'Lost visual, I'm in the crowd.'

– This is 4. We got you, we're up on the plaza. We have eyes on him, he's just turned off into the alleyway after the Freshness Burger. You're about twenty metres behind. –

Itō took out his badge and started shouting his way through the crowd. It drew dumb stares but did little to help him. The heat was starting to get to him now, his knees burning. *Excitement*, he panted in his own mind. *Need to remember that I don't actually like excitement.*

Reaching the Freshness Burger, he snuck a glance up the alley – empty. 'Four – did he go left or right?'

– Unclear. He's in a hurry, though. –

'I noticed.'

At the end of the alley Itō dodged a woman with a pram. Holding the phone to his ear, he simulated amiable conversation. At one end of the street a truck driver was angrily remonstrating with one of the marathon officials. At the other Itō saw Miyake slip down another alley by a 24-hour parking unit. 'Got him.'

Itō was sprinting now, the rain a fine haze. Lurching into the alleyway, he clattered into a man sifting through a recycling bin. Plastic bottles rattled loudly and the man shouted at him, but Itō was already gone, his footfalls smacking the wet concrete, his breath wheezing.

Reaching the end, he skidded to a halt then casually took the corner. He saw Miyake across the road. 'Subject entering the fish market. Southern entrance. I'm gonna have a heart attack.'

– Copy, we're there in ninety seconds. –

Snatching an 'I ♥ Tokyo' cap from one of the souvenir shops, Itō pulled the brim down low and eased his way into the herd. The fish market was already thronging, workers and tourists alike. The stalls were packed so closely together wares on either side of the street almost touched. Scooters buzzed through browsers. High above the oily yellow awnings, seagulls from Tokyo Bay circled. The sun was starting to stab through the hot, ashen sky.

Miyake was a good ten metres ahead. Suddenly, he stopped and looked over his shoulder. Itō swerved his eyes at the last second then strolled over to one of the stalls. He ordered a sea-urchin bun from a portly man in a tracksuit who had the look of a market lifer. Itō paid and bit into the ink-black bun, the creamy orange urchin filling his mouth.

– Buzzard 6, do you still have visual? –

'Copy. He's stopped by the whale-skewer stand. On the phone again.'

– Any further detail? –

'Yeah, the sea-urchin buns are insanely good. All right, he's moving.' Itō took one last bite and tossed the snack before returning to Miyake's blind spot. He snatched a plastic apron out of a bin and put it on, wiping away the fish guts.

Bells rang out in the distance now and an announcement

for the auction came on the PA system. Miyake veered left, as if responding to the call.

'He's heading for the auction, I think.'

Up ahead, the level crossing started to clang. The barrier to the train track that separated the tourist street-food area with the wholesale market was closing. Miyake slipped through just in time. Itō hit the barrier as the train trundled through.

'Shit! I've lost him – the train.' Itō counted a full thirty seconds until the barrier lifted again. Sprinting into the merchant's compound, his head swivelled.

Electric transport carts bleeped around him. A small group of visitors in high-vis jackets gawked and shuffled out of the way. Pink-cheeked workers in rubber boots grumbled to themselves. On either side of the ice-slick concrete expanse men were tossing empty blood-stained polystyrene boxes, angular snowdrifts piling up, pink liquid pools forming beneath. Fish shipments were being rushed in on forklifts, urgent as donor organs.

Itō tried to get his bearings. The building to the left was abandoned, large signs marking it as scheduled for demolition. To the right, the warehouse was still operational. Two choices, but one Miyake. Swearing, Itō headed for the sound of the auction.

Inside the warehouse it was cold. It smelled like an aquarium, but there was blood on the air. Itō followed the noise. Through the gaggle, he saw thirty massive bluefin-tuna carcasses laid out neatly, black and pink gold, the most expensive flesh on earth. The auction was under way.

The caller musically screeched out numbers and, immediately, unintelligible hand gestures flickered into the air. Notes were scribbled, blind bidders consulted, split-second calculations made. It was a room where men had always done the same thing the same way; the only inconstant here was the price.

Itō saw no signs of Miyake. The other two surveillance cops appeared at the opposite end of the warehouse now, both of them holding clipboards. *Nice touch*, Itō thought. He itched his ear and turned the gesture into an arrow pointing towards the other building. Two imperceptible nods.

Itō exited through a loading bay and crossed the clearing, taking care not to slip on the ice. Now that he was out in the open, he couldn't allow himself to hurry.

He reached the abandoned warehouse. Skipping over the KEEP OUT barriers, he fumbled with his fly for show. The main entrance was sealed shut but one of the loading bays was still open.

Inside, it was empty and silent. Most of the bare stalls hadn't been taken down yet. Too many hiding places to count. *Why would he hide?* A few of the lights were still on, for some reason.

Itō scanned the gloomy expanse and wondered why he felt fear. He could see his breath on the air. Easing deeper into the warehouse, he glanced around the thick concrete pillars, a century of fish oil in their cracks. The echo of his footsteps made him wince and he avoided puddles like they were landmines. Droplets from rusted metal pipes above sniggered all around him.

Where are you?

Itō heard voices now. Not too far away. His heart was hammering. At the end of the stalls, amid the old crate stacks, the voices were clearer. One was Miyake, insistent, hateful. The other voice was quieter, softer.

Itō crept up to the last pillar, just a few metres away from the stacks. 'Buzzard 4,' he whispered. 'I have him in the abandoned warehouse. He's talking to someone –'

Something had shifted in the conversation now. Miyake was shouting, his tone transformed.

Itō glanced around the pillar. Miyake's hands were out; he was backing away from a short man with a hood. The knife thudded into Miyake's neck and was ripped out a second later. There was a flashing red spray followed by pink mist.

'Police! Stop!'

The man looked up, just the bottom half of a face. Then he was running.

Itō ran over to Miyake, who was gurgling, his eyes wide and unfocused. He clutched his throat as though gravely offended. 'Oh, fuck me. Buzzard – whatever damn number you were – Miyake is down. Repeat: Miyake is down. Stabbed by an unknown male, roughly 165 centimetres in height. He has a knife. I'm in pursuit.'

Slipping on blood, Itō fumbled out his gun and gave chase.

He felt like a child. He had never really intended to become a policeman. He had never wanted to look death in the face. All Itō wanted from life was to drink coffee, read books and listen to punk music. How could he be the one chasing a murderer now? How could he be the tip of the spear that was the MPD? It should have been Iwata, or Ideguchi – anyone but him.

Shut the fuck up, Itō, Itō told himself. *He's getting away.*

At the end of the warehouse the hood had shoulder-slammed his way out of the fire exit. Grey light punctured in. Itō's legs felt like mallow; fear consumed him. He ran through the exit, into the light, momentarily blinded. The back lot was a football pitch of empty concrete, broken crates and polystyrene scraps rolling in the breeze. Itō saw the hood up ahead. 'Stop! I'm armed!'

The hood was fast. He reached the chain-link fence a good forty metres ahead. A distant horn resounded, followed by a familiar clanging. Lungs burning, head whirling, Itō traversed the lot. He crashed into the fence and started climbing. At the top, he reminded himself to flick off the safety on his gun. As he did this, it dropped. Reaching for it, his balance went.

Itō landed by the train tracks, an awkward fall. *Train coming, got to move back.* He dragged himself to his feet just in time to register the man in the hood standing there. He was holding a rock. A moment passed between them, then the rock smashed into Itō's temple.

Itō sank back into the fence. He realized there was no longer any sound. He felt no pain, only the warm eddies of the train through his hair. He watched the man disappear out of view, taking his consciousness with him.

25. Just a Guy

In Shindo's office, Iwata was once again staring through a window out of which nothing could be seen. Lynch was languidly smoking, watching the two men. Shindo was openly coughing blood now, unembarrassed. Necking some pills, he shook his head bitterly. 'I can't believe I let you talk me into letting this prick out on bail.'

'You're the one with all that faith in me, boss.'

'Don't get smart with me, Iwata. I'm dying, but I'm not senile. This felt like a bad move.'

'I didn't foresee that Miyake would have enemies.'

'So the one good suspect we've got is now another murder victim. Well, that's wonderful. When this comes out the press will want me castrated.'

'It's my face out there, not yours, boss.'

'That makes no difference in the end. You *are* me.' He fumbled for a cigarette he didn't have. 'We'll have to play it as a mugging gone wrong for as long as we can.'

Lynch double-tapped some ash into a coffee cup. 'Where was Miyake going? That's what I want to know.'

Iwata shrugged. 'He was heading in the direction of home, at least. He takes a taxi, traffic is blocked, he gets out, down into the subway, but then he gets a call. Whatever was said, he changed direction completely. Seemed to be in a rush.'

'So he was meeting someone.'

'Impossible to tell. He looked desperate to the surveillance guys.'

'Or spooked,' Shindo offered.

'Either way, he was dead within ten minutes of receiving the call.'

'Coincidence?' Lynch handed Shindo the rest of her smoke.

'Maybe it's not connected at all.' Shindo took it gratefully. 'What about those accusations in the past? You said there was rape, or something?'

'Again, possible.' Iwata nodded. 'But we're talking almost ten years ago and the woman in question has since left the country. So if it's a reprisal, why now?'

Lynch sat in the window frame and rested her chin on her drawn-up knees. 'Iwata, you said he was dead soon after receiving the call. But what about the press conference?'

'That's true. Looked at from another angle, he's also dead within two hours of being associated with the Skye Mackintosh murder. We didn't release his name, but someone might have leaked it.'

'So who benefits?' Shindo cut in. 'Not Skye's killer. He just lost a good fall guy.'

'Assuming Miyake *wasn't* Skye's killer.'

Shindo sighed, a man too old for headaches.

'How's Itō doing anyway?' Lynch asked.

'Pretty nasty hit to the head, but he'll be okay.'

Shindo chuckled smoke out. 'Maybe the perp knocked some sense into him.'

'*A short man in a hood* was the best Itō could do,' Iwata mused. 'Another shadow.'

There was a timid knock at the door. Negishi bowed. 'Commissioner, Consultant.'

'Come in.'

'Sir, something just came through on the hotline. That

missing can-crusher? Ueda? Well, one of the Minami-Senju cops thinks they know where he is.'

Iwata and Lynch parked near Ueno station and walked under the metal arch of Ameya-Yokochō. To Lynch, it seemed lifted straight out of *Akira*, all cyber-punk grime and retro shops huddling under the rusty iron buttresses of the Yamanote Line. The cold stench of fish wafted through the stalls. Vendors held up their marine wares, scales and claws glistening, thick tentacles spilling over thick fingers as prices were slashed.

Everything here was for sale: counterfeit cosmetics, holistic herbs, knock-off Rolexes, T-shirts with poorly translated English slogans.

Endless left turns, endless right turns, through minuscule alleys, minuscule back streets – to Lynch it seemed as if Iwata were leading them in circles. Between a lack of sleep and a lack of food, she felt as if she were floating. The city was above her, it was beneath her, it was hiding from her in plain sight.

Finally, Iwata stopped at a net café. 'This is the place.'

The sign read: **WEB24/7**. Four cops were loitering in the alleyway behind it.

'Consultant Iwata, it's just been confirmed by Forensics. The murder weapon? It belongs to him. Ueda's prints are all over it.'

Iwata led the way down into a tiny basement reception, where he showed his *techou*. The woman behind the counter pointed down the corridor. 'He's in the one on the end.'

People were walking in and out, rolling suitcases behind them: men and women in office attire, young backpackers, sex workers just passing through – those who could not make rent, those who could not afford to put down roots, those stuck in between.

The corridor was dim except for two plastic neon strips on the floor, as if it were an aeroplane cabin. On either side there were black faux-wood cubicles, wardrobe-sized. The cubicles had no ceiling; a man of average height could stand up and look into the world of his neighbour.

Lynch saw computers, ashtrays, tissues, mounds of dirty laundry, plastic packaging. She smelled disinfectant, sweat, cigarette smoke, feet, perfume. A gentle, tinkling muzak played, as if this were all normal.

'What is this place?' she asked.

'A net café.'

'Looks like an emergency shelter.'

'It is, in a way. Only here, you pay. Some call these people the "cyber homeless" – refugees in their own country. Anyway, look – that must be him.'

Lynch saw blackened trainers outside the last cubicle. Without a word, they stood on either side of the flimsy door and heard canned laughter from a TV show inside. Iwata knocked. The door slid open and a scruffy, slender man looked up at the detectives.

'Takashi Ueda?'

He nodded.

'Open your mouth, please.'

The man frowned, but complied.

Seeing buck teeth, Iwata flipped open his *techou*. 'Takashi Ueda: you are under arrest on suspicion of murder under Article 199 of the Penal Code.'

Takashi Ueda was 175 centimetres tall, thirty-nine years old, of no fixed address. He had a small face and bright eyes. His skin was field-work dark and his buck teeth gave him a comical air when he puffed on his cigarette.

Ueda had been brought to Minami-Senju police station, as arranged. The interrogation room was tiny, but the first thing Ueda did when he was handcuffed to the fixed table was to joke that it was an improvement on his net-café cubicle.

Already, the press had got wind of another arrest. Outside, the first vans were double-parked, aerials protruding like slug antennae. Iwata ordered the blinds shut then had several of the Team A detectives dress up in uniform, as if they were just police moppets keeping the suspect company, waiting for the real detectives to show up.

They fed Ueda a constant stream of barley tea, smokes and small talk. Ueda smiled for no reason as he chatted, almost fading in and out of embarrassment at his own words in the face of all the attention. He made the disguised detectives laugh frequently, gesturing with his large hands, his thick, grey fingers moving like Swiss army knife tools unfolding.

'What's it like living in that place?' one of the cops asked.

'The lap of luxury.' Ueda toasted the memory of it.

The disguised detectives laughed again. One by one, they emerged from the interrogation room, shrugging their shoulders as they took off the spare uniforms.

Iwata had had enough.

In his experience, interrogation at smaller police stations mostly involved shouting and snarling. Depending on the subject, Iwata chose sharper tools: listening and building rapport, presenting himself as the single empathetic ear in the suspect's perilous new world.

Iwata wasn't obliged to give the Minami-Senju detectives the keys to the interrogation room, but they were, after all, the ones who had looked for Ueda.

'Chief Inspector Mizunaga,' Iwata said across the station. 'Would you like to conduct preliminary questioning of the suspect at this stage?'

Mizunaga, cauliflower ears, the most senior detective in Team A, stood slowly, the weight of the world on his shoulders. Licking his lips, he glanced towards the closed blinds. He knew what was out there. It wasn't just local news now – the world was converging on his little police station.

'Thank you, Consultant Iwata.'

He beckoned for Daiki Numa, the young detective with the port-wine stain, to follow him. The two of them headed for the interrogation room.

Iwata, Lynch and the rest of Team A gathered at the two-way mirror. Mizunaga and Numa entered the chamber, small and hot as a submarine bunk. The younger detective leaned against the wall and folded his arms; the older man sat at the table. He dispensed with the formalities and set down a sheet of blank paper on the table.

'Takashi Ueda, you understand why we've arrested you?'

He nodded. 'It's to do with the English girl.'

'*To do with?*' Numa snorted. 'I see you've mastered the art of the understatement, along with crushing your little cans.'

Ueda looked at the floor.

Mizunaga tapped the page. 'Do you know what I want you to write here?'

Ueda shook his head but, immediately, Numa was there, hissing in his ear. 'Answer him, shit for brains. Use words. It's very simple.'

'I don't know.'

Mizunaga sighed. 'Mr Ueda, we know you murdered the girl. We have witnesses. We have the murder weapon. Now, we can pursue this with or without you. But I'm giving you this chance – a confession is the only thing that will help you.'

Ueda shook his head. 'I–I don't . . .'

Numa snapped his finger in his face. 'Speak up, rolling stone. You're on camera. Try and make a good impression for the judges.'

'I didn't kill her. It must have been that other guy you arrested. The one they talked about on the news.'

Mizunaga rubbed his eyes, unmoved. 'We have your scooter on CCTV. Your own boss confirms you made the pizza delivery. We have eye witnesses at the scene of the crime who have described you. We have members of your, uh, community under the freeway confirming you crush cans. And we have the murder weapon with the victim's blood on it. What's the point in denying this, Ueda? Fighting us will only make it worse.'

Numa circled, chuckling to himself. 'Inspector Mizunaga is being diplomatic, pal. What he means is that you, you dumb fuck, have created an international incident. The whole world is watching us now. Ordinarily, you'd just get life. But for your extra effort? Well, the Detention House can always fit one more. You know what they do in the Detention House? It's not the kind of detention you get out of.'

'I don't understand all this. I–I did deliveries, yes. But I never killed anyone.'

'So why were you hiding out in the net café?'

'I wasn't hiding out. It's better than being under the

238

freeway, that's all. The heat is unbearable at this time of year and I had some money.'

'Then explain the delivery to the victim on 7 July.'

'July the 7th?'

'Is there an echo in here?' Numa tapped Ueda on the head. '*Answer* him.'

'Well then, you must be talking about someone else because I sold my scooter the day before – on the 6th.'

Mizunaga glanced at Numa. It was improbable, but they both knew Ueda's face had never been caught on the CCTV – the driver had been wearing a helmet. Mizunaga looked down at his notes. 'A blue Yamaha Zuma 2011 model?'

'Yes.'

'Registration plate 0780-P?'

'Yes.'

'Who did you sell it to?'

'Just a guy.'

'*Just a guy*, huh?'

'He was paying cash. We didn't share life stories.'

'Your boss at the pizza place confirms you were still delivering pizzas the day after.'

'He can't have confirmed that because I had nothing to deliver it with. He wanted to get rid of me anyway, and I wanted to leave.'

Mizunaga realized now that the manager had never actually confirmed seeing Ueda pick the pizza up. Just that it was picked up.

'The manager told us you were on shift.'

'I didn't turn up. One of the other guys must have filled in. He's in the kitchen anyway, he doesn't see who comes and goes.'

'Bullshit,' Numa barked. 'You fucking killed her.'

'I understand you want to solve this murder, but it's the truth. I don't have my scooter any more. You searched my things, though. You saw I have money. I didn't make that crushing cans.'

'What about the staff at the love hotel who say the crime scene was rented by a man your height who looked homeless and had buck teeth?'

'I don't know, but it wasn't me.'

'Ueda, stop wasting our time. We have your tamper. Your prints are all over it. So if you didn't go to that love hotel and if the scooter was no longer yours by then, help us understand why the hell your tamper is dripping with brains.'

'I don't know! It went missing. I thought maybe it was stolen.'

'You think we're fucking idiots? *Your* tamper. *Her* brains.'

'You can ask anyone at the camp; I was searching for it before I decided to move on to the café. I've never been to any love hotel in my life. Let alone killed someone.'

Mizunaga and Numa had turned up expecting a sitting duck and found instead a fox. The shouting began.

26. All the Bad Luck in the World

Iwata and Lynch entered the interrogation room. Ueda, pale from the onslaught, flinched as the door shut behind them. Iwata reeled off his name for the camera before turning his attention to the thick file in front of him. He leafed through it for several minutes.

Ueda fumbled for cigarettes he'd run out of long ago and shakily drained the last of his tea instead. Lynch didn't take her eyes off him. A suspect shitting himself in an interview room looked the same here as it did six thousand miles away in London.

'Mr Ueda, help me understand something.' Iwata spoke with the tone of a man trying to crack a Sudoku puzzle. 'How does a guy like you end up living under the freeway?'

'What's that got to do with the English girl?'

'Answer the question, please.'

'My luck was bad. Things didn't work out.'

'Simple as that?'

'Simple as that.'

'How long have you been living on the street?'

'As far back as I can remember.'

Iwata held up papers from the file before him in sequence. 'Payments on an apartment in Yokohama five years ago. The certificate of ownership for your scooter, brand new at the time. Social security records from your last job at Nakata Corp. Doesn't your memory go back that far?'

'That part of my life doesn't exist any more.'

'Judging by the dates of your redundancy, I'm guessing it was the massive product recall that did it for you. A batch of faulty seatbelts sold to the Americans, wasn't it? That was the scandal, right? Your corporation was killed by the compensation payouts in the end. Not your fault, of course. But it's always the little guy who gets it in the neck.'

Lynch realized Ueda had stopped shaking. He was glaring at Iwata.

'This is all correct so far, isn't it, Mr Ueda?'

'So what?'

'Oh, nothing. I'm just trying to understand how a smart guy like you ends up in your situation. A respected engineer working for Nakata Corp. Then, five years later, you're delivering pizzas and crushing cans?'

'Sometimes life's shit.'

'We'll come back to that. Now this is my colleague, Detective Constable Anthea Lynch from the London Metropolitan Police. She's going to ask you a few questions.'

Ueda ran his tongue across his teeth. 'What's she doing here?'

'People don't grow on trees, Mr Ueda. When they have their heads smashed in, concerns are raised. It's the same in England, you see.'

'Well, I don't speak any English so –'

'Mr Ueda.' Addressing him in Japanese, Lynch took out a photograph of Skye Mackintosh, the smile everyone knew by now. 'My question is very simple. Did you know this woman?'

'Never seen her before.'

Lynch shuffled photographs. Now Skye's eyes were dead, the hole in her skull gaping. 'You're sure?'

242

'Positive.' He looked away, as if there were something else in this room to see.

'Did you ever go to the Starlet love hotel?'

Trying to contain his scowl, Ueda shook his head.

'Did you ever go to Room 806?'

'No, because I was never there.'

'You've never been to that love hotel?'

'What did I just say? Damn it, couldn't you find some-one who understood Japanese or –'

'Mr Ueda, I would ask you to answer my questions directly.'

'*No*, like I said, never been there. You think I have any reason to go there?'

Iwata held up the ownership certificate now. 'And you maintain that you sold *this* scooter – a blue Yamaha Zuma 2011 model – to an unknown individual on 6 July.'

'Yes. It's written right there.'

'Mr Ueda, why would someone buy your scooter and deliver a pizza for you, all in the same forty-eight-hour period that your tamper goes missing?'

Ueda shrugged. 'I guess to frame me.'

'Who?'

'I don't know. If you say my scooter went to the love hotel, then the guy who bought it must have gone there.'

'Sir, if you didn't know the man, why would he frame you?'

'I guess that's your job to find out.'

Iwata was still mulling over the employment records before him. 'I just don't get it, Ueda.'

Noting the dropping of the honorifics, Ueda replied with a tight jaw. 'What's to get?'

'Well, I just mean a guy like you – good job, married with a nice apartment, a nice kid – how did you lose all that and end up by the river in a box?'

'I told you, life's –'

'Shit, yes. But there's shit and then there's losing *every-thing*. I mean, Ueda, you really threw your whole life down the toilet. For most people, that'd be a lifetime's supply of bad luck. And yet, if what you say is to be believed, you managed to go one better. You managed to sell your scooter to a guy paying cash who turns out not only to be a murderer but one who wants to frame you. That's all the bad luck in the world.'

'Well, it's what happened. Look, when can I –'

'There'll be a chance for you to speak later. Right now, it's important you just focus on answering our questions. Now, let's talk about this buyer. You'd never seen him before?'

'No. I told you that.'

'But he wanted to frame you? Why?'

'How would I know?'

'Well, I mean I suppose it's *possible* a mystery man fell from the heavens offering cash for a ten-year-old scooter belonging to a homeless guy he doesn't know in order to frame him for a murder. But for *no reason* whatsoever? I've heard some old chestnuts, but that's something else.'

Ueda put his face in his hands and spoke through his fingers. 'You're asking me to give you reasons I don't know anything about. I can only tell you it wasn't me.'

'The mystery man, then. He paid in cash?'

'Yes.'

'Did you get a good price?'

'Yes.'

'You didn't think to question it?'

'If you're thirsty and someone offers you water, do you drink?'

244

'What did he look like?'

'I don't know.'

'You don't know?'

'He wore sunglasses and a surgical mask. The kind you see everywhere. I told the other detectives that.'

'You didn't think that was strange?'

'Where I live that's all there is.'

'Tall? Short?'

'He was tall.'

'How tall?'

'A hundred and eighty-three centimetres. Maybe 185.'

'Describe what you could see despite the mask and sunglasses.'

'Dark hair, I think. Softly spoken. He had an accent.'

'What kind of accent?'

'I don't know. Foreign. American, I think.'

Iwata looked down at his notes. 'Do you know who Sonoda Takuma is?'

Ueda paused. 'He's the middle man who organizes the can collection under the freeway. So what?'

'Here's the problem, Ueda. He's in the next interview room right now. Under threat of being charged as an accessory to murder, he confessed that you asked him to hide your scooter behind his house. Officers are recovering it as we speak. So I know there was no cash sale.'

Ueda blanched.

'Here's another problem with your cash-buyer theory. You just said he was tall. Maybe 185 centimetres. Yet the CCTV shows a man your height on your scooter. And, yes, there's a helmet. But if it wasn't you delivering that pizza, then how can it be that the receptionist at the love hotel described *a slender man, around 174 to 178 centimetres, scruffy, with buck teeth, looked homeless?* More terrible luck, I suppose.'

Ueda was biting his lips violently now. 'I didn't kill her.'

'You know what every cop in this building thinks? That you're just a pathetic little rat who lost his job, lost his home, lost his family and ended up crushing cans. You were pissed off with the world, then you saw that pretty foreign girl alone in the room. You thought, *Why shouldn't old Ueda get his end away with a fine piece for once? I've got the gift of the gab, after all. Used to be a time when women didn't recoil at the sight of me.* Though in the fantasy you gloss over your teeth, of course.'

Ueda leapt up. 'Fuck you! It's a *scandal*, that's what it is. Nobody does anything for me when my life turns to shit. But one dead white slut and the army is mobilized! There's no fucking sense any more, no fucking decency!'

'Ueda, sit down.'

'No! I happen to be in the wrong place at the wrong time and they send a smiling queer and a fucking black bitch to question *me*?'

Iwata saw the anger inside him now, the real Ueda. He was a hornet in a jar, unrelenting resentment. Crushing cans all day, he glared at the world as it passed him by, as it changed around him, as it left him behind. He snarled at Iwata and Lynch, not seeing a man or a woman, or police inspectors. He only saw blank canvasses for painting what was wrong with the world.

Iwata pointed at the chair until Ueda, chest heaving, finally sat.

'Mr Ueda, wittingly or unwittingly, you are implicated in the murder of Skye Mackintosh. I know you were there. You just said so yourself: *Wrong place, wrong time*. But if you're suggesting someone else was responsible, then now is the time for clarity. Whatever he threatened you with won't be worse than the noose. So I'm going to ask you for the last time. Did you or did you not kill the girl?'

'No.'

'Then talk.' Iwata had exposed him, had drawn out the anger like a venom. Now it was out, the shell of Ueda was just a small, exhausted man in poor health.

'Okay.' Chewing his dirty nails, Ueda spoke quietly. '... There was a man.'

'Like the man you described? Tall, masked?'

'Yes.'

'Go on.'

'He approached me and asked me to rent a room for him at a love hotel in San'ya. Said he was too embarrassed, that he'd pay me a lot of money. I did it; he paid me. A few days later he approaches me again and asks me to deliver a pizza to the same place.'

'And when he initially approached you, what did he say to you? Word for word.'

'I think it was "Do you want to make money?" I said yes. He asked if I would rent the room for him as he was too shy. I figured, what the hell. Later on he came to me again. Said there was a girl he liked and she was staying at the same place. Would I deliver a pizza to her room? I told him that's what I did as my job anyway, why would he pay me for that? But he said he wanted to put something inside the delivery box, like a surprise. He wouldn't say what.'

'When you saw the news about the murder, you realized he'd set you up. So you tried to think of a reason for your presence in the love hotel and for having the money. You came up with the scooter-sale story – figured you'd try and pin it back on to him?'

Ueda nodded into his empty cup.

'Okay, so how did it go down on the 7th?'

'I picked up the pizza, met the guy at the drop-off point, he gave me the money. I then drove to the love hotel, went up, made the delivery and left.'

'You saw the girl?'

'No. I was instructed to leave the pizza outside, knock and leave. That's what I did.'

Iwata shook his head. 'You must think we're stupid.'

'I'm not lying!'

'So how did this strange man know where to find you? And how did he know you delivered pizza, for that matter?'

'. . . I can't answer that.'

'You can't because *you* killed her, Ueda. You killed her with your own tamper. You had the weapon. You had the scooter. You went to her room. You put a hole in her head. And you admitted to fabricating alibis to the police a second ago. Told us you'd never been to Starlet. Are we really to believe that version A was just fiction, but version B is the honest truth? I'm sorry, but you're finished, Ueda. Like my colleagues said earlier, we can do this with or without you. Why not have the balls to admit it? Impress us all. It'll be the only way this gets better for you.'

'But I'm telling the truth!'

'Then explain the tamper.'

'It was in my scooter, then it was gone. Look, I know – I know how this sounds. But someone *took* it.'

'Last chance: who was the man who gave you the money?'

'I fucking told you! I don't know!'

Iwata stood. 'Then we're done here.'

*

In the basement of Minami-Senju police station the two detectives sat in an empty room, in silence. Word had come through: Ueda was going to be charged with the murder of Skye Mackintosh. Somewhere upstairs a champagne bottle popped open.

Lynch was sipping barley tea, conflicted in her feelings. Ueda's charge would mean her time in Japan was coming to an end. Iwata was at the back of the room, lying on a sofa, expressionless.

'Sounded like he was going to confess,' she offered.

'They have twenty-two days left with him,' Iwata said absently. 'He'll confess sooner or later.'

'You think we have enough?'

'Conviction rate in this country is 99.99 per cent. He's finished.'

'Then well done, Iwata. You called it.'

'What did I call?'

'What do you mean? The tamper in the river which led us to Ueda.'

'I took a punt, that's all. The wound signature was strange, and then I saw the can-crushers. The river is close to the crime scene and a logical dumping ground. But it would have been dredged sooner or later.'

'Either way, you caught the murderer of Skye Mackintosh.'

'Did I? I'm not so certain.'

'You're not serious?'

Iwata sat up. 'What about the money? Like Ueda said, he didn't make that crushing cans or delivering Hawaiian pizzas.'

'That money could have come from anywhere.'

'For a guy like him? How?'

249

'I don't know, but he was lying his arse off in there.'

'Everybody lies. Not all lies are covering murder, though. And, another thing, the disposal of the murder weapon is off. This is a killer who leaves no trace at the crime scene. You're telling me that same guy then walks a mile and casually tosses the murder weapon into the river right by where he lives?'

'Okay, so he got lucky at the crime scene. But things caught up with him at the river.'

'Then why toss it in full view of the people who live under that freeway? Moreover, why did he go out of his way to leave nothing at the crime scene, only to toss the weapon into the water in a waterproof bag, ensuring evidence would be preserved?'

'Look, Ueda might have been an engineer, but he obviously isn't a criminal mastermind.'

'That's the point, Anthea. You really think *Ueda* could leave no traces if he tried? He's not the type to get lucky in anything. What's more, we saw him drive away on the CCTV. Someone else disposed of the weapon in the bag. Unless Ueda found a way of growing ten centimetres in twenty minutes.'

'Has it occurred to you that you're overcomplicating this?'

'The old man under the freeway told us the individual who threw the bag looked like *George Harrison*. Now, we know Unknown Male Three is tall. Yet Ueda is 175 centimetres tall. So if he *did* kill Skye, then somebody else disposed of the weapon for him. Who would do that?'

'So he paid someone to dispose of it for him. Probably unwittingly. Look, I don't know, but that old man doesn't know what year it is. If you take away his testimony, then it's just CCTV of a person with a green bag crossing a bridge. We can't be sure it's even the same bag. Ueda had the weapon, Ueda was at the scene, Ueda went into hiding.'

Iwata checked his watch. 'None of that proves he killed Skye.'

'I don't understand you, Iwata. We have to announce the arrest. You're saying Ueda will go down for it, but you don't believe he's the killer. And you don't care?'

'There's something else we still have no explanation for. The spider.'

'Oh, for fuck's sake. You want me to tell my boss we've arrested the bloke at the scene of the crime who owned the murder weapon and then did a runner but you've still got doubts due to the local fauna not adding up?'

'What I think now doesn't matter. The prosecutor wants Ueda. He'll get Ueda.'

'But you believe the killer is out there, and what? You're just going to walk away?'

Iwata's phone buzzed. It was a message from Ozawa:

MINISTER HISAKAWA WILL RETURN HOME TONIGHT.
FORMAL PRESENTATION IN CABINET TOMORROW.
PERHAPS GOOD TIME TO CONGRATULATE HIM?

Daiki Numa stumbled into the room with a grin on his face and two mugs of champagne in his hand. 'Detectives, a little gesture of gratitude from Team A.'

'You see, Anthea?' Iwata snatched one of the mugs and downed the champagne. 'I've done my part.' Then he was gone.

27. Between Dog and Wolf

Assistant Inspector Itō arrived at Minami-Senju police station and scrambled from floor to floor in search of Iwata. But nobody in Team A had seen him since he left the interrogation room several hours ago.

Shindo had been very clear: *Give Iwata everything he needs, stick close to him.* Itō wasn't about to slack off now. Especially with his own role in Kappa Unit up in the air. Not to mention he'd let Miyake's killer vanish into thin air. The last thing he wanted was to be sent back to Traffic. *So where the hell is Iwata?*

Finally, Itō found Lynch in the basement. To his dismay, she was alone.

'Itō, are you all right?' She nodded at his head bandage.

'Detective Constable,' he fought to catch his breath. 'Do you know where Consultant Iwata is?'

'He left a while ago.'

'I've been calling him non-stop, but his phone is off.'

Lynch frowned. 'Why, what's up?'

Itō wondered if she had meant to use such informal phrasing, as if they were friends. It took him a moment to look past her long limbs and striking face to recall the matter at hand. 'One of our undercover officers in Kabukichō has made an arrest.'

Lynch raised her eyebrows then said something in English about buses that Itō didn't understand.

*

Deep inside Shinjuku police station, Inspector Tanigawa was pacing the corridor, popping his knuckles. Seeing Lynch and Itō walking towards him, he shook his head.

'Where the hell is Iwata?'

Itō cleared his throat. 'We can't find him, sir. He took the car.'

Tanigawa clucked his tongue. 'We could find him with the GPS tracker, in theory. But I'm not sure it's going to matter now.' He glanced uncertainly at Lynch. 'Meantime, I suppose you'd better come with me.'

Tanigawa led them downstairs to a small interrogation room and they stood at the two-way mirror. Inside the room, Inspector Ideguchi was looming over the suspect, playing his usual role, class bully.

In the hot seat was an average-looking man wearing a mid-range grey suit. Lynch could tell his hair had been cut recently, his nails trimmed short. He looked pleasant, vaguely concerned yet patient – a man caught up in a mis-understanding. Yet her intuition told her that, for the first time, they had trapped a real butterfly in their net – not just bugs.

Inside the interrogation room, Ideguchi sighed. 'Okay, Sato. Let's go over this again. You're saying you were in Kabukichō just to unwind. Unwind how? Why do you go there?'

Mr Sato shrugged awkwardly. 'Sometimes just a drink, sometimes a bit more, you know.'

'Be specific, please.'

'I mean I like conversation. Female company.'

'Do you go for sex?'

'In the past.'

'How often do you go?'

'Once in a while.'

'One night a week? Three times a month?'

'Once every few months.'

'Why tonight?'

'Spur of the moment.'

'What does your wife say about all this?'

Sato looked at the floor. 'She doesn't know.'

'What a surprise.' Ideguchi referred to his papers, indifferent to the suspect's shame. 'So why did you take your car tonight? Not so easy to drive around that area.'

'I was just feeling lazy, that's all. Besides, the train is so expensive these days.'

'So let me get this straight. You took the train home. Then you picked up your car and drove all the way back into the city because you were feeling lazy?'

'It was spur of the moment, as I said. I only decided to go once I was nearly back home.'

Ideguchi pursed his lips. 'Mr Sato, you should know we've questioned the young girl who got into your vehicle and she's admitted to being a sex worker in the area. She says you asked her to get into your vehicle and the price of intercourse was discussed. Do you understand you've been charged with soliciting under Article 3 of the Anti-prostitution Law?'

'That's not what happened.'

'So you asked the girl into your car for strictly non-sexual purposes, I suppose?'

Sato glanced at the two-way mirror, then down at the floor again. 'I understand the way this seems. And I know you must hear all kind of lies in this room. I'm not saying I'm perfect, but I assure you, Inspector, you have this all wrong.'

'What is it, then, you decided to become a taxi driver for fun?'

'The girl was just standing out there and I thought she was too young – all right? Anything could happen to her in Kabukichō. So, yes. I stopped to ask her if she was okay. She wanted to hop in, and I didn't think there was any harm in it. At least she'd be safe that way.'

Ideguchi snorted. 'Mr Concerned Citizen.'

'That's what happened.'

'She's lying, then?'

'I don't want to brand her a liar, but she's young, she doesn't want to get in trouble. She'd probably say anything.'

'Don't you realize that we all know this girl, dickhead? She's in here every week. Offers me and my buddies a special discount. Her snatch is practically blue by now. So why would she lie to us about you?'

Sato frowned. 'I'm sorry, Inspector, I'm not sure I understand. You're saying she's admitted to being a sex worker but you're already aware of this because your colleagues engage her services?'

'You smug fuck,' Ideguchi snarled. 'Are you calling *me* a liar now?'

Sato shook his head vigorously. 'Of course not. I just don't understand. Prostitutes lie.'

'How'd she get that bruise on her face, then?'

'She was bruised when I saw her. That's part of the reason why I was concerned for her.'

'Cut the shit, Sato.' Ideguchi sighed. 'All right, let's back up. You ever been to a love hotel called Starlet?'

'No.'

'How about a hostess bar called Black Widow?'

'Never.'

'If I look into those places, I won't find you're lying to me?'

'You absolutely won't.'

'Your vehicle is a silver Toyota Sienta, registration plate 51-26B. How long have you had it?'

'A little over a year.'

'Pretty new, then. Any problems with it?'

'No.'

'Even anything minor?'

'No.'

'In that case' – Ideguchi held up a piece of paper – 'this is an inventory of all the items in your vehicle. Why have you got so much starter fluid in your new car, Sato?'

'I just like to be prepared.'

'Prepared for what?'

'I don't know what you mean.'

'I'm asking you what you use the starting fluid for.'

Sato blinked furiously, then composed himself. 'I keep it in my car for winter. What else?'

Ideguchi sized him up. 'You know what I do for a living, sir?'

'You're a police inspector.'

'That's my job title. What do I *do*?'

'You catch criminals.'

'A more accurate description would be that I'm an asshole purveyor, Sato. A regular fucking *sommelier*. Now, the city pays me for my expert eye. And when I cast that eye, I only ever see two kinds of people. Those caught up in a misunderstanding. And deviants who break the law.'

'Am I to understand you consider me part of the second bracket?'

'I'll tell you what you are to understand, you little prick.

I think you come to Kabukichō to pick up girls, knock them out with the starter fluid then rape them.'

Mr Sato shook his head. 'I'm sorry, Inspector. But I've never hurt anybody in my life. I certainly didn't hurt the girl tonight.'

'Come *on*, Sato. You're scum. We caught you. We see your kind in here every single day.'

'I'm not a perfect person, I told you this. But I know you have no evidence against me for any crime, whatever the hooker is telling you.'

'Fucking smart-ass —' Ideguchi smashed his fist down on the table.

Mr Sato flinched for appearances then sat back with the satisfaction of a man trying to conceal his winning hand.

Despite his theatrics, Ideguchi glanced at his colleagues beyond the two-way mirror as if to say: *This is a waste of time.*

In the room next door Itō looked at Tanigawa. 'You think he's involved in this, sir?'

The senior detective shrugged. 'No idea. Hatanaka is working those missing hookers. He might want to keep an eye on this guy. But we can't connect him to the English girl. Ueda has been charged now and the surveillance operation is already winding down. No sense in wasting any more time here.'

Lynch was going through the personal effects found on Mr Sato. The contents of the man's wallet were completely unremarkable. A photograph of a little boy. Credit cards. A season ticket for the train. A breakfast bill from Denny's settled in cash. Receipts for petrol and household items: fresh fruit, socks, invoices for a child's violin lessons, a sales slip for home-improvement materials: soundproofing, paint, a metal stepladder.

'What do you think, Detective Constable?' Itō asked, trying not to blush.

Lynch met his eyes.

'When Inspector Ideguchi asked him about the starter fluid it looked like he was going to faint. And I don't like the way he keeps smiling.'

'But as Inspector Tanigawa said, there is no connection to the Skye Mackintosh case and no evidence of any crime beyond soliciting.'

'I know. He just seems . . . strange.'

Tanigawa laughed. 'Strange? He's just a garden-variety pervert. I don't know about London, but we have them everywhere here. Now if you want to make yourself useful, why don't you go and find Consultant Iwata?'

Lynch peered at the Denny's receipt again and saw a little doodle of a cat. Slipping the receipts in her pocket, she stood. Lynch looked through the two-way mirror one last time. Mr Sato was alone now, seemingly humming a tune to himself. He glanced down at his watch.

Den-en-chōfu. Iwata stuck to the shadows gifted by the murky twilight. He thought of what the French called this time: *between dog and wolf.* In his pocket, the revolver felt lighter than it had before. But then he hadn't been drinking heavily last time.

Iwata didn't stop in the twenty-four-hour coffee shop. There was nothing to weigh up any more. As he staggered through the dark, he thought about his mother. The clear memories Iwata had of her were mostly of her second life, in America, after she had come back for him at the orphanage. He was well into his teenage years the first time he saw her laugh. The memories of his mother before America were only snatches – wailing, silence, bruises. Beneath his drunkenness, Iwata felt fear. The little boy locked inside screamed out the only solution he knew: *run away*.

The street was picturesque, beautiful houses behind elegant gating, orderly gingko trees like a silent cortège. And now Iwata saw his father's house. The lights were on.

Trembling badly, he slipped into the same shadow he had stood in before. Dread quaked in his guts. He wanted to turn and flee – find the nearest convenience store and drink it dry. But he knew he could not. There was a blood debt to be paid.

Iwata had been created in violence, in hatred. His own life had blighted his mother's. How could he let Ryoma Hisakawa get away with that? Iwata's entire life had been a cloud of fear and confusion. But here, at last, was clarity. Here was retribution.

Iwata drained the last of his pocket bottle of vodka. Then, taking deep breaths, he pulled the gun out of his pocket. The grip was slick with sweat. But before he could take a step forward he felt an impact. At first Iwata thought it was a car. But now he understood – it was the two black suits. One of them was twisting his arm behind his back. The other one lining up the punch. The shot to the solar plexus took Iwata's breath away, the pain wondrous. He had been hit before, but this was professionally administered. Adrenalin wasn't going to help him here.

One of the suits was short with slicked-back hair, a crooked nose and indifferent, serpentine eyes. The other was a blue whale with a bovine face and a keen sense of job satisfaction. They dragged Iwata back into the shadow. Then it was kicking.

When the introductions were out of the way, Snake lit a cigarette. 'At last we meet.'

'Yeah,' Iwata grunted from the foetal position. 'My pleasure.'

Whale didn't bother to stop laughing as he crunched a boot into Iwata's ribs. 'Why are you here? You got a mystery boyfriend in the area?'

'Yes. And we're very exclusive –' Iwata reached for his gun but Snake kicked it and it snickered away into the darkness. 'Who you working for, asshole? Start talking.'

'I'm afraid I can't do that. The Colonel has entrusted me with the recipe for the eleven secret herbs and –'

Whale jackhammered a boot into his gut. Iwata's eyes lolled shut, but Snake clicked his fingers for attention. 'Answers now. American government? Chinese?'

'American. Or was it American Samoan? My memory goes blank in stressful situations.'

'All right.' Snake sighed and turned to Whale. 'Just go get the van.'

Whale flicked his cigarette at his new-found friend and hurried away.

Iwata rolled on to his front, his nose dripping blood into the rain-swollen gutter.

'Okay, my friend. We're going to take a little ride –' Snake slipped out a long, thin sashimi knife from his sleeve. 'We'll park somewhere quiet and I'll carve you a beautiful cunt where your balls used to be. Then we'll see if you're still a comed—'

Footsteps – fast over the wet concrete.

Snake snapped his head around as the trash-can lid smashed into it. He dropped.

Iwata looked up, blinking in the hot rainfall. At first he

thought the suits had turned on each other. But now he saw Lynch standing there like an angry spirit.

Snake scrambled up from the floor, but she was already pointing Iwata's revolver at him. It gleamed onyx in the night. Lynch spoke one word in Japanese: 'Leave.'

He glared at Iwata then ran. She kept the gun on him.

When he was gone, Lynch dragged Iwata up from the floor and sat him on the low wall nearby. 'Mates of yours?'

'Passing acquaintances,' Iwata slurred.

'You owe money or something?'

'Lend me a few thousand, would you?'

Lynch laughed. They sat in the shadow, the rain pattering around them, the adrenalin seeping away. Somewhere nearby, a vehicle screeched off into the night. After a while, she looked at the revolver in her hand then sidelong at her partner.

'Iwata. Why are you here?'

His bloodshot eyes were still on the house across the road. 'You couldn't understand.'

'You're right, as it goes, I don't understand. I don't understand why you're lurking around suburbia. To be honest, I don't even know why you're in this country. I don't think you give a shit about the case. Maybe you're just jaded. But then I see you with your gun in your hand walking towards that house. Next thing I know, you're getting the shit beaten out of you by two heavies and we both know it's not the first time you've seen them. So give me something, Iwata. You owe me that much.'

He looked at her. Then he pointed at the house across the road. 'The man who lives there ruined my mother's life. My life.'

They regarded the house together and listened to the rain for a while.

'Iwata?'

'Yeah.'

'You have someone waiting for you back home, don't you?'

'I have a kid.'

'Then you're wrong. I don't know what he did to you or your mother. But if you have a kid now, your life isn't ruined. Not unless you go in there and do something stupid.'

Iwata cast his eyes down at the gutter.

'Forget this man. Live the life you have now. Go home to your kid.'

Iwata thought about Santi. He pictured him playing records, flicking between RPM speeds and laughing at the distorted singing. Having to stop him eating family-sized jars of pickles. Staying to the end of Dodgers games just to hear Randy Newman's 'I Love LA.'

Iwata gave a single nod. 'You're right, Anthea. Again.'

Even though his words were spoken honestly, he knew he was not finished with Ryoma Hisakawa. He would be back soon.

Lynch handed him back the revolver. 'You still have work to do. You have to help the Mackintosh family.'

Iwata saw his blood spill into a puddle, the droplets hitting the concrete like a moment of tiny dance. For the first time, he thought about Skye Mackintosh as a person. He couldn't bring her back, he couldn't fix a thing, but he could give her parents somewhere for their lost love to go. Maybe that's what justice was.

'How did you find me?'

262

'I went to your capsule. The only thing in there was a scrap of newspaper with an address on it – Itō pointed out that the Altima's GPS reading was close to that.'

'I didn't really consider . . . afterwards. Tanigawa will have questions.'

'You were here chasing down a lead. Turned out to be a false tip. Then you startled some burglars who caught you cold.'

Embarrassed, Iwata thanked her quietly.

'Come on.' Lynch linked her arm around his shoulder and hefted him to his feet.

The two detectives arrived at Den-en-chōfu station. Seeing them, Assistant Inspector Itō hurried over.

'Not now, Itō. Please.'

Though he was taken aback by the sight of Iwata's face in the streetlight, he was undeterred. 'I'm afraid I have to talk to you. It's not good news.'

28. Commiserations

Commissioner Isao Shindo was in the west wing of the fourth floor of JSDF Central Hospital. His body had finally given out. The doctor had put it in layman's terms: a massive heart attack, his condition critical. There was no question of survival; it was simply a case of going out as cleanly as possible.

Iwata entered the room and left the light off. He sat in a chair by the bed, shocked at how small Shindo was outside of his dirty suit and oversized desk.

A decade ago, it had been Iwata in this hospital after Hideo Akashi's knife had ripped through his stomach. Shindo had visited him back then and made small talk which, for him, was about as close to grapes and flowers as it got. They had discussed the ramifications of Akashi's arrest, the exposure of the corruption in the MPD. And they had spoken of the future, which, Iwata supposed, was what they were in now.

He looked at his boss, never a friend, never a mentor, never more than an old man taking a punt due to a lack of options. But they had come to trust each other. Shindo had taken risks for him. And they had both lost Noriko Sakai. Few could claim to understand that.

Iwata supposed the old man was one of the few people in this world who meant something to him.

He grasped Shindo's small, withered hand. Iwata couldn't

remember ever touching it before. It was cold. 'Boss. I'm here.'

There was no reply, only the steady mechanical rhythm of the machines, an occasional beep, like a dream. The grim resolve, the bitter single-mindedness, the dogged components that constituted Shindo – all of that was gone. What was left was a human pincushion of plastic tubes: nasogastric, tracheal, IV.

'I let you down, Shindo . . . But I'm going to make things right.' Closing his eyes, Iwata resolved to find the killer. For Shindo. For the Mackintosh family. For Skye.

The door burst open and a scuffle spilled into the room. Lynch was trying to hold a man in a suit back – it was Ozawa, his face angry and smug at once.

'Anthea, it's okay.'

With a glare, she withdrew.

'Hello again, Inspector.' The government man blithely smoothed down his jacket. 'We need to talk.'

Outside, they walked along the beige corridor until they came to a shadowy recess. Ozawa scrutinized Iwata's face for a moment. 'I thought you said you didn't drink?'

'Just tell me what you want.'

'The new Justice Minister sends his commiserations.' Ozawa dipped his head with exaggerated solemnity. 'However, as it seems you're prone to going AWOL, I was asked to speak to you in person. Given the media attention surrounding all this *untidiness*, my superior has turned his attention to Commissioner Shindo's department as a matter of urgency.'

'What are you saying?'

'The old man is gone.'

'Shindo has barely been in here more than –'

'It's very simple, Iwata. He's gone, same as the *former* Justice Minister. Both of them are yesterday's news. *Today's* front page, however, is clear to everyone: the Skye Mackintosh task force is a shambles.'

Iwata felt rage, but after the beating he had taken, he could barely lift his hands above his waist.

'Ozawa, listen to me. A suspect has already been charged. This happened within a few days of me taking over this investigation.'

'Ah, yes. The infamous can crusher. Located thanks to an anonymous tip, if I'm not mistaken. Hardly astounding detective work, Iwata. In any case, the damage was already done. Shindo's decision to delay the investigation until you arrived was catastrophic. Ever since then you've been trying to catch up while the world looked at us and shook their heads.'

'What about Ryoma Hisakawa? We had a deal.'

'No. You had a window, Inspector. And now it's gone.'

'These two suits turned up out of nowhere –'

Ozawa held up his manicured hand. 'It doesn't matter. The minister has already rubber-stamped Inspector Tanigawa as the stand-in commissioner until a more senior man can be appointed. Ideguchi will become superintendent. In the meantime, Hatanaka will assume command of the Mackintosh investigation. What's left of it, anyhow.'

'*Hatanaka?* What about his missing sex workers?'

'We live in a world of priorities. When things have died down a little, I'm sure that will be investigated thoroughly. Now, as for you, Iwata – please hand over your credentials to Acting Commissioner Tanigawa immediately. Your friend Sherlock Holmes can hang around until the case is

266

officially closed, but she's wallpaper. She comes nowhere near the case.'

'This is a sham.'

'Look on the bright side. At least you saved on that new suit, eh?' Ozawa winked. 'Safe journey back.' The government man turned on his heel, his footsteps curt, an order of business in human form.

Iwata stood outside the hospital, wet and numb. Streetlamps were only shy polyps of orange in the rainy mist. *Division One is all I've got left.* That's what Shindo had said.

Now Division One was broken, bartered away by baby-kissers and partisan interests. Consultant Iwata continuing on the case was in no one's interests, at least no one beyond Commissioner Shindo and the Mackintosh family. And what could be done about it? The wind blew, the grass bent.

Safe journey back.

Soaked through and feverish, Iwata saw familiar figures inside the bar across the road. They were laughing. Flustered waitresses in dirndls were ferrying over platters of sausages and pitchers of beer. Tanigawa and Ideguchi were raising a glass for Hatanaka's toast.

Beneath the bruises, Iwata felt a new anger unfurling. He limped across the road, barely dodging traffic. Maybe he couldn't stop anything, but he wasn't about to let these two-faced careerists celebrate their promotions without making them hear some home truths.

At the entrance to the bar, a cop in uniform blocked his way. 'Sorry. Private party tonight.'

Iwata flashed his *techou*.

'I know who you are.'

'Stand aside.'

'Or what?' The uniform smirked.

Swearing, Iwata went to the window where the detectives were sitting and motioned for Tanigawa to come out. Turning the corner, he waited in the alley, pacing up and down, resentment thumping through his empty stomach.

Eventually, it was Hatanaka who emerged, mug of beer in his hand, scowling up at the rain as if it were the single fly in the ointment of his good mood.

'Heard about Shindo. Terrible news.'

'Yeah, seems like you're grieving. Where's Tanigawa?'

'He figured it was better if I spoke to you. You know, given our *closeness*.'

'I need to speak with –'

'He's not interested, Iwata. Oh, and while I remember, I'm going to have to ask for your *techou*. Sorry.'

A bitter silence fell, admixed with the sound of the rain on concrete.

Iwata relinquished his badge. 'Now tell Tanigawa to come out.'

'No, I don't think I will.'

Iwata looked at his old apprentice now. His face was red with beer, a large fleck of cheese on his chin.

'Boss, if I'm not mistaken, you're giving me a funny look.'

'Shindo's up there dying, and you're celebrating.'

'I take no pleasure in this situation. But Shindo is old. That's life.'

'You've been biding your time.'

Hatanaka shrugged. 'This case is a mess. Though I won't deny it, I do appreciate the new minister's trust.'

'Trust?' Iwata couldn't help but laugh. 'Who would trust you?'

Hatanaka gave a strange smile. '*There* he is. Beneath the greys, the old Iwata, sneering and arrogant, as ever was.'

'You don't know this case. You don't understand what's happening.'

'*I* don't know the case?' Hatanaka hurled his mug against the wall. 'Fuck you. I was the first detective on the *scene*.'

'This isn't about you or me –'

'You're going to say it's about the case. And you're right. But there's really not that much to comprehend here.' Hatanaka regained his composure. 'You see, the minister found out about Ueda: the last person to see her alive, the person who owned the murder weapon, but a person who, somehow, you were against formally charging. Well, see, I'm not so reticent.'

'There's something bigger than Ueda going on here. I don't have the whole picture yet, but I just need to –'

'Everything is a big conspiracy theory to you, isn't it? Little grey men and UFOs.' Hatanaka unzipped and pissed against the wall. 'Not me. I'll do whatever needs to be done.'

'I didn't come here to fight you. Listen, you could talk to them. Maybe we could –'

'Life has a sense of humour.' Hatanaka smiled wryly as he zipped up. 'Now you're begging *me* for a chance? I'm sorry, Iwata. You had your shot and now you're out. Ueda killed the girl. End of story.'

Iwata nodded. 'So, this is who you are now?'

'Me? *You're* the one who doesn't belong here. But you couldn't stay away, could you? The ingenious Inspector Iwata had to investigate. Had to get your name in the papers. Avenge the *gaijin* sluts. Well, things have changed. The results are there for the taking and, this time, everyone will know the name *Hatanaka*.'

Iwata thought back to the press conference at the embassy, the media ambush. '. . . It was you, wasn't it? You were the one leaking to the press.'

'Shindo wasn't making sense any more, I did what I had to do.'

'Because you wanted this case.'

'This case *should* be mine. You're just a fucking tourist, Iwata.'

He stepped into Hatanaka's space and jabbed a finger into his chest. 'You only exist here because of me. Ten years ago, I needed someone to carry my laundry. You were situational. That's all you'll ever be.'

Hatanaka shunted Iwata against the wall then lifted him up by the lapels against the slimy bricks. His fat cheeks were quivering with rage. 'You're forgetting something, boss,' he hissed. 'I saved your life. I saved your fucking *life*.'

Iwata struggled, but his body was compromised and Hatanaka was the larger man.

'Not once did you thank me. I got nothing for stopping Akashi. Nobody even fucking *realized* I was up there on that bridge. I knew what he was capable of and I still went up there. For *you*, Iwata. To save you.' Hatanaka dropped him, out of breath. 'But it doesn't matter now. Look at you. I'm the one who's finally made it.' He stumbled back towards the bar.

'You're right.'

Hatanaka stopped, his back still to him. 'What?'

'I said you're right.' On the floor, Iwata rubbed his neck. 'Truth be told, I wasn't grateful for being saved back then.

270

Still, I should have thanked you, that was wrong of me. But Hatanaka? Something has happened to you. You're not right any more.'

'Go back to America.'

Iwata looked up at the rain. He had nothing now; no badge, no power. He'd thrown away a decade of sobriety. The only thing left in his pockets was a gun, an old ferry ticket and a decomposing spider. Closing his eyes, Iwata considered the men in the web of Skye Mackintosh's murder. The dead landlord, Miyake. Unknown Male Three. The unfortunate Ueda.

It would be Ueda who paid tonight. But what of the unknown males of tomorrow? Hatanaka and his cohorts weren't like Shindo. They had no interest in the truth, felt no duty to their city. They were happy to lead goats into the wilderness then pat each other on the back. Hatanaka, Tanigawa, Ideguchi – they were not Homicide men. They were bureaucrats. Shindo had known it. And when the moment came, it was not them he had called upon.

Iwata opened his eyes and looked up at the hospital across the road. He felt shame for deceiving the old man, offering him false hope. *You'll find him. You'll find this son of a bitch just like you found the others.* That's what Shindo had said.

Groaning, Iwata dragged himself to his feet.

Distant thunder cracked behind the mountain. Rain was hissing through the forest. Up in the darkness of the branches, hiding under his tarp, Mr Sato was shivering with fury. *How dare they stop me? Question me?*

He had taken every precaution. Cleaned up after himself religiously. Refused to fall into any discernible pattern.

And still, somehow, the police had managed to snare him. He was outraged.

Although Mr Sato had managed to escape their clutches with just a warning in the end, the damage had been done. They'd telephoned his wife. She was waiting up for him when he got home. In tears, she had banished him to the country house. He'd driven through the night.

As soon as he reached Ōkuromori, he'd thought about going to bed; after all, his cabin stood empty. It pained Mr Sato to think of it vacated, grumbling and gurgling at him the same way an empty stomach would. But now the clockwork order of his life was disjointed he knew sleep would be impossible.

Up in his tree stand, six metres above the detritus, Mr Sato was holding his rifle. He had decorated his perch with branches from coniferous trees and his view of the deer trail was unhindered.

Of course, hunting was only a pretext. The truth was he wanted to make sure he wasn't being followed. It was unlikely. Tokyo cops would hardly be traipsing about the forests of Ibaraki at 2 a.m.

So then how did they find you? Mr Sato reasoned the detectives had simply chanced a few observations about the starter fluid and his presence in the red-light district in the hope that he would confess. They couldn't have had anything substantial on him. No, they must have been investigating something else and he simply happened into their trap; after all, why else would they let him walk free?

Still, Mr Sato couldn't shake the fear that they were on to him. The detective had practically accused him. Wasn't it possible they were trying to trick him now? Give him the illusion of freedom only to catch him in the act? Mr

Sato knew he couldn't return to the pig pen ever again. Evidently, Kabukichō was off limits now. He even wondered if he should return to his cabin.

Mr Sato's hands tightened around the rifle butt, strangling the stock in silent fury. *And all of this because the little bitch blabbed before she could become Number Eight. Now I'm in limbo.*

He couldn't stop thinking about the caveman detective. *He knew I was hiding something.* Knew *it. Maybe I should stop now, before it's too late. My wife will leave me. That's no surprise, the bitch hasn't loved me for years, even if she doesn't realize it herself. She was only good for cover anyway, and now she'll be doubting everything — fat lot of good she'll be from here on in . . . But what about the boy?*

Thinking about his son filled Mr Sato with immediate, sharp panic. Just picturing his beautiful face now tore open a dam of regret and self-loathing. *How could I give in to my own impulses this way? I've risked everything.* It had been different before. Things had been on track. Risk had been minimal. The Mixture was going to be made and Mr Sato's project would be completed. But now? *I can't let him grow up without a father. He needs me, he won't make it without me.*

There was a gentle rustling somewhere below. Silently, automatically, Mr Sato raised his rifle. A small doe padded cautiously into view. She flicked her ears, then her tail, the spots on her wet coat milky white. Her nose twitched shiny black in the night. Mr Sato had set up his tree stand years ago. Neither the sight nor the smell of it alarmed her. She began to nibble the bark of a nearby tree.

Eyes on the doe, Mr Sato lowered the rifle. For once, he felt no joy in visualizing the blood. The doe raised her head. With glassy, dark eyes, she looked up at Mr Sato and opened her mouth. It was his father's voice that spoke to him.

Itsuki.

Mr Sato froze. '. . . Father?'

I see you're still pathetic as ever.

'Forgive me.'

Just keep your mouth shut and listen. Still munching a shard of bark, the doe eased over a few metres. *You think the boy won't make it without you. Well, I'm telling you he'll be fine. Didn't your mother leave you? You snivelled for years, but even you made it through in the end.*

'But Father . . . this is different. Mother died. And this –'

She was weak, Itsuki. They all are. It's not a characteristic, it's what they are. You inherited that from your mother and I tried my best to cut it out of you. But you're not a boy any more. So answer me this. If your mother loved you so much, don't you think she would have fought to stay by your side a little harder?

'. . . She was sick.'

I can see you think I'm being harsh, but I'm *here for you, boy. I always have been. That's the truth of the matter. This is my land. And you are my blood.*

Mr Sato began to weep. 'I miss you, Father.'

I know. Now stop blubbing and tell me: are you going to avenge me?

Mr Sato nodded angrily and wiped away hot tears. He took aim. The shot rang out in the dark forest. *Father is right. I can't stop now. The* matsuri *is upon us. Time's running out, but there is only one girl left to add to the Mixture.*

Mr Sato began his climb down from the tree. He couldn't return to Kabukichō, but he knew where he would go instead.

29. A Spider with no Business in Tokyo

Mr Sato parked outside his house but stayed in the car. Now he had been kicked out by his wife, the neighbourhood seemed different somehow, as if he was just a stranger who had never belonged. That was, of course, the truth.

'Father, do we have to bring the boy? I don't want him to see . . . what needs to be done.'

Don't get weak on me now, boy. On the digital album display, Huey Lewis was smiling back at him. *The child helps you blend in. If he doesn't show at the* matsuri*, people will ask questions.*

Mr Sato took a breath then got out of the car. The front door was unlocked, which, he thought, was a good sign. He nudged it open and his wife was sitting on the stairs. She lifted her face from her hands, eyes puffy. 'Hello.'

He entered the house and stood in the *genkan*, not taking off his shoes. 'Hello.' He looked at the floor. 'Thank you for allowing me to see him.'

'He's your son, Itsuki.' It was a statement of fact and an accusation all at once.

Mr Sato nodded. 'Are you okay?'

She raised her eyebrows at this question, as if to say: *Do you really want to go there?* He didn't, nor could he think of any safe ground. Mr Sato fell to his knees and pressed his face to the floor. 'I'm going *crazy* without you. Without the boy.'

Mrs Sato had never seen her husband speak so openly, so vulnerably. She was shocked to see tears in his eyes.

'Hitomi, I know what I did was wrong. It was foul . . .' he whiffled. 'But I've just been under so much stress lately, so many late nights . . . I don't know what came over me.'

'I don't know. What you did . . .' She shook her head, not having the words for it. 'I shouldn't even let you back in here, but the boy . . . He's been looking forward to the *matsuri*. I don't have it in me to forbid him from going.'

'I'll have him back the minute it's over.'

Mrs Sato fixed her face then called for the boy. He shuffled down the stairs and stood in front of his father, who patted his cheek now. 'I've left the music on in the car for you.'

'Bye, Mother.' He glanced over his shoulder at his parents before slipping out.

'Hitomi, before I go –'

'I don't want to hear it.'

'Please, just another moment. I just wanted to say that I know I don't deserve another chance. You've always deserved more than me, Hitomi. Maybe one day you might even think this is for the best. I'm ashamed about a great deal. But one thing I'll never regret . . .' He nodded outside in the direction of the boy. 'He's the best thing I've ever done. Without him I would be nothing. Without you. I know that. One day, things will be better.'

Mrs Sato put her face in her hands and started to cry.

'I love you. I'm sorry for everything.' Mr Sato stepped outside. Getting into the car, he looked back at his son.

'Everything all right?'

The boy nodded, though there was a strange expression on his face.

'What is it?'

'. . . Father?'

'Yes?'

'What's that sound?'

'What sound?'

'That banging sound from the boot.'

'Nothing, the engine is on the way out, that's all. Now put your seatbelt on, we have to go.' Mr Sato cranked the volume all the way up. The Toyota Sienta screeched out of its space then lurched away, Shakespears Sister's 'You're History' blaring.

It was 8 a.m. and Shinagawa station was alive with commuters: black jackets, black laptop bags, black heads of hair – night tulips under greenhouse lamps. Every day, a ceaseless undertow of suits passed through Shinagawa, brought in each morning like nutrients, carried out at night like waste.

The Central Institute for Arachnological Studies was in a drab alley, east of the station, hiding behind hulking hotel towers and office super-blocks, announced only by a small sign. Inside, the receptionist gestured to the elevator.

The institute was a medium-sized office on the top floor with a modest lab at the back. It was empty except for a woman with short hair and heavy eyeliner. She looked up at him.

'Help you?' she asked, taking out her earphones.

'I hope so.' Iwata took out the baggie containing the spider and placed it on her desk.

She glanced down at it, unimpressed. 'Have you tried a library?'

Iwata replied by flashing his private licence.

'This is in English.'

'It says I'm a professional investigator in California. Are you the senior arachnologist?'

'No, but I'm the only person here. What's this to do with?'

'Murder.'

The woman sighed. Putting on her glasses, she opened the bag and gently eased the spider out with tweezers. 'Hm, dead a while . . . What do you want to know?'

'I'm not sure yet. Could you give me a general run-down?'

She pursed her lips. 'You're not going to tell me the spider was used as a murder weapon?'

'Nothing so imaginative.' One half of Iwata's mouth curled up. 'His colours seem too vivid for a Tokyo spider?'

'*Her* colours.' The arachnologist flipped down the magnifiers on her glasses and peered at the spider. '*Argiope amoena*, or *kogane-gumo*. Found throughout much of the world, usually in temperate or tropical environments.'

'Is she dangerous?'

'Only a handful of spiders are genuinely life-threatening. As for the *Argiope*, their venom is essentially harmless to humans.' She took off her glasses. 'General rundown? We're talking a moderately-sized orb-weaver. Females are larger. They sit in webs often built fairly close to the ground for catching hopping prey – grasshoppers, crickets, that kind of thing. Note the distinctive black and yellow markings.'

'Why have the legs folded up that way?'

'A spider's muscles draw its legs in, but they're unable to extend them again.' The arachnologist took a pen and

278

gently eased its legs outwards, back into its natural X-shape. 'To do this, they pump a liquid into their legs to push them out again. After death, that fluid is no longer present and they end up curled up this way.'

'I've never seen one around Tokyo.'

'They'll tend to stick to the south-west regions of Japan. In Tokyo, you're mostly looking at money spiders, house spiders – the usual suspects in urban environments.'

'So it's possible someone brought her to the city?'

'I can't be 100 per cent certain, but gun to the head? This spider has no business in Tokyo.'

Iwata thought about this. 'So how did she get here?'

'Someone brought her. It wouldn't have to be particularly high-tech, we're not dealing with an exotic rarity here. Most likely a polystyrene box with some wet cotton wool for fluid. You could even mail her.'

Iwata carefully returned the spider's corpse to the baggie, which he put back in his inside pocket. He thanked the arachnologist, then left. Outside, he crossed the road. As he looked over his shoulder, he caught a glimpse of a grey sedan. He waved at Whale, who waved back. Snake, sporting two black eyes, did not.

Senior Inspector Kento Sugino of Ibaraki Prefectural Police followed the flies. Human beings were a mess of motivations, infinitely oscillating between attractions and resentments. Not so with a fly. Flies were simple. A fly's entire life hinged on finding decaying meat; that's what a fly's existence *was*. Sugino couldn't argue with that kind of expertise.

This forest was normally empty and quiet. But today, it was full of new life. Forensics officers wearing blue overalls, hair nets and face masks were buzzing through the trees: crawling, peering, prodding, photographing, discussing. They bowed to Sugino as he passed.

The area up ahead was cordoned off, illuminated by remote area lamps. The flies knew the way by heart. And now Sugino saw it too.

Only one part of the corpse was visible. A single finger, its nail blackened, raised up through the dirt as if asking for the check. It was the finger that the mushroom-picker's dog had discovered.

The dead woman had most likely been young. Little granules of soil had collected in the eye sockets and at the meeting of the lips. She was naked except for one trainer and a baby-blue work blouse. An improbable pile of leaves had been heaped over her head. Sugino didn't think she had been dead long. Even so, muscular stiffening had reached her scalp and her hair was sticking up – goose-flesh in death.

The shallow grave was pathetic, a child's half-hearted attempt at burying treasure. Sugino carefully crouched down over the body. The sweet, mouldy pungency crept down his throat, a perfume of rotten leaves and bad meat. Like every single other corpse he had seen, its frailty in death was unequivocal. This one was cut and torn, missing parts, a ragged road map to madness – existence completely vacated, empty as a rowboat on a winter lake.

One of the men in blue overalls approached and bowed. 'Morning, sir.'

Sugino nodded.

'We don't think she's been in there long. Two days at most. Obviously, she was buried, but there's very little soil in the soles of her shoe and her exposed foot is also relatively clean. Death by strangulation, we think. Traces of sexual assault, though there doesn't seem to be any semen present. There are no drag marks anywhere, nor any signs of a struggle. Sir, given the remoteness of this area, we think that the killer likely used a vehicle. The nearest road is some three kilometres away so he must have carried her.'

Sugino thanked him, and the forensics officer respectfully retracted. In this line of work, these men and women saw and smelled and tasted death far more than the average citizen. Yet even here, Sugino felt a hushed discomfort.

Perhaps it was the uncertainty of the ever-after that made death unmentionable. Humanity had reached the moon, it had split the atom, it had created life itself in test tubes. But no technological advance could ever bridge that unknowable. And so humanity buried death, silenced it, burned it away with flames.

Sugino cast his eyes down at the woman once more. Already, her tissues were breaking down, little fragments of nitrogen compounds released into the soil that had surrounded her. Death feeding life, only to die anew. At least now she could be mourned and cremated like anyone else.

Delicately wafting away the flies, Sugino brushed away some soil and saw a name tag. In life, the woman had been a waitress at Denny's.

Iwata stood outside Kaori Harada's apartment once more. The portly housing officer opened the door.

'Kaori's still not back. And I suppose you're not here to cover her unpaid rent.'

Iwata ignored him. Inside Kaori's room, he closed the

door behind him and looked around. It was bare now, the cobwebs cleaned away. Iwata sat on the chair, the empty room swarming with his contemplations. And then he noticed something.

The window was open. And through it, the droning of cicadas – a metallic buzzing, the sound of Tokyo summers.

Iwata hurried downstairs and found the housing officer in the kitchen. 'What was it you said before? About the strange sound that came from Kaori's room?'

'Oh, that? It was only sometimes.'

'Describe it.'

'It was low and constant buzzing. I told you, I thought it was mood music.'

'Like cicadas or crickets?' Iwata opened the window and the sound came whirring in.

'Now you mention it, I guess it did sound similar. But why would Kaori have crickets in her room?'

Iwata had already left.

Walking the short distance to Asagaya station, Iwata took out his phone. Concluding he had nothing to lose at this stage, he dialled.

'Negishi? It's Iwata. I'm sorry to bother you, but I'm afraid I need your help.'

'If this is about the English girl –'

'Please just hear me out. There's a young woman named Kaori Harada. Part-time student at Rikkyo University. She also worked at Black Widow. She was friends with Skye –'

'Iwata, I'm sorry they got rid of you, but I can't –'

'*Anything I can do to help*. That's what you said. Look,

Negishi. Skye is dead and now her friend is missing. All I'm asking you to do is a few rudimentary searches. Relatives, criminal records, educational background, place of birth – basic stuff. Her name is Kaori Harada.'

Negishi sighed.

30. London Calling

Iwata arrived at Black Widow at 2 p.m. Madam Madoka was in her office. The power suit was gone, replaced with a rushed ponytail and gym clothes. 'You again.' She didn't bother to falsify a smile. 'I thought our business was concluded.'

'I'm here for Kaori this time.'

Madam Madoka frowned. 'Kaori Harada?'

'What can you tell me about her?'

'Not much. She left a few months ago. That was no great loss – a sort of pretty girl, but strange. No good with the customers.'

'I need a photograph.'

The woman rustled through a plastic binder then removed the passport-sized photograph and handed it over. Kaori Harada was looking beyond the camera, her cheekbones pronounced, her hair in a ponytail, the stray strands babyish on her forehead. Her large lips were pursed as if in apprehension, with no real attention paid to the photograph being taken. There was a scar on her chin. Her features were pleasant individually but somehow at odds with each other.

'No good with the customers – why?'

'Her heart wasn't in it. Don't get me wrong, nobody's is, but she was so obviously disinterested in the punters, distracted all the time. By the end she was hardly getting a single request. Still, I quickly realized she was useful in other ways. Kaori took care of the spiders for me. Turns out she was a regular expert. As you've seen, we have dozens of spiders here. It's our theme, after all. And Kaori was great with them. With her around, they grew nice and big. Never died on us. She fed them, made sure they were happy.'

'Where could I find her?'

'She didn't leave a forwarding address. What's this about?'

'I think she may be missing. You wouldn't know anything about that, would you?'

'Of course not.' There was no theatricality in the denial. Iwata knew counterfeit horror well. There was none of it in the woman's tone.

'You said Kaori fed the spiders? Crickets, cicadas – that sort of thing, I presume?'

'That's right.'

'Where did she get her supplies?'

'Little place in Nishiwaseda. I never understood that myself – there must be a million pet shops between here and there, but what do I know?' Madam Madoka shrugged. 'Spiders are more complex creatures than men.'

Iwata took the Seibu-Shinjuku Line to Takadanobaba. Not feeling like making the changeover, he exited the station and decided to walk.

Iwata soon joined the narrow path flanking the Kanda River. Immediately, the Tokyo thrum softened. Afternoon rain tittered through wax myrtles. Rich green ivy streamed down flood walls. Cherry trees grazed the water's surface. A bluebottle rested on an islet of mud, its wings black-pearlescent sails. Iwata saw crayfish, night heron, soft-shelled turtles. The Kanda River snaked through the city, criss-crossed by train lines and freeway flyovers but teeming with creatures – a concrete safari.

Turning off the river, he cut through an empty lot, its old brick walls plastered with peeling posters endorsing local politicians. Those on the left smiled confidently; those on the right held up triumphant fists.

Iwata emerged on to the main road. The pet shop was old and cluttered, an olfactory free-for-all. One half of the shop was normal enough: puppies in cages, ordinary supplies, goldfish bowls. The other, however, seemed to cater to the pet owner looking to spoil their animals as if they were children: prams for dogs too lazy to walk, a whole array of tasteful outfits (according to season), even a few different highchairs allowing master and pet to dine together.

The back door opened to loud chirruping and an elderly lady emerged holding a box of soiled newspaper.

'Afternoon,' Iwata said, looking around the shop.

'And to you, young man. Anything catch your eye?'

'It all does. Your stock is . . . interesting.'

'You can laugh, but the newfangled stuff has expanded my clientele threefold. Used to be I'd just get parents in here looking to buy for their kid. Now it's a constant stream of oddballs.'

'Odd how?'

'I guess half of them don't realize that their pet is just that: an *animal*. To them, they're replacement babies.'

'Isn't that good for business?'

'Sure it is. But a lot of the time it isn't good for the animals. See, I get a lot of part-time owners in here. Literally part-time. These folks only have time on the weekends so

286

they'll, say, rent a dog for Saturday and Sunday. While they have the dog, they want to pamper it as much as possible.' She nodded to her prams and highchairs.

Iwata frowned. 'But if they're renting, how do they know they'll get the same pet?'

'They don't. These animals bounce from owner to owner. I know one guy who can only rent dachshunds because his girlfriend thinks he owns one. He lives in fear of the day when the rental company runs out.' The woman laughed. 'Anyway, never mind me. What can I do for you?'

Iwata took out the photograph. 'I'm looking for Kaori Harada.'

The woman's demeanour shifted. 'I thought you were being too friendly.'

'I'm an investigator.' Iwata took out his credentials. 'When did you last see her?'

'A few days ago. Kaori is a regular. What's this all about?'

'Mam, she could be in danger. Did she say anything out of the ordinary?'

'Nothing. Just the usual supplies for spiders.'

'Way I heard it, she's a big fan.'

'That's putting it lightly.'

'Do you have an address for her, a number, credit card details – anything like that?'

'No, she only ever paid cash.'

'Was anything different last time? Did she seem anxious? Nervous? Say anything about going away?'

'She seemed normal enough.'

Iwata plucked out a page of newspaper from the bin liner and held it up. 'Mam, you see these people? Those are the parents of the English woman who was murdered.

Now I believe Kaori may have been known to the man who killed Skye Mackintosh. And I'd rather not go into detailed descriptions of what he did to her to try and persuade you to help me. I understand that you think you're protecting Kaori. But I promise you she may be in danger.'

The old woman sighed. 'What I said was true. She didn't say anything about leaving.'

'You know *something*.'

'Okay, look. Kaori asked me if I knew any pet shops in Old Town Kirishima. Although she didn't say anything, I got the sense she was going away.'

'Why Kirishima?'

'No idea. I told her about my friend's place there, Watanabe Pets. That's all I know.'

Iwata thanked the woman and headed south to Waseda station. He took the Tozai Line five stops and walked the short distance to Tokyo station – its Bavarian palace façade containing one of the busiest train stations in the world.

Iwata bought a ticket for the 4.10 p.m. bullet train to Kagoshima via Hakata. He boarded, took his seat and wondered if there was anything money wouldn't buy you in this city. Part-time pets, part-time priests, part-time playmates.

At exactly 4.10, a uniformed man on the platform blew his whistle and bowed to the train as it pulled out of Tokyo station.

Lynch sat on the edge of her hotel bed, watching the breaking news: human remains had been found in the mountains east of Tokyo. A large, awkward man appeared onscreen now:

Senior Inspector Kento Sugino – Ibaraki Prefectural Police

'So far, we can only confirm that the decedent is female and that the death is being treated as suspicious. For now, that's all I can say.'

The broadcast cut to a map of a mountainous region east of Ibaraki, a red dot where the body had been found. Lynch leapt out of bed and picked up the phone.

After a few rings Assistant Inspector Itō picked up. 'Detective Constable?' He switched to English. 'You hear news.'

'About the dead woman, yeah.'

'Woman? No – Ueda.'

'What about him?'

'The suspect kill himself. Last night.'

'Oh. Well. Shit.'

'Yes.'

'Then I guess it's finished.'

'Due to Ueda death, Inspector – ah, Senior Inspector Hatanaka begins close of Skye Mackintosh case this morning.'

'What about this dead woman in the mountains? It's on the news. Do you know anything?'

'Victim is waitress. Lead inspector – Sugino – I know him. I grow up in Ibaraki.'

'I just saw him on the TV. Itō, listen. I need to talk with you. Can you meet me?'

'Meet?'

'Yeah. Now.'

'After shift end I must visit doctor for head scan.'

'After, then. Do you know a place?'

Itō gave this some thought then told her to write down an address.

At 11.40 p.m. Lynch was wedged into the corner of London Calling, a tiny dive bar with bare bulbs and red walls covered in ragged band stickers. The back wall of the bar doubled as a cinema screen, the projector playing *This is England* on mute. The owner, a burly man with a pink mohawk in a Dead Kennedys T-shirt, was laughing with two American students.

Itō returned from the bar with two glasses of Guinness. His bandage was off now. He sipped his drink and nodded at the bespectacled salaryman manically skanking in the tiny gap he had made his own dance floor.

'This man arrives to this place every week. Ska night today.'

'*Tonight*,' Lynch corrected.

'Tonight. Sorry. I am bad.'

'No, you're good. Much better than my Japanese.'

Embarrassed, Itō returned his gaze to the skanking salaryman. 'I believe false, Detective Constable. Your Japanese is good.'

The song changed now, 'Pressure Drop' by Toots and the Maytals. 'So, Itō. You like this music a lot, yeah?'

'I like. But more I like punk. Good energy. *No god, no master!*' Itō gave Lynch a two-finger salute and stuck out his tongue. 'Sid Vicious, you know?'

'Yeah, mate.' She laughed. 'Very good.'

As though nervous at the success of his joke, Itō looked up at the screen. 'Detective Constable –'

'Anthea. It's Anthea.'

'Andy-ah?'

'Andy is fine. And you're wondering why the fuck I've dragged you out here after a long shift and a head scan, I know. Well, I won't muck you about, Itō. I want to ask you about the body in the mountains.'

'I don't know very well.'

'You said she was a waitress. Did she work near Kabukichō?'

'No. She belongs to Denny's. North of here. Place name is —'

'Takahagi.' Lynch smacked the table. 'I'm right, aren't I?'

Itō frowned. 'How you know this?'

'You answer my question first: that guy with the Toyota Sienta who was questioned the other night at the Shinjuku nick – uh, police station?'

'Itsuki Sato. Yes. He belongs to Kunisawa Corp.'

'Why did he say he went to Kabukichō in the first place?'

'For relax until return to home. You suspect him, I know. But please, Andy, understand. Sato make no payment in areas where women have abduction. He buys no gas for car near this places. We check his parking permits, he enters with car into city infrequently. No evidence against Sato. Only police connection is gun licence, which he registers. But there is no illegality.'

Lynch necked her Guinness. If Ueda was guilty *and* dead, she'd be on a plane home soon. Her job was done; one pint wouldn't change that. 'Okay, so tell me something else, Itō. Why does Sato drive at all?'

'Why?'

'Well, he admitted to going to the red-light district to relax, right? *Sexu*, yeah? All right, fair dos. His story was that he went home to the other side of the city then returned again in the car on the spur of the moment. But his office is just a few kilometres away from the red-light district. Why didn't he just walk, find a girl, then go to a love hotel? Why go back for the car at all? Does it make any sense to you?'

'. . . Maybe no.'

'And another thing. Why did Sato pay for an annual rail pass at all? Plus the parking permits in Central Tokyo? Paying for both seems a little pointless to me. But if he takes the train to and from work and only comes into the city with his car when he wants to pick up girls, well now, that does make sense. Especially if he's not planning on letting them go afterwards.'

Itō thought about this.

'One Step Beyond' by Madness started and the salary-man leapt up from his table and started skanking once again.

'If he's a registered gun-owner, you have his address, yeah?'

'Yes. Sato must, uh, register with police. He takes rifle. We inspect this every year. Sato live close to Haneda Airport. Also has house in small village Ōkuromori.'

Lynch took out her tourist map and spread it on the table. She'd marked the location of the dead waitress with a blue biro dot. 'Where is that village?'

Itō pointed to a location very close to the dot and stared at it for quite some time.

'To answer your question' – Lynch took out the Denny's receipt she'd kept from Sato's wallet and held it up – '*This* is how I knew it was in Takahagi. Sato went there recently.'

The diner's address was printed on the bottom. There was a doodle of a cat in the corner.

'Andy, you take?'

'Yeah. And this other receipt from the hardware shop. They've got his details on them.'

'Why?'

'I just had a feeling about him. Anyway, forget that for a minute. Itō, the case that Hatanaka was handling before, the missing prostitutes – are there any bodies?'

'No, no body find.'

'Well, what if that's because the bodies are up in those mountains?' She tapped the blue biro dot.

Itō was still staring at the receipt, in awe of the catch Lynch might have just made.

'Come *on*, Itō. I know you're signed off for the next few days with your head, and it's not like anyone's going to care if I'm not about. I want to take a look at this Sato wanker.'

Itō downed his drink then puffed his chest out. 'Detective Constable Andy Lynch, do you have available tomorrow?'

'Just so happens I do, Assistant Inspector Itō.' 'Rat Race' by The Specials was playing now. 'Fuck's sake, I love this one. Come on.'

'Excuse?'

Lynch downed her Guinness and grabbed him by the wrist. 'Come on!'

'Please. I do not.'

'Oh bollocks, you come here every week. It's a pile of piss, come *on*!'

'Piss?'

'I mean it's *easy*.' She led him to the tiny dance floor and started bopping about manically.

'Andy!' He shouted over the music. 'You only jump!'
'Then fucking jump, Itō!'
'Junya!' He started to bop with her. 'Junya! My name!'
Elated, the salaryman was among them now, skanking for all he was worth.

31. 'Girl A'

Iwata observed Japan through the train window. Honey-comb towns clustered by the tracks, little more than blurry moments for the passengers travelling at 180 mph. The late afternoon was an empty blue, interrupted only by cirrus clouds and, eventually, the solitary perfection of Mount Fuji.

Somewhere past Nagoya, the landscape became more rustic, yellow fields bordered by the deep green of conifer-ous forests, old villages like moving postcards, rice paddies glinting pink in the dusk. The constant metallic rumble of the bullet train lulled Iwata into closing his eyes.

It was his childhood home he dreamed of; sitting in the corner of his room, the silence all through the house like a sickness. As it got later and later, the dread in the pit of his stomach grew. He shut his eyes and scrunched up his toes in his socks, hoping the door would not slam.

But it always did – and then a sticky sound down the corridor, the *squelch-splat* of his father's slippers, growing closer and closer. And now there was his mother's muffled voice. She spoke and spoke and spoke. Iwata had learned quickly: the more she said, the worse it would be. When the screams came, and they always came, he would open his window and think about jumping out.

Iwata jolted awake as the train slowed. He arrived at Hakata station at 9.10 p.m., exactly five hours after leaving Tokyo. His connecting train was due to leave in eight min-utes. As Iwata waited on the platform, he took the spider out of his pocket and held it up to the light. Then he noticed something that had fallen out after it. Bending down, he picked up the dog-eared piece of paper. It was the ticket for Golden Koi hydrofoil ferry from Busan to Hakata dated 6 July.

On a whim, he approached the platform attendant and asked if he could take a later train to Kagoshima on the same date of travel. The man told him that there would be a fee to pay but that, so long as there was room on board, there shouldn't be any problem.

Leaving the station, Iwata took a taxi to Hakata harbour. Fifteen minutes later, he approached the passenger ferry terminal. Iwata walked along the waterfront until he came to the Golden Koi ferry building. The last crossing had already disembarked and only a few employees remained, smoking outside the terminal.

An old man was manning the security booth. Iwata held out his ID.

'Private investigator?'

Iwata nodded. 'Though I was a Homicide inspector not so long ago.'

'I was on the force once, too. Thirty years.'

'I'm not surprised. You give off that air.'

The old man smiled. 'What can I help you with, son?'

Iwata held up the ticket from his pocket. 'I'm working a case and this was found near the crime scene.'

'Yes, that's one of ours.'

Iwata nodded at the empty ferry moored nearby. 'Do you mind if I take a quick look around?'

'Well, we've closed for the night. And the cleaners are on board . . .' The security guard weighed it up. 'What the hell, follow me.'

It was a relatively small vessel, with bad carpet that clashed with the chairs, the TV screens still playing commercials despite the lack of passengers. Under the guard's supervision, Iwata looked around without knowing what to look for. He didn't even know if the ticket had belonged to Skye's killer.

Feeling like he had wasted his time, Iwata thanked the guard warmly. As they disembarked, the tannoy was still replaying the same message.

WELCOME TO JAPAN. THANK YOU FOR CHOOSING GOLDEN KOI.

A muzak version of 'Somewhere beyond the Sea' was playing beneath it. Annoyed, and with the song now stuck in his head, Iwata took a taxi back to Hakata station.

At 10.24 p.m. he boarded the Shinkansen *Mizuho* 611. As it pulled out of the station his phone rang. Hurrying out to the smoking compartment, he answered.

'Iwata, it's me.'

'Negishi. Glad to hear from you.'

'I still don't know why I'm helping you, but I think I've found something. This girl you're looking for? There's a reason why not much turned up on her. Kaori Harada is an assumed identity.'

'Come again?'

'Get this: she murdered her father years ago. Stabbed him over a hundred times. Self-defence, it was said. The court referred to her as "Girl A" to protect her identity.'

'Shit. I think I remember that.'

'Wouldn't surprise me. It was a huge case at the time; the newspapers had a field day with it. Anyway, she was kept in a psychiatric facility for a few years, granted a new identity then released.'

'*Girl A*, huh.'

'I assume you thought she was missing because of Skye's murderer. But Iwata, do you think she had something to do with the crime itself?'

'I don't know. It's possible. Seems Kaori disappeared around the time of the murder. And now we know she has killed before, one way or another.'

'I won't tell you the kind of rocks I had to look under to get this.'

'I'm in your debt, Negishi.'

'No, I think you have enough of that as it is. Good luck, Iwata.'

A little before midnight, Iwata arrived in Kagoshima. The station was busy despite the hour. It felt familiar some-how, even though he had never been here before. Or maybe he had, somewhere he had passed through while on the run with his mother – a thousand nameless bus terminals, a thousand nights spent at train stations.

Iwata walked a mile through the city and sat on a water-front bench. Across the bay, Sakurajima, an active volcano, looked back at him. The city was illuminated, the volcano only a silhouette.

Iwata was exhausted, but he didn't want to dream about his mother, his father, or even Shindo. Instead he bought a can of coffee from a vending machine and decided to watch Sakurajima while he waited for the morning. It was calming somehow, a city that faced its own destruction every day, like some ancient prophecy.

*

Lynch and Itō got out of the rented car. It was a mauve dawn and, up in these mountains, almost freezing. They followed the marked path quite a distance until they reached the lonely forest clearing. Portable lamps illuminated the Forensics tent where investigators were working. Seeing the pair, Senior Inspector Kento Sugino waved them over. Itō awkwardly introduced Lynch and conveyed the need to discuss a matter of great potential importance.

Sugino looked at his former colleague doubtfully but motioned towards a dim clearing where camp tables had been set up. They sat and he poured green tea, as though they were at some miserable picnic. Lynch produced the receipt she had taken from Sato's wallet and Itō cleared his throat. 'We're looking into an individual from Ōkuromori.'

Sugino nodded. 'Does this man have any connection to my victim?'

'We're really not sure but' – Itō tapped the address on the receipt – 'this is where she worked, correct?'

'That's right.'

'Well, this was found in the individual's wallet two days ago. He was arrested for soliciting in Kabukichō.'

'That could be something.' Sugino pursed his lips. 'Then again, it could be nothing. That particular Denny's is only an hour north of here. All that shows is that he went for breakfast there recently. Maybe the victim served three hundred men in the last few days.' Despite his words, he still peered at the receipt. 'What's this all about anyway, Itō?'

'Some girls in Tokyo have gone missing. Mostly runaways and sex workers. We think this individual may be involved.'

'What's his name?'

'Itsuki Sato. He lives in Tokyo, but the family home is up in Ōkuromori.'

'Does he have a car?'

'Yes.'

Sugino cupped his craggy jaw. 'How many women are missing?'

'At least seven that we know of. Possibly more.'

'So, if Sato is so good at abducting women, we can assume he also knows what he's doing when it comes to disposing of them. After all, seven missing and no bodies so far? That would mean he's no amateur.' He motioned to the tent behind them. 'Yet this was very sloppy. Very rushed.'

'Well, he *was* arrested. Could be it sent him into a panic.'

As Sugino mulled it over he saw a fly circle above them. 'Tell you what. Why don't you spend the day around Ōkuromori? See the sights, if you know what I mean. We'll call it a day trip.' Kento Sugino handed back the receipt and left.

Lynch pocketed the receipt. 'What did he say? I didn't catch that last bit.'

'He says we go to investigate Sato. Today only.'

Iwata caught the 5.39 a.m. Nippō mainline train and looked out of the window as it curved its way around the bay then passed through green-gold rice fields. Three-quarters of an hour later he arrived in Old Town Kirishima. Iwata was the only person to disembark. The platform afforded him a good view of the town, a quaint collection of traditional houses surrounded on all fronts by dense forests and roving hills. There were no signs of Olympic fanfare here.

Iwata tucked his shirt in for warmth and went in search of coffee, but nothing was open yet. Nor was the place he had travelled all this way for, Watanabe Pets. With a few hours to kill, he headed north past the old red-brick town hall and followed the river, twinkling in the dawn.

Iwata made his way into the wood and arrived at the secluded shrine at 7.30 a.m. It was a magnificent building, framed by the jade of the forest, its joists and columns vermilion lacquered. Only a few elderly tourists were present, offering prayers to the 800-year-old cedar tree nearby.

Iwata explored the forest behind the shrine, the ancient trees luminous with thick moss. He found some silver honeysuckle and ate a meagre nectar breakfast watching a stream gush by, its waters absolutely clear, the grass on its bed undulating at him in greeting. All around him, stone figurines that had crumbled eons ago were being reclaimed by the land. Above him, ravens perched on dead branches inclined their heads to blink at him, their *kraa kraa* calls different somehow to those in Tokyo. The rising sun shone through the canopy in shards of grainy light. He took out his phone and sent a text to Santi saying he missed him. Immediately, the boy's response appeared: *Loser.* Then, a few seconds later he sent another: *Me too.* Iwata wished he could have been here in other circumstances.

At 9 a.m. Iwata arrived back at the pet shop. The lights were still off. He knocked on the door and tried calling, but he could hear the phone inside ringing. That's when he noticed the little sign in the window.

CLOSED TODAY

Eight hundred miles and the guy takes the day off. Iwata kicked a pebble. As he started to walk away, a postman on a red

301

scooter pulled up outside the pet shop, unlocked his tail box and took out some letters.

'Excuse me, do you know where I can find Watanabe?'

'He'll be at the town hall for the spider battle. Everyone here is crazy for it. If I were you, I'd get out while you still can.' With that, the postman got back on and buzzed away.

Iwata walked the short distance to the town hall. Inside, the event was packed. Big yellow vinyl banners hung everywhere. Several school trips had descended on the spider tournament, two hundred little faces pressed up against glass tanks. Children's paintings adorned the walls, the yellows vibrant. Visitors posed for photographs, spiders crawling over their hands, their shoulders, their faces. Facts about spiders were being played over the public address system:

> Our nation's fondness for the humble spider goes back many centuries. It is believed that General Shimazu Yoshihiro began the first contest in the 1500s to boost morale among his troops.

The main assembly space had been repurposed for seating, fold-up chairs already occupied by the expectant audience. On the stage was the tiny arena itself, a sort of small wooden gallows painted red, without any noose.

Tournament officials were checking the equipment, all of them wearing yellow-and-black striped jackets in homage to the stars of the show, the Argiope spiders. The contestants were off to one side, their eight-legged prize fighters still in their mesh tubes.

There were two main contests: the beauty pageant, where spiders were judged on colour, shape, pattern and general loveliness, and the main attraction, the round-robin battle.

Did you know that ancient fortune-telling customs involved placing a spider inside a box? When the spider wove its web, a person's fortune could be read through it.

A man appeared on stage. With him, an excited hush broke out among the crowd.

'Good morning. This is a final reminder for anyone wishing to register their specimen for today's competition. We will be beginning in exactly ten minutes so please proceed immediately to Registration. Remember, female spiders only.' He returned to the mic. 'I almost forgot to mention, this year's prize is ¥1 million!'

There were audible gasps. Iwata took a seat at the back of the room next to an old woman wearing a hat with furry spider legs. 'First time?'

Iwata nodded.

'You won't regret it! The fights themselves are usually over within ten seconds, so it's frenetic stuff. The rules are simple: a spider loses when she's bitten, wrapped up in her opponent's web, or if her thread is cut.'

Iwata scanned the crowd. 'Any idea who Watanabe is? He has a pet shop in town.'

'That was him just now. He's this year's host. As he is every year, sadly –'

Iwata was already heading backstage. Behind the curtain there was a small green room where the contestants were chatting quietly among themselves. Watanabe was collecting the last of the registration forms and checking his watch. Iwata was about to approach him when he noticed someone standing alone. Someone short. Wearing a hood.

He eased closer. And now, beneath make-up, Iwata saw the small scar on her chin. The young woman was at the back by the fire exit, in the shadow, whispering to the spider in the palm of her hand.

Down the ages, spiders came to be associated with love. Women writing poetry to their partners would employ a spider theme to keep relationships secret.

'Kaori Harada!' Iwata called out.
She turned and met his eyes. It was a silent starter pistol.
She ran.

32. Carp on the Cutting Board

Lynch and Itō heard Ōkuromori – the booming of taiko drums in the distance – before they saw it. They parked on the outskirts of town and donned their backpacks – two friends on a hiking trip.

The townsfolk were all out decorating the main street with paper streamers and pinwheels. Wooden apparatus boxes were being dusted off for another year. Booths were being put up for souvenirs, snacks, pools for goldfish scooping. The drummers were down practising by the lake, their sound carried by the water. At the other end of it, pedaloes were being dragged out of the boathouse. Everyone was smiling, excited for the big day to come.

Sitting among the locals, Lynch and Itō ate a breakfast of roasted rice-flour balls in sweet sauce and made subtle inquiries regarding Mr Sato. Many claimed not to know him; others said they didn't have much to say about him. A handful seemed glad that a man as meticulous as he was organizing the *matsuri*. One or two called him a good man, though their tone was non-committal.

After a while, one of the young volunteers took them to one side.

'I don't know why you're asking about Sato, but if you really want to know, I'd try at the tea house.' He looked down at his rubber boots. 'Once you're finished, please leave. This is meant to be a time of celebration for us.'

Lynch frowned at Itō. 'That was weird.'

He nodded. 'Maybe yes.'

The tea house was empty except for an elderly couple playing a card game. Itō greeted them, explaining that they had been told to ask here about Sato.

'Ask the old-timers, huh?' The man clucked his tongue. 'It doesn't surprise me they don't want to talk about him. After what happened, the Sato family have become callouses on the ears of Ōkuromori.' He sipped his tea and considered the two outsiders. 'What's Sato to you?'

Itō revealed his *techou* and the old man nodded, as if he had been waiting for the day. 'That idiot has never had to lift anything heavier than chopsticks all his life. I'm not surprised you're here. What has he done?'

'I'm afraid I can't get into that, sir.'

'Well, you must know what the father did?'

Itō shook his head.

'He used to be the dentist here. When the old mayor passed away, he ran for office. It was a surprise; Sato was a stern man, didn't say much, but everybody trusted him. He won and, for a while, things were good. When it came to light that he was embezzling, nobody could believe it.' The old man motioned out of the window to the empty lot at the bottom of the hill. 'That's what's left of his dental clinic. Set it alight while he was still inside.' He smiled with satisfaction, as if the natural order of things had been confirmed. 'So that was the father. Like I say, I'm not surprised you've come for the son. A berry only ever falls to its roots.'

'Is Mr Sato friendly with anyone in town?'

'Talk to the man who runs the gas station. They were friends in school.'

Itō thanked the couple and turned to leave.

'Inspector, are you going to arrest Sato?'

'Unfortunately, I can't answer that.'

For the first time, his wife opened her mouth. She spoke quietly. 'His house is up in the cursed woods. If you go there, take this.' She handed Itō a small cloth pouch. 'That forest is full of *yōkai*. Step carefully.'

Itō bowed and left. Outside, the heat had picked up. The skies were blue but, to the north, heavy clouds formed a black whirlpool.

'What was that about?' Lynch asked.

'She gives gift. *Omamori*.' He handed the old stone amulet to her. 'Make protect for evil spirit.'

'What, like ghosts?'

'*Yōkai*.'

Lynch put it in her pocket. 'You're having a giraffe, aren't you?'

'What?'

'I mean, you don't believe in that shit, Junya?'

'I do not believe.'

'But you don't *disbelieve*?' She smirked.

'Maybe no.'

The gas station was at the top of the hill and one of the few places still open in town. There were just two pumps and a small convenience counter selling drinks and snacks. The building doubled as a hardware store, from which a woman in her mid-thirties emerged.

'Morning.'

'Morning.' Itō flashed his *techou*. 'We're looking for the proprietor.'

'He's on a supply run for the festival. I'm his wife.'

Itō smiled. 'Looks like it's going to be quite a day.'

'Is everything all right?'

307

'Oh yes, I just wanted to ask your husband a few questions. Perhaps you could help.'

The woman led them inside the hardware shop. Unsure of where to go next, she stood behind the counter.

'We're here about Itsuki Sato.'

The woman seemed to stiffen. 'I know him, yes. Though not well.'

'He's a friend of your husband's?'

'At school they were closer, I think. Now he comes in every once in a while. Maybe every month. He's a good customer, more than anything.'

Lynch took out the receipt from Sato's wallet. 'Is this from your shop?'

'Yes.'

'What does he buy?'

'Gardening equipment, mainly. Home-improvement basics. A few padlocks. A lot of soundproofing material.'

The detectives glanced at each other. 'Do you have a record of what you've sold to him?'

'No, nothing like that, I'm afraid. My husband suspects he doesn't need half the stuff he buys and he's just being kind to us.'

'Mam, we've heard some things about him in town . . .'

She sighed. 'Itsuki is a nice man, whatever his father did. Once that all came out, though, that was it for him. From then on, he was carp on the cutting board. Completely unfair, but that's life. Yet despite the way they've treated him, he still makes an effort with everyone. He's even organizing the traditional communal stew for us all.'

Itō thanked the woman for her time, but Lynch lingered.

'So, he's a nice man?'

'Yes, that's what I said.'

'But do you like him?'

She looked at the floor. 'He *is* nice. I just . . . I don't know. Perhaps this is unfair, but he always gave me the creeps. I guess he just looked at me for a second too long.'

As Iwata bolted out of the town hall he felt the tremendous rumble in the distance. Up ahead, Kaori Harada's head was down, arms pumping, dirty plimsolls slapping the pavement. Iwata was still weak from his beating, but adrenalin was flooding him. Immediately, his chest was hammering, his breath coming only in snatches. *She's fast. Can't let her escape.*

Kaori had reached the end of the street and was turning right. Iwata took the corner just in time to see her enter the area fenced off for the cable car up to the mountain. He heard another distant detonation. A siren resounded and the public address system kicked into life, imploring people to remain calm and to get to the designated safe areas as soon as possible. People began to surge away from the cable car, panic rising. Iwata dodged them. He sailed through the entrance of the cable car loading area and right into the butt of a traffic cone.

Badly winded and doubled over, he looked up at Kaori. She was standing over him, panting with fear and fury all at once. Her voice was soft but unequivocal. 'No more warnings.'

She carried the cone over to the control booth, where the cable-car operator was on the phone. Iwata tried to call out but could barely wheeze. Kaori hit the operator over the head and he slumped to the floor. Frantically scanning the control panel she hit some buttons. There was a hydraulic whirring and she ran out of the control booth towards the cable car.

'Kaori, wait –' he gasped, but she was already inside. A coloured bulb flashed green and the car clanked away, sharply climbing up into the air.

Iwata got to his feet and staggered over to the operator, who was mumbling. 'How long till the next car?'

'Muh?'

'How long!?'

'Only one car . . .'

Iwata stumbled back into the street. The postman from earlier was trying to help a group of elderly tourists. Iwata hopped on to the scooter and sped away, up towards the mountain.

Mr Sato's house was large and beautiful: long exterior hallways, a tiled roof with broad, majestic eaves and an impressive view of Ōkuromori below. It was surrounded by stone walls. Behind the house, there was only dense forest.

Lynch rang the bell. They waited a minute before trying again.

'Maybe Sato does not go to home.'

'Bollocks to it.' Lynch shrugged off her backpack and pushed Itō against the wall. Though shocked, he didn't struggle. Then she cupped his hands in front of his stomach and used them to boost herself up to the top of the gate.

'Andy, please –' Itō hissed. 'Very bad.'

Reaching down, she offered her hand to him. 'Don't be a fanny all your life.'

'No. I cannot.'

'Suit yourself.' Lynch dropped into the garden, crept into the bush and waited. There was no movement, no sound. She scanned the windows, listened. Then, satisfied, she unlocked the gate from the inside. A grumbling Itō slinked through.

'Very bad.'

'Junya, you take the garden, yeah?'

Lynch hurried over to the house and slipped inside. Shaking his head, Itō searched the garden. He saw nothing out of place, and it didn't escape his attention how wonderfully kept it was. Lanterns, a lotus-laden pond, irises, harmonious rock compositions. It hardly seemed possible that a man who kept such a garden could abduct and murder women.

Looking around, Itō felt doubt. All they had was a receipt and some village gossip – this man had a life. Plus, if Itō was caught trespassing now, what would that do to his career? He resolved to never speak of the day trip with the English detective to his colleagues.

Then he saw a shed. It was set away from the house, hidden by a tree, easily missed. Heart thudding, Itō approached. His service weapon was in his backpack. He didn't take it out but reminded himself it was there.

The shed, quite predictably, was locked. Itō recognized the brand of padlock on sale at the hardware store from earlier on. The idea of breaking in gave him a sick feeling in the pit of his stomach. Then again, Itō had already crossed the line by entering Sato's property. Itō picked up a stone. 'No gods, no masters,' he whispered. Then he crashed it down on the lock. The door creaked open. In the dimness, Itō saw soundproof cladding all over the walls.

'Hello?' He stepped inside.

There were no women, no bloodstains, no bodies. Just a small desk, a small stand and sheet music. In the corner, a shiny violin case.

Swearing, Itō left the shed. 'Andy!'

'Over here!' she called back.

He found her at the side of the house, standing by the garage. 'Andy, there is nothing here. Anti-sound material is just for neighbour consideration. Child plays violin.'

'Yeah? The nearest neighbour is a kilometre away. Consideration for who?'

'Andy, please –'

Lynch didn't reply; she merely pointed to the ground. There, between them, were bloody drag marks leading into the garage. Itō took out his gun and nodded. *Ready.*

She crept to the side of the garage and pressed the button. The door rumbled open. Itō took deep breaths. Sunlight flooded in. Body parts were strewn all over the floor. Hooves, ribs, a tail, the head of a deer. In the blood, there were tyre tracks leading out of the garage.

'Jesus.'

Itō let his gun drop. 'Sato takes animal.'

'The woman earlier mentioned he's cooking a stew. Where?'

Lynch and Itō left the house and closed the gate behind them. As they walked back to the rental car, an overweight man in luminous running gear approached them.

'Good morning.' His irritated curiosity had turned the phrase into a question. 'Are you friends of –'

Itō stuck his *techou* in the man's pink face. 'Sato. Where is he?'

The man blinked. 'He's at the old community hall. But why –'

Lynch and Itō were already in the car.

By the time Iwata had reached the top of the mountain the postman's scooter was sputtering. Ash was raining down, the sky a thick, billowing grey. Covering his face with a rag from the tail box, he came to the cable-car exit. The car was humming, but the door was open. There was a message on the side of the car, in colourful letters.

PLEASE ENJOY OUR BEAUTIFUL
MOUNTAIN SCENERY.

'Kaori!' Iwata's voice couldn't travel through the haze.

He followed the hiking trail up the mountain. There was no way of seeing the villages below, or even understanding the altitude. The ash made it seem as if Iwata were alone, floating through a gaseous world.

He climbed for half a mile through the ash storm, coughing all the while, until he passed a red sign:

NO-ENTRY ZONE –
DANGER – VOLCANIC ACTIVITY

On it there was a small handprint – someone had stopped here to rest. Another low rumble resounded, like subterranean thunder.

A few hundred yards further up, the path levelled out and Iwata saw the information centre. It was just a small Portakabin at the edge of a sheer drop. Inside the cabin, Kaori Harada was standing by the window, her back to the door. Her clothes were filthy, her hair was lank, she was struggling to breathe, her face completely grey with ash.

'Kaori.'

She stiffened but did not face him.

'My name is Kosuke Iwata. I'm not here to hurt you. I

was investigating the murder of Skye Mackintosh. You knew her, didn't you?'

She glanced over her shoulder. 'I saw you in the paper.'

'I've come for the truth, Kaori. I have to know what happened to her.'

She turned to face him, tears slicing through the ash like pink wax. 'Truth? There's only one: Skye is gone.'

'Was it you, Kaori? Did you hurt her?'

'Hurt *Skye*?'

'You know what it takes to kill, you've done it before.'

Kaori looked away. 'That was different. My father was a cruel man. I just snapped one day.'

Iwata took a cautious step forwards, his hand outstretched. 'Is that what happened with Skye?'

Kaori screwed up her face in disgust at the idea. 'I *loved* Skye. I could never hurt her.'

Iwata stopped still. Instinctively, he knew he was hearing the truth. 'You loved her.'

'I loved Skye like I've never loved anyone else. And Miyake took her away . . .'

'Miyake? . . . It was you. You killed the landlord.'

'Is that who you think he was?' Her face hardened. 'Miyake was scum. He was paying Skye for sex. From the beginning he was jealous of us. Always trying to poison us with money. Threatening to evict her. No, I couldn't let him hurt anyone else.'

Iwata's head was whirling. He recalled the notes from the case file. The only other individuals to visit the eighth floor of the love hotel prior to the discovery of the body were a couple who stayed for an hour and a young woman by herself who didn't stay for long.

'You went up to the love hotel, didn't you?'

'Yes, that's where I saw . . . Skye. And what Miyake had done to her.'

'Why Starlet? Why at that particular love hotel?'

'I don't know. Skye just sent me a message asking me to meet her.'

'*She* asked you to come?'

'Yes. Said it was important. But when I got there . . .' Kaori began to cry now.

'What about this?' Iwata took out the dead spider from his jacket.

'That's not mine.'

'But you love spiders, and this was found near Skye's body.'

She wasn't listening any more. She opened the window and stepped up into the frame.

'Kaori, wait.'

'. . . Why?' She was shaking, the rivulets of sweat down her arms cutting through the ash. 'All I had was Skye and Manami. Skye is dead, and I left Manami behind.' She closed her eyes and teetered in the grey wind. 'Manami was going to win.'

'Listen to me. I believe you didn't kill Skye. Just come down and we can talk.'

'But I did kill Miyake. They'll send me back to jail.'

'There will be consequences, I can't hide that, but –'

'Then I'd just be Girl A all over again.'

'Wait –'

'No, I think I'd rather stay as Kaori.' Kaori Harada let herself drop into the raging sea of ash below. A few seconds later there was a tremendous subsonic rumble. In the distance, across the mountains and across the bay, Sakurajima erupted.

33. Cruel Summer

Mr Sato was working frantically in the kitchen of the old community hall, stopping every few seconds to gag on the smell. His work was all but complete. All over the counter, his ingredients: little mountains of yellowed nail clippings, fun-sized plastic pop bottles filled with semen and saliva, zip-lock bags brimming with pubic hair. His cold box containing toes, fingers, nipples, earlobes and eyelids. A small pile of ground bone, a dull cream colour, off to one side, ready for seasoning. On the hi-fi, Bananarama's 'Cruel Summer' was playing full blast.

The stew was bubbling away in the large iron cauldron, the smell of the venison clashing with the rich stench of human flesh. Mr Sato, checking his stopwatch, tossed in a toe, then added some more of the poisons. He had quite the selection – hemlock, nightshade, arsenic, various rodenticides. Scratching a few numbers on a scrap of paper, he made the calculations and applied the necessary masking agents and sweetness enhancers. He whistled along with the music, the excitement rumbling in his gut.

'Father?' His son peeked around the door.

Mr Sato flinched. 'I told you not to come in here.'

'I'm sorry, but –'

'You're meant to be keeping a lookout.'

'I know –'

'So what the fuck are you doing here?'

'There are two people here. They're asking for you.'

Mr Sato's stomach clenched. 'Police?'

'I don't know. One of them is a foreigner.'

How could they even know I'm here? Snarling, Mr Sato snatched up his sports bag, grabbed his son by the arm and marched out of the kitchen.

The old community hall was a dank chamber that contained only shadows and the village's unwanted items: things that had broken, things that were no longer fit for purpose.

The two outsiders were waiting by the door. The male was plain-looking, around Sato's height. He kept his hands in his pockets, a friendly smile on his face. The female was tall, black, with no expression at all.

'Good afternoon.' It was the male who spoke, noting Sato's sports bag and his grip on the boy's arm.

'Who are you?'

'I'm Assistant Inspector Junya Itō, and this is my colleague. I understand you were interviewed by Shinjuku Police recently. We're just following up, sir. Completely routine.'

'What do you want?'

'We're looking into another case and we'd like to eliminate you from it. You haven't visited the Denny's restaurant in Takahagi in the last few days, have you, sir?'

'No.' Mr Sato was blinking rapidly. 'Do I look like the type to eat that sort of shit?'

Lynch took out the receipt from her pocket.

Mr Sato recognized the little cat doodle and smiled to himself. 'All right, I suppose I'd better explain –' In one rapid movement, he pulled his rifle from his bag and stabbed it into the small of the boy's back. 'This is how it goes. You obey, or I kill him.'

Itō put his hands out. 'We're only here to talk to you, sir.'

'Talk about what? My hanging? Now, your gun – drop it and kick it over to me.'

Itō complied. The boy's eyes were closed, the denim over his crotch darkening. Mr Sato let him go and aimed his rifle at Itō. He glared at the detectives in a strained silence. Every chest in the room rose and fell rapidly. Earlobes burned. Stomachs churned.

'My work here is almost finished.'

'Sir, your son is very scared.'

'Then he's a fucking coward, just like his mother.'

'It would be better if you let him leave.'

'No, he'll be coming with me.'

Itō shook his head. 'Not gonna happen, Sato. We'll work something out, but you have to let the boy go.'

'You're wasting my time. I wasn't planning on killing you, but I can't allow you to interfere –'

Lynch stepped forward. 'Take me.'

'You?' Mr Sato snorted. 'And who the fuck are you, anyway?'

'Detective Constable Anthea Lynch of the London Metropolitan Police.' From inside her pocket, she fired twice.

One shot cracked over Sato's head; the other hit him in the thigh. The boy threw himself to the floor. Sato dropped the rifle and reeled backwards. Itō rushed him.

But Sato was too quick. He snatched up Itō's surrendered pistol from the floor and fired. The bullet hit him in the side. Itō went down. Lynch returned fire and threw herself behind a column. Sato did the same. Both of them panted in the ringing silence.

Then there was a grunting noise, Itō crawling behind cover, dragging the boy with him.

'Junya?' Lynch shouted out. 'Hold on.'

He groaned in response. Lynch tried to centre herself. She closed her eyes and demanded deep breaths. Then, as if a referee had called time, Sato fired another volley in her direction and ran for it. Now he was back in the kitchen, the metal door clunking shut.

Hurrying over to Itō, Lynch took off her raincoat and covered his wound as best she could. She glanced at the boy, who was just staring off into space, as if on pause. Lynch cupped his cheek. 'You're okay. Stay here, understand?'

He looked up at her in a daze.

'Itō, tell him that you will protect him and that he's going to be okay.'

Lynch took her phone out and dialled Iwata. *Straight to voicemail*. She tried Kento Sugino. When he answered she explained the situation in two sentences, gave their location then hung up.

Sato had taken the sports bag, but the rifle was still on the ground. Lynch grabbed it and put it in Itō's hands. She left her phone next to him. 'Junya, look at me.'

He was pale now. 'Yes.'

'Hold this, yeah? If he comes back, you know what to do.'

'Yes.'

'You're gonna be all right.'

'Maybe yes.'

Lynch checked her rounds, stood, then went for the kitchen door.

As she reached it, Itō called out. 'Andy.'

'Yeah?'

He gave her a blood-soaked thumbs-up. 'Good luck.'

Lynch grasped the metal door handle. It was heavy, but

relented. Immediately, she gagged on the butcher-shop stink. All around, there were dark splotches on the floor – a thick brown liquid. Instinctively, she sensed horror but didn't allow herself to take in any details.

The rear exit was ajar. A slice of light cut through the kitchen's gloom. Nudging the door open, she poked her head outside. Sato's Toyota Sienta was there, engine running, its doors open. There was some kind of cauldron next to it. In the distance, she could hear the beat of the taiko drums pounding gleefully, the madness of a tin whistle squealing above them.

Lynch cleared her corners then dashed over to the empty car. Sato had to be in the forest beyond it. She took a deep breath and realized where the foul stench was emanating from: the cauldron. Unable to stop herself, she looked inside.

'Oh Christ . . .' As she struggled to contain her vomit, something exploded in the forest. Lynch snapped her head round. A hundred metres in, there was a papery noise, like firecrackers. After a brief silence, thick red smoke billowed through the trees.

Coloured smoke bombs?

Another one went off deeper into the wood, this one bright green.

Boom boom boom – pop pop pop

Lynch ran into the forest, her heart thudding like taiko. The red and green smoke mixed together now, and she coughed on it. She could only see a few trees up ahead, only hear the distant drums.

Lynch ran deeper and deeper into the wood – through pinks, purples, oranges, through the pounding thrum, beneath the distant rumble of thunder. As the vivid smoke swirled around her she saw faces in the commingling colours, she heard a guttural laughter in the popping. *Which fucking way did you –*

A shot rang out. The bark above her head showered down. Lynch fell to the ground and fired back into the miasma. There was a yelp.

Sweating and trembling, she belly-crawled towards it. Up over a muddy crest, down a little cascade of dead leaves, then under a fallen trunk.

The smoke cleared at last. And there, right in front of her face, was Itō's pistol. *Sato dropped it.* There were spots of blood all around it. Lynch scrambled to her feet.

Mr Sato staggered past the familiar sequence of chinquapin trees, dripping blood as he went. The woody tang of the forest smelled like death. He caught his breath behind a tree and tried to inspect his wounds. As a keen purveyor of harm, Mr Sato had visited many different types of pain on a human body, but the effects of being shot were unexpected. The bullet wound in his thigh felt hot, like a deep blister. But the new one in his chest felt dull, like he'd been punched by a heavyweight boxer wearing knuckledusters.

At least I got one of those bastards. Got him good. Mr Sato grinned. Then he heard his father. *The whore. She's still after you. You're bleeding, and she'll get you.*

'Not me,' he hissed. 'Not *me*.'

Mr Sato pushed himself off the tree and hurried down to the lake. The water was a powder blue, the sky curdling low. Kicking off his shoes, he careened his way to the shore. The mud was warm and fluffy, like running through sponge cake. *That's it, bitch. Right this way. You're about to go on a wonderful journey. Follow us to our island; you'll like it there. We'll make you feel right at home.*

In the reflection of the water he saw it was his own mouth moving, his own words he was hearing. But Mr Sato had no time to consider this; he had reached the jetty. As he stepped up on to it, he cried out. The pain in his thigh was now spine-tingling agony. 'Just give up,' he whispered to himself. 'Stop now. You're bleeding out.'

There was a large cormorant perched on the final mooring. It threw its head back and squawked. Mr Sato looked up at it. In its black, expressionless face, he saw his own eyes, blinking rapidly. It opened its beak and his father's words screeched out.

Not yet, boy. Not yet. Stop your blubbing and do what you swore to do.

Grimacing, Mr Sato dragged himself along the jetty. He reached his rowboat and untied it, the water already disturbed from the growing wind. With great effort, he lowered himself into the boat. Mr Sato moaned as he began to row, the motion enflaming his wounds. The collected water in the deck turned pink with his blood. The pain and numbness were scaring him now. *Just got to get to the cabin. I have my things there.*

There were three loud, hollow cracks. Two plumes of water flew up next to the boat and another shot bit into the stern. Mr Sato looked up and saw the foreign woman marching down the jetty, gun outstretched. She was lining up another shot now.

He flung himself into the water. The shock of the cold cleaved through him. He felt water slip into his bullet holes. Mr Sato screamed.

*

Lynch was out of bullets. She watched Sato swim away from the sinking rowboat. Pacing back and forth, saw him get smaller and smaller. *He's gonna get away.* She had left her phone behind. Lynch knew she should just wait for Sugino, wait for help. But how long would he take?

'Bollocks.' She kicked off her shoes and dived into the lake.

As Lynch swam, she pictured the council-flat bathroom where it had all gone down. She recalled the sound of cracking finger bones. She heard Chief Superintendent Powell's words as he killed two birds with one stone: *Japan is a long way away, after all. You'd be going above and beyond, I'd say.*

Lynch opened her eyes. In the silent murk there was only serenity. She wanted to stay there, in the cold peace, but already her lungs were burning.

She surfaced and the thrum of reality roared back in.

Reaching the overturned rowboat, she propped herself up. Sato was nowhere to be seen. It was raining now, a hard and sudden summer downpour. The clouds above the islet were black. Its mudbanks were gleaming in the rain, the branches of its scraggy trees waving in welcome.

Lynch waited, but there was no other movement. She turned to look back at the jetty, hoping to see police, even hoping to see Itō, but there was no one.

She heard a loud, wet thump and felt an impact between her shoulder blades. Then deep, rasping pain. *He doubled back and hid behind the boat.*

Lynch kicked out. Sato drew the gutting knife back again as she lurched away. The blade hammered into the wood. She tried to punch him but went under. Lynch opened her eyes and saw her own blood drifting out around her. The leakage felt cold.

Above her, Sato had one of the oars. It hit her in the stomach, and now he was forcing her down, down, down. Lynch screamed then spun away. Sato was descending, knife out in front of him, his blood wafting all around him like some lake monster.

Lynch fumbled for something, for anything. *No time.* She blocked the knife as they sank deeper and deeper. The lack of air was turbine-loud in her head, the pain in her back impossible to process. The murk was so thick it was as if there had been an eclipse.

Lynch fought to retain logic. But this was a place people were not meant to go, the deep wretchedness feared from childhood.

Above, Sato's eyes were fixed on her. In the green-black he seemed to be moving his head, a small, determined nodding as he tried to press the knife into her. Lynch had run out of strength. *This is it. He's going to kill me.*

She remembered swimming lessons at Swiss Cottage pool, drifting off from the rest of the class to the deep end, where she'd practise holding her breath. In those last few seconds before surfacing, in the roaring, in the burning, there was a thrill – it felt like she'd pop completely.

Lynch opened her eyes and saw the stone amulet necklace that the old lady had given Itō around her neck. She stabbed it into one of Sato's bullet holes. A torrent of bubbles came out of his mouth. Lynch kicked away desperately.

She broke the surface, sobbing air back into her lungs. Lynch swam madly, anywhere, *away.* And then she was dragging herself through the shallows and straight into a bush. Heart clobbering in her chest, she tried to contain her breath. Her clothes were sopping wet, her hands trembling. To her horror, she realized she was on the island. In the mist of the storm, she couldn't even see the mainland.

Crawling into a small cave, Lynch closed her eyes.

34. This is the Day

Iwata travelled back to Tokyo in a sleepless daze. Throughout the journey, he thought about Kaori, he thought about
spiders, he thought about Skye Mackintosh. Many things
bothered him but he kept coming back to one detail.
Holding the dead spider up to the light, he asked himself:
If Kaori didn't leave you there, then who did?

Back at the capsule hotel, lying in the warm darkness,
he remembered her words: *I loved Skye. I could never hurt her.*

His dreams were turbulent, frequently interrupted by
moments of lucid wakefulness: *Why did Skye ask Kaori to
meet her at the love hotel? Who called in anonymously to report the
body? To report Ueda's location? Why would Unknown Male want
to put something in the box for Skye? And why the spider?*

Finally, Iwata woke at dawn and went up to the bath on
the top floor. Standing naked, looking out over the grey,
drizzly Tokyo cityscape, he asked himself the question
he'd asked on day one: *What if the killer left the spider there
intentionally, as a message? But a message to mean . . . what?*
Beyond taunting the police, Iwata had no idea.

After a breakfast of white rice with salted seaweed, Iwata
dressed in his black suit and took the Fukutoshin Line
heading south. At Jiyugaoka station, he switched on to the
Tokyu-Oimachi Line, getting off four stops later at
Todoroki. It was a short walk to Ravine Park, an enclave
of tranquil water, ancient trees and sprawling moss.

Taking the stone stairs down, Iwata heard the flow of the river, the wind through the bamboo groves, the distant *clank-clank* of footsteps over the boardwalk. The smell of earth and wet stones felt alive. Iwata passed little waterfalls, bridges and ancient statuettes, faces worn down by time.

Given the weekday morning rain, it would have been half-empty here, were it not for the Mackintosh family and the press pack that followed them. It was looking thinner these days.

Philip, Karen, Geraldine and Dylan White were laying flowers for Skye's birthday. Fiery pink camellias drifted slowly downstream.

Seeing Iwata now, Philip Mackintosh began marching towards him, snarling despite the tears in his eyes. Immediately, Dylan tried to hold him back, reminding him about the press.

'*Let* them see!' Philip shouted. 'Bastard has the gall to show his face! Today, of all days!'

'Phil, come on.' Dylan had him around the chest. 'It's done now.'

'No thanks to this charlatan.'

'I know, I know. Come on, let's go.'

Philip Mackintosh let himself be led away.

When he was gone, Karen stood next to Iwata. They watched the camellias drift away.

'He's not angry at *you*. He just needs someone to . . . you know.'

'I understand.'

'He doesn't think you do. He doesn't think anyone does.'

'Some years ago . . . I also lost a child.'

She looked at him with new eyes. 'I didn't know.'

Iwata bowed. 'I came to pay my respects.'

'I – *we* do appreciate what you've done for us. Whatever those jackals said about you.' Karen took a Skye T-shirt from her bag and gave it to him. 'Goodbye, Inspector.'

And Geraldine arrived and slipped her arm around her mother's shoulder. She looked at Iwata pointedly. 'Come on, Mum. Let's get out of this rain.'

'Mrs Mackintosh, you used to live in a place called Hatfield?'

She nodded uncertainly.

'When you get back to England you should go to your old house. There's a chestnut tree in the field behind it. Skye buried a watch by it. It may still be there.'

Mrs Mackintosh pursed her lips and thanked him wordlessly.

'Geraldine,' Iwata called. 'One last thing?'

'What now?'

'Did Skye ever talk to you about Kaori Harada? A friend of hers?'

'No.' She looked away. 'No, she didn't.'

Iwata watched them go. He felt sure of it: the sister had just lied to him.

Lynch woke with a start. She was still in the cave. Something smelled vaguely fetid. It reminded her of the fishmonger's on Queen's Crescent. For some reason, recalling home made her want to cry.

Lynch tore her shirt into a tourniquet and tried not to shout out as she fastened it between her shoulders. She was covered in blood, her white bra now grey and pink. Emerging from the cave, she listened. She heard only drums, thunder, rain.

He could be dead . . . Picking up a good-sized rock, she hurried along the beach. *He could also be very fucking not dead.* Lynch began to circle the islet. She wasn't about to let this bastard creep up on her again.

Halfway around, she saw it: an A-frame cabin, enshrouded by knotweed. It was small, completely hidden from the mainland. She felt wet sand beneath her bare feet and the cold, crippling fear of death in her gut. Lynch knew instinctively, hell itself was in that cabin.

He's in there waiting for you. If you go inside, you'll never leave this place. Just get back in the water and get out of here.

Trembling, Lynch turned away and waded into the lake. She was up to her knees when she heard something. It was a loud but nebulous noise, a collage of sounds emerging from the cabin. *Music?* She heard an accordion now, a mix of melancholic euphoria. Soon it was unmistakable: 'This is the Day' by The The. *The fucker is playing music.*

Lynch stared at the lake, its surface undulating in the storm. It would be safe in there. Peaceful. Warm, even. But there was something stopping her. It was the memory of 19 May – finding the broken little body of the child. Lynch had snapped then, drawn her baton, locked herself in the bathroom with the father. That moment had brought her here.

She thought about Skye Mackintosh on the autopsy table. The waitress from Takahagi she had seen that morning buried in a shallow grave. Like hands beneath the lake, they gripped her ankles and whispered to her. Anthea Lynch's fear of death was replaced by something deeper.

Rage.

Screaming, she waded back towards the island.

Clambering through the knotweed, rock in hand, she charged the cabin. The door was open. Music was blaring out.

She entered. The stench was overwhelming. There were footsteps over wooden floorboards. Lynch turned. Snarling, Sato rushed her with a scalpel, his hair wild, his teeth pink with blood. She threw herself at him. The scalpel thumped down into her shoulder as the rock smashed into Sato's temple.

He fell to the floor, one eye rolling back. Crawling to the dentist's examination chair, he curled up in the foetal position. He was wheezing, his face white, blood pooling around his body.

Lynch reached back and pulled the scalpel out of her shoulder blade. She looked around the stinking cabin. It was decorated with student ID cards, underwear, strips of leather material from handbags, used tampons and Polaroids of rape, torture, execution. There was a camcorder on a tripod in the corner. Next to it, a large crate of discs and flash drives was divided into numbers: 1–7.

Lynch crouched down over Sato and pointed the scalpel at his face.

Eyes wide, Sato tried to drag himself away from her, but his muscles weren't responding any longer. 'Please . . . please . . .'

'Did *they* say please? Beg for their lives?'

'I need help . . .'

'The waitress from Denny's. They found her this morning. Seven other missing women. Did you kill Skye Mackintosh, too?'

He began to weep.

'I tried, Father. I tried . . .'

'You're going to tell me why, Sato.'

He looked up at her now, as if seeing her for the first time. His eyes were red. '. . . Ōkuromori . . . They took him from me . . . Then pushed me away . . .'

'What's that got to do with these women? Tell me why you killed them.'

'I just wanted to be inside . . .' His eyes fell shut. '. . . Inside.'

'Inside what?'

Sato stopped breathing. The song ended. Lynch turned off the tape.

The old community hall was surrounded – ambulances, police cars, a helicopter whirring overhead. Storm exhausted, the deepening dusk was as pink as the flashing turret lights. Lynch was sitting in the back of an ambulance, wrapped in a shock blanket.

Kento Sugino sat next to her and handed her a bottle of water. 'You all right?'

'Fine. How's Itō?'

'He should be okay. He was lucky.'

Relief overwhelmed her but she could only nod. Police tape was being rolled out around the hall. Crime-scene technicians were fanning out, a joyless parade descending on these quiet outskirts of Ōkuromori.

'We found body parts in the kitchen. Enough poison to murder the whole village . . . Did Sato say anything to you?'

She nodded. 'He said he wanted to be inside.'

'What does it mean?'

Lynch shrugged.

Sugino looked off into the forest and shook his head. 'Detective Constable, what was going on here?'

Lynch saw the cauldron off by the Toyota Sienta. A tent was being put up around it. Above it, a swarm of flies were sparring. 'I don't know.' She spoke quietly. 'But I don't ever want to.'

35. Nothing Personal

In the steam room of the members-only club near the National Diet Building, Ozawa was leaning back on his elbows, the sweat streaming down his neck. At this time of day it was usually dead – one of the few places in this city he could let his guard down.

He was something approaching relaxed when the door opened. A man entered, large as an orca whale, and struck up a conversation. After a minute of his prattle, Ozawa admitted defeat and excused himself. Back in the changing room, the lights were off. Ozawa switched them on but evidently the power was out. Swearing, he squinted through the gloom to fiddle with his locker.

'Seems like you see well in the shadows.'

Ozawa flinched. 'Who's there?'

A smaller, serpent-like man edged out of the darkness. 'No need to be so jumpy.'

'If you're looking for friends –' Ozawa looped his tie around his neck '– there's a guy in the steam room who I'm sure would be happy to indulge you.' The steam room door opened and the large man stood there.

From behind, Whale snapped the tie up against Ozawa's windpipe and pulled him off balance. 'Actually, we already know each other.' The government man hacked and flailed, but Whale's grip was obstinate. 'Though we're more colleagues than friends.'

Snake slipped out a blade from his jacket. 'It seems the

three of us work in a similar field, Mr Ozawa. The weird thing is, though we've asked around about you, nobody seems to know much. It's as if you just *appeared* one day. Now, I know this is a place of relaxation but my companion and I are keen to talk shop.'

Whale dropped him to the floor and Ozawa scuttled away. With nowhere to go, he leaned back against a locker, holding his neck. 'You guys have it all wrong.'

'Do we? In that case, I must apologize.' Snake bent down and slashed the blade across his chest. As Ozawa squealed, Whale wedged the locker room door shut with a bench.

'Kosuke Iwata,' Snake wiped his blade clean. 'Talk.'

Panting, Ozawa tried to stem the bleeding with his towel. He was shaking badly. 'There's nothing to say. Iwata is a nobody.'

'Oh, Mr Ozawa, we don't think that's quite right. In fact, he was your great hope, wasn't he? You were the voice in his ear. You gave him Ryoma Hisakawa's scent then let him off the leash. Even when you took away his badge, you didn't demand his gun. No, you were *praying* he'd lose control.'

Pale with fear, Ozawa looked up at his tormentors. 'I didn't meet with Iwata in the name of philanthropy. I never pretended otherwise. But you know as I well as I do, his father is a cancer.'

'We don't make those calls, Mr Ozawa. And it's our job to make sure foreigners don't, either.'

'Listen to me. With his new powers in Defense, Hisakawa will do great damage. I know you're both doing what you think is the right thing but –'

Snake silenced him by pressing the tip of the blade

against his shoulder. 'This isn't a conversation. Who are you with? Chinese? North Koreans?'

For once Ozawa had no smile. Only silence.

Snake booted the blade through bone. Ozawa's scream mixed with the metallic screech of the locker behind him. Whale took the blood-soaked towel and covered Ozawa's face with it until the screaming had subsided. When it was just whimpers, he let it drop. Ozawa was crying, his body skewered against the locker behind.

Snake lowered his mouth to the spy's ear. 'I won't ask again.'

Ozawa spat blood, then nodded once. 'Whatever you do to me is nothing compared to what will happen to me if you send me back.'

'Is all this really worth it? For your Dear Leader?'

'Your question implies I had a choice.'

Snake looked at Whale. 'How long until clean-up arrives?'

'About five minutes.'

'Okay.' Snake stood on the bench and punched out the smoke detector. Then he took out three cigarettes and handed them around. Ozawa's arm was completely dead so Whale lit up for him.

'You know,' Snake squinted through his smoke. 'I've always been fascinated by your culture, Ozawa. Not that that's your real name, of course. But I'm curious, is it really like they say?'

'I don't know what you want me to tell you.'

'Well, paint us a picture. Did you always want to be an undercover operative, ever since you were a little kid?'

Whale sniggered.

'Seriously, though. What was it like growing up there?'

Considering the end, Ozawa's eyes glazed over with his

past. 'My earliest memory is the sound of Party broadcasts from lorries washing over me. In my village, there was a big red banner that read: *victory on all fronts.*' He took a drag then laughed out bitter smoke. 'They shot a man for eating his own grandchild under that banner. That was the choice in the winter, dying of cold or dying of hunger. Classrooms half full in the spring.'

'But you survived, didn't you. That's what you are, right? I've always known how. When I was a kid they used to call me the Rat King. In the mountains above my village, people would set fires to drive out the rats then cook them in a stew. But I was smarter than that. I could see the value in them. Rats are highly organized, after all. So I would find their holes and dig away from above. I would unearth them and steal their stores of maize and corn. Each little rat hole would give me a handful. Then, when I had taken everything, I would tie string around its neck and force it to lead me to the next lair. If I found babies, I would let them grow so that they would soon work for me too. I recruited them. Just as how the Party recruited me.'

'Why does your country want to target Hisakawa?'

'The Americans have been badgering the PM for years now over militarization. Engage and contain us by arming Japan. Three years ago, he made himself quite clear. He wanted to fundamentally alter the constitution – completely overhaul Article 9 – thereby removing the impediment to Japan's ability to wage war for purposes beyond self-defence. Ryoma Hisakawa was brought into the Cabinet to help this along. His unshakable view is that the best deal lies with the Americans. It just so happens this would lead to tidy profits for US weapons manufacturers. And of course, him, too.'

'So you procured work as the senior aide for a government minister who happens to hate Hisakawa. Still, he has to be discreet about it. But you found an alternative solution. You were banking on Iwata to kill him. Everyone wins.'

'Hisakawa is a dangerous man. He will rot that Cabinet from the inside out. Every time a jet is scrambled, every time a missile is tested, Hisakawa will be there, whispering the word "war" in the Prime Minister's ear. It was my job to stop him.'

Whale's phone rang now. He answered without speaking. Hanging up, he nodded once.

Putting out his cigarette, Snake faced Ozawa. 'Ready?'

The spy took one last drag. 'For everything I said about my country, at least we know what we're living for. Yet I've been living among you people for years. You're all empty. Your struggles mean nothing. So do what you've come to do.'

Snake smiled. 'I liked your story about the rats, Ozawa. But it sounds like you owe them a nice dinner. And I think it's about time you settled. Nothing personal, you understand.'

36. Her Name

Kosuke Hisakawa loved everything about these rare car journeys — the smell of the leather, the gleaming dashboard, the seatbelt's embrace against his chest. But most of all he loved to watch the city flashing past him. Sometimes weeks would pass without him leaving the house. To the boy, Tokyo was more magnificent each time he saw her. Tokyo was freedom. But Tokyo never lasted. She winked at him, smirked. *Goodbye, little one. You didn't belong here anyway.* Still, for once, this car journey would not be returning to his father's house.

Kosuke's childhood was only terror. Yet, looking through the bus window, he consigned it to the past. That large house he had tiptoed through was behind him and now he felt it only when he closed his eyes: a slap ringing out, a scream, a cup smashing, the sound of his mother against the wall, his father's bellowing from downstairs, the unbearable tension of a dinnertime, being scrutinized for the most minor mistake.

His father had devised a jail solely to crush his mother's spirit, to punish her for her own nature. At every turn he used little Kosuke as his pawn against her, always reminding her the boy was nothing more than a disappointment.

Nozomi had started with the pills long ago. Kosuke was familiar with the changes in her by now — the slowness of her blinking, her grinding teeth, entire days spent in bed. When it started, it was as if she had found a secret way out and was abandoning him to his father.

That was when he began to answer back. To provoke Ryoma in small, subtle ways. Deflect attention towards himself. Kosuke would establish evidence of transgressions throughout the house, ensuring they would be discovered – attempt to enter forbidden rooms, open letters, leave the phone receiver slightly askew, raising the possibility that he had tried to call for help. He inherited the beatings and whippings, and they became routine, the sound of the blows trouncing his flesh like a heavy rain on a thin roof.

And so Kosuke began to hone his instincts. He became hyper-aware of clues in his father's mood, intentions. He began to fathom the world beyond his prison through newspapers left out, snatched moments of television, a collection of mystery books forgotten by an old tutor.

Then this morning his mother had simply put his Captain Tsubasa backpack in front of him and told him to collect only his favourite books. The taxi drove them to the terminal. They got on the first bus that came. With nowhere to go, anywhere would do. By sunset, Kosuke's surname had been erased. Hisakawa was gone for ever, replaced by his mother's – Iwata.

When the money ran out they lived hand to mouth. They relied on the kindness of strangers, on the mercy of strange cities. When that ran out, too, Nozomi searched for scraps or stole. She would leave Iwata in libraries, in department stores, in small recesses. *Your mother needs to go and do something.* And every time Nozomi left, Iwata terrified himself with the thought that she would not come back.

On the first day of 1986 that moment arrived. Nozomi left

him in a bus station in the mountains north of Kyoto. That was the moment that established in Iwata a deep-rooted and consuming resentment of his mother. Throughout his years in the orphanage he all but blocked out his father, purged him from memory and consigned the blame instead to Nozomi. Even well into manhood, long after his mother had come back into his life, he had lived that lie, nourished himself in its simplicity.

Then, five years ago, he had come into possession of her diaries. Regained the truth. Reality roared back, in nightmares, in daydreams. And now all that was left was Ryoma Hisakawa, standing in the dark hallway of his mind.

Den-en-chōfu. Night. Heart thudding against his ribs, Kosuke Iwata climbed the exterior wall and landed in the unlit front garden, quiet as blood. The house was modern, all glass and sustainable materials, a piano seen through the tall vertical window. It was the sort of place an Ikea executive might have owned by some remote Swedish lake. Iwata saw the security alarm blinking. They would be here soon. But he knew that true revenge could not be stopped by any system.

Iwata approached the back of the house. The garden was large and elegant. He crossed gravel, the crunching sound making him feel sick. He weaved through neat shrubs, granite slabs, raked sand swirls. Finally, Iwata saw him.

The old man was sitting in a large armchair, a drink in his hand, his feet up on a stool. Iwata begin to tremble violently but, before he could stop himself, he was drifting over to the sliding door. He knocked on the glass.

Ryoma Hisakawa opened his eyes, rubbed them, then

frowned. Iwata fought the need to piss as Hisakawa stood up and slid the door open. He entered the massive lounge, staring at Hisakawa. The proportions were all wrong – too small, too old.

'You must be with the new security detail. Another false alarm is it?' The man's voice was ragged now, weaker, but it was the one Iwata knew so well – the rhythm of his nightmares.

'No.' Iwata tasted bile. 'The house looks different.'

'Different to what?'

'To how I remember it.'

'It's changed. A while ago, now.' Hisakawa's lips twitched. Then he simply returned to his chair and took a sip of his drink. 'Have one, if you want.'

Iwata looked around the room, took in the indoor koi pond, the ornamental stones, the black sculptures. The pleasant scent of the lounge revolted him. 'Is there anyone here?'

'My wife is on vacation.' Hisakawa rattled his ice cubes in a miniature celebration.

'Children?'

'Grown up. Are you going to tell me who you are?'

'You know who I am.' Iwata took out his gun.

'Oh.' Hisakawa took another sip, fear beneath the gesture visible now. 'You've come for an apology?'

'No.' Iwata flipped off the safety on the gun. 'You wouldn't be capable anyway.'

Hisakawa stood and turned to face the garden. He could reach the phone. Iwata picked up the handset and smashed it against the wall. Hisakawa flinched then; in the black reflection, he closed his eyes. The skin on his head was creased and speckled, horrifically babyish somehow.

'Do you remember me . . . ?' Iwata's tone wavered. 'What you did?'

'Kosuke . . .' Hisakawa's voice was a toneless croak. 'I barely remember you.'

'What about my mother? Do you remember what you did to her?'

Hisakawa grunted fondly. 'How is Nozomi?'

Iwata grabbed him by the nape and slammed his face into the glass door. Hisakawa's head bounced off and he landed on his back. 'You don't speak her name.' Iwata sounded like someone else.

Hisakawa tried to drag himself away.

'You never speak that name again.'

'No no no I won't I won't.'

Iwata rolled him back over. Blood was streaming from one nostril, he was quivering, his hands held up in fear. Corralling his rage, Iwata breathed deeply. 'Hisakawa, I'm going to tell you something I've never told anyone before. My earliest memory is a joke. *You* making a joke. Do you remember this?'

'I–I don't know.'

'You asked me if I loved you and when I said no you started to cry. I felt bad – can you imagine? I even put my hand on your shoulder. Then I saw you were laughing. You were laughing so hard at me. Do you remember?'

'No, no, I wouldn't –'

'Over and over I asked my mother, at least in my own mind: *Why stay? Why stay for so long?* But I was asking the wrong thing to the wrong person. Never once did I wonder why *you* were violent. Never once did I pray that *you* would change. I simply accepted that's how you were. That you were evil. That there was no choice.' Iwata put the gun to the man's face. 'I realize now there was a choice. You didn't have to be what you were. But time passes, Hisakawa. Seeds become saplings. And now I have a choice, too.'

The old man closed his eyes. 'Make it quick.'

'No. This will not be over quickly. Get up.'

'Please –'

'Hisakawa, get up.'

Whiffling, the old man dragged himself to his feet.

'Put your hands behind your back.'

Hisakawa feebly offered his hands; rugose, liver-spotted, but strangely dainty. *How could these hands cause so much pain for so long?* It didn't matter any longer.

Iwata flipped the safety on his gun back again. He took out his handcuffs and snapped them around the old man's wrists. 'Ryoma Hisakawa, I'm arresting you on suspicion of rape under Article 177 of the Penal Code. It is your right to maintain silence and to have an attorney at trial. Do you understand these rights?'

'W–what?'

'Do you understand these rights?'

Realizing he wasn't about to be killed in cold blood, Hisakawa laughed scornfully. 'You come here – to the *Defense Minister's house* – and arrest me on a bullshit charge, years beyond the statute of limitations? You don't even have a warrant.'

'Article 210 of the criminal code of procedure; *kinkyu taiho.*'

'You're going to quote the code at *me* –'

'The article provides that police may arrest, without warrant, a person who, if there is a sufficient reason to believe, has committed a crime punishable by imprisonment

343

for three years or more, when there is an urgent need to arrest and there is no time to apply for a warrant.'

'Listen to me, you little fucker, you have to apply for the warrant immediately, and the judge will turn this down, which means I'll be released immediately.'

'Maybe so. Now move before I change my mind.'

Iwata marched him out of the house.

Hatanaka was staring at his new phone on his new desk. Division One was half empty tonight, some kind of hubbub up in Ibaraki prefecture. Tanigawa and Ideguchi had stormed out earlier, cursing Assistant Inspector Itō and the English detective. But Hatanaka had no interest in that. He was waiting for his phone call.

Surely it will come soon. Ueda did us all a favour by burying the English girl's murder. And that was on my watch, I solved it. Ideguchi was promoted. Tanigawa is Acting Commissioner. That only leaves me. The minister will call me and tell me that Kappa Unit is now under my supervision permanently as Senior Inspector.

The phone on his desk started ringing. Hatanaka took a breath. 'This is Hatanaka.'

'Inspector, please come down to Booking. We have a, uh, problem.'

'What's that got to do with me?'

'It's a . . . delicate situation.'

Swearing, Hatanaka hung up and marched over to the elevator. As he descended, he realized how hungry he was. *MOS Burger? Freshness Burger? Or treat myself to Chatty Chatty Burger? I'll get whatever this is sorted out and then leave early. Maybe get a massage afterwards.*

Downstairs, the doors dinged open and Hatanaka's mouth fell open. At the custody suite, Iwata was remonstrating

344

with a terrified clerk amid a pile of papers, while he held the Defense Minister slumped against the counter.

'Iwata, what the fuck are you doing?' Hatanaka hurried over to the minister, already fumbling for the key to the handcuffs.

'I've got it from here, thanks.'

Hatanaka laughed incredulously. 'You're insane. Your arrest is legally invalid – you're not a cop any more, you're not even a fucking *consultant*. And even if you were, I know you don't have a warrant for this madness.'

'He's guilty. Under Article 210 –'

Hatanaka pushed Iwata hard and he stumbled back. Turning to the clerk, he thundered. 'You lose those papers *right now*. A word of this and you're finished, understand?'

The clerk immediately collected the papers between frantic bows.

'As for you, Iwata. I warned you. You should have left. Article 210? He's a *Cabinet minister*, you mad bastard.' Unlocking the handcuffs, Hatanaka grovelled before Hisakawa and led him to the elevator. He turned to look at Iwata. 'You've done it this time.'

The doors closed and the clerk busied himself among the shelves to avoid eye contact. Iwata put his hands in his pockets and walked out of the police station.

Tetsuya Suda was waiting for him, standing next to a photographer. 'How'd it go?'

'As well as you would imagine.'

Before going to Ryoma Hisakawa's house, Iwata had met the journalist at his capsule hotel. In the empty cafeteria, over bowls of vending-machine ramen and coffee, Iwata laid out all the details of his plan to arrest the Defense Minister, while Suda chain-smoked Hope cigarettes. Iwata was calm in his discourse: his mother's past, the rape, the coercion, the years of abuse. Suda recorded everything. Afterwards, Iwata seemed almost tranquil.

Now, standing outside the police station, Suda was grinning from ear to ear.

Iwata nodded at the photographer. 'How did I look?'

'You'll always be beautiful to me.' Suda laughed. 'Hisakawa getting into government was a travesty. Everyone knows he's rotten, he was always just too smooth for anything to touch him. But now? Iwata, he's finished.'

Suda bowed and, along with the photographer, got into the waiting car. Iwata watched it go. He was about to head off when the police station doors opened and Negishi emerged.

'Iwata.'

'Negishi, working late for a change?'

She smiled. 'We need to talk.'

'So let's get out of here.'

They walked a few blocks until the police HQ was out of view then ducked into a minuscule curry house. They ordered two potato curries, Negishi drank beer while Iwata went for a vegetable juice. 'Did you find Girl A in the end?'

Iwata nodded.

'And did she have answers?'

In his mind, Iwata saw Kaori Harada sailing into the ash. 'Only that I don't think she killed Skye Mackintosh.'

'You heard about the English detective and Assistant Inspector Itō, right?'

'Did he ask for her hand in marriage?'

'You *haven't* heard?' Eyes widening at the joyful prospect of being able to tell such a story, Negishi recounted the discovery of Sato. Iwata asked a few questions and she answered as best she could.

When they were finished, she shunted her plate aside and puffed out her cheeks.

'Hit the spot?'

'Hit everything.' Negishi finished her beer then looked at him.

'Iwata, you've been all over this city, this country, you've been dragged through the mud in the press, you've faced down Tanigawa and the rest. And I don't even want to know where those bruises came from.'

'Why do you mention all this?'

'Because I don't think you would have done all that if you thought Ueda was the one who killed Skye Mackintosh. Same goes for Miyake.'

'You're perceptive. Watch that – could get you into trouble in this line of work.'

'Iwata, the subpoenas? Hatanaka forgot to cancel them. NTT Docomo finally released Skye's call logs.' Negishi took a folded page out of her handbag. 'And I don't think Ueda or Miyake killed her either.'

Iwata unfolded a list of numbers, dates, times. He looked up at Negishi. 'Someone has been using her phone.'

'Yes. It's been turned on periodically for between two and ten minutes pretty much every night since her murder. Even yesterday morning. It's been pinging all over Tokyo. No calls, message or internet usage, though. Whoever has it is just browsing through her phone.'

'Can we trace it to a location?'

'For an exact location, I need an hour. But –' She took out a Google Maps print-out. 'It's coming from somewhere near here.'

347

Iwata recognized the area at once. Crushing her in a bear hug, he leapt up.

'Get off!'

He paused at the door. 'Negishi, you're the best damn cop in this city.'

37. A Masterful Plan

On the taxi journey to the Mackintoshes' hotel, Iwata realized now he'd been wrong all along. While the spider *had* been left as a message, it was not intended to taunt the police.

His phone beeped with Negishi's message now. Skye's cellphone had been pinging from just a few miles away from Shibuya HQ the whole time. Iwata took a breath, then opened the message. The exact location had been pinpointed. It was as he suspected. He closed his eyes and felt the warmth of the rising sun on his face. The serenity of finally understanding the truth filled Iwata.

In the lobby, the Mackintosh family were checking out, surrounded by their suitcases. A Foreign Office representative was with them. The press were nowhere to be seen. Lynch had arrived, her shoulder bandaged beneath her jacket. Looking up, she gave Iwata a tired smile.

Outside, they embraced awkwardly, Iwata trying to avoid her injuries. 'How are you doing?'

'Tip-top. Sato didn't slice through anything too valuable in the end. Doc says I've got another week or so before he'll sign me off for travel.'

'Well, thanks for coming.'

'All in the spirit of openness. So, you gonna tell me what you dragged me out of hospital for?'

Iwata unfolded the cellphone record Negishi had given

him then explained the situation. Lynch shook her head. 'It can't be.'

He nodded.

'Christ.' She took the page and went into the empty meeting room, as if she needed solitude to fully comprehend the truth.

Iwata approached the family now. Before Philip Mackintosh could say anything, Iwata bowed deeply. 'Mr Mackintosh, there is still one final thing to discuss. Though I need to warn you now, it may be something of a shock. I'd ask you please to go with your wife and daughter into the meeting room. DC Lynch will explain.'

'Fine.' Philip Mackintosh sighed. 'I need to get Dylan; he's still upstairs.'

'It's okay, I'll talk to him.'

'All right. Room 1210.'

Iwata took the elevator to the twelfth floor. At the end of a grey, dim corridor, he knocked on the door.

'Come in.'

Dylan White was sitting on the edge of the unmade bed, staring blankly out of the window, humming 'Somewhere Beyond the Sea'.

'Oh, Inspector.' He gave a fatigued smile. 'Didn't think I'd see you before we left.'

'I wanted to say goodbye.' Iwata sat at the table, setting down his gun and his wallet. 'You don't mind if I rest here for a moment, do you, Dylan?'

'Not at all. You must be exhausted.'

'Work, work, work.'

'I know. Strange to think that in a few days I'll be back at the travel agency.'

Iwata smiled neutrally and they were silent for a while

until he spoke again. 'Skye's family. They're downstairs, I think they're ready to go.'

'I know. It's just such a long journey; I'm tired just thinking about it.'

Iwata nodded. 'At least all this is over.'

The younger man gave a sad smile. 'I'm not sure it will ever be over, Inspector.'

Iwata stood and walked to the window. He looked out across Tokyo for a long while. In his peripheral vision, he eyed Dylan White's suitcase now, several luggage tags around its handle.

PUS – Gimhae International Airport, Busan
LHR – London Heathrow
NRT – Tokyo Narita

'You know, Dylan' – Iwata kept his tone even, despite his dawning understanding – 'I think we can take five minutes before we head down.'

'I could do with a breather, to be honest.'

Iwata went over to the sink, poured himself a glass of water and returned to the window, his back to Dylan. 'I do need to ask you something, though. And I need you to be honest with me.'

'Of course.'

'Why did you kill Skye?'

'. . . What?'

'You discovered that Skye had met someone else, I know that. So what was it? Did she confide in her sister? Because I'm guessing that if Geraldine knew, then that's how you found out.'

'I don't understand what you're –'

'Yes, you do. You understand. You murdered Skye and you tried to pin it on her girlfriend.'

'Girlfriend? What are you *talking* about?'

'You're a smart kid, Dylan. That's true. But you're a bad actor.'

Dylan stood. 'I *loved* Skye.'

'Oh, I don't doubt that. You did love Skye. But somewhere along the way, I think love turned into lustful hatred. She left you, didn't she? That's why she's dead. Now I know *how* you did it. It was very clever – killing three birds with one stone. You almost managed it.'

'You've gone mad.'

'Have I?' Iwata took out his phone and dialled a number. In the next second, an electronic ringtone came from Dylan's backpack. It was a jaunty electronic tune, so happy, so artificial, it hardly seemed possible it could ever incriminate a man. Yet Dylan White slumped on to the bed at the sound of it.

Iwata ended the call. 'You had Skye's phone on you the whole time.'

He nodded.

'To look at the pictures? Read her messages? Maintain control over her, even in death?'

Dylan opened his backpack and took out Skye's phone. He looked at it lovingly, as though it were Skye herself. Iwata took it from him.

'You posed as Kaori in order to get Skye to come to the love hotel. That was the first step. Next you tracked Ueda down. Wouldn't be hard to find him – you knew the poor bastard from your volunteering days. And you remembered his temper, didn't you? Wouldn't shock me if he'd got on the wrong side of you once or twice. You knew he'd need the money, but you didn't want him to recognize you. That's why you hid your face when you found him. You paid him to deliver the pizza with the dead spider inside. But tell me, Dylan. Why Starlet?'

'I knew it from my volunteering days. I'd spoken with local police before when searching for missing homeless people. They always complained that the CCTV was spotty around that area, that nobody took any notice of anybody else.'

'So Skye went to the room you had Ueda book for you. Then he delivered the pizza. You told him to leave it outside the door and go before she could explain she hadn't ordered anything. Confused, she takes the box in, maybe thinking it's Kaori's idea. She opens it and sees the spider. Now she's scared – you knew she would be. Skye didn't understand – spiders were *Kaori's* thing. But Kaori was nowhere to be seen. I'm betting you got off on scaring her. It made you feel good. I would have guessed you were watching, but I know that you weren't. Because while Ueda was upstairs making the delivery you were downstairs stealing the iron tamper from his scooter. Now, of course, Ueda's involvement looked incidental. Just a pizza delivery guy and an attempted rape that got out of hand. But it was *you* who went upstairs. You who finally got your revenge on Skye. So, tell me: did her shock delight you? Arouse you?'

'Shut up.'

'You smashed her skull in with Ueda's tamper then you tossed it in the river near his shack, knowing that both the delivery and the weapon would implicate him. But Ueda wasn't the main course for you, was he? You also arranged for Kaori Harada to come to Starlet after the murder. Not only did you force her to see her girlfriend dead, but you also placed her at the crime scene. You gave us two good suspects and then you let us work it out for ourselves, happy with whichever result we came to. You must have been laughing your ass off when Miyake got thrown into the mix.'

Looking out of the window again, Iwata shook his head, as if marvelling at Tokyo itself. 'I know all of this to be fact. But I want you to tell me why.'

Dylan shrugged. His voice had a different tone now, harsher, more nasal, his words much faster. It was as if the relief of shedding a weight had accelerated his speech. 'I knew from the beginning she would leave me. *Course* she fucking would – you saw what she looked like.'

'Tell me, Dylan. I'm listening to you.'

Dylan leapt at the invitation, unblinking, spittle flying out of his mouth. 'I knew Skye was the best it was ever going to be for me. There was no point in anything else. But I also knew I was never more than a distraction for her.' The hardness in his face filtered away and his eyes softened. For a moment he looked fragile again. 'Loving someone – truly loving them – is hopelessness itself.'

'Skye had power over you.'

'For a time. But then I realized. Control *could* be mine. See, Inspector, if she wasn't going to be my world' – he picked up the revolver from the table – 'then she wasn't going to be in the world at all.'

Iwata faced him. 'What are you doing, Dylan?'

'I saw you look at my luggage tags. That was clever. The one little shitty detail I forgot: the Korean luggage tag.'

Iwata's tone was full of admiration. 'You hid it from me at the medical examiner's office when I tried to help

354

you with your bags. I didn't think anything of it at the time . . .'

'You really do want to know how I did it, don't you?'

'Of course' – Iwata humoured him – 'it was a *masterful* plan.'

Trembling with pride, Dylan began to pace the room. 'It didn't cross a single detective's mind – that I might have been in the country *at the time of Skye's murder.* Not even yours, Iwata.'

'. . . You came to Japan by sea. You flew from London to Busan. From there, you took the jetfoil to Hakata. Then the train to Tokyo, to arrange with Ueda and carry out the murder soon after. You threw your ferry ticket away outside Starlet, knowing it couldn't prove anything. Then you simply went back the way you came, all the way back to London. Tight schedule, but you could have made the entire trip in just a few days.'

The younger man grinned. 'Just in time to join her stupid fucking mess of a family for the flight out here as the terrible news broke. Which, of course, I broke. I was planning to let some cleaner find her body initially, but what can I say? I got tired of waiting.' He aimed the gun at Iwata. 'Not that any of this matters now. I'll be on the plane before they even realize you're dead.'

'And then what, Dylan? Go on the run?'

'If it came to it, I could live that way. You know my planning capabilities.'

'But first tell me *why*. So Skye left you. She didn't love you any more. All of that, much as it hurts, is just a part a life, Dylan.'

'*Just a part of life?!*' He was red in the face now, tears in his eyes. 'Skye *was* my fucking life. And she left me. She *left* me.' An icicle of snot hung from his lip. 'I loved her so much I thought maybe the world might be worth something after all. That maybe I wasn't all wrong inside . . .' He bared his teeth as tears betrayed him, then tried to laugh away the pain. 'Deep down, I knew it was impossible. Even so, I couldn't help myself. Couldn't not love her. I should've run away, I know. But I was so tired of being myself. Of being alone. It's like I was in a dark room somewhere and Skye was a rising sun in my world, so *bright*. How could I not give in?'

'You know what I think, Dylan? I think everything you said is bullshit. That's why you chose the love hotel, isn't it? It was your way of telling the world what you thought of Skye. *She's trash. She's merchandise. She's a whore.* But the truth is, you try to control because you are weak. And you don't know which you hate more: women or yourself.'

'You see a lot, Inspector.' Dylan wiped away his tears and snorted up his snot. 'But our five minutes are over and you're trying to stall me.' He lined up the shot. 'I'm sorry, Inspector, but you've given me no choice.'

Iwata nodded, as though the transaction had been concluded. He marched towards the younger man, who pulled the trigger. The hammer snapped down.

And nothing.

He pulled the trigger once more. Again, nothing.

Iwata calmly took away the empty gun, a mother confiscating a toy. He pocketed it then held up his phone – the record app was running. Pressing SEND, Iwata downed the rest of his water. He took his glass to the sink, washed it out and headed to the door. He stopped there, as if something had just occurred to him. 'Dylan?'

'Yes?' he whispered.

'What you said earlier was right. It won't ever be over. Not for you.'

Iwata left the room. A moment later, four officers in dark blue uniforms filled the doorway.

38. Forever Yours

Two turgid weeks of humidity and storms passed. Then, as if forgetting itself, Tokyo woke to a clear, brisk August morning. The Olympic closing ceremony would take place the next day.

Kosuke Iwata checked out of the addiction treatment centre and travelled back to the city. Across the road from Kaori Harada's apartment building, in a little neighbourhood park beneath zelkova trees, he was crouching over the small grave he had fashioned in the mud. The cicadas were ringing loudly. A breeze was blowing.

When Iwata felt shadow fall across his face, he opened his eyes. Snake and Whale were standing there, the former's black eyes now a light green. Neither one of them wore any kind of expression.

'Inspector, we looked into this Ozawa individual, as you suggested. Ended up taking him for a drive.'

Whale nodded. 'Japan appreciates your vigilance.'

'Always happy to do my civic duty.'

Without another word, Snake and Whale turned away. Iwata watched them get into a black van. When they were gone, he went back to the small handmade plot.

Iwata took the desiccated spider out of his pocket, removed it from the plastic bag and laid it carefully to rest. He placed the photograph of Kaori Harada next to the spider then put in the Skye Mackintosh T-shirt. He buried them together and looked up at the sky. It was vivid and sharp, as though a god had tunnelled her way from one realm to another, leaving behind only cream mist and blue wonder.

You left me here alone. In Tufnell fucking Park. The grey bedsit you tried to make 'bijou'. No explanation, no discussion, just a Post-it note – <u>Sorry</u>. Not even the decency of 'I am' or 'I'm so'. The same sort of brevity I'd get from an accidental push on the Northern Line.

How <u>dare</u> you let me think you loved me? And let's be honest, I know the 'sorry' wasn't for me. It was just enough to make it clear. To make sure I wouldn't mount a campaign. Get the police involved. Guess it's ironic, then.

I kept that note, you know. Not that you put any thought into it. Scribbled the first thing that flew into your beautiful little head, I'm sure. I ignored it at first. Told myself it was a mistake. That you'd walk through the door and explain it away. But you were already halfway around the world.

What was I meant to do? I drank in the grotty Irish pub around the corner where you always made friends. I slept with an abandoned scarf that probably still holds your perfume, wondering if the fact that you left it behind was a clue to a warm destination. I passed the kebab shop in Kentish Town where we'd do Turkish accents and laugh at the neon knife cutting the neon meat for ever. We cherished the dreariness of London. The crumbling pubs where old men watched horse races. The freezing winter walks in Clissold Park. Fishfinger sandwiches with reduced bread in front of Question Time. I lied to myself, convinced myself that all this had meant happiness.

How stupid of me, to think I could withstand you. Anywhere in this world you ever walked, in whatever corresponding language, people could only ever look at you and think the word *beauty*.

Even holding up the milk to check the sell-by date was an act of elegance in your hands. As you reached back to unclip a bra, the folding skin between your shoulder blades was a tapestry of shadows. If you furrowed your brow in concentration over an email, how could I not think of my cum jetting out across your face? When you wanted new pillows from Habitat you couldn't afford and asked me if I minded getting them, how could I be anything other than happy that there would be more things in the house to smell of you?

Sorry.

I loved you until debasement, barely able to let myself watch you undress, as though each bedtime, each bath, were somehow a reminder of my inadequacy – my vulnerability. But early on you suggested living together. Weekend getaways. Fucking in bushes. Adventures and admissions. The weight of your stupid sleeping head on my shoulder in some night bus made me float. But for you it was A to B. Quickly, you said 'Love you' – although it was always in a breezy sing-song. You never said 'I'. Your *love yous* never contained 'I'.

Sorry.

And yet, even after all you've done to me – the abandonment, the lies, the pathetic theatre of our relationship: all of it – I'm not angry with you. I'm angry at myself. Because I always knew you didn't love me. Stupid to think you could. Anything as beautiful as you could only ever love yourself. That's how this world is.

Tells us cages are bad when nothing else will keep
beauty close to us.

Of course, I raged in the beginning. Explaining to the
landlord I couldn't pay your half of the rent as he pitied
me. Explaining it to our neighbours. How humiliating it
was to watch them fill in the blanks. Worse – explaining it
to my parents, who had loved you, who had offered my
grandmother's ring for us one day. You would've liked
that ring, I think. Would have fit in with that bullshit
vintage aesthetic you worshipped. Then again, you couldn't
have given a fuck about my grandmother's ring.

So I swore I would hurt you back, somehow. Tried
calling your friends but realized they were all my friends.
I walked the streets. Got buses and sat on the top deck, like
you always wanted. London – never-ending – a stony
infinity of all those who were not you. To me that dark
orange streetlight is the loneliest colour in the world.

I woke up in the mornings, went to work. Did what I was
expected to do. Stood up from my desk at the end of a long
day selling emptiness to the empty and headed home to
nothing. No more Skye Mackintosh in my world.

I tried to acclimatize to your leaving. But everything
reminded me of your rejection. It never truly went away.
That's the arrogance of beauty, though. Knowing full
well its effect on mediocrity but being happily oblivious
to its true impact.

Well, you were always beautiful, Skye, but you weren't
so clever. It was your sister who gave it away. Of course,
you know that fat bitch would betray you in an instant
if I wanted her. But you'd probably just be happy for us.
A better fit, eh? Low runs into low.

Well, Skye. You made your fucking choice, and so did I. They say there's a chance I'll hang, though the lawyers think it's unlikely. In the mornings they give me newspapers, but anything relating to my case (or is it our case?) is redacted, of course. Prison here really isn't that bad, except for the boredom. You don't see anyone else. Not that I care; there's no one else I'd want to see in this world anyway.

I realize now that Inspector Iwata only had me on possessing your phone. He just gambled and tricked me into confessing. I was angry at myself at first, but now I've made my peace with it. Maybe I wanted to tell the world, deep down. In a way, I'm glad. Everybody knows what I did to you now. Never again can you be mentioned without the thought of me being there inside your memory. That can't be taken away from me ever. <u>I killed you</u>. Me.

So this is my confession, Skye. The judges will want to know, I was told. Well, you know it all already. I suppose there's only one thing left to say. So here it is:

<u>Sorry.</u>

Forever yours,
Dylan White x

39. Sayōnara Means For Ever

Narita International Airport. Anthea Lynch and Kosuke Iwata were sitting at the bar, their eyes on the TV screen. The news was breaking: a new Defense Minister had been appointed to replace the disgraced Ryoma Hisakawa. Footage of the old man in handcuffs now appeared on the screen. Lynch sipped her cold barley tea, oblivious to the scandal. 'When do you fly back to LA?'

'In a few days.' Iwata looked away from the screen. 'Shindo's funeral is tomorrow.'

They were silent for a while. With tired, glassy eyes, Lynch watched planes taxiing, some coming home, some visiting, some leaving for ever.

'You know, I couldn't sleep last night,' she said. 'Kept thinking about Sato and Dylan.'

'Oh?'

'I've been in the murder game for a while now, but I never really thought too much about the actual *people* themselves, you know what I mean? Murderers were just part of the job. But last night I was going round and round it – why Sato is the way he is, how Dylan could travel half the way round the world to kill his ex-girlfriend. I thought about why people call them monsters. You know what I realized? They're just broken. After that, I closed my eyes and fell straight to sleep.'

Iwata nodded. 'There aren't any monsters in this world. We'd see them coming. Instead, people like Sato, people like Dylan, they blend in with the rest of us.'

Lynch sipped her tea. 'When I first looked at Sato, something deep down told me: *He's not right*. I don't know why, he just seemed so at ease in that interrogation room. But *Dylan*' – she shook her head – 'I never looked at him twice. So what was it for you?'

Iwata shrugged. 'I didn't know anything for sure; it was Negishi's phone records that confirmed it. But I suppose it was the little things. He brought those T-shirts with him. I suppose that struck me as a little odd, that level of acceptance, that level of preparation. Then there was the language he used. Within a few minutes of seeing the photos of Skye's dead body, he said: *She loved jays*. Immediately, she was in the past tense. Of course, there's no script for normal behaviour in shock and grief, but a lot about Dylan White didn't sit right with me.'

'You know, Iwata. Out of the two, Sato's the unicorn. Multiple victims, all strangers. Intelligent, methodical, absolutely addicted to killing. Some of the things they've found in his cabin . . . Yet for all that, it's Dylan who scares me. I don't know why. Maybe cos there's a shitload more Dylans out there than Satos.'

'For all his intelligence, Dylan White is just another tiny ego, another terrified man shouting: *Women can't hurt me*.'

Lynch ordered an Orion beer. It arrived as a table with a view of the runway opened up. They sat by the window together and shared an exhausted silence. In the reflection of the glass, they looked at each other. For the first time, it wasn't incidental, it wasn't connected to a murder case, to ulterior considerations. They had been thrown together haphazardly, more for PR and reputation management than the integrity of an investigation. And yet it had worked.

Discordant sounds together, played long enough, some-times formed a rhythm.

'You know, Iwata, I still don't know the first thing about you.'

He shrugged. 'I'm forty-five years old. I like cooking and going on morning runs. I like old records, old cars. I'm not a great person, but I'm an okay father.'

Lynch laughed. 'Give me some colour. Tell me a story.'

Iwata thought about this. 'Hm, okay. I had this teacher at my orphanage. I hated him. But like most conmen, he told good stories. He had this one about the devil I always liked.'

'I went to a Catholic school, remember. I'm listening.'

'Okay. So. Once in a while, when the devil was feeling generous, he'd pull one of his minions close and whisper in their ear – *What would you like?* And the answer would always be the same. *Entertainment! Entertainment! Entertainment!* And so the devil would sweep his hand across the town and take the roof off all the houses so they could watch the people. Their secrets. Their sins.'

'Yeah, go on.'

'That's it. The end. I never really found any meaning in it, I just always remembered it.'

'You realize he was trying to warn against masturba-tion, yeah?'

Iwata laughed. 'As detectives, I guess that's what we do, too. We take the roof off and look inside.'

Lynch smirked. 'We're disciples of the devil?'

'Well, I don't know about you, but I'm not exactly an angel.' He crunched on a rice cracker. 'Now you tell me something. Why'd they send you out here?'

'You mean you didn't assume I'm the best the Met has got to offer?'

366

'I mean you're carrying something with you. Something's in those nightmares.'

She took a sip of her beer and lost her smile. 'There was this case, back in London. A young Angolan girl . . . Nuria. She was beautiful, Iwata.' Lynch had been replaying it in her mind since the day it happened; it was always there in the background, regular as a radio jingle on the hour. 'The smell raised the alarm before her absence at school did. Later, teachers would say it wasn't noted because she was often in Angola visiting family. There were no visits, of course . . . I was the first one to see her body. The damage was horrific. Two ingested teeth resulting from the beating her father gave her. A torn frenulum. Several rib fractures.' Lynch looked at Iwata now, her eyes wet with fury. 'The pathologist explained that this would have required significant brutality as children have pliable ribs. *An extremely forceful compression* – I could quote you her report like it was poetry.'

Iwata held out his hand and Lynch squeezed it hard.

'When we broke down the door the father was sleeping. 'Course, he blamed the mother. She was shit scared; she didn't contradict him. And then something inside me just *went*. I led that man into the bathroom and took out my baton. By the time they got that door down I had beaten Nuria's father half to death. My CO practically carried me out of there, saying it would be okay, over and over. But his face told me otherwise. The press had a picnic outside Scotland Yard and I was put on leave. This – Japan, Skye, the whole thing – it was meant to be a second chance. But they'll get rid of me. The disciplinary hearing is next week. Truth of the matter is, I don't know if I even care.'

Iwata ordered Lynch another beer. 'I had a case like that

once. Long time ago. Some cases wash away in time. Others stay in your bones for years. Like love, maybe.'

She nodded. 'The thing that really got me? A Kit-Kat. The only contents of her stomach, her last meal. I don't know why, but there was something so lonely about that. I could hear the little snapping of the biscuit.

'Iwata, I've seen a lifetime of sad, horrible shit. But that was the loneliest I ever felt. For that little girl, that was life. That was all it was.' Lynch downed her beer and cracked open her new one. 'I'm not religious, but when I saw Nuria's little body it was like God himself told me: *Kill that man.* Afterwards, I lied. Said it was self-defence. I wanted to make sure he was put away.' Lynch wiped away a self-conscious tear. 'It was the right thing to do. I know it was. But I also know I sold my soul as a copper.'

'You did what you had to do. That's not always free.'

Lynch sloshed her suds from side to side. 'Maybe not. But that's just it. I don't think I can do whatever *that* is any more.'

'I wasn't there for that. But here? You found the needle in a haystack, Anthea. You saved lives. You're luminous.'

'Piss off.'

'Look, if you're done with the police, I get that. I really do. But why not wait and see what the outcome of the hearing is and go from there? You found Sato in a second language surrounded by goons. God knows what you're capable of in your own city.'

Hiding her blush, Lynch swatted his arm. 'There it is.'

'What?'

'That charm you mentioned back in the hostess club. I wasn't convinced it existed.'

Iwata laughed. 'So,' he said. 'Everything Calvin?'

She grinned. 'Proper Calvin.'

The departure screen updated and the gate started flashing.

'That's you.'

'That's me.' Lynch stood. 'Mind how you go, Inspector Iwata.'

'If you're ever in Los Angeles, look me up.'

She laughed at the thought. 'And if you ever come to London, give me a bell.'

'I'll do that.'

'Before I go, I've been meaning to ask you. That thing you were going to do the night when I found you. Did you do it?'

Iwata shook his head. 'At least, not with the gun.' They embraced now, briefly but forcefully. Lynch grimaced through the pain but was grateful for the contact.

'Hey, I almost forgot.' Iwata took out a boarding pass from his inside pocket.

'I've already got one.'

'Actually, it is yours. I upgraded you online.'

'Now I owe you.'

'*Shou ga nai*, Anthea Lynch. *Shou ga nai*.'

'Wanker.' She smiled. That was always, that was everything – a smile on the precipice of goodbye. '*Sayōnara* means for ever, doesn't it?'

'Friends say: *See you later*.' Iwata held out his hand.

'Then I reckon' – she shook it – 'I'll be seeing you later, mate.'

Iwata watched her leave the bar then mingle into the crowd until she'd been replaced completely with a million other faces.

*

Two hours later, Santi came through the Arrivals door, embarrassed by his unaccompanied minor lanyard. Curling his earphones behind his ears, he embraced Iwata awkwardly.

'You've grown.' Iwata spoke in Spanish.

'And you look older,' Santi replied in English.

Laughing, Iwata crushed him to his side and made him stumble for a few steps. 'Come on, let's get out of here. You tired?'

'Kinda.'

'Hungry?'

'AF.'

'I'll feed you if you stop using that damn word.'

'Okay. Then I wanna hit the arcades.'

'All right, but when I kick your ass, you don't get to blame it on the jet lag.'

40. Tokyo Will Miss You

Shindo's funeral was attended by many powerful men in the upper echelons of law enforcement and politics. One lone surviving cousin had made the trip down from Hokkaido. It was a funeral full of ceremony and dignity on a quiet, grey morning. Every man wore a black suit, a black tie. Not a single tear was shed.

When it was over Iwata stood outside. He lit a cigarette, his first smoke in years, a tiny fire to honour Shindo's big fire. He coughed from time to time and watched the fragments of blue dusk through the grey clouds.

When he was done, he stubbed it out against the brick and brushed ash from the breast of his black jacket. Another funeral, another loss.

Hatanaka appeared now, hands by his sides.

Iwata had no fight left in him. 'What do you want?'

'Do you have a minute? I need to talk with you.'

Iwata sighed. 'I was going to walk back to my hotel anyway.'

They walked in silence for a few blocks and passed Shinagawa station. Ascending a steep hill, they passed through a plush neighbourhood of free-standing houses. A few yards away from the Embassy of Brunei, Iwata and Hatanaka sat on a low wall, looking south.

Far below, they could see workers pouring out of offices, little grey and black specks of lint in a city of suits. *That's what this place is*, Iwata thought. *Black suit city.*

Hatanaka mopped his balding head with his rag. 'Did you hear? I've been credited for solving the Skye Mackintosh murder. Though I know it had nothing to do with me.'

'I'm not so sure it matters in the end.'

'It matters. Iwata . . . I don't know how to say this –'

'Then don't.'

Hatanaka seemed at once relieved and hurt by the answer. He shifted on the wall and took in the Tokyo panorama as if only now comprehending it. 'All this time, I've been resentful of Shindo, my colleagues – above all, you. And now I'm Senior Inspector and people look to me for leadership, but I don't know what the hell I'm doing . . .'

'You took the path you took. You can't undo that. But it's done now. Accept it, throw yourself into it head first.'

Hatanaka nodded and bit his thick lips, as if trying not to cry. The sky had darkened, the few remaining clouds carnation red. The skyscrapers were illuminated, cruise liners sailing through a sea of glass.

'You know, Iwata, this might sound strange, but it was only this morning that I realized he was gone. I understood it, but I only *felt* it today.'

Iwata nodded. 'In my experience, losing someone is understood by the head and the heart at differing paces.'

'Without Shindo, I wouldn't be where I am today. He knew I wasn't a good detective. But I always looked up to him. To you, too.'

'Just do your best. For what it's worth, I think you'll be okay.'

Hatanaka stood. He seemed to search for something else to say, something deeper, but the words were hiding in plain sight.

'Take care of yourself, Hatanaka.'

As if dismissed, he bowed deeply, turned and ambled down the hill, muttering to himself as he went.

An hour passed. Then another. Finally, as Iwata was getting ready to leave, he saw something. In the Persian-blue darkness above the city, bolts of brilliant gold were streaking silently through the sky.

Iwata smiled. *A meteor shower.*

He thought of Nozomi and felt the deep concoction of the love and sorrow of mothers.

To the south, somewhere over Tokyo Bay, the blimp lingered over the city. In the last few days, the message on its electronic display had changed:

TOKYO WILL MISS YOU!

*

It was Iwata's final day in Japan. Still wearing his black suit and black tie, he boarded a mid-morning service heading east with Santi. It was a clear day of gentle warmth. The train passed through the purlieus, sleeper cities with no history, identikit houses, canals that had been concreted over. When Tokyo finally ran out, there were only forests, rice paddies, miniature level crossings, bamboo groves, small huddles of houses too small to be hamlets.

While Santi played on his handheld console Iwata took in the green landscapes blurring by, feeling the unfulfillable longing of the world. He committed the details to memory – unsure of when he'd be passing through this way again.

A few hours later, they arrived in Chōshi. Getting off

373

the train, Iwata didn't look at the biscuit-coloured hotel where he had cheated on his wife all those years ago. Nor did he look at the police squad car sitting outside the station, just like the one he had driven back then.

Iwata and Santi walked north along the main road, past the old shopping arcades, past failed businesses, past rusting shutters, until they reached the Tone River. The water was calm today. Sitting on a bench on the promenade, Iwata took out two bananas from his bag and they watched the boats sailing out to sea.

At 4 p.m., Iwata and Santi were back at Chōshi station with flowers and incense. Trainspotters scurried around the platform for the perfect shot of the grand old single-carriage Dentetsu train. Iwata boarded after Santi and wondered about a world gentle enough to devote oneself to pet topics. The train passed through fields that farmers had given up on a long time ago, bobbing sunflowers, warped forests, level crossings clanging for no one.

Twenty minutes later, Iwata and Santi got off at Inobuh station. In the distance, they saw the lighthouse. It was a brilliant white in the late-afternoon light. They heard the ocean distantly crashing against the rocks, they smelled salt on the air. The windows of the seafront hotel in the sun were like silver flames.

It had been so long, it took a moment for Iwata to remember the way. And then he found it, the steep path leading down to the bamboo grove that gave out to the sea. Dragonflies glinted over a rocky stream that cut through it. At the bottom, there was a small cemetery surrounded by wizened trees, beaten by eons of ocean fury. But the water was still today.

Iwata found the grave of his wife and child.

'Santi, I want you to meet Cleo and Nina.'

Together, they cleaned it thoroughly then placed the flowers and the incense in the stone stand. Iwata did not speak to ones he had lost as he worked, he did not feel their presence, but he did think of them, remember them.

When it was done Santi went down to the shoreline. Iwata sat down next to the grave and watched him. His whole life, he had dreaded facing up to his father. Now it was done and, for the first time in his life, he felt ready to let go of the past.

Even so, he realized that he would be returning to Japan. Maybe not soon, but he would be back. There were plenty of missing here, too. A hundred thousand, Hatanaka had said.

Iwata closed his eyes and thought about those who had passed through his life. He thought about Cleo. He thought about Nina. He thought about his mother. He thought about Noriko Sakai. He thought about Hideo Akashi. He thought about his disgraced father. He thought about Mara Zambrano. He thought about Skye Mackintosh. He thought about Itsuki Sato. He thought about Dylan White. And he thought about Anthea Lynch.

Looking into the distance, Iwata asked the ocean if any of them meant anything, if the particular composition of these people in his own existence was a symphony or a scream. He knew there would be no answer. The only conclusion was chaos.

Even so, he saw merit in the maelstrom. Value in the void. And, above all, beauty – beauty everywhere.

Kosuke Iwata stood and touched the grave of his wife and child. 'See you,' he whispered. Taking out his *techou*, Iwata hurled it deep into the forest.

'Santi!' he called. 'Let's go home.'

The boy skimmed a final stone into the ocean. 'Yeah, Dad.'

The wind blew and Iwata felt the first cries of the newborn autumn in the small of his back. Fallen leaves scurried and chased each other for a while until they landed on the surf. There they floated for a moment, in a fraught, poetic balance, until they were finally overwhelmed by the waves.